What People Are Saying
about the Left Behind Series

"This is the most successful Christian-fiction series ever."
—Publishers Weekly

"Tim LaHaye and Jerry B. Jenkins . . . are doing for Christian fiction what John Grisham did for courtroom thrillers."
—TIME

"The authors' style continues to be thoroughly captivating and keeps the reader glued to the book, wondering what will happen next. And it leaves the reader hungry for more."
—Christian Retailing

"Combines Tom Clancy–like suspense with touches of romance, high-tech flash and Biblical references."
—The New York Times

"It's not your mama's Christian fiction anymore."
—The Dallas Morning News

"Wildly popular—and highly controversial."
—USA Today

"Bible teacher LaHaye and master storyteller Jenkins have created a believable story of what could happen after the Rapture. They present the gospel clearly without being preachy, the characters have depth, and the plot keeps the reader turning pages."
—Moody Magazine

"Christian thriller. Prophecy-based fiction. Juiced-up morality tale. Call it what you like, the Left Behind series . . . now has a label its creators could never have predicted: blockbuster success."
—Entertainment Weekly

Tyndale House products by Tim LaHaye and Jerry B. Jenkins

The Left Behind book series
Left Behind®
Tribulation Force
Nicolae
Soul Harvest
Apollyon
Assassins
The Indwelling
The Mark
Desecration
The Remnant—available summer 2002

Other Left Behind products
Left Behind®: The Kids
Devotionals
Calendars
Abridged audio products
Dramatic audio products
Graphic novels
Gift books
and more . . .

Other Tyndale House books by Tim LaHaye and Jerry B. Jenkins
Perhaps Today
Are We Living in the End Times?

For the latest information on individual products, release dates, and future projects, visit www.leftbehind.com

Tyndale House books by Tim LaHaye
How to Be Happy Though Married
Spirit-Controlled Temperament
Transformed Temperaments
Why You Act the Way You Do

Tyndale House books by Jerry B. Jenkins
And Then Came You
As You Leave Home
Still the One

ASSIGNMENT: JERUSALEM, TARGET: ANTICHRIST

ASSASSINS

LARGE PRINT EDITION

TIM LaHaye
JERRY B. JENKINS

Tyndale House Publishers, Inc.
WHEATON, ILLINOIS

Visit Tyndale's exciting Web site at www.tyndale.com

Discover the latest about the Left Behind series at www.leftbehind.com

Left Behind series designed by Catherine Bergstrom
Designed by Julie Chen
Cover photo illustration by Julie Chen

Published in association with the literary agency of Alive Communications, Inc., 7680 Goddard Street, Suite 200, Colorado Springs, CO 80920.

ISBN 0-8423-6555-9

Library of Congress Cataloging-in-Publication Data

LaHaye, Tim F.
   Assassins / Tim LaHaye, Jerry B. Jenkins.
     p.   cm.
   ISBN 0-8423-2920-X (hardcover)
   ISBN 0-8423-2927-7 (softcover)
   ISBN 0-8423-6555-9 (large print ed.)
   I. Jenkins, Jerry B.   II. Title
PS3562.A315A94   1999
813'.54—dc21   99-23466

Printed in the United States of America

06   05   04   03   02
8   7   6   5   4   3   2   1

To Dr. John F. Walvoord
For more than fifty years,
he has helped keep
the torch of prophecy burning

THIRTY-EIGHT MONTHS INTO THE TRIBULATION

The Believers

Rayford Steele, mid-forties; former 747 captain for Pan-Continental; lost wife and son in the Rapture; former pilot for Global Community Potentate Nicolae Carpathia; original member of the Tribulation Force; an international fugitive now in exile at the safe house in Mount Prospect, Illinois

Cameron ("Buck") Williams, early thirties; former senior writer for *Global Weekly*; former publisher of *Global Community Weekly* for Carpathia; original member of the Trib Force; editor of cybermagazine *The Truth*; fugitive in exile at the safe house

Chloe Steele Williams, early twenties; former student, Stanford University; lost mother and brother in the Rapture; daughter of Rayford; wife of Buck; mother of ten-month-old Kenny Bruce; CEO of the International Commodity Co-op, an underground network of believers; original Trib Force member; fugitive in exile, safe house

Tsion Ben-Judah, late forties; former rabbinical scholar and Israeli statesman; revealed conversion to Christ on international TV—wife and two teen-agers subsequently murdered; escaped to U.S.; spiritual leader and teacher of Trib Force; cyber audience of more than a billion daily; resides at safe house

Dr. Floyd Charles, late thirties; former physician for the GC; exiled at the safe house

Mac McCullum, late fifties; pilot for Nicolae Carpathia; resides in the GC palace complex, New Babylon

David Hassid, mid-twenties; purchasing/shipping/receiving director for the GC; palace complex, New Babylon

Leah Rose, late thirties; head administrative nurse, Arthur Young Memorial Hospital, Palatine, Illinois; lives alone

Tyrola ("T") Mark Delanty, late thirties; owner/director, Palwaukee Airport, Wheeling, Illinois

Mr. and Mrs. Lukas ("Laslos") Miklos, mid-fifties; lignite mining magnates; Greece

Abdullah Smith, early thirties; former fighter pilot; Jordan

The Enemies

Nicolae Carpathia, mid-thirties, former president of Romania; former secretary-general, United Nations; self-appointed Global Community Potentate; GC palace, New Babylon

Leon Fortunato, early fifties; Carpathia's right hand; supreme commander; GC palace, New Babylon

Peter Mathews, late forties; former cardinal, Cincinnati archdiocese; self-appointed Pontifex Maximus, Peter II, head of Enigma Babylon One World Faith; Temple Palace, New Babylon

The Undecided

Hattie Durham, 30, former flight attendant, Pan-Continental; former personal assistant to Nicolae Carpathia; safe house

Dr. Chaim Rosenzweig, late sixties; Israeli botanist and statesman; discoverer of a formula that made Israeli deserts bloom; former *Global Weekly* Man of the Year; Jerusalem

PROLOGUE

A VAST network of house churches had sprung
up—seemingly spontaneously—with converted
Jews, clearly part of the 144,000 witnesses,
taking leadership positions. They taught their
charges daily, based on the cyberspace sermons
and lessons from the prolific Tsion Ben-Judah.
Tens of thousands of such clandestine local house
churches, their very existence flying in the face
of the all-inclusive Enigma Babylon One World
Faith, saw courageous converts added to the
church every day. . . .

●   ●   ●

Buck Williams had long been anonymously
broadcasting his own cyberspace magazine,
The Truth, which would now be his sole writing
outlet. Ironically, it attracted ten times the largest
reading audience he had ever enjoyed as senior

staff writer for *Global Community Weekly*. He worried for his safety, of course, but more for his wife Chloe's. . . .

●　　●　　●

Nicolae Carpathia's litany of achievements ranged from the rebuilding of cities and roads and airports to the nearly miraculous reconstruction of New Babylon into the most magnificent city ever built. "It is a masterpiece I hope you will visit as soon as you can." His cellular/solar satellite system (Cell/Sol) allowed everyone access to each other by phone and Internet, regardless of time or location. All this merely ushered in the superstructure necessary for Nicolae to rule the world. . . .

●　　●　　●

The day would come when the sign of the cross on the forehead would have to say everything between tribulation saints. Even pointing up would draw the attention of enemy forces.

The problem was, the day would also come when the other side would have its own mark, and it would be visible to all. In fact, according to the Bible, those who did not bear this "mark of the beast" would not be able to buy or sell. The great network of saints would then have to develop its own underground market to stay alive. . . .

● ● ●

Global Community Supreme Commander Leon
Fortunato introduced His Excellency, Potentate
Nicolae Carpathia, to the international television
audience. Tsion Ben-Judah had warned Rayford
that Nicolae's supernatural abilities would be
trumpeted and even exaggerated, laying a founda-
tion for when he would declare himself God
during the second half of the Tribulation. . . .

● ● ●

Raucous laughter or silliness just didn't have
a place in the lives of the Tribulation Force.
Grief was wearying, Rayford thought. He looked
forward to that day when God would wipe away
all tears from their eyes, and there would be no
more war. . . .

● ● ●

"I feel such compassion for you," Tsion told
Hattie, "such a longing for you to come to
Jesus." And suddenly he could not continue.

Hattie raised her eyebrows, staring at him.

"Forgive me," he managed in a whisper, taking
a sip of water and collecting himself. He continued through tears. "Somehow God has allowed
me to see you through his eyes—a scared, angry,
shaken young woman who has been used and
abandoned by many in her life. He loves you with

a perfect love. Jesus once looked upon his audience and said, 'O Jerusalem, Jerusalem, the one who kills the prophets and stones those who are sent to her! How often I wanted to gather your children together, as a hen gathers her chicks under her wings, but you were not willing!'

"Miss Durham, you know the truth. I have heard you say so. And yet you are not willing. . . . I look at your fragile beauty and see what life has done to you, and I long for your peace. I think of what you could do for the kingdom during these perilous times, and I am jealous to have you as part of our family. I fear you're risking your life by holding out on God, and I do not look forward to how you might suffer before he reaches you."

●   ●   ●

Rayford's life as an accomplished commercial pilot seems eons ago now. It was hard to comprehend that it had been fewer than three years since he was just a suburban husband and father, and none too good a one, with nothing more to worry about than where and when he was flying next.

Rayford couldn't complain of having had nothing important to occupy his time. But the cost of getting to this point! He could empathize with Tsion. If the Tribulation was hard on a regular Joe like Rayford, he couldn't imagine what it must be like for one called to rally the 144,000 witnesses and teach maybe a billion other new souls. . . .

●　　●　　●

Buck loved talking with Tsion. They had been through so much together. It hit him that he was whining about his wife's complicated pregnancy to a man whose wife and children had been murdered. Yet somehow Tsion had the capacity for wisdom and clear thinking and had a calming effect on people. . . .

"So Trumpet Judgment Six is next," Buck said. "What do you expect there?"

Tsion sighed. "The bottom line, Cameron, is an army of two hundred million horsemen who will slay a third of the world's population."

Buck was speechless. He had read of the prophecy, but he had never boiled it down to its essence. ". . . Whatever we have suffered," Tsion continued, "whatever ugliness we have faced. All will pale in comparison to this worst judgment yet."

"And the ones after this get even worse?"

"Hard to imagine, isn't it? Only one-fourth of the people left behind at the Rapture will survive until the Glorious Appearing, Cameron. I am not afraid of death, but I pray every day that God will allow me the privilege of seeing him return to the earth to set up his kingdom. If he takes me before that, I will be reunited with my family and other loved ones, but oh, the joy of being here when Jesus arrives!"

●   ●   ●

"One woe is past. Behold, still two more woes are coming after these things. Then the sixth angel sounded: And I heard a voice from the four horns of the golden altar which is before God, saying to the sixth angel who had the trumpet, 'Release the four angels who are bound at the great river Euphrates.'

"So the four angels, who had been prepared for the hour and day and month and year, were released. . . ."

Revelation 9:12-15

ONE

RAGE.

No other word described it.

Rayford knew he had much to be thankful for. Neither Irene—his wife of twenty-one years—nor Amanda—his wife of fewer than three months—had to suffer this world any longer. Raymie was in heaven too. Chloe and baby Kenny were healthy.

That should be enough. Yet the cliché *consumed* came to life for Rayford. He stormed out of the safe house in the middle of a crisp May Monday morning, eschewing a jacket and glad of it. It wasn't anyone in the safe house who had set him off.

Hattie had been her typical self, whining about her immobility while building her strength.

"You don't think I'll do it," she had told him as she raced through another set of sit-ups. "You way underestimate me."

"I don't doubt you're crazy enough to try."

"But you wouldn't fly me over there for any price."

"Not on your life."

Rayford stumbled along a path near a row of trees that separated a dusty field from what was left of the safe house and the piles of what had once been neighboring homes. He stopped and scanned the horizon. Anger was one thing. Stupidity another. There was no sense giving away their position just for a moment of fresh air.

He saw nothing and no one, but still he stayed closer to the trees than to the plain. What a difference a year and a half made! This whole area, for miles, had once been sprawling suburbia. Now it was earthquake rubble, abandoned to the fugitive and the destitute. One Rayford had been for months. The other he was fast becoming.

The murderous fury threatened to devour him. His rational, scientific mind fought his passion. He knew others—yes, including Hattie—who had as much or more motive. Yet Rayford pleaded with God to appoint him. He wanted to be the one to do the deed. He believed it his destiny.

Rayford shook his head and leaned against a tree, letting the bark scratch his back. Where was the aroma of newly mown grass, the sounds of kids playing in the yard? Nothing was as it once was. He closed his eyes and ran over the plan one more time. Steal into the Middle East in disguise. Put himself in the right place at the precise time. Be God's weapon, the instrument of death. Murder Nicolae Carpathia.

● ● ●

David Hassid assigned himself to accompany the Global Community helicopter that would take delivery of a gross of computers for the potentate's palace. Half the GC personnel in his department were to spend the next several weeks ferreting out the location of Tsion Ben-Judah's daily cyberspace teaching and Buck Williams's weekly Internet magazine.

The potentate himself wanted to know how quickly the computers could be installed. "Figure half a day to unload, reload, and truck them here from the airport," David had told him. "Then unload again and assume another couple of days for installation and setup."

Carpathia had begun snapping his fingers as soon as "half a day" rolled off David's tongue. "Faster," he said. "How can we steal some hours?"

"It would be costly, but you could—"

"Cost is not my priority, Mr. Hassid. Speed. Speed."

"Chopper could snag the whole load and set 'em down outside the freight entrance."

"That," Carpathia said. "Yes, that."

"I'd want to personally supervise pickup and delivery."

Carpathia was on to something else, dismissing David with a wave. "Of course, whatever."

David called Mac McCullum on his secure phone. "It worked," he said.

"When do we fly?"

"As late as possible. This has to look like a mistake."

Mac chuckled. "Did you get 'em to deliver to the wrong airstrip?"

"'Course. Told 'em one, paperworked 'em another. They'll go by what they heard. I'll protect myself from Abbott and Costello with the paperwork."

"Fortunato still looking over your shoulder?"

"Always, but neither he nor Nicolae suspects. They love you too, Mac."

"Don't I know it. We've got to ride this train as far as it'll take us."

● ● ●

Rayford didn't dare discuss his feelings with Tsion. The rabbi was busy enough, and Rayford knew what he would say: "God has his plan. Let him carry it out."

But what would be wrong with Rayford's helping? He was willing. He could get it done. If it cost him his life, so what? He'd reunite with loved ones, and more would join him later.

Rayford knew it was crazy. He had never been ruled by his feelings before. Maybe his problem was that he was out of the loop now, away from the action. The fear and tension of flying Carpathia around for months had been worth it for the proximity it afforded him and the advantage to the Tribulation Force.

The danger in his present role wasn't the same. He was senior flyer of the International Commodity Co-op, the one entity that might keep believers alive when their freedom to trade on the open market would vanish. For now, Rayford was just meeting contacts, setting up routes, in essence working for his own daughter. He had to remain anonymous and learn whom to trust. But it wasn't the same. He didn't feel as necessary to the cause.

But if he could be the one to kill Carpathia!

Who was he kidding? Carpathia's assassin would likely be put to death without trial. And if Carpathia was indeed the Antichrist—and most people except his followers thought he was—he wouldn't stay dead anyway. The murder would be all about Rayford, not Carpathia. Nicolae would come out of it more heroic than ever. But the fact that it had to be done anyway, and that he himself might be in place to do it, seemed to give Rayford something to live for. And likely to die for.

His grandson, Kenny Bruce, had stolen his heart, but that very name reminded Rayford of painful losses. The late Ken Ritz had been a new friend with the makings of a good one. Bruce Barnes had been Rayford's first mentor and had taught him so much after supplying him the videotape that had led him to Christ.

That was it! That had to be what had produced such hatred, such rage. Rayford knew Carpathia was merely a pawn of Satan, really part of God's plan for the ages. But the man had wreaked such havoc, caused such destruction, fostered such mourning, that Rayford couldn't help but hate him.

Rayford didn't want to grow numb to the disaster, death, and devastation that had become commonplace. He wanted to still feel alive, violated, offended. Things were bad and getting worse, and the chaos multiplied every month. Tsion taught that things were to come to a head at the halfway point of the seven-year tribulation, four months from now. And then would come the Great Tribulation.

Rayford longed to survive all seven years to witness the glorious appearing of Christ to set up his thousand-year reign on earth. But what were the odds? Tsion taught that, at most, only a quarter of the population left at the Rapture would survive to the end, and those who did might wish they hadn't.

Rayford tried to pray. Did he think God would answer, give him permission, put the plot in his mind? He knew better. His scheming was just a way to feel alive, and yet it ate at him, gave him a reason for breathing.

He had other reasons to live. He loved his daughter and her husband and their baby, and yet he felt responsible that Chloe had missed the Rapture. The only family he had left would face the same world he did. What kind of a future was that? He didn't want to think about it. All he wanted to think about was what weapons he might have access to and how he could avail himself of them at the right time.

●　　　●　　　●

Just after dark in New Babylon, David took a call from his routing manager. "Pilot wants to know if he's to put down at the strip or at—"

"I told him already! Tell him to do what he's told!"

"Sir, the bill of lading says palace airstrip. But he thought you told him New Babylon Airport."

David paused as if angry. "Do *you* understand what I said?"

"You said airport, but—"

"Thank you! What's his ETA?"

"Thirty minutes to the airport. Forty-five to the strip. Just so I'm clear—"

David hung up and called Mac. Half an hour later they were sitting in the chopper on the tarmac of the palace airstrip. Of course the computer cargo was not there. David called the airport. "Tell the pilot where we are!"

"Man," Mac said, "you've got everybody chasin' their tails."

"You think I want new computers in front of the world's best techies, all looking to find the safe house?"

Mac tuned in the airport frequency and heard the instruction for the cargo pilot to take off and put down at the palace strip. He looked at David. "To the airport, chopper jockey," David said.

"We'll pass 'im in the sky."

"I hope we do."

They did. David finally had pity on the pilot, assured him he and Mac would stay put, and instructed him to come back.

A crane helped disgorge the load of computers, and Mac maneuvered the helicopter into position to hook up to it. The cargo chief attached the cable, assured Mac he had the size and power to easily transport the load, and instructed him how to lift off. "You've got an onboard release in case of emergency, sir," he said, "but you should have no problem."

Mac thanked him and caught David's glance. "You wouldn't," he said, shaking his head.

"Of course I would. This lever here? I'll be in charge of this."

TWO

EARLY after noon, Buck sat at his computer in the vastly enlarged shelter beneath the safe house. He and his father-in-law and Dr. Charles had done the bulk of the excavating work. It wasn't that Dr. Ben-Judah had been unwilling or unable. He had proved remarkably fit for a man with his nose in scholarly works and his eyes on a computer screen the majority of every day.

But Buck and the others encouraged him to stay at his more important work via the Internet— teaching the masses of new believers and pleading for converts. It was clear Tsion felt he was slacking by letting the other men do the manual labor while he toiled at what he called *soft work* in an upstairs bedroom. For days all he had wanted to do was join the others in digging, sacking, and carrying the dirt from the cellar to the nearby fields. The others had told him they were fine without his help, that it was too crowded with four men in the cramped space, that his ministry was too crucial to be postponed by grunt work.

Finally, Buck recalled with a smile, Rayford had told Tsion, "You're the elder, our pastor, our mentor, our scholar, but I have seniority and authority as ersatz head of this band, and I'm pulling rank."

Tsion had straightened in the dank underground and leaned back, mock fear on his face. "Yes, sir," he said. "And my assignment?"

"To stay out of our way, old man. You have the soft hands of the educated. Of course, so do we, but you're in the way."

Tsion had dragged a sleeve across his forehead. "Oh, Rayford, stop teasing me. I just want to help."

Buck and Doc stopped their work and joined, in essence, in ganging up on Tsion. "Dr. Ben-Judah," Floyd Charles said, "we all really do feel you're wasting your time—*we're* wasting your time—by letting you do this. Please, for our sakes, clear our consciences and let us finish without you."

It was Rayford's turn to feign offense. "So much for *my* authority," he said. "I just gave an order, and now Sawbones pleads with him yet again!"

"You gentlemen are serious," Tsion said, his Israeli accent thick as ever.

Rayford raised both hands. "Finally! The scholar gets it."

Tsion trundled back upstairs, grumbling that it "still does not make any sense," but he had not again tried to insert himself into the excavation team.

Buck was impressed with how the other three had melded. Rayford was the most technologically astute, Buck himself sometimes too analytical, and Floyd—despite his medical degree—seemingly content to do what he was told. Buck teased him about that, telling him he thought doctors assumed they knew everything. Floyd was not combative, but neither did Buck find him amused. In fact, Floyd seemed to run out of gas earlier every day, but he never slacked. He just spent a lot of time catching his breath, running his hands through his hair, and rubbing his eyes.

Rayford mapped out each day's work with a rough sketch amalgamated from two sources. The first came from the meticulously hen-scratched spiral notebooks of the original owner of the place, Donny Moore, who had been crushed to death at the church during the great wrath of the Lamb earthquake nearly eighteen months before. Buck and Tsion had discovered Donny's wife's body in the demolished breakfast nook at the back of the house.

Donny had apparently planned for just such

a future, somehow assuming that one day he and his wife would have to live in seclusion. Whether he feared nuclear fallout or just hiding from Global Community forces, he had crafted an expansive plan. His layout enlarged the tiny, dank cellar at the back of the house to extend beneath the entire other side of the duplex and far out into the yard.

The other source Rayford had consulted was the late Ken Ritz's refinement of the original plan. Ken had honed his image as a clod-kicking blue-collar bush pilot. It turned out he was a graduate of the London School of Economics, licensed in all manner of high-speed jets, and—as these schematics showed—a self-taught architect. Ken had streamlined the excavation process, moved Donny's support beams, and devised a central communications protocol. When all was in place, the shelter should be undetectable and the various satellite linkups, cellular receivers and transmitters, and infrared computer interfaces easy to access and service.

While Buck worked with Doc and Rayford, and Tsion wrote his masterful daily missives to his global audience, Chloe and Hattie busied themselves with their own pursuits. Hattie seemed to work out every spare moment, madly building tone and endurance and adding weight to what had become her emaciated frame.

Buck worried she was up to something. She usually was. No one in the house was certain she hadn't already compromised their location with her ill-conceived effort to buy her way to Europe months before. So far no one had come nosing around the place, but how long could that last?

Chloe spent the bulk of her time with baby Kenny, of course. When she wasn't sneaking in a nap to try to regain her own strength, she used her free moments to work via the Net with her growing legion of Commodity Co-op suppliers and distributors. Already believers were beginning to buy and sell to and from each other, in anticipation of the dark day when they would be banished from normal trade.

The pressure of close quarters and lots of work, not to mention dread of the future, was Buck's constant companion. He was grateful he could do his own writing and help Rayford and Doc with the shelter while still getting time with Chloe and Kenny. But somehow his days were as long as ever. The only time he and Chloe had to themselves was at the end of the day when they were barely awake enough to talk. Kenny slept in their room, and while he was not the type to bother the rest of the household, both Buck and Chloe were often up with him in the night.

Buck lay awake one midnight, pleased to hear

Chloe's deep rhythmic breathing and know she
was asleep. He was mulling how to improve the
efficiency of the Trib Force, hoping he could
contribute as much as the other men seemed to.
From the beginning, when the Force consisted
of just the late Bruce Barnes, Rayford, Chloe,
and him, Buck felt he had become part of a
pivotal, cosmic effort. Among the earliest believers following the Rapture, the Tribulation Force
was committed to winning people to Christ,
opposing Antichrist, and surviving until the
reappearing of Christ, now just over three and
a half years away.

Tsion, whom God had provided to replace
Bruce, was a priceless commodity who needed
to be protected above all. His knowledge and
passion, along with his ability to communicate
on a layman's level, made him Nicolae Carpathia's number one enemy. At least number
one after the two witnesses at the Wailing Wall,
who continued to torment unbelievers with
plagues and judgments.

Chloe astounded him with her ability to run
an international company while taking care of
a new baby. Doc was clearly a gift from God,
having saved Hattie's life and keeping the rest
of them healthy. Hattie was the only unbeliever
and understandably selfish. She spent most of
her time on herself.

But Buck worried most about Rayford. His father-in-law had not been himself lately. He seemed to seethe, short-tempered with Hattie and often lost in thought, his face clouded with despair. Rayford also had begun taking breaks from the house, walking nowhere in the middle of the day. Buck knew Rayford would not be careless, but he wished someone could help. He asked Tsion to probe, but the rabbi said, "Captain Steele eventually comes to me when he wants to reveal something. I do not feel free to pursue private matters with him."

Buck had asked Doc's opinion. "He's my mentor, not the other way around," Floyd said. "I go to him with my problems; I don't expect him to come to me with his."

Chloe begged off too. "Buck, Daddy is a traditional, almost old-world father. He'll give me all the unsolicited advice he wishes, but I wouldn't dream of trying to get him to open up to me."

"But you see it, don't you?"

"Of course. But what do you expect? We're all crazy by now. Is this any way to live? Going nowhere in daylight except to Palwaukee once in a while, having to use aliases and worry constantly about being found out?"

Buck's compatriots all had reasons for not confronting Rayford. Buck would have to do it. *Oh, joy,* he thought.

●   ●   ●

David Hassid sat in the passenger seat of GC Chopper One, watching with Mac McCullum. The ground crew at New Babylon Airport hooked a thick steel cable from the helicopter to three bundled skids containing 144 computers. The crew chief signaled Mac to begin a slow ascent until the cable was taut. Then he gently lifted off, ostensibly to deliver the cargo to the Global Community palace.

Mac said, "The skids should take care of themselves, provided you keep away from that release lever. You wouldn't really do that, would you?"

"To delay my own staff from finding Tsion's and Buck's and Chloe's transmission point? You bet I would, if it was the only way."

"If?"

"C'mon, Mac. You know me better than that by now. You think I would trash that many computers? I may be only about a third your age—"

"Hey!"

"All right, a little less than half, but give me some credit. You think the number of computers we ordered was lost on me?"

Mac held up a finger and depressed his radio transmitter. "GC Chopper One to palace tower, over."

"This is tower, One, go."

"ETA three minutes, over."

"Roger, out."

Mac turned to David. "I figured that's why you ordered a gross. One for every thousand witnesses."

"Not that it'll parcel out that way, but no, I'm not going to crash them in the desert."

"But I'm not putting down at the palace either, am I?"

David smiled and shook his head. From their position he had a view of the sprawling palace complex. Acres and acres of buildings surrounded the great gleaming castle—what else could he call it—Carpathia had erected in honor of himself. Every imaginable convenience was included, thousands of employees dedicated to every Carpathia whim.

David dug his secure phone from his pocket and punched a speed number. "Corporal A. Christopher," he said. "Director Hassid calling." He covered the phone and told Mac, "Your new cargo chief for the Condor."

"Do I know him?"

David shrugged and shook his head. "Yes, Corporal Christopher. Is the Condor hold accessible? . . . Excellent. Be ready for us. . . . Well, I can't help that, Corporal. You may feel free to speak with Personnel, but my understanding is that you have no say in that."

David held the phone away from his face and turned it off. "Hung up on me," he said.

"Nobody likes the cargo job for the two-one-six," Mac said. "Not enough work. You trust this guy?"

"No choice," David said.

●   ●   ●

Buck had temporarily moved his computer to the kitchen table and was rapping out a story for *The Truth* when Rayford returned from his morning walk. "Hey," Buck said. Rayford only nodded and stood at the top of the stairs to the cellar.

Buck's resolve nearly left him. "What's the plan today, Ray?"

"Same as always," Rayford muttered. "We've got to start getting walls up down here. And then we've got to make the shelter invisible. No apparent access. Where's Doc?"

"Haven't seen him. Hattie's in the—"

"Other side, of course. Training for a marathon, no doubt. She's going to wind up getting us all killed."

"Hey, Dad," Buck tried, "way to look on the bright side."

Rayford ignored him. "Where's everybody else?" he said.

"Tsion's upstairs. Chloe's on her computer in the living room. Kenny's napping. I told you where Hattie is; only Floyd is AWOL. He might be downstairs, but I didn't notice him go down."

"Don't say he's AWOL, Buck. That's not funny."

It was unusual for Rayford to chastise him, and Buck hardly knew how to respond. "I just mean he's unaccounted for, Ray. Truth is, he hasn't looked well lately and looked awful yesterday. Wonder if he's sleeping in."

"Till noon? What was the matter with him?"

"I saw a little yellow in his eyes."

"I didn't."

"It's dark down there."

"Then how'd you see it?"

"Noticed last night, that's all. I even said something to him about it."

"What'd he say?"

"Some joke about how honkies always think the brothers look strange. I didn't pursue it."

"He's the doctor," Rayford said. "Let him worry about himself." That, Buck decided, was a perfect opening. He could tell Rayford that he didn't sound like his usual compassionate self. But the moment passed when Rayford took the offensive. "What's *your* schedule today, Buck? Magazine or shelter work?"

"You're the boss, Ray. You tell me."

"I could use you downstairs, but suit yourself." Buck rose.

●   ●   ●

Mac delicately lowered the skids onto the pavement at the east side of the hangar that housed the Condor 216. The hangar door was open, the cavernous cargo hold of the Condor also agape. David jumped out before the blades stopped whirring and hurried to unhook the cable from the cargo. Out from the hangar sped a forklift that quickly engaged the first load, smoothly tilted it back against the truck, then spun in a circle and shot back into the hangar. By the time Mac joined David and they shut the hangar door, the forklift operator had shut the Condor cargo hold and was replacing the forklift in a corner.

"Corporal Christopher!" David shouted, and the corporal whirled to face him from a hundred feet away. "Your office, now!"

"Doesn't look too pleased," Mac said as they walked to the glassed-in office within the hangar. "No salute, no response. Negative body language. Gonna be a problem?"

"The corporal is my subordinate. I hold all the cards."

"Just the same, David, you have to give respect to get respect. And we can trust no one. You don't want one of your key people—"

"Trust me, Mac. It's under control."

The name on the office door next to Mac's had just been repainted: "CCCCC."

"*What* is that?" Mac said.

"Corporal Christopher, Condor Cargo Chief."

"Please!" Mac said.

David motioned Mac to follow him into the corporal's office, shut the door, and sat behind the desk, pointing to a chair for Mac. The older man seemed to sit reluctantly.

"What?" David said.

"This is how you treat a subordinate?"

David put his feet on the desk and nodded. "Especially a new one. Got to establish who's boss."

"I was taught that if you have to use the word *boss* with an employee, you've already lost 'em."

David shrugged. "Dark ages," he said. "Desperate times, desperate measures . . ."

Footsteps stopped outside the door, and the knob turned. David called out, "Surely you'll knock before walking in on your boss and your pilot, won't you, Corporal?"

The door stopped, open an inch.

"Shut the door and knock, Corporal!" David hollered, his hands behind his head, feet still on the desk.

The door shut, a little too loudly. Then a long pause. Finally, three deliberate and loud raps on the door. Mac shook his head. "This guy even knocks sarcastically," he whispered. "But you deserve it."

"Enter," David said.

Mac's chair scraped as he bolted upright in the presence of a young woman in fatigues. Under her cap showed short cropped black hair, cut almost like a man's, but she was trim and comely with large dark eyes, perfect teeth, and flawless skin.

Mac whipped off his cap. "Ma'am."

"Spare me, Captain," she said, then turned her scowl on David. "I'm required to knock to enter my own office?"

David had not moved. "Sit down, Mac," he said.

"When the lady sits down," Mac said.

"I'm not giving her permission to sit," David said, and Corporal Christopher waved Mac to his seat. "Captain Mac McCullum, this is Corporal Annie Christopher. Annie, Mac."

Mac started to rise again, but Annie stepped and shook his hand. "No need, Captain. I know who you are, and your Neanderthal chauvinism is noted. If we're going to work together, you can quit treating me like a little woman."

Mac looked at her and then at David. "Maybe you treat her with the respect she deserves," he said.

David cocked his head. "Like you said, Mac. You never know whom you can trust. As for this being your office, Corporal, everything of yours is mine as long as you're under my command. This space has been parceled to you to facilitate your doing what I tell you. Understood?"

"Clearly."

"And, Corporal, I'm not even military, but I know it's a breach of protocol to keep your head covered in the presence of your superior."

Annie Christopher sighed and let her shoulders slump as she whipped off her cap. She ran a hand through her short hair and moved to the window between the office and the rest of the hangar. She closed the blinds.

"What are you doing?" David said. "There's no one out there, and I didn't give you permission to—"

"Oh, come now, Director Hassid. Do I need your permission for everything?"

David lifted his feet off the desk and sat upright as Annie approached. "As a matter of fact, you do."

He opened his arms and she sat on his lap. "How are you, sweetheart?" she said.

"I'm good, hon, but I think Mac's about to have a heart attack."

Mac slid to the edge of his chair and leaned forward, elbows on knees. "You're both brats," he said. "Forgive me, Miss Christopher, if I check your mark."

"Be my guest," she said, leaning across the

desk so he could reach her. "You can bet that's what David and I did the day we met."

Mac cradled the back of her head in his palm and ran his other thumb across the mark on her forehead. He cupped her face in his hands and kissed her gently atop the head. "You're young enough to be my daughter," he said, "sister."

Annie moved to another chair. "And for the record, Captain McCullum, I can't stand working for either of you. Personnel has a standing request from me, demanding that I be reassigned. The director of my department is condescending and unbearable, and the captain of the Condor is unbearably sexist."

"But," David said, "I have informed Personnel that she is not to be catered to. Annie has caused trouble in every department she's served, and it's payback time for her. They love it."

Mac squinted at her, then at David. "I can't wait to hear your stories," he said.

● ● ●

Buck postponed his heart-to-heart with his father-in-law when Rayford spread the plans under a light in the basement and asked his advice on how to make the entrance impossible to detect.

"Thought you'd never ask," Buck said. "Actually, I *have* been noodling this."

"I'm all ears."

"You know the freezer in the other duplex?"

"The smelly one."

Buck nodded. They had discarded the spoiled food, but the stench inside remained. "Move that over here, stock it with what looks like spoiled food but only smells that way because of the residue, and hinge the food trays at the back. Anyone who looks in there will be repelled by the smell and won't look close at what they assume is spoiled food. They'll never think to lift the food trays, but if they do, they'll find a false bottom that opens to the stairs to the shelter. Meanwhile, we put a wall over the current basement door."

Rayford cocked his head, as if searching his mind for a flaw. He shrugged. "I like it. Now if there was a way to keep it from Hattie."

Buck looked around. "So I was right? Floyd's not down here?"

● ● ●

Mac's beeper vibrated. "Fortunato," he said. "Terrific. May I use your phone, Corporal?"

Annie said, "It's not my phone, sir. It's merely been parceled out to me. . . ."

He phoned Fortunato's office. "Mac McCullum returning his call. . . . Yes, ma'am. . . . Friday? . . . How many guests? . . . No, ma'am. You may tell him there was some sort of a snafu about that shipment. He'll have to talk with the purchasing director, but no, those were not available to be delivered to the palace. . . . Perhaps when we return from Botswana, yes, ma'am."

●   ●   ●

Dr. Floyd Charles's bedroom door was shut. Buck saw Tsion at his computer in the next room, forehead in his hand, elbow on the desk. "You OK, Tsion?"

"Cameron! Come in, please. Just resting my eyes."

"Praying?"

The rabbi smiled wearily. "Without ceasing. We have no choice, have we? How are you, my friend? Still worried about your father-in-law?"

"Yeah, but I'll talk to him. I was wondering if you'd seen Doc today?"

"We usually share an early breakfast, as you know. But I was alone this morning. I did not hear him in the basement, and I confess I have not thought about it since. I have been writing. Cameron, we have no idea how long this lull may last between the fifth and sixth woes. I am trying to decide myself whether what John saw in his vision is real or symbolic. As you know—"

"Dr. Ben-Judah, forgive me. I want to hear this—"

"Yes, of course. You should check in on Floyd. We will talk later."

"I don't mean to be rude."

"You need not apologize, Cameron. Now go. We will talk later. Call if you need me."

Buck had never grown used to the privilege of living in the same house as the man whose daily words were like breath to millions around the world. Though Tsion was usually within a few dozen steps, when he was too busy or too tired to talk, the others in the household downloaded his messages from the Net. The best part about living with him was that he was as excited about the messages as were his audiences. He labored over them all morning and most of the afternoon in preparation for transmitting no later than early evening. All over the world sympathetic translators converted his words into the languages of their people. Other computer-literate believers invested hours every day in cataloguing Dr. Ben-Judah's information and making it easily accessible to newcomers.

When Tsion came across some startling revelation in his study, Buck often heard him exult and knew he would soon pad out to the top of the stairs. "Listen to this," he would call out, "anyone who can hear me!" His knowledge of the biblical languages made his commentary the absolute latest thought on a given passage by the world's most astute Bible scholar.

Buck couldn't wait to hear what Tsion was wrestling with about the prophesied sixth woe. But for now he worried about Doc. He tapped lightly on his bedroom door. Then louder. He turned the knob and entered. It was the middle of the afternoon, the spring sun high in the sky. But the room was dark, the shades pulled. And Doc Charles was still in bed. Very still.

●　　●　　●

"Goin' to Africa Friday," Mac said. "Fortunato's agreed to a face-to-face request by Mwangati Ngumo. 'Course Ngumo thinks he's meeting with Nicolae. Bet Mwangati's wonderin' when Carpathia's gonna make good on his promises."

Annie Christopher snorted. "Imagine what the potentate must have promised him to get him to give up the secretary-generalship."

"We'll know Friday," Mac said. "At least I will."

Annie looked at Mac. "They let you sit in on these meetings?" she said.

Mac glanced at David. "You haven't told her?"

"Feel free," David said.

"Come with me, Corporal," Mac said.

She and David followed him out. "I'll keep calling you *Captain* or *Mr. McCullum*, even in private," Annie said. "I let you check my mark and kiss me on the head. But the most formal thing you're allowed to call me from now on is *Sister.*"

"I don't know," Mac said. "I'd better keep it formal, just so I don't slip up in front of somebody." She followed him into the cockpit.

●　　●　　●

"Doc?" Buck said, approaching the bed. He detected no movement. He didn't want to scare him.

Assuming the light would be less blinding than sunshine, Buck flipped it on. He sighed. At least Floyd was breathing. Perhaps he had merely had trouble falling asleep and was catching up. Floyd groaned and turned.

"You all right, Doc?" Buck tried.

Floyd sat up, his face a mask of puzzlement. "I was afraid of this," he said.

"I'm sorry," Buck said. "I just—"

Floyd whipped off the blankets. He sat on the edge of the bed in a long terry cloth robe that fell open to reveal him fully clothed in flannel shirt, jeans, and boots. He had sweat through it all.

"Was it that cold last night?" Buck said.

"Open those drapes, would ya?"

Floyd covered his eyes as the light burst into the room.

"What's the matter, Floyd?"

"Your vehicle in running order?"

"Sure."

"Get me to Young Memorial. My eyes still yellow?"

He squinted at Buck, who bent to look.

"Oh, Floyd," Buck said. "I wish they were."

"Bloodshot?"

"That's an understatement."

"No white showing?"

Buck shook his head.

"I'm in trouble, Buck."

THREE

DAVID, Mac, and Annie Christopher sat in the luxurious lounge of the Condor, twenty feet behind the cockpit. "So," Annie said, "the what-did-you-call-it reverse thingie—"

"Reverse intercom bug," Mac said.

"—lets you hear *everything* in the cabin?"

Mac nodded. "Lounge, seats, sleeping quarters, lavs—everywhere."

"Amazing."

"Somethin', ain't it?" Mac said.

"Amazing you haven't been caught."

"You kiddin'? They discover it now, I disavow knowledge of it. I had nothing to do with it, Rayford never told me it was here, I never stumbled upon it. They already see him as a traitor. And neither they nor I know where he is, do we?"

Annie moved to a couch behind a highly

polished wood table. "This is where the big man himself watches TV?"

David nodded.

She turned back to Mac as if she had just thought of something. "You have no trouble lying?"

Mac shook his head. "To the Antichrist, you serious? My *life* is a lie to him. If he had a clue, I'd be tortured. If he thought I knew where Rayford was, or Ray's daughter and son-in-law, I'd be dead."

"End justifies the means?" Annie said.

Mac shrugged. "I sleep at night. That's all I can tell you."

"I'll sleep a little better myself," she said, "knowing you've got Carpathia under surveillance."

"At least when he's on board," Mac said. "Actually, Leon's more entertaining. There's a piece of work."

"Wish I could go with you," Annie said.

"Me too," David said. "But unless we're in the cockpit, we wouldn't hear anything anyway. Speaking of that, Mac, you still worried your first officer's on to you?"

"Not anymore," Mac said. "Got him promoted. He's gonna be Pompous Maximum's pilot."

Annie laughed. "I love it! I got in trouble for forgetting part of his title once. It's His

Excellency Pontifex Maximus, Peter the Second, isn't it?"

Mac shrugged. "I call him Pete."

"You should see the plane he's ordered," David said. "Nicolae and Leon are beside themselves."

"Better'n this one?" Mac said.

"Way better. Fifty percent larger, costs twice as much. Used to belong to a sheik. I'm taking delivery in a week."

"They approved it?"

"They're setting him up," David said, "letting him hang himself. Will his new pilot be able to fly it?"

"He can fly anything," Mac said. "I liked him. Good skills. But a total Carpathia loyalist. Much as I wanted to get to him—you know, really talk to him—I didn't dare give myself away. He was already getting pitched by a believer in C sector."

"Maintenance?" Annie said. "I didn't know we had any believers over there."

"We don't anymore. My guy ratted him out. Would've done that to me too. God's going to have to reach him some other way."

David stood and ran his fingers along the base of the wide-screen TV. He turned it on, muted the sound, and idly watched the Carpathia-controlled news. "Amazing reception inside a metal building," he said.

"Nothing surprises me anymore," Mac said. "Turn that up."

The news mostly carried stories of Carpathia's accomplishments. The potentate himself came on, smooth and charming as ever, praising some regional government and humbly deferring praise for his own reconstruction project. "It is my privilege to have been asked to serve each and every member of the Global Community," he said.

"There you are, Mac," David said, pointing out the pilot in the background as Carpathia was welcomed to yet another former Third World country that had benefited from his largesse. "And there's Peter's new pilot. You bringing in a believer to replace him?"

"If I can sneak him past Personnel."

"Anybody I know?"

"Jordanian. Former fighter pilot. Abdullah Smith."

● ● ●

Buck's Land Rover bounced along toward Palatine. Floyd Charles lay across the backseat. "What is it, Doc?" Buck said.

"I'm a fool is all," Floyd said. He sat up, settling directly behind Buck. "I felt this coming on for months, telling myself I was imagining it. When the vision started to go, I should have contacted the Centers for Disease Control. It's too late now."

"I'm not following you."

"Let's just say I figured out what almost killed Hattie. I contracted it from her somehow. In layman's terms, it's like time-released cyanide. Can gestate for months. When it kicks in, you're a goner. If it's what I've got, there'll be no stopping it. I've been treating the symptoms, but that was useless."

"Don't talk like that," Buck said. "If Hattie survived, why can't you?"

"'Cause she was treated personally and daily for months."

"We'll pray. Leah Rose will get what you need."

"Too late," Doc said. "I'm a fool. A doctor is his own worst patient."

"Are the rest of us in trouble?"

"Nah. If you haven't had symptoms, you're in the clear. I had to have gotten it when delivering her miscarriage."

"So, what about Leah?"

"I can only hope."

Buck's phone chirped.

"Where are you?" Chloe asked.

"Running an errand with Floyd. Didn't want to bother you."

"It bothered me to hear you take off and not

know where you were going. Errands in broad daylight? Daddy's not happy. He was supposed to go see T at the airport today."

"He can use Ken's car."

"Too recognizable, but that's not the point. No one knew where you guys went. Tsion's worried."

Buck sighed. "Floyd's not well and time is crucial. We're on our way to Young Memorial. I'll keep you posted."

"What's—"

"Later, hon. OK?"

She hesitated. "Be careful, and tell Floyd we'll pray."

● ● ●

"We shouldn't be seen together a lot," Mac said, and David and Annie nodded. "Except what would be normal. Anybody know you're here now?"

Annie shook her head. "I've got a meeting at ten tonight."

"I'm clear," David said. "But there's no normal workday anymore, in case you hadn't noticed. You've got to wonder when Carpathia sleeps."

"I want to hear you guys' stories, David," Mac said. "I know you still have family in Israel. Where you from, Annie?"

"Canada. I was flying here from Montreal when the earthquake hit. Lost my whole family."

"You weren't a believer yet?"

She shook her head. "I don't guess I'd ever been to church except for weddings and funerals. We didn't care enough to be atheists, but that's what we practiced. Would have called ourselves agnostics. Sounded more tolerant, less dogmatic. We were tight. Good people. Better than most religious people we knew."

"But you weren't curious about God?"

"I started wondering after the disappearances, but we became instant devotees of Carpathia. He was like a voice of reason, a man of compassion, love, peace. I applied to work for the cause as soon as the U.N. changed its name and announced plans to move here. The day I was accepted was the happiest of my life, of our whole family's life."

"What happened?"

"Losing them all happened. I was devastated. I'd been scared before, sure. Knew some people who had disappeared and some who had died in all that happened later. But I had never lost anyone close, ever. Then I lose my mom and dad and my two younger brothers in the earthquake, not to mention half our town, while I'm merrily in the sky. We wind up landing in the sand at Baghdad Airport, see other planes

go down. I find out GC headquarters is demolished, finally report to the underground shelter,
and see the ruins of my little suburb on CNN.
I was a mess for days, crying, praying to who-
knows-who, pleading with Communications
for word about my family. They were slower
than I was on the Internet, so I just kept searching. I finally found dozens of names I knew on
the confirmed dead list. I didn't even want to
look under C, but I couldn't stop myself."

Annie bit her lip.

"You don't have to talk about it if—"

"I want to, Mr. McCullum. It's just that it
seems like yesterday. I checked into un-enlisting,
going back for memorial services, looking into
claiming the bodies. But that wasn't allowed.
Mass cremations for health reasons. There wasn't
even anyone left to commiserate with. I wanted
to kill myself."

David put a hand on her shoulder. "Tell him
what you found on the Net."

"You must know," Annie said, looking up
with moist eyes. Mac nodded. "I first saw all the
rebuttals of Dr. Ben-Judah coming from the shelter. That was even before I found his Web site.
When the GC made noises about making it illegal
to even access that site, I had to see it. I was still a
blind loyalist, but Carpathia preaches individual
freedom even while he's denying it. The whole

praying thing scared me. I had never given God a second thought. Now I wished he were there for me. I had no one else."

"So you found Tsion."

"I found his home page. I couldn't believe it. A number in the corner of the page—you must have seen it—showed how many people were accessing the site every so many seconds. I thought it was exaggerated, but then I realized this was why the GC was already trying to counter him. Someone gaining that vast an audience was a threat. I clicked through the site and read that day's message from Ben-Judah. I recalled having heard of him when he declared his conversion over international TV. But that's not what impressed me. And I didn't too much understand what he was communicating that day on the Net either. It looked like Bible stuff and was beyond me, but his tone was so warm. It was as if he were sitting there next to me and just chatting, telling me what was going on and what to expect. I knew if I could ask him questions, he would have answers. Then I saw the archives. I thought, *Archives already?* I mean, how old could the site be?

"I clicked through the listings, amazed that he had posted a significant teaching message every day for weeks already. When I came upon one called "For Those Who Mourn," I nearly fainted.

I felt warm all over, then a chill. I locked my door
and hoped the GC hadn't begun monitoring our
laptops. I had the greatest sense of anticipation
ever. Somehow I knew this man had something
for me. I printed out that message and carried
it with me for months, until David and I discovered each other and he warned me I shouldn't
be caught with it. So I memorized it before I
destroyed it."

Mac shot her a double take. "You memorized
an entire Ben-Judah message?"

"Pretty much. Want to hear the first para-
graph?"

"Sure."

"He wrote, 'Dear troubled friend, you may
be mourning the loss of a loved one who either
disappeared in the Rapture or has been killed
in the ensuing chaos. I pray God's peace and
comfort for you. I know what it is to lose my
immediate family in a most unspeakable manner.
But let me tell you this with great confidence:
If your loved ones were alive today, they would
urge you to be absolutely certain you're ready
to die. There is only one way to do that.'"

David could tell Mac was moved.

"Dr. Ben-Judah explained God and Jesus and
the Rapture and the Tribulation so clearly that
I desperately wanted to believe. All I had to do
was look back at his other teachings to realize

that he was right about the Bible prophecies.
He has predicted every judgment so far."

Mac nodded, smiling.

"Well," she said, "of course you know that.
I switched back to the archived message and read
how to pray, how to tell God you know you're
a sinner and that you need him. I laid facedown
on my bed and did that. I knew I had received
the truth, but I had no idea what to do next.
I spent the rest of the day and night, all night,
reading as much of the teaching as I could. It
became quickly obvious why the GC tried to
counter Dr. Ben-Judah. He was careful not to
mention Nicolae by name, but it was clear the
new world order was the enemy of God. I didn't
understand much about the Antichrist, but I
knew I had to be unique among GC employees.
Here I was, in the shelter of the enemy of God,
and I was a believer."

"That's where I come in," David said. "She
thought I was making eyes at her."

"Don't get ahead of the story," Annie said.
"The next time I went out into the employee
population, I was afraid I *looked* like a believer.
I thought anybody I talked to would be able to
tell that I had a secret. I wanted to tell somebody,
but I knew no one. I had arrived in the middle
of chaos and was assigned quarters, given a uniform, and told to report to Communications. I

was working several levels below David, but I noticed him looking at me. First he seemed alarmed, then he smiled."

"He saw your mark," Mac said.

"Well, yeah, but see, I had not gotten far enough into Tsion's teachings to know about that. Anyway, David sent word down through the various supervisors that he wanted to meet with me. I said, 'Personally?'

"As soon as I got in there and the door was shut, he said, 'You're a believer!'

"I was scared to death. I said, 'No, I—a believer in what?'

"He said, 'Don't deny it! I can see it on your face!' He had to be fishing, so I denied it again. He said, 'You deny Jesus one more time, you're going to be just like Peter. Watch out for a rooster.'

"I had no idea what he was talking about. I couldn't have told you that Peter was a disciple, let alone that he had denied Christ. David had guessed my secret, mentioned someone named Peter, and was jabbering about a rooster. Still I couldn't help myself. I said, 'I'm not denying Jesus.'

"He said, 'What do you call it?'

"I said, 'Fearing for my life.'

"He said, 'Welcome to the club. I'm a believer too.'

"I said, 'But how did you know?'

"He said, 'It's written all over you.'

"I said, 'But really, how?'

"And he said, 'Literally, God wrote it on your forehead.' That's when I knew I had stepped off the edge."

●　　●　　●

As soon as Buck and Floyd Charles entered Young Memorial, the teenage receptionist called out, "Miz Rose, your friends are here."

"Keep your voice down!" Leah said, hurrying from her office. "Gentlemen, I'm not sure I can do anything for you today. What's the trouble?"

Floyd whispered it to her quickly. "God help us," she said. "This way. Grab that."

"Have you had any symptoms?" Doc said.

She shook her head. Buck appropriated a wheelchair and pushed Floyd behind Leah. She led them down a short ramp, past the main elevators, and around a corner to the service elevator. She used a key from a huge, jangly ring to access it. "If you see anyone, hide your face," she said. "Just don't make it obvious."

"Yeah, that wouldn't be obvious," Buck said.

She glared at him. "I know you know what real danger is, Mr. Williams, so I'd appreciate it if you'd not underestimate mine."

"Sorry."

They boarded and the doors shut. Leah used her key again and held the sixth floor button. "Don't know if this'll work," she said. "On the other one you can bypass other floors by turning the key and holding down the button."

It didn't work. The car stopped on two. Buck immediately knelt before Doc as if chatting with him. That blocked both their faces from the door. "Sorry," Leah told the people waiting. "Emergency."

"Oh, man!" someone said.

The same thing happened on five and elicited an even more frustrated response.

"This is not good," Leah said as the doors shut again. "Be prepared for people in the hallway on six. We're going left."

Fortunately, the trio was ignored as Leah led the way to an empty room. She shut the door and locked it, then closed the blinds. "Get him into the bed," she told Buck, "and get those wet clothes off him. You sleep that way, Doctor?"

Doc nodded, looking tired.

Buck hated the bright red around his dark pupils. "What's wrong with him, Leah?"

She ignored Buck, grabbing a gown from a cabinet and tossing it to him. "If he needs to use the bathroom, now's the time. He's not likely to get out of that bed again."

"For how long?" Buck said.

"Ever," Doc slurred. "She knows what's going down here."

Leah pushed the speaker button on the wall phone and continued working as she talked. "CDC delivered some antivenin yesterday. Get me two vials to 6204."

"Stat?" her receptionist said.

Leah made a face. "Yes, stat!" she said. "Like now."

"You've got a phone call."

"Do I sound free to take a call? *Stat* was your word, girl. Would you hurry please?"

"OK," the girl said. "Don't say I didn't tell you."

Leah tugged Buck's sleeve and pulled him close to Doc's bed. "I need to ask him some questions. When that girl knocks, just take the medicine and shut the door."

He nodded.

"Now, Doctor," she said. "First symptoms?"

"Quite a while ago," he mumbled.

"Not good enough. When?"

"I'm a fool."

"We know that. How soon after you brought that miscarriage in here?"

"Maybe six months."

"You've done nothing about it?"

He shook his head. "Just hoped."

"That's not going to work."

"That's what I was afraid of."

"You know the closest CDC can get to an antidote is antivenin, and no one knows—"

"It's too late anyway."

Leah looked at Buck and shook her head. "He's right," she said. "The antivenin won't even let him die comfortably."

"What're you telling me?" Buck said. "He hasn't even got a chance?"

Doc shook his head and closed his eyes.

"The maximum antivenin dosage will be like spitting into the wind," Leah said. "What can you see, Doctor?"

"Not much."

Leah pressed her lips together.

There was a knock at the door. Buck opened it, reached for the medicine, and the girl pulled back. He made a lunge for it and ripped it from her hands.

"Miz Rose," she called over his shoulder. "That call was from GC!"

Buck shut the door, but Leah pushed past him and called after her. "GC where?"

"Wisconsin, I think."

"What'd you tell them?"

"That you were busy with a patient."

"You didn't say who, did you?"

"I don't know who. 'Cept he's a doctor."

"You didn't say that, did you?"

"Shouldn't I have?"

"Wait right there."

"I'm sorry."

"Just wait there a second."

Leah returned and quickly filled two syringes. She drove them into Floyd's hip, and he didn't even flinch. "Have her come in here," Leah told Buck.

He looked down the hall and signaled for the girl. She hesitated, then came slowly. "C'mon!" he said. "No one's going to hurt you."

As soon as she poked her head in the door, Leah said, "Bring me my purse as fast as you can, will you?"

"Sure, but—"

"Stat, sweetheart. Stat!"

The girl ran off.

"What's happening?" Buck said.

"Get your vehicle and bring it around the back. There's a basement exit, and that's where I'll come."

"But if he's dying, how can y—"

Leah grabbed his arms. "Mr. Williams, Doctor Charles and I have not just been talking. This man could be dead before we get him to the car. If you want to bury him or cremate him or do anything with him other than have him found here, I'll deliver him to the back door. GC in Wisconsin ring any bells? That's where he

worked, remember? That's where he's AWOL
from. They've been nosing around, watching for
him, figuring he's in this area and might show up
here sometime. They don't know—at least from
me—that he was already here once. I've been
lying through my teeth. They find him here,
dead or alive, we're all in trouble. Now go!"

"Any chance you can save him?"

"Get the car."

"Just tell me if he's better off here or in
the c—"

Leah whispered desperately, "He's dying. It's
just a matter of when. Where is irrelevant now.
The best I can do for him I have already done.
The absolute worst would be his being discovered
here."

●   ●   ●

Mac looked at his watch. "Just enough time for
you two to tell me how you got together, you
know, romantically."

"I think you've heard enough details,
Captain."

"C'mon! I'm an old romantic."

"It hasn't been easy," David said. "Obviously
I kept her from you and Rayford."

"Yeah, what's that all about?"

"At the time we believed the fewer who knew
the better."

"But we need all the comrades we can get."

"I know," David said. "But we're both so new at this, we don't know who to trust."

"If you wondered about Ray and me, you sure never showed it."

"It was a good exercise, let me just say that. What's going to happen when the brass start looking for a mark that's not there, rather than not seeing a mark that is?"

"There'll be no hiding then, kids."

●   ●   ●

Buck took the main elevator to the first floor and realized he had to exit past the receptionist. The last thing he wanted was to have her see his Rover. He planned to distract her with a fake emergency, but as he breezed through the lobby toward the front door, a substitute was in her place, a thick, middle-aged woman. Of course! The original girl was taking Leah her purse. Leah had thought to divert her.

Buck hurried to his car. As he pulled around the side of the building toward the back, he saw the substitute standing at the window, staring at him. He only hoped Stat Girl had not told her to find out what he was driving.

Buck skidded to a stop on an asphalt apron that led to a basement exit. He leapt from the Rover and opened the door as Leah, her bag over her shoulder, rolled out a gurney containing Floyd Charles with a sheet to the top of his head.

"He's gone already?" Buck said, incredulous.

"No! But people kept their distance, and nobody's going to identify him, are they?"

"Only your receptionist."

Buck lowered the back seat and Leah slid the whole bed in. "You're stealing that?" he said.

"I put more in my purse than that bed's worth," she said. "You want to debate ethics or fight the GC?"

"I don't want either," he said, as they climbed into the front seat. "But we're committed now, aren't we?"

"I don't know about you, Williams, but I'm in with both feet. This hospital has been GC-run for ages. How long was I going to be able to work for Carpathia when there's no way I'd ever take the mark of the beast? I'd die first."

"Literally," Buck said.

"Well, I just appropriated a bed and a lot of medicine from the enemy. If you have a problem with that, I'm sorry. I don't. This is war. All's fair, as they say."

"Can't argue with that. But, um, where am I taking you?"

"Where do you think? Take a left, and I'll take you out around the long way. Nobody will see you from the front of the building."

"Then where?"

"My place."

"What if the GC are there?"

"Then we'll just keep going."

"But if they're not, you'll try to nurse Floyd back to—"

"You're not thinking, Mr. W—"

"Quit with the formality, Leah. You put a dying friend in my car, so just run down the program for me."

"All right," she said. "If we can beat GC to my apartment, I'm going to grab as much of my stuff as I can in sixty seconds. You know they're on their way, as soon as they find me gone from Young."

"Then where do I take you?"

"Where do you live?"

"Where do *I* live?"

"Bingo, Buck. I need to hide out. You and yours are the only people I know who have a place to hide."

"But we're not telling anyone wh—"

"Oh, yes, you are. You're telling me. If you can't trust me after all we've been through, you can't trust anybody. I helped you discharge your patched-up pilot, Ritz. And I helped Doc with the miscarriage of guess-who's baby. How's that young woman doing, by the way?"

"Getting better."

"There's irony. Doc helps her beat the poison, and it's going to kill him."

"We lost Ritz."

"Lost him?"

"Killed in Israel. Long story."

Leah suddenly fell silent. She pointed directions and Buck lurched along, double-clutching and shifting till he thought his arm would fall off. "I liked that guy," she managed finally.

"We all did. We hate this, every bit of it."

"But you're taking me in, cowboy. You know that, don't you?"

"I can't make that decision."

She glared at him. "What are you going to do, leave me at the corner blindfolded while you and your compatriots vote? You owe me and you know it. This isn't like me, inviting myself. But I've risked my life for you, and I have nowhere else to turn."

Doc's death rattle began. His labored, liquid breathing pierced Buck. "Should I pull over?"

"No," she said. "There's nothing I can do now but shoot him full of morphine."

"That'll help?"

"It'll just make him pain free and maybe knock him out before he dies."

"Something!" Floyd called out in a mournful wail. "Give me something!"

Leah spun and knelt in her seat, digging

through her bag. Buck slowed involuntarily as he tried to watch. This was too much. Floyd was going to die while Buck was racing around in the car! No good-byes, no prayer, no comforting words. Buck felt as if he hardly knew the man, and he had been living with him for more than a year.

"Watch the road," she said. "This will quiet him, but he's never going to leave this car alive."

Sobs rose in Buck's throat. He wanted to call Chloe, to tell her and the others. But how do you do that on the phone? *Doc's dying and I'm bringing a nurse to live with us?* Pulling into the safe house without notice, carrying Floyd's corpse and a new houseguest wouldn't be much easier. But Buck had run out of options.

Leah's neighborhood, what was left of it, crawled with GC vehicles. The morphine had quieted Floyd. Leah slid onto the floor under the dash, and Buck avoided her street. He headed to Mount Prospect, hoping Floyd might at least have the privilege of dying in his own bed.

FOUR

DAVID Hassid walked Mac McCullum back to his quarters in the GC palace residential annex late that night. "There are things I haven't told even Annie," he said.

"I knew you had somethin' to tell me, kid. Otherwise, you'd be walking her back, wouldn't you?"

"We're trying to not be seen together. I don't even know if her meeting's over."

"So, what's up?" Mac said as they stood in the corridor outside his door.

"You know I was on the palace antibugging installation task force."

"Yeah, how'd you wangle that appointment?"

"Just kept telling Leon how important I thought it was to ensure total impregnability. I came in as a starry-eyed idealist, and they still see me that way. You know about the installation?"

Mac nodded. "Best in history and all that."

"Yeah, except it needs constant monitoring."

"Naturally."

"I volunteered for that, and everybody was glad to let me have it," David said.

"I'm listening."

"So am I."

"What?"

"I monitor the antibugging devices in Carpathia and Fortunato's offices."

"Go on."

"My job is to find out if anyone's trying to listen in. Well, I'm staying on top of it. And in the process I hear anything I want, any time I want."

Mac shook his head. "I wouldn't have minded not knowing that. Man, David, you're sitting on a time bomb."

"Don't I know it. But it's untraceable."

"Guaranteed?"

"In one way it's simple. In another it's a miracle of technology. The stuff is actually being recorded onto a miniature disk embedded in the central processing unit of the computer that runs all of New Babylon."

"The one people like to call the Beast."

"Because it contains so much information about every living soul, yeah. But we both know the Beast is no machine."

Mac folded his arms and leaned against the

wall. "One thing I've learned in surveillance work is that you never want to have hard copies of anything. Anything can eventually fall into the wrong hands."

"I know," David said. "Let me tell you how I've protected it."

Mac looked around. "You sure we're secure here?"

"Hey! I'm in charge of that. What we're saying could wind up on my disk, but no one else will ever hear it. *I* won't hear it unless I choose to. If I do, it's all categorized by date and time and location. And the fidelity is unparalleled."

Mac whistled through his teeth. "Someone had to manufacture this for you."

"That's right."

"Someone you trust with your life."

"You're looking at him."

"So how'd you make sure no one ever finds it?"

"I'm not guaranteeing that. I'm saying they will never be able to access a thing from it. The disk is slightly smaller than an inch in diameter and, because of supercompression digital technology, can hold nearly ten years of spoken conversation if recorded twenty-four hours a day. Well, we don't need that much time, do we?"

Mac shook his head. "They've got to have checks and balances."

"They do. But they aren't going to find anything."

"What if they do?"

David shrugged. "Say someone catches on to
me and starts looking for my bugs. They find
'em, trace 'em to the CPU, tear the whole thing
apart, and find the disk. It is so heavily encrypted
that if they tried random number combinations at
the rate of ten thousand digits a second around
the clock for a thousand years, they would have
barely begun. You know, even a fifteen-digit
number has trillions of combinations, but theoretically it could be deciphered. How would
you like to try to match an encrypted number
containing three hundred million digits?"

Mac rubbed his eyes. "I was born too early.
Where do you kids come up with this craziness?
How can *you* access your disk if it's that
encrypted?"

David was just warming to his subject. "That's
the beauty of it. I know the formula. I know what
pi to the millionth digit has to do with it and how
the date and time to the current second have to
be used as a multiplier, and how those figures
float forward and backward depending on various random factors. The number that would
unlock it now is different from the number a
second from now, and it doesn't progress rationally. But let's say someone *were* to get far

enough into my disk where the only step left was to match the encryption code, a miracle in itself. Even if they *knew* the number, only a lightning-speed computer grinding away for more than a year could enter it."

"Has what you've heard been worth the work?"

"It will be to the Tribulation Force, don't you think?"

"But how can you transmit it to them without jeopardizing your security or theirs?"

David pressed his back to the wall and slid to sit on the floor. "All that's encrypted too, though certainly not to where it takes them forever to get into it. So far we have been able to communicate by both phone and Carpathia's own cellular-solar technology on hidden scrambled bands. Of course, he's constantly on me to find ways to monitor all citizens."

"For their own good, no doubt."

"Oh, absolutely. The potentate merely cares deeply about the morale of his global family."

"But, David, can't anything transmitted also be intercepted?"

David shrugged. "I like to think *I* can bug anything. But I've tested my own stuff against my tracing power, and unless I drop enough bread crumbs along the road, I'm powerless too. Random scrambling and channel switching, coordinated with miniaturization and speed that makes fiber optics look like a slow boat . . . well, nothing is beyond possible anymore."

Mac stood and stretched. "Ever wonder about this stuff? Like what Dr. Ben-Judah says about Satan being the prince and power of the air? Transmitting through space and all that . . ."

"Scares me to death," David said, still sitting. "It means I'm on the front lines against him. I didn't know what I signed on for when I became a believer, but I wound up on the right side, didn't I? It's too late to change my mind. I walk the same halls with Antichrist himself, and I play around in the air with the devil. I'm careful, but the mark of the beast will change everything. There won't be *any* believers working here after that, unless they find a way to fake the mark. And who would want to do that?"

"Not me," Mac said, unlocking his door. "We're all going to wind up in one safe house or another one of these days. I sure hope mine's the same as yours."

David was so moved by that compliment that he was too stunned to respond. "Long flight Friday," Mac added. "I've got to find out who's tagging along with Leon and whether I can get Abdullah in here in time to help."

The tension of his role, exciting as it should have been for a young man, weighed on David.

But he headed toward his own quarters with a lighter step.

●　　　●　　　●

Floyd was quiet. The morphine must have done its work. Buck slowed as he drew within a mile of the safe house. He peered in the rearview mirror. He had not been followed. His phone startled him. "Buck here," he said.

"You were going to keep me posted," Chloe said.

"Almost home. A few minutes."

"Is Floyd with you?"

"Yeah, but he's not well."

"Hattie and I changed his bed and freshened the room."

"Good. I'm going to need help with him."

"Is he all right, Buck? Are you?"

"I'll see you soon, hon."

"Buck! Is everything all right?"

"Please, Chloe. I'll see you in a minute."

"All right," she said, sounding displeased.

He clicked the phone shut and dropped it in his pocket. He glanced at Leah. "Is he going to last the night?"

"I'm sorry, Buck. He's gone."

Buck slammed on the brake and they lurched forward as the Rover slid in the dirt. "What?"

"I'm sorry."

Buck turned in his seat. Leah had covered Floyd's face again, but the sudden stop had pressed his body against the back of the front seat.

"Do you know who this man is?" Buck said, his own desperate voice scaring him.

"I know he was a good doctor and courageous."

"He risked his life to tell me where the GC took Chloe. Came there himself to help her escape. Stayed up for days with Hattie. Saved her life. The miscarriage. Delivered our son. Was never too big to pitch in with the hard work."

"I'm so sorry, Buck."

Buck pulled the sheet from Floyd's face. In the darkness he could barely make it out. He turned on the inside light and recoiled at the death mask. Floyd's teeth were bared, his eyes open, still filled with blood around the pupils. "Oh, Doc!" he said.

Leah turned in her seat and rummaged in her bag for latex gloves. She carefully closed Floyd's eyes and mouth, massaging his cheeks until he looked more asleep than dead. "Help me with that shoulder," she said. Buck took one side and Leah the other, and they tugged at the body until Floyd looked more naturally reposed. Buck drove slowly, avoiding ruts and bumps.

When he pulled up to the safe house, the

curtain parted and he saw Chloe peer out. She was nursing Kenny. He drove around the side but stopped short of the backyard. "Give me a minute," he said. "You don't mind staying here with him—"

"Go," Leah said.

Chloe held open the back door with one hand, Kenny now over her other shoulder. "Who's with you?" she said. "I didn't see Floyd."

Buck was spent. He leaned forward to peck Chloe on the cheek, then did the same to Kenny, just as the baby burped. "Can you put him down?" he said.

"Buck—"

"Please," he said. "I need to talk to everybody."

The others were already waiting in the kitchen. Chloe went to put the baby down and quickly returned. Rayford sat at the table, and it was clear from his clothes he had spent hours working in the basement. Hattie sat on the table. Tsion, with a sad, knowing look, leaned against the refrigerator.

Buck found it hard to speak, and Chloe came to him, wrapping an arm around his waist. "We have another martyr," he said, and told the story, including that Leah was waiting in the car with Floyd's body.

Tsion hung his head. "God bless him," he said, his voice thick.

Hattie looked stricken. "He caught that from me? He died because of me?"

Chloe wrapped Buck in her arms and wept with him. "Are any of us susceptible?"

Buck shook his head. "We would have had symptoms by now. Floyd had symptoms but didn't tell us."

Buck stole a glance at Rayford. They would all look to him. Tsion would pray, but Rayford would walk them through the decision on Leah, the burial, everything. Yet Rayford had not moved. He sat without expression, forearms on the table. When Rayford's eyes met his, Buck sensed he was demanding to know what was expected.

Where was Rayford the Leader, their take-charge guy?

"We, ah, shouldn't leave Leah out there long," Buck said. "And we're going to have to do something with the body."

Rayford still stared at Buck, who could not hold his gaze. Had Buck done something wrong? Had he any choice other than to race off with Floyd to the hospital, then bring him back, Leah in tow?

"Daddy?" Chloe said softly.

"What?" Rayford said flatly, turning his eyes on her.

"I just . . . I'm . . . we're wondering—"

"What?" he said. "What! You're wondering what we're supposed to do now?" He stood, his chair sliding against the wall and rattling onto its side. "Well, so am I!" Buck had never before heard him raise his voice. "So am I!" Rayford railed. "How much can we take? How much are we supposed to take?"

Rayford picked up his chair and slammed it upright so hard that it bounced. He kicked it against the wall again and it flew back toward the table, chasing Hattie into Tsion's arms.

"Rayford," Tsion said quietly.

The chair would not have hit Hattie. It hit the edge of the table and spun, coming to rest next to Rayford. He yanked it to where he could sit again and slammed both fists on the table.

Tsion released Hattie, who was shaking. "I think we should—," he began, but Rayford cut him off.

"Forgive me," he said, clearly still fuming and seemingly unable to look anyone in the eye. "Get Leah in here and then let's get the body buried. Tsion, would you say a few—"

"Of course. I suggest we make Leah comfortable, then have the burial, then spend more time with her."

Rayford nodded. "Forgive me," he said again.

Buck backed the Rover into the yard, then brought Leah in and introduced her to everyone.

"I'm sorry for your loss," she said. "I didn't know Dr. Charles well, but—"

"We were about to pray," Tsion said. "Then we'd like to get to know you."

"Certainly."

When Tsion knelt on the hard floor, the others followed, except Hattie, who remained standing. "God, our Father," Tsion began, his voice weak and quavery. "We confess we are beyond our strength to keep coming to you at terrible times like this, when we have lost one of our family. We do not want to accept it. We do not know how much more we can bear. All we can do is trust in your promise that we shall one day see our dear brother again in the land where sorrow shall be turned to singing, and where there shall be no more tears."

When the prayer was over, Buck moved toward the cellar stairs.

"Where are you going?" Rayford said.

"To get shovels."

"Just bring one."

"It's a big job, Ray. Many hands—"

"Just bring one, Buck. Now, Ms. Rose, I want to be clear on this. Floyd died from the poison Carpathia used to try to kill Hattie, is that right?"

"That's my understanding."

"Straight answer, ma'am."

"Sir, I know only what Dr. Charles told me.

I have no personal knowledge of how Hattie was poisoned, but it seems clear that Floyd was contaminated by her, yes."

"So Nicolae Carpathia is responsible for this death."

Buck was impressed that Leah did not appear obligated to reply.

"This was murder, people," Rayford added. "Pure and simple."

"Rayford," Tsion said, "Carpathia likely has never heard of Doc Charles, and so, technically, while it is safe to say he tried to have Miss Durham killed—"

"I'm not talking court-of-law guilty," Rayford said, his face flushed. "I'm saying the poison Carpathia intended to kill someone killed Doc."

Tsion shrugged resignedly.

"Now, Buck," Rayford said, "where's my shovel?"

"Please let me help," Buck said

Rayford stood and straightened. "Save me from saying one more thing I'll regret tomorrow, would you, Buck? This is something I want to do myself. Something I need to do, all right?"

"But it should actually be deeper than six feet, so close to the house and—" Buck held up both hands in surrender to Rayford's out-of-patience look. He found the biggest shovel in the cellar.

While Rayford toiled in the backyard, Leah

talked about the most sanitary way to prepare the body. Unable to find lime with which to line the grave, she concocted a substitute made from kitchen products. "And," she told Buck, "we should wrap the body in a plastic tarp." She distributed gloves for those who would touch the body and prescribed a solution for disinfecting the Rover and the gurney.

Buck was amazed at what Rayford accomplished, considering he had worked all day in the shelter. He dug a hole seven feet long, three feet wide, and more than eight feet deep. He needed help to be hoisted out, covered with mud. The three men lowered Floyd's tarpaulin-shrouded body into the hole, and Rayford allowed the others to help fill it back in.

The group, save the sleeping baby, stood around the grave in the low light emitted from the house. Chloe, Hattie, and Leah were bundled against the cool night air. The men, sweaty from the shovel work, soon shivered.

Buck never ceased to be amazed at Tsion's eloquence. "Blessed in the sight of the Lord is the death of a saint," he said. "Floyd Charles was our brother, a beloved, earnest member of our family. Anyone who would like to say a word about him, please do so now, and I will pray."

"I knew him to be a gifted physician and a brave believer," Leah said.

Buck said, "Every time I think of him I'll think of our baby and of Chloe's health."

"Me too," Chloe said. "So many memories in such a short time."

Hattie stood shaking, and Buck noticed Rayford looking at her, as if expecting her to say something. She glanced at him and then away, then shook her head.

"Nothing," Rayford said. "You have nothing to say about the man who saved your life."

"Rayford," Tsion said.

"Of course I do!" Hattie said, her voice pinched. "I can't believe he died because of me! I don't know what to say! I hope he's gone to his reward."

"Let me tell you something else," Rayford said, his anger evidently unabated. "Floyd loved you, Hattie. You treated him like dirt, but he loved you."

"I know," she said, a whine in her voice. "I know you all love me in your own w—"

"I'm telling you he loved you. *Loved you.* Cared deeply for you, wanted to tell you."

"You mean—? You couldn't know that."

"He told me! I think he'd want you to know."

"Rayford," Tsion said, putting a hand on his shoulder, "anything else you would like to say about Floyd?"

"This is a death that must be avenged. Like Ken's and Amanda's and Bruce's."

"Vengeance is the Lord's," Tsion said.

"If only he would include me in that," Rayford said.

Tsion looked hard at him. "Be careful about wishing for things you don't really want," he said. "Let me close in prayer." But Buck could not hear him. Rayford had begun to weep. His breath came in great heaves and he covered his mouth with his hand. Soon he could not contain the sobs, and he fell to his knees and wailed in the night. Chloe rushed to him and held him.

"It's all right, Daddy," she said as she helped him up and walked him into the house. "It's all right."

Rayford pulled away from her and rushed up the stairs. Buck took Chloe in his arms, and the mud that had transferred to her from her father also smeared his clothes.

● ● ●

Rayford was thankful for the well and the generator-run water heater as he stood under the steaming shower in the safe house. His muscles were finally untying. What a day! The inexplicable anger that had sent him marching into the morning air had been building for months. Working in the cellar had not dented it, especially when he found himself alone all day. The awful news about Floyd had finally made him erupt in a way he hadn't since a loud fight with Irene fifteen years before. And that had been the result of too much alcohol.

While he felt bad about mistreating the others, something about this anger seemed righteous. Was it possible God had planted in his heart this intolerance for injustice for the sole purpose of preparing him to assassinate Carpathia? Or was he deluding himself? Rayford didn't want to think he was losing his mind. No one would understand a man like him trying to rationalize murder, even the murder of the Antichrist.

Rayford turned the dial to as hot as he could bear it and hung his head beneath the spray. His prayers had become entreaties that God allow him to do the unthinkable. How much was a man supposed to endure? The loss of his wife and son were his fault. He could have gone to heaven with them, had he been a man of faith and not pride. But losing Bruce, then Amanda, then Ken, now Doc—ah, why should he be surprised? It was a numbers game now. Did he expect to be among the last standing at the Glorious Appearing? He certainly wouldn't be if he took a shot at Nicolae Carpathia. But he probably wouldn't survive either way. Might as well go out with guns blazing.

Rayford stepped out of the shower and looked at himself in the steamed-up mirror, a towel

draped over his shoulders. As the vapor dissi-
pated and his face became clearer, he hardly
recognized himself. Even a year ago he had
felt all right, and Amanda seemed impressed
with his mature look. Now *mature* would be
a compliment. He looked and felt older than
his years. Everyone did now, of course, but
Rayford believed he had aged more quickly
than most.

His face was lean and lined, his eyes baggy,
his mouth turned down. He had never been much
for ascribing depression to every blue period or
downtime, but now he had to wonder. Was he
depressed? Clinically depressed? That was the
kind of thing he might have discussed with Floyd.
And with the thought of his name came that stab
in the gut. People around him were dying, and
there would be no end to it until Jesus returned.
That would be wonderful, but could he last? If
he responded like this to someone he had known
as briefly as Floyd, what would happen when,
if, if . . . he didn't want to think about it. Chloe?
The baby? Buck? Tsion?

This woman from the hospital, Leah, would
she be worth talking to? Trying out a few ideas
on a professional, a virtual stranger, seemed
easier than raising the same things with anyone
else in the house. In a peculiar way, Hattie knew
him as well as the others. But she was still an

outsider, even more than the newcomer was. He could never reveal his deepest thoughts to her.

Of course, he wouldn't say anything about his Carpathia plot to Leah Rose either. But he might get some insight into his own mind. Maybe she had dealt with depressed people, or knew doctors who had.

Rayford realized as he dried his hair that he recognized neither the man in the mirror *nor* the man inside anymore. The schemes playing at the edges of his mind were so far afield from the Rayford Steele he thought he was that he could only imagine what Chloe would say. And she knew only the half of it.

His new abruptness was hardly hidden from the rest of the Trib Force. They had all forgiven each other countless times for pettiness. All except Tsion, of course. It seemed he never offended, never had to be forgiven. Some people had the ability to live with grace despite untenable conditions. Tsion was one.

But Rayford had stepped beyond selfish behavior in an enclosed environment. He had threatened the status quo, the way of life—difficult as it was. And he was supposed to be the leader. He knew he was in charge only in the manner of the manager of a baseball team. Tsion was the Babe Ruth, the one who won ball games. But still Rayford had a vital role, a position of authority, a spiritual responsibility of headship as an elder would in a church.

Was he still worthy? Part of him was sure he was not. On the other hand, if he wasn't going bats and if he really *had* been chosen of God to have a part in a centuries-old assassination plot, he was someone special after all.

Rayford pulled on a huge robe and stepped out of the bathroom. *So I'm either anointed or a megalomaniac. Great. Who's going to let me know?* The old Rayford Steele fought to jar himself to his senses, while the rage-filled, righteously indignant, grieving, depressed, frustrated, caged member of the Tribulation Force continued to entertain thoughts of grandeur. Or at least revenge. *I'm a sick man,* he told himself. And he heard voices downstairs. Praying.

● ● ●

Mac McCullum moved steadily along on his daily jog as the sun rose orange over the radiant city of New Babylon. He couldn't get over the beauty and what a privilege it might have been to be there under other circumstances. State-of-the-art, first-class, top-drawer, all the clichés came to life when someone considered this gleaming new megalopolis.

But with his secret conversion, Mac had become a mole, subversive, part of the rebellion.

A lifetime of military training, self-discipline, chain of command, all-for-one-and-one-for-all thinking was now conflicted. Having reached the pinnacle as a career big-plane pilot, he now used every trick and wile he had ever learned to serve the cause of God.

Whatever satisfaction came with that was akin to the satisfaction he got that he could still clip off six brisk miles a day at his age. To some that was impressive. To him it was a necessity. He was fighting time, gravity, and a malady of physical attacks that came with mere longevity. That's just how he felt in his job. He should feel fulfilled, but the enemy was his employer. And as a valued, crucial plant for the other side, he should exult in the fact that he knew without doubt he was on the right side—the winning side.

But fear precluded any joy. The second he began to enjoy his role, he was vulnerable. Living on the edge, knowing that the one slip that gave him away would be his last, took all the fun out of the job. A measure of satisfaction came with the knowledge that he was good at what he did, both overtly and surreptitiously. But to wonder constantly when the other shoe would drop, when you would be found out—that was no way to live.

As the sun cleared the horizon and Mac felt the sweat on his weathered head and face, he knew that his exposure would likely be accomplished long before he was aware of it. That was the curse of it. Not only did he not know when or if he would be found out, but there was also one thing he was sure of: he would be the last to know. How long would Carpathia, Fortunato, any of them, let him twist in the wind, still trying to ply his trade when they already knew the truth? Would they let him hang himself, implicate the comrades he loved and served, allow him to make a mess of the precarious safety he tried to protect?

It was possible he had been exposed already. How could one know? The end of a traitor is like the end of a star—the result is always seen long after the event has taken place. He would just have to watch for the signs. Would something indicate to him that he should run, flee to the safe house, put out the SOS to the stateside Tribulation Force? Or would he be dead by the time they knew he had been compromised?

With a mile to go, he made the last curve, now with the sun at his back. His last encrypted message to Abdullah Smith had put the Jordanian right into Mac's own boat: "Personnel will ask straight out about your loyalty to the cause, to the Global Community, to the potentate. Remember, you are a frontline warrior. Tell them what they want to hear. Get yourself this job by whatever means you can. You will be in a position to help thwart the worst schemes of the evil one and see men and women come to Christ in spite of everything.

"If you wonder what to say, how to phrase it, just align yourself with me. Say without hesitation that you share Mac McCullum's views of the Global Community and are as wholly committed as he is to the policies and direction of the leadership. A truer word will never be spoken.

"I'm not saying it will be easy. The pay is exorbitant, as you know, but you will not enjoy one cent of it. The perquisites are like none you ever dreamed of, but you will constantly feel in need of cleansing. Praise God, that cleansing is there, because we are under assignment from the Almighty. It's short-term work, because Tsion Ben-Judah is right: When the mark of the beast is required for buying or selling, you know it'll be a requirement for being on the payroll here. We'll go from senior members of the staff to international fugitives overnight.

"I need you, Abdullah, that's all I can say. You and Ray and I cooperated in the past. This won't be as fun, but there won't be a dull moment. I'll look forward to once again sharing the cockpit with a respected airman and a brother I can trust. All the best, Mac."

●   ●   ●

Buck sat next to Chloe on the couch. Tsion sat nearby, as did Leah. Here she was, brand-new in the house and already involved in a prayer meeting about their leader. Buck prayed hesitantly and not without guilt. Should they not have simply confronted Rayford? Wasn't this akin to spiritually talking behind his back? Surely Tsion would approach Rayford in due time.

FIVE

RAYFORD hated feeling isolated from the others. With his dream of eliminating Carpathia (even temporarily) he ironically had more in common with Hattie than with anyone. It was his own fault for losing control and making them tread carefully around him. But what was going on downstairs at midnight? All of them praying together always encouraged Rayford. But did this constitute a meeting of the Trib Force without him? Should he be offended?

Of course they were free to meet in any combination of brothers and sisters they wished. It wasn't like they were conducting business. What was the matter with him? When did he start caring about such trivia? Rayford tiptoed down so as not to disturb them. Sure enough, they sat on the couch and in chairs in the living room, heads bowed, praying. Everyone but Hattie.

Rayford was moved and suddenly wanted to
join them. His motive wasn't pure. He wanted to
reconcile with them without having to apologize
again. Inserting himself in a spiritual exercise
would speak volumes. He could even pray for
forgiveness for his outbursts. . . .

As he slipped into the living room, Rayford's
conscience was suddenly crushed. What a fool!
How small! To be so blessed of God despite
wrenching pain and then to want to use prayer
to manipulate. . . . He nearly retreated but now
wanted to join them for the right reasons. He
didn't even want to pray aloud. He just wanted
to agree with them before God, to be part of this
body, this church. He knew he would feel worthy
to lead them again only when he realized that
he was *not* worthy aside from the gift of God.

He was the object of the prayer meeting. First
one, then another, mentioned his name. They
prayed for his strength, for peace, for comfort
in his grief. They prayed for supernatural con-
tentment when that was humanly impossible.

He could have been offended, to be, in essence,
gossiped about in prayer. But he was ashamed. He
had been worse than he had feared. Rayford knelt
silently. Eventually the emotion and fervency of
the prayers so humiliated and humbled him that
he was powerless to hide anymore. He pitched
forward onto his elbows and wept aloud. He was

just sorry, so sorry, and grateful they believed him worth the effort to restore.

Chloe was the first to rush to Rayford, but rather than lift him, she merely knelt with him and embraced him. He felt Buck's tentative hand on his back and wished he could tell his son-in-law not to worry, that his support meant everything. Tsion laid his warm hand on Rayford's head and called on God "to be everything this man needs you to be during the most difficult season anyone has ever been asked to endure."

Rayford found himself sobbing for the second time that night, only now he did not wail the mournful cries of the hopeless. He felt bathed in the love of God and the support of his family. He had not given up the idea that God might still use him in the comeuppance of Nicolae Carpathia, but that was—at least briefly—less important than his place within the group. They could handle his not always being strong. They would stick with him when he was human and worse. They would support him even when he failed. How could he ever express what that meant to him?

It was not lost on Rayford that Leah, though she had understandably not felt comfortable enough to touch him, had prayed for him. She did not pretend to know the problem, only indicating a recognition that he was apparently not himself and needed a touch from God.

When the prayers finally fell silent, Rayford could muster only "Thank you, God." Tsion hummed a familiar tune. First Chloe, then the others, sang. *Blest be the tie that binds our hearts in Christian love. The fellowship of kindred minds is like to that above.*

The four of them rose and returned to where they were sitting. Rayford pulled up a chair. "Thought I was getting voted out of the club," he said.

Tsion chuckled. "We would not even let you resign," he said. "I would like to ask you, Leah, if you would mind waiting until tomorrow to tell us your story. I think we have all been through enough for one day, and we would like to give you our full attention."

"I was going to suggest the same," she said. "Thank you."

"Do you have any aversion to staying where Floyd used to sleep?" Rayford said.

"Not unless anyone else has a problem with it," she said. "And I know this sounds weird, but I won't sleep well unless I have a sense of the rest of the place. Could I get a quick tour, just so I know where everything is?"

"Chloe and I will be happy to show you," Rayford said, hoping to start a connection that would facilitate conversation.

"I'll check on the baby," Buck said.

Tsion rose wearily. "Good night, all."

Rayford was impressed that Chloe knew enough to ignore the cellar. She started in the back of the duplex, where Leah had come in. "There's nothing in the other flat," she said. "It was more structurally damaged anyway. You came through the nook area here. This has been rebuilt since the earthquake when a tree smashed it and killed the wife of the owner. Her husband was at our church at the time and died when that collapsed.

"Then the kitchen, of course, and off to the left the living room. Then the dining room, where we never eat but a lot of us work. Past the stairs there is a bathroom and the front room where Buck and I sleep with the baby."

Upstairs they showed her the other bath, Rayford's room, Tsion's, and Floyd's.

"Thanks," she said. "And where did Ritz stay?"

Rayford and Chloe looked at each other. "Ah," he said, "I wasn't aware you knew he had lived here."

"Was it a secret?"

"The whole place is."

"I'm not supposed to know he lived here? I knew Dr. Charles and Mr. Williams and Hattie lived here."

"I just didn't know you knew, that's all," Rayford said. "I hope it doesn't make me sound suspicious."

She stopped. "Of what? You want to examine my mark? Something gave you the confidence to bring every emergency my way. If I wasn't trustworthy, would I have risked my life for all of you?"

"I'm sorry, I—"

"Really, Mr. Steele. If I was working for the GC I could have tipped off the potentate when his lover miscarried his child while I attended her. I could have reported Dr. Charles when he incinerated the remains rather than follow legal procedure. I could have tipped off the authorities when your son-in-law got me to release Ritz with a gaping head wound. You think I didn't know who you people were and why no one could know where you lived?"

"Miss Rose—"

"It's Mrs. Rose, and frankly the reason I assumed Ritz lived here was because I knew the airport had been virtually demolished. And, in case you don't remember, he was with you when you brought Hattie in. Was I to assume you came from your hiding place and he rendezvoused with you from somewhere else?"

"You're right. I'm just—"

"There'll be infiltrators, Mr. Steele. I don't know how they'll do it, but I wouldn't put anything past the GC. But until they perfect some sort of a foolproof replica of the sign we can see only on each other, I can't imagine a spy foolish enough to waltz in here. Run me through any grill you want, but I'll thank you to never again admit you're suspicious of me just because I assumed a man lived with you whose first name I don't even remember."

Rayford looked pleadingly at her. "Would a tough day be an excuse?"

"I've had one too," she said. "Tell me you're not afraid of me before I turn in."

"I'm not. I'm sorry."

"I am too. Forgive me if I overreacted."

So much for bonding, Rayford thought. "Don't give it another thought."

"You trust me then."

"Yes! Now go to bed and let us do the same. Feel free to use the bathroom before the rest of us."

"You're telling me you trust me."

Rayford could tell even Chloe was losing patience with Leah. "I'm tired, Mrs. Rose. I apologized. I'm convinced. OK?"

"No."

"No?" Chloe said. "I have to get to bed."

"You think I'm blind or stupid or what?" Leah said.

"Excuse me?" Chloe said.

"Where's the shelter?"

Rayford flinched. "You don't want me to be suspicious and now you ask about a shelter?"

"You don't have one?"

"Tell me how you would know to ask."

Leah shook her head. "This is worse than your thinking me subversive. You think I'm daft."

"Not anymore I don't," Chloe said. "Tell me how you know there's more here, and I'll show it to you."

"Thank you. If I hid out in a safe house, I'd assume its security would one day be compromised. Either you have a place to run to on a moment's notice, or this place turns upside-down. Plus, and this is so obvious it offends me to have to raise it, am I to assume Hattie sleeps outside?"

"Hattie?" Rayford said.

"Yeah. Remember her? No seal on her forehead, but fairly visible here until you all get spiritual? Where does she sleep?"

Chloe sighed. "Go to bed, Dad. I'll show her."

"Thank you!"

They turned to head down the stairs.

Rayford couldn't resist. "You can be obnoxious, Mrs. Rose, you know that?"

"Daddy!" Chloe said, her back still to him. "We deserved that and you know it."

Leah stopped and turned to face him. "I respect everyone here," she said. "But that was sexist. You'll call me a feminist, but you would not tell a man, insulted like I was, that his response was obnoxious."

"I probably would," Rayford said. "But the point is taken."

"Thanks for making me feel like a creep," Leah said. "I spoke to your son-in-law earlier in a way I have rarely spoken to anyone. And now I've done it again. I don't know what's happening to me."

Rayford felt exactly the same but didn't care to admit it. "Promise me tomorrow we can discuss a truce," he said.

"That's a deal."

The women descended, and Rayford was finally able to get to bed. He hung his robe and lay back on the cool sheets, feeling morning-after soreness from his work in the cellar and the back-yard, and it wasn't even morning yet. He locked his fingers behind his head and within minutes felt himself drifting—until he heard footsteps on the stairs, then a knock at his door.

"I was showing Leah the cellar," Chloe said, "where Hattie sleeps. Only she's not there."

"Hattie?"

"Where could she be? She's not in the house. Not outside as far as we can see. And, Dad, a lot of her stuff is gone. She took a heavy load."

Rayford rose and pulled on his robe again, wondering if he had the energy to deal with yet one more crisis before collapsing. "Check the shed for Ken's car. Make sure Buck's is still in the yard. She couldn't get far on foot. Buck and I can each take a vehicle and start looking for her."

"Dad, we have no idea when she left. She might have been gone since the burial. I don't remember seeing her since, do you?"

He shook his head. "We can't let her out of here with all she knows."

"Talk about vulnerable. If she got someone to pick her up somewhere, you'll never catch her."

They followed footprints to what had once been the street in front of the house. Now it was just a dirt path strewn with chunks of asphalt and dotted with potholes. She could have headed either direction. Rayford fired up Ken Ritz's Suburban, and Buck threw dirt from all four wheels on his Land Rover. He sent Buck north and headed south.

When it became clear Hattie was nowhere in Rayford's vicinity, he called Buck. "Nothing here either," Buck said. "I've got a bad feeling about this. It's not like we can report her missing."

"I've got one other idea," Rayford said. "I'll see you back at the house."

Rayford called Palwaukee and reached the answering machine. He said, "T, this is Ray. If you're there, I need you to pick up." He waited a few moments, then reluctantly dialed Delanty's personal cell phone. Rayford was greeted with a groggy hello.

"Sorry, T. Did I wake you?"

"Of course you did. 'Sup, Ray? I don't want this to be an emergency, but if it's not I'm gonna ask why you called now."

Rayford filled him in. "So I was just wondering if Tweedledee and Tweedledum are still kicking around out there."

"Ernie and Bo? Haven't seen Ernie for almost a year. Kind of miss him, even if he was an idiot. I heard he headed west. Beauregard Hanson still hangs around trying to exercise his 5-percent stake in the place. Why?"

"Just wondering if Hattie might have used him to get somebody to fly her out of there."

"I left at six. Had a guy in the tower till nine. We shut down after that."

"Any way I can find out if a big plane left there this evening?"

"Ray, I can't call a guy at this time of the morning and ask him that."

"Why not? I just did."

"Yeah, but you were pretty sure I wouldn't hate you for it."

"Don't you?"

"I'm not allowed to say. We're brothers, remember?"

"Speaking of that, you're the only 'brother' brother I've got left, if you catch my meaning."

"What?"

Rayford told him about Doc.

"Oh, man! I'm sorry, Ray. You don't suspect Hattie . . . ?"

Ray told him Floyd's own theory on how he contracted the poison. "But still, I've got dire reasons to know where she is."

"I'll check the log."

"I don't want you to go out at this hour."

"I can do it from here, bro. Just a minute."

Rayford heard T's bed squeak and then computer sounds. He came back on the phone. "I'm scrolling through here. Not much traffic tonight. Mostly small stuff, business planes, couple of GC. Hmm."

"What?"

"There *is* a unique entry here. Oversized Quantum, that's like a huge Learjet, different manufacturer, arrived pilot only at 2230. Left 2330 hours with a fuel top-off, no cargo, one unidentified passenger, destination unreported."

"That's all?"

"Well, we've got a column here that asks whether it was paid, charged, or OK'd. This one was OK'd by BH."

"I don't know the specs on the Quantum," Rayford said. "What kind of speed and range?"

"Oh, fast as a heavy but probably needs one more top-off before going overseas. How far you figure your escapee's going anyway?"

"I wouldn't put it past her to think she can march into Carpathia's office and personally give him what for. Well, there'll be no catching or intercepting that craft, will there?"

"Nope. What is it, almost one? That thing's been airborne, I assume at maximum speed, an hour and a half. Even with twenty minutes on the east coast for landing, fuel, and takeoff, it's still gonna be too far away by now."

"You got enough information that I could radio the craft?"

"Think about it, Rayford. Whoever's flying that plane is not going to answer unless he knows who's calling."

"Maybe I could spin him a yarn, urge him to put down in Spain due to a fuel irregularity or something that turned up here or wherever he refueled."

"You're dreaming, Ray. And I'd like to be."

"Thanks for nothing, friend."

"You're going to have to go round her up yourself or turn some of your contacts onto her over there."

"I know. I appreciate it, T. I'll try to get out to the strip for some co-op business tomorrow."

"Today, you mean?"

"Sorry," Rayford said.

"I might bring a couple of people from our house church. We want to get behind this thing in a big way."

For all Rayford knew, Hattie had the power
to blow the lid off the co-op too.

●   ●   ●

Mac McCullum had a full morning. After tipping
his cap to Annie Christopher as he passed her
office in the hangar, he arrived at his own office
to three messages. The first was a list generated
by Leon Fortunato's secretary, outlining personnel
authorized on the flight to Botswana in three days.
The supreme commander, his valet, an assistant,
a cook, and two servers would make up the GC
contingent. Two aides would accompany President
Ngumo of Botswana. "Note that the Supreme
Commander has decreed that the plane shall be
stationary while the Botswanians are aboard."

The list also included captain and first officer in
the cockpit, with an asterisk after the latter. At the
bottom of the page the asterisk referred to a note:
"The Supreme Commander believes you will be
pleased by the resolution of this matter."

Mac was. The second document was a note from
Personnel regarding the application of Abdullah
Smith for Condor 216 first officer. Not only had
he been ranked high in every technical aspect save
verbal acuity ("Somewhat laconic" read the sum-
mary), but he had also been judged "an outstanding citizen, loyal to the Global Community."

Fortunato himself had scribbled in the margin,

"Congratulations on a wonderful find, Mac. Smith will make a great contribution to the cause! S. C. L. F."

If you only knew, Mac thought.

Mac's third missive was from David Hassid. "Important message for you, Captain," it read. "In person, please."

Mac and David had learned to appear impersonal and professional in front of staff. Their difference in age helped. The entire GC complex, though ostensibly antimilitary because of Carpathia's avowed pacifism, was pseudomilitary in its organizational structure. Mac felt comfortable with the chain of command, having spent so much of his life in uniform. And David often deferred to Mac's counsel because David had come to the GC from the private sector. Now the two were on equal footing in separate branches, and it appeared their occasional face-to-faces attracted no attention.

David's secretary ushered Mac into David's office. "Captain," David said, shaking his hand.

"Director," Mac said, sitting.

When the secretary left, David said, "Get this," and turned around his laptop so Mac could read it. The captain squinted at the screen and read Rayford's account of the previous day's activities at the safe house in Illinois. "Oh, man," he said, "that doctor. The girl lives, the doctor dies. Beat that."

"It gets worse," David said.

Mac reached the news of Hattie's disappearance. He settled back in his chair. "Does he really think—"

David held up a finger to stall him. "Let me get rid of this while I'm thinking of it." With a few keystrokes the heavily encrypted file had been trashed. "That she'll come here? I can't imagine. I understand she's ditzy, but how far does she think she'll get? It's a miracle she survived this long with all the things Carpathia has tried to get rid of her. She shows her face in New Babylon, she's history."

Mac nodded. "She's got to be holing up somewhere, waiting to surprise him."

"I can't see her getting close."

Mac shook his head. "I know. Your people loaded two sets of metal detectors on the two-one-six last week."

"Plan is to use them even for dignitaries. 'Course, that's due to a basic distrust of Pete Two, you know."

"I know firsthand. Fortunato's got all ten kings, excuse me, regional international sub-potentates—or whatever Saint Nick is allowing them to call themselves this week—primed for that snuffing. It's almost like he wants them willing to do the deed themselves."

"Like those guys would agree on anything,"

David said. "How many of 'em you think are really loyal to Carpathia?"

Mac shrugged. "More than half. Not more than seven, though. I know three who would usurp given half a chance."

"Would they take him out?"

"In a New Babylon minute. 'Course, Pete would too."

"You think?"

Mac sat forward and pressed his palms together. "I've heard him say it. He rubs Carpathia raw with his brashness, but he pretends to be cooperative. Carpathia makes nice with him all the time, as if they handpicked each other. I'll tell you what: if Leon doesn't get rid of Mathews soon, he's going to have to answer. It's a directive clear as if it were on paper."

David stood and pulled some files from a drawer behind him, then spread them on the desk. "In case anyone's watching," he said, and Mac leaned over as if studying them.

"They're upside-down, you idiot," Mac said, controlling his smile.

"Wouldn't want to be distracted," David said.

"You know what Rayford used to dream out loud?"

"Tell me."

"Crashing on purpose with Carpathia aboard."

David straightened and cocked his head.

"That's not even biblical, is it? I mean, if he's who we think he is, he's not going to die till the forty-second month, is he? And even then he doesn't stay dead."

"I'm just telling you."

"Doesn't even sound like Captain Steele. He always seemed so even and sensible."

"Didn't mean to spoil your image of him."

"Believe me, you didn't. I can't deny I've fantasized about how I'd do it."

Mac stood and headed to the door. "Same here," he said.

SIX

EMOTIONAL turmoil took as much out of Buck as did physical labor. Often, after toiling all day with Rayford and Floyd in the underground shelter, he had trouble falling asleep. But now he had taken to bed his grief over Floyd, fear of how Hattie could imperil the Tribulation Force, and dread over the strange behavior of his father-in-law. Buck was exhausted beyond measure. Lying next to his damaged but resilient wife, he fought to stay awake and listen to her.

He and Chloe had so little time to talk anymore, despite spending most of their days in the same house. She lamented not being as involved as she once had, housebound with the baby, slowed by her injuries from the earthquake.

"But no one else could do what you're doing with the co-op, babe," he said. "Imagine the millions who will depend on you for their lives."

"But I'm on the periphery," she said. "I spent most of today comforting you and Daddy and taking care of the baby."

"We needed you."

"I have needs too, Buck."

He draped his arm across her. "Want me to watch Kenny so you can go with your dad to see T tomorrow? They're talking co-op business."

"I'd love that."

Buck thought he had responded. He had meant to. But when Chloe removed his arm from her and turned away, he realized he had drifted off. She had said something more; he was aware of that now. He tried to muster the energy to force his eyes open and apologize, finish the conversation. But the more he tried, the more jumbled his thoughts became. Desperate that he was missing a huge opportunity to be to his wife what she needed him to be, he slipped over the edge of consciousness.

● ● ●

Late in the afternoon in New Babylon, David was urgently ordered to the office of Global Community Supreme Commander Leon Fortunato. Leon's opulent quarters comprised the entire seventeenth floor of the new palace, only one below His Excellency, the potentate's.

Though David reported directly to him, a face-to-face with Fortunato had become rare. The organization chart, as Mac had mentioned more than once, had to look like a spaghetti bowl. Ostensibly, Carpathia himself had only one subordinate—besides his secretary and the ever-present gaggle of obsequious lackeys—and that was Fortunato. But the entire administrative wing of the palace was filled with sycophants who dressed like the potentate and the supreme commander, walked like them, talked like them, and bowed and scraped in their presence.

David, the youngest member of the management staff, seemed to have garnered the respect of the brass with what appeared only appropriate deference. But for the moment, he was in trouble.

As soon as Fortunato's door was shut, before David could even sit in the gargantuan room, Leon started in on him. "I want to know where those computers are and why they aren't being installed as we speak."

"The, uh, gross of—"

"The biggest single shipment of hardware since we equipped the castle—excuse me, the palace," Leon said, planting his meaty frame in the throne-like leather chair behind his desk. "You know what I'm talking about. The more you hem and haw, the more suspicious—"

"No, sir, of course I know. We took delivery of those yesterday and—"

"Where are they?"

"—they're not in position to be directly moved into th—"

"What's wrong with them?" Leon barked, and finally pointed to a chair.

David sat. "It's a technical thing, sir."

"A glitch?"

"It's a, an orienting problem. Positioning renders them inoperative in the palace."

Leon glared at him. "Do they need to be replaced?"

"That would be the only solution, yes, sir."

"Then replace them. You understand me, don't you, Director Hassid?"

"Yes, sir."

"You get my drift?"

"Sir?"

"When I get exercised, you understand it's not just me?"

"I know, yes, sir."

"His Excellency is eager that I—you—that we get a handle on this. He has confidence, because I assured him he could, that you will complete this assignment."

"We will get that equipment installed as soon as humanly possible."

Leon shook his head. "I'm not talking about just the blamed installation! I'm talking about tracing the opposition."

"Of course."

"His Excellency is a pacifist, as you know. But he also knows the only power a man of peace has is information. That's why he monitors those two crazy preachers in Jerusalem. Their day will come. They have admitted as much themselves. And sympathetic as he is to variant views, a small but influential faction has the attention of those rebellious to the new world order. Would you not agree?"

"Agree, sir?"

Fortunato looked frustrated. "That His Excellency has reason to be concerned about this Ben-Judah character and his own former publisher, who is spewing anti-GC propaganda!"

"Oh, yes, absolutely. Dangerous. I mean, if there were just small pockets of these types out there, who cares? But, they seem to have rallied under the banner of—"

"Exactly. And they're harboring the mother of His Excellency's child. She must be found before she tries to abort, or worse, reveal information that could damage . . ."

Leon let his thought trail off. "Anyway," he said, "replace that order or fix that orientation or whatever problem, and get people on this."

● ● ●

Buck was grateful to have awakened before Chloe. He kissed her cheek and straightened her blankets.

He left a note on the bedside table: "Sorry I drifted off. Go with your dad today. I'll cover here. I love you."

He padded to the kitchen, where Tsion sat alone, shoulders hunched, eating breakfast. "Cameron!" he whispered. "If I had known you were coming, I would have fixed something for you."

"No need. Gonna get a head start on my writing so I can watch the baby." Cameron poured himself a glass of juice and leaned against the counter. "Chloe's going with Ray to see T about the co-op."

Tsion nodded wearily. "I miss Floyd. I knew something had to be wrong when he did not get up with me yesterday." He sighed. "Doc had a good mind. Many questions."

"I don't have that mind, but I do have questions. You were working on your commentary about the second woe, the sixth Trumpet Judgment."

"Which I am late on," Tsion said. "With everything that happened, I was unable to post it yesterday. I hope to have it done this morning. And I hope my absence for a day did not cause panic among the audience."

"Everybody prays you will not be taken off the Net."

"David Hassid assures me we can stay ahead of

Carpathia technologically. Yet when he explains how he bounces our signal from satellite to satellite and cell to cell, I am lost. I just thank God he knows what he is doing."

Buck rinsed out his glass. "You were wrestling with something yesterday."

"I still am," Tsion said. "For centuries scholars believed prophetic literature was figurative, open to endless interpretation. That could not have been what God intended. Why would he make it so difficult? I believe when the Scriptures say the writer saw something in a vision, it *is* symbolic of something else. But when the writer simply says that certain things happen, I take those literally. So far I have been proven right.

"The passage I am working on, where John sees—in a vision—200 million horsemen who have the power to slay a third of the remaining population, seems by necessity figurative. I doubt these men and animals will be literal beings, but I believe their impact will be very real nonetheless. They will indeed slay a third of the population."

Buck squinted, and the teacher looked away. "This is a new one," Buck said. "You really don't know, do you?"

Tsion shook his head. "Yet I feel a great responsibility for the readers God has entrusted to me. I do not want to get ahead of him, but neither do I want to hang back in fear. All I can do is to be honest about how I am tussling with this. It is time many of these believers start interpreting the Scriptures for themselves anyway."

"When is this judgment supposed to happen?"

"All we know for sure is that it comes next chronologically and that it must occur before the midpoint of the Tribulation. Unless God himself makes it happen in an instant, it appears it could take several weeks."

Tsion had, the day before, merely transmitted the Scriptural passage he would comment on the next day. Running the body of text alone resulted in the largest cyberspace audience in history, awaiting Dr. Ben-Judah's fearful teaching on Revelation 9:15-21:

So the four angels, who had been prepared for the hour and day and month and year, were released to kill a third of mankind.

Now the number of the army of the horsemen was two hundred million; I heard the number of them.

And thus I saw the horses in the vision: those who sat on them had breastplates of fiery red, hyacinth blue, and sulfur yellow; and the heads of the horses were like the heads of lions; and out of their mouths came fire, smoke, and brimstone.

By these three plagues a third of mankind was killed—by the fire and the smoke and the brimstone which came out of their mouths.

For their power is in their mouth and in their tails; for their tails are like serpents, having heads; and with them they do harm.

But the rest of mankind, who were not killed by these plagues, did not repent of the works of their hands, that they should not worship demons, and idols of gold, silver, brass, stone, and wood, which can neither see nor hear nor walk.

And they did not repent of their murders or their sorceries or their sexual immorality or their thefts.

● ● ●

David returned to his office conflicted by the fear Leon had engendered and the thrill of having toyed with the man once again. From his laptop, ignoring a flashing Message sign, he ordered another gross of the computers, directing that they be delivered to the palace airstrip. No sense drawing further suspicion. He could thwart whatever his experts detected by planting viruses in the equipment or merely misinterpreting their findings.

●   ●   ●

Buck sat with the others at a meeting of the stateside Tribulation Force at 11 A.M. Tuesday. He
reported he'd just gotten word from David that
Abdullah Smith was to be Mac's new first officer.
Rayford raised a fist of celebration.

Then Rayford said, "A couple of updates.
We're getting the word to people we trust to keep
an eye out for Hattie. She can do us more harm
than anyone I can think of. I'm calling a break
on work in the cellar for a day. Chloe and I are
meeting with T this afternoon. All right, Mrs.
Rose, the floor is yours."

Leah stood to speak, which seemed to surprise
the others as much as it did Buck. They scooted
their chairs back to soften the angle as they
looked up at her. She spoke softly and seemed
more self-conscious than when she had met them
the night before. Her story came in a monotone,
as if she were covering her emotions.

"I gather that you people were fairly normal
before the Rapture, except that you weren't
believers. I was messed up. I grew up in a home
where my dad was an alcoholic, my mother a
manic-depressive. My parents' fights were the
neighborhood entertainment until they divorced
when I was twelve. Within three years I smoked,
drank, slept around, did drugs, and nearly killed
myself more than once. I had an abortion when

I was seventeen and then tried to drink away the horror of it. I dropped out of school and lived in a friend's apartment. I consumed more booze and dope than food, and when I found myself wandering the streets and passing blood in the middle of the night, I came to the end of myself.

"I knew I was a bum and that if I didn't do something about it, I would soon be dead. I didn't want that because I had no idea what came next. I prayed when I was really in trouble, but most of the time I didn't even think about God. I went into a free county rehab center and wondered if I dared live without junk in my system. When I finally began to think rationally, the people there discovered I had a brain and had me tested. I had a high IQ, go figure, and proclivities—whatever that meant—for the sciences.

"I was so grateful to those people that it sparked in me some latent soft spot for the needy. I got back into school, graduated a year late with almost straight A's, and worked as a nurse's aide and a signer for deaf students to pay for community college. I met my husband there, and he put me through state school and a nursing program. I was unable to bear children, so after about six years of marriage we adopted two boys."

As soon as she tried to say their names, Leah clouded over and could barely speak. "Peter and Paul," she whispered. "My husband had been raised in a religious home and, though he hadn't gone to church for years, had always wanted sons with those names. We wanted to expose the boys to church, so we started going. The people were nice, but it might as well have been a country club. Lots of social activities, but we didn't feel any closer to God.

"At the hospital where I worked one of the chaplains tried to convert me. Though he seemed sincere, I was offended. And the woman who ran the day care center our boys went to gave me literature about Jesus. I assured her we went to church. I was incensed when my sons came home with Bible stories. I called the woman and told her they went to Sunday school and that I wished she'd stick to just watching them."

Leah's voice was husky with emotion. "I found my boys' beds empty the morning after the Rapture. It was the worst day of my life. I was convinced they had been kidnapped. The police couldn't do anything, of course, because all children were gone. I hadn't heard of the Rapture, but it was quickly put forth on the news as one of the possibilities. I called the hospital chaplain, but he had disappeared. I called the day care center, but the director had vanished too. I raced over there, but no one knew anything. In a rack in the waiting room I found more pamphlets like the ones the director had given me. One, titled 'Don't Be Left Behind,' said that someday true believers would disappear into heaven with Jesus.

"That was in my purse when I got home and discovered my husband in the garage with the door shut and his car running." Leah paused and collected herself. "He had left me a note, saying he was sorry but that he was frightened out of his mind, couldn't live without the boys, and knew he had no answer to my grief."

Leah stopped, her lips trembling.

"Do you need a break, dear?" Tsion asked.

She shook her head. "I tried to kill myself. I swallowed everything in the medicine cabinet and made myself violently ill. God must not have wanted me dead, because apparently much of what I ingested countered whatever else I took. I awoke hours later with a horrible headache, stomachache, and rancid taste. I crawled to my purse to find some mints and came across that pamphlet again. Somehow it finally made sense.

"It predicted what had happened and warned the reader to be ready. The solution—well, you know this—was to seek God, to tell him I knew I was a sinner and that I needed him. I didn't know if it was too late for me, but I prayed just in case. I don't know how I found the energy, but as soon as I could get myself out of the house, I looked for other people like me. I found them in

a little church. Only a few had been left behind,
but they knew why. Now there are about sixty
who meet in secret. I'm going to miss those
people, but they won't be surprised I've disappeared. I told them what was going on, that
I had treated a GC fugitive and all."

"We'll get word to them that you're safe,"
Rayford said, clearly overcome.

"*Am* I safe?" Leah said, sitting down with a
sad smile. "Do I get to stay?"

"We always vote," Tsion said. "But I think you
have found a home."

●   ●   ●

Early in the evening in New Babylon, David sat
in his office after hours, missing Annie. Being
alone with her was risky, so they spent time on
their secure phones and computers. He built into
his unit the capability to erase both their transmissions, to serve as a backup if she forgot. He
couldn't imagine that either of them would forget
to remove from their computers evidence of their
relationship and especially their faith.

"Maybe we should reveal our love," she
transmitted. "By policy I would be forced to
move to a department outside your supervision,
but at least we could see each other without
suspicion."

He tapped back: "It's not a bad idea, and we

could use another pair of eyes in other departments. Where you are right now is strategic, though, because of what we can smuggle out of here and into believers' hands in other countries. Keep thinking, though. I can't stand being apart from you."

Suddenly the TV monitors in his area—all of them—came on. That happened only when GC brass believed something was on that every employee would want to see. Most of the time it meant that Carpathia or Fortunato was addressing the world, and it didn't make any difference whether anyone in a sector was working. If there was a TV there, it came on.

David spun in his chair and leaned back to watch the monitor in his office. A GC CNN anchorman was reporting a plane crash. "While neither the plane itself, reportedly a large private aircraft, nor the pilot or passenger have been sighted, personal belongings have washed ashore in Portugal. Listen to this Mayday call, recorded by several tracking stations in the region."

Mayday! Mayday! Quantum zero-seven-zero-eight losing altitude! Mayday!

"Radar trackers lost sight of the craft soon thereafter, and rescuers searched the area. Luggage and personal effects of two people, a man and a woman, were discovered. Authorities assume it will be just a matter of time before the wreckage and bodies are discovered. Names of the victims are being withheld pending notification of next of kin."

David squinted at the screen, wondering why GC brass thought this newsworthy until the victims were known. Then the internal caption scrawl appeared on the screen:

ATTENTION GC PALACE PERSONNEL. PROBABLE VICTIMS IN THIS CRASH, ACCORDING TO RESCUE AUTHORITIES, ARE AS FOLLOWS: PILOT SAMUEL HANSON OF BATON ROUGE, LOUISI- ANA, UNITED STATES OF NORTH AMERICA, AND HATTIE DURHAM, ORIGINALLY OF DES PLAINES, ILLINOIS, U.S.N.A. MS. DURHAM ONCE SERVED HIS EXCELLENCY THE POTENTATE AS PERSONAL ASSISTANT. CONDOLENCES TO THOSE WHO KNEW HER.

David phoned Mac. "I saw," Mac said. "What an obvious fake!"

"Yeah!" David said. "The pilot must be cash- ing in a huge insurance policy, and Hattie has to be somewhere in Europe."

"Maybe they're shopping for more Stupid

pills," Mac said. "Are we supposed to believe Carpathia and Fortunato fell for this?"

"Surely not," David said. "Unless they engineered it. Maybe they found Hattie and had her killed, and now they're covering. They'd better come up with wreckage or bodies."

David heard the ping that told him he had a new message. "I'll get back to you, Mac."

●   ●   ●

Rayford and Chloe sat in T's office at the base of the Palwaukee tower with T and two men from his house church. Chloe outlined how she planned to link the major players on the co-op network and start testing the system before actual buying and selling got under way. "We have to keep it secret from the beginning," she said. "Otherwise we'll be grouped with all other commodities brokers and put under the GC's aegis."

The others nodded. Rayford's phone beeped. It was Buck. Rayford laughed aloud as Buck recounted the strange news report. "Turn on the TV, T," he said. GC commentators mournfully discussed the tragedy, though names had not been revealed outside New Babylon and so far nothing but papers and belongings had been found. Rayford shook his head. "Someday Fortunato, or whoever tried to take advantage of this, is going to embarrass himself beyond repair."

Chloe tugged at his sleeve and whispered. "At least we can be pretty sure Hattie's all right for now."

"The question," he said as the meeting broke up, "is where she is. She's not smart enough to get any thinking person to believe she went down in that plane. Could she still surprise Carpathia?"

When the churchmen were gone, Rayford, Chloe, and T jogged upstairs to quiz the tower man about the 11:30 flight the night before. He was fat and balding, reading a science fiction book.

"Sounded southern to me on the radio, though I never saw him," the man said. "Bo signed off on the landing and takeoff."

"He was here?" T said.

"No, he called me about eight to preapprove it."

"I didn't see the plane's numbers on the computer."

"I wrote 'em down. I can still enter 'em." He rummaged under a pile of papers. "Oh-seven-oh-eight," he said. "And I guess you know it was a Quantum."

"Can we find out who that's registered to?" Rayford said.

"Sure can," the man said. He banged away at

his computer keyboard and drummed his knee as the information was retrieved. "Hm," he said, reading. "Samuel Hanson out of Baton Rouge. He's got to be related to Bo, doesn't he? Isn't Bo from Louisiana?"

SEVEN

REUNITING with Abdullah Smith warmed Mac.
In his earliest days as first officer to Captain
Rayford Steele, Mac had met the former fighter
pilot from Jordan. Abdullah had lost his job
when Carpathia confiscated international weap-
onry, but he quickly became one of Rayford's
leading black market suppliers.

Abdullah had been disgraced four years before
the Rapture when his wife had become a Christian. He divorced her and fought for custody of
their two small children, a boy and a girl. When
he could not get relief from months of travel at
a time for the Jordanian air force, he was denied
custody and took up full-time residence at the
military base.

A man of few words, Abdullah had once
revealed to Mac and Rayford that he was heart-
sick to the point of suicide. "I still loved my

wife," he said with his thick accent. "She and the children were my world. But imagine *your* wife taking up a religion from some mysterious, faraway country. We wrote long letters to each other, but neither could be dissuaded. To my shame, I was not devout in my own religion and fell into loose morals. My wife said she prayed for me every day that I would find Jesus Christ before it was too late. I cursed her in my letters. One sentence pleaded with her to renounce the myths and return to the man who loved her. The next accused her of treachery and called her despicable names. Her next letter told me she still loved me and reminded me that it was I who had initiated the divorce. Again, in my anger, I lashed out at her.

"I still have the letters in which she warned me that I might die before finding the one true God, or that Jesus could return for those who loved him, and I would be left behind. I was enraged. Just to get back at her I often refused to visit my children, but now I realize I hurt only them and myself. I feel so guilty that they might not know how much I loved them."

Mac recalled Rayford's telling Abdullah, "You will be able to tell them one day." Abdullah had merely nodded, his dark eyes moist and distant.

Abdullah became a believer because he saved his wife's letters. She had meticulously explained the plan of salvation, writing out Bible verses and telling him how she had prayed to receive Christ. "Many times I crumpled up the letters and threw them across the room," Abdullah said. "But something kept me from tearing them or burning them or throwing them away."

When Abdullah heard that his wife and children had disappeared, he had lain prostrate on the floor in his quarters in Amman, his wife's letters spread before him. "It had happened as she said it would," he said. "I cried out to God. I had no choice but to believe."

Because of his Middle Eastern look and his fondness for a turban and a blowsy, off-white top over camouflage trousers and aviator boots, the diminutive Jordanian was the last person anyone suspected of being a Christian. Until the conversion of the 144,000 Jewish witnesses from all over the world and their millions of converts of every nationality, most assumed they could identify a Christian. Now, of course, only true believers knew each other on sight, due to the mark visible only to them.

Abdullah, thin and dark with large, expressive features, was as quiet as Mac remembered him. He was also extremely formal in front of others, not giving away that he and Mac were both spiritual brothers and old friends. He didn't pretend they had not met, for Mac had concocted a former military connection. But they did not embrace until they were alone in Mac's office.

"There's someone I want you to meet," Mac said, calling Annie from her office. She knocked and entered, breaking into a smile.

"You must be the infamous Abdullah Smith," she said. "You have a custom mark reserved for Jordanians."

Abdullah gave Mac a puzzled look, then stared at Annie's forehead. "I cannot see mine," he said. "Is it not like yours?"

"I'm teasing you," she said. "Yours merely works better with your coloring."

"I see," he said, as if he really did.

"Go easy on the American humor," Mac said.

"*Canadian* humor," Annie said. She spread her arms to hug Abdullah, which seemed to embarrass him. He thrust out his hand, and she shook it. "Welcome to the family," she said.

Again Abdullah looked questioningly at Mac.

"Actually, *she's* the newest member of the family," Mac said. "She's just welcoming you to this chapter of the Tribulation Force."

Abdullah left some of his stuff in his small office behind Mac's, then two laborers from Operations helped take the rest to his new quarters. As he and Abdullah followed the men, Mac said, "Once you get unpacked you can get your feet wet by plotting our course to Botswana

Friday. We'll leave here at 0800, and they're an hour earlier, so—"

"Johannesburg, I assume," Abdullah said.

"No, north of there. We're seeing Mwangati Ngumo in Gaborone on the old border of Botswana and South Af—"

"Oh, pardon me, Captain, but you must not have been there recently. Only helicopters can get in and out of Gaborone. The airport was destroyed in the great earthquake."

"But surely the old military base—"

"The same," Abdullah said.

"Carpathia's reconstruction program has not reached Botswana?"

"No, but with the . . . the, pardon me, regional potentate of the United States of Africa residing in Johannesburg in a palace not much smaller than this one, the new airport there is spectacular."

Mac thanked the helpers and unlocked Abdullah's apartment. The Jordanian's eyes widened as he surveyed the rooms. "All of this for me?" he said.

"You'll grow to hate it," Mac said.

With the door shut, Abdullah looked at the bare walls and whispered, "Can we talk here?"

"David assures me we can."

"I look forward to meeting him. Oh, Captain, I nearly referred to the African potentate as the king! I must be so careful."

"Well, *we* know he's one of the kings, but those two wouldn't have had a clue. I thought Potentate Rehoboth—what's his first name—?"

"Bindura."

"Right—was going to move his capital more central, like back up to his homeland. Chad, was it?"

"Sudan. That was what he had said, but apparently he found Johannesburg preferable. He lives in such opulence, you could not believe it."

"All the kings do."

"What do you make of that, Captain?" Abdullah was whispering. "Has Carpathia bought their cooperation?"

Mac shrugged and shook his head. "Wasn't there some sort of controversy between Rehoboth and Ngumo?"

"Oh, yes! When Ngumo was secretary-general of the U.N., Rehoboth put tremendous pressure on him to get favors for Africa, particularly Sudan. And when Ngumo was replaced by Carpathia, Rehoboth publicly praised the change."

"And now he's his neighbor."

"And Rehoboth is his king," Abdullah said.

●   ●   ●

Late Thursday night in Illinois, Rayford finally found himself alone in the kitchen with Leah

Rose. She sat at the table with a cup of coffee. He poured himself one.

"Settling in?" he said.

She cocked her head. "I never know what you're implying."

He pointed to a chair. "May I?"

"Sure."

He sat. "What would I be implying?"

"That I shouldn't get too comfortable."

"We voted you in! It was unanimous. Even the chair voted, and I didn't have to."

"Had it been a tie otherwise, how would the chair have voted?"

Rayford sat back, his cup in both hands. "We got off on the wrong foot," he said. "I'm sure it was my fault."

"You ignored my question," she said.

"Stop it. Voting in a new sister would never result in a tie. Hattie was here for months, and she's not even a believer."

"So is this our truce chat, or are you just being polite?"

"You want a truce?" he said.

"Do *you?*"

"I asked you first," he said.

She smiled. "Truth is, I want more than a truce. We can't live in the same house just being cordial. We've got to be friends."

Rayford wasn't so sure, but he said, "I'm game."

"So all that stuff you said . . ."

He raised his chin. ". . . that exposed me for the crank I am?"

She nodded. "Consider this an all-inclusive pardon."

He hadn't asked forgiveness.

"And for me?" she pressed.

"What?"

"I need a pardon too."

"No you don't," he said, sounding more magnanimous than he felt. "Anything you said was because of what I—"

Leah put a hand on his arm. "I didn't even recognize myself," she said. "I can't put that all on you. Now, come on. If we're going to start over, we have to be even. Clean slates."

"Granted," he said.

"I've got money," she said.

"You always switch subjects so fast?"

"Cash. We'd have to go get it. It's in a safe in my garage. I am not going to be a freeloader. I want things to do, and I want to pay my way."

"How about we give you room and board in exchange for medical care and expertise?"

"I'm more about care than expertise. I'm no replacement for Floyd."

"We're grateful to have you."

"But you need money too. When can we get it?"

Rayford pointed to her cup. She shook her head. "How much are we talking about?" he said.

When she told him, he gasped.

"In what denominations?"

"Twenties."

"All in one safe?"

"I couldn't fit another bill in there," she said.

"You think it's still there? The GC must have torn the place apart looking for you."

"The safe is so well hidden we had to remind ourselves where it was."

Rayford rinsed out the cups. "Sleepy?" he said.

"No."

"Want to go now?"

● ● ●

Mac and Abdullah met with David Friday morning. Once introductions were out of the way, David asked if either had an idea where the 144 computers in the Condor cargo hold could be put to use for the cause.

"I can think of lots of places," Mac said. "But not one on the way to Africa."

"I can," Abdullah said. "There is a huge body of underground believers in Hawalli. Many professionals, and they could—"

"Hawalli?" David said. "In Kuwait?"

"Yes. I have a contact in cargo—"

"That's east. You're flying southwest."

"Only slightly east," Abdullah said. "We just need a reason to stop there."

"Virtually right after takeoff," Mac said. "That'll arouse suspicion." They sat in silence a moment. "Unless . . . ," he said.

David and Abdullah looked at him.

"How far is our flight?"

"Here to Kuwait?" Abdullah asked, pulling out his charts.

"No, to Africa."

"More than four thousand miles."

"Then we need a full fuel load to go nonstop. We want to save the GC money, so we're going to make a quick detour for fuel at a good price."

"Excellent," David said. "I'll negotiate it right now. All I need is a few cents' break per pound of fuel and it'll be worth the detour."

"What will my contact need to get the cargo?" Abdullah said.

"Big forklift. Big truck."

●   ●   ●

"Why'd you leave a note?" Leah asked Rayford as he pulled the Land Rover away from the house toward Palatine. "Surely we'll be back before anyone wakes up."

"It wouldn't surprise me," he said, "if someone was peeking at the note already. We hear everything in that house. In the dead of night we hear sounds in the walls, sounds from outside. We've been fortunate so far. We only hope for some warning so we can hide out below before we're found out. We always tell each other where we go. Buck didn't the other day when he rushed Floyd to see you, but that was an emergency. It upset everybody."

Rayford spent the next forty minutes maneuvering around debris and seeking the smoothest man-made route. He wondered when Carpathia's vaunted reconstruction efforts would reach past the major cities and into the suburbs.

Leah was full of questions about each member of the Trib Force, how they had met, become believers, got together. "That's way too much loss in too short a time," she said after he had brought her to the present. "With all that stress, it's a wonder you're all fully functioning."

"We try not to think about it. We know it's going to get worse. It sounds like a cliché, but you have to look ahead rather than back. If you let it accumulate, you'll never make it."

Leah ran a hand through her hair. "Sometimes I don't know why I want to survive until the Glorious Appearing. Then my survival instinct kicks in."

"Speaking of which . . . ," Rayford said.

"What?"

"More traffic than I'm used to is all."

She shrugged. "This area wasn't as hard hit as yours. No one's hiding here. Everybody knows everybody else."

They agreed Rayford should park a couple of blocks away and that they should move through the shadows to Leah's town house. He pulled a large canvas bag and a flashlight from the back of the Rover.

At the edge of her property, Leah stopped. "They didn't even shut the door," she said. "The place has to be ransacked."

"If the GC didn't trash it, looters did," Rayford said. "Once they knew you were on the run, your place was fair game. Want to check it out?"

She shook her head. "We'd better be in and out of that garage fast too. My neighbors can hear the door going up."

"Is there a side entrance?"

She nodded.

"Got the key?"

"No."

"I can break in. No one will hear unless they're in there waiting for you."

● ● ●

When Mac met Abdullah in the hangar to bring him up to speed on the Condor 216, Annie was already there, supervising cargo handlers. "More, Corporal?" Mac said.

"Yes, Captain. The purchasing director would like us to transport this tonnage of surplus food-stuffs to Kuwait. He got a spectacular deal on fuel, so while you're taking on fuel, you can off-load this."

Abdullah was silent inside the plane until they reached the cockpit and Mac showed him the reverse intercom bug. "Imagine the methods of our dismemberment if they found out," he said.

At ten to eight in the morning, Mac and Abdullah finished their preflight checks and contacted the palace tower. Three figures in white aprons ran toward the plane. "Kitchen staff," Mac said. "Let 'em in."

Abdullah opened the door and lowered the stairs. The cook, a sweating middle-aged man with stubby fingers, carried a steaming pan covered with foil. "Out of the way, out of the way," he said in a Scandinavian accent. "Nobody told me the commander wanted breakfast aboard."

Abdullah stepped back as the cook and his two aides hurried past. "Then how did you know?" he said.

The cook hurried into the galley and barked orders. Distracted by Abdullah's hovering, he turned. "Was that rhetorical, sarcastic, or a genuine question?"

"I am not familiar with the first two," Abdullah said.

The cook leaned on the counter as if he couldn't believe he was about to waste his time answering the first officer. "I meant," he said slowly, as if indulging a child, "that no one told me before now, and then the supreme commander him*self* told me. If he's looking forward to eggs Benedict once airborne, it's eggs Benedict he'll get. Now, was there anything else?"

"Yes, sir."

The cook looked stunned. "There is?"

"Would you like to impress the supreme commander?"

"If I didn't I wouldn't have run to the plane with a tray of hot food, would I?"

"I happen to know Commander Fortunato does not mean airborne when he says airborne."

"Indeed?"

"No, you see, we have a brief stop in Kuwait after takeoff, and that would be the perfect time to serve him. Quieter, more relaxed, no danger of spilling."

"Kuwait?"

"Just moments after takeoff, really."

"Children!" the cook hollered to his aides. "Keep it hot. We're servin' breakfast in Kuwait!"

●　　●　　●

As Rayford expected, the side door to Leah's shared garage was flimsy enough to be forced open without a lot of racket. But when he crept inside and asked her to point out the safe, he was alone. Rayford caught himself before he called to her, not wanting to compound the situation if something was wrong. He turned slowly and tiptoed back to the door. At first Rayford didn't see her, but he heard her hyperventilating. She was kneeling near him in the moist grass and mud, her torso heaving with the strain of catching her breath. "I—I—I—," she gasped.

He crouched beside her. "What is it? Are you all right? See someone?"

She wouldn't look up, but in the darkness she fearfully pointed past Rayford. He took a good grip on the flashlight and whirled to see if someone was coming. He saw nothing.

"What did you see?" he said, but she was whimpering now, unable to say anything.

"Let me get you inside," he said.

Helping her up and getting her into the garage was like picking up a sleeping child. "Leah!" he said. "Work with me. You're safe."

She sat on the floor, pulling her knees up to her chest and hugging her legs. "Are they still out there?" she said. "Can you lock the door?"

"I broke the door," he said. "Who's out there?"

"You really didn't see them?"

"Who?" he whispered loudly. She was shivering. "You need to get off that cold floor."

He reached for her, but she wrenched away. "I won't be able to leave," she said, covering her face with trembling fingers. "You'll have to bring the car for me."

He hadn't expected her to be this high maintenance. "Too risky."

"I can't, Rayford! I'm sorry."

"Then let's get the money and get going."

"Forget the money. I wouldn't be able to work the lock now anyway."

"Why not?"

Again she pointed outside.

"Leah," Rayford said, as soothingly as he could, "there's nothing out there. We're safe. We're going to get your cash and go straight back to the car and go home, all right?"

She shook her head.

"Yes, we are," he said, and he grabbed her elbow and pulled her up. She was incapacitated. He guided her to the wall and gently pushed her back until it supported her. "Tell me what you saw."

"Horses," she said. "Huge, dark horses. On the ridge behind the house, blocking the whole horizon. I couldn't make out the riders because the horses breathed fire and smoke. But they just sat there, hundreds of them, maybe more, huge and menacing. Their faces! Rayford, their faces looked like lions with huge teeth!"

"Wait here," Rayford said.

"Don't leave me!" she said, grabbing his wrists, her fingers digging into flesh.

He peeled her hands away. "You're safe."

"Don't go near them! They're hovering."

"Hovering?"

"Their feet are not touching the ground!"

"Tsion didn't think they were real," Rayford said.

"Tsion saw them?"

"Didn't you read his message about this?"

"I don't have a computer anymore."

"These have to be the horsemen of Revelation 9, Leah! They won't hurt us!"

"Are you sure?"

"What else can they be?"

Leah seemed to begin breathing easier, but even in the faint glow of the flashlight, she was pale. "Let me go check," he said. "Think about the safe and the combination."

She nodded, but she didn't move. He hurried to the door. "To the east," she stage-whispered. "On the horizon." Though he felt he was safe, still he kept the door between him and the horizon. The night was cool and quiet. He saw nothing. He stepped away from the door and moved up a small incline, peeling his eyes to peer between buildings and into the open. His heart pounded, but he was disappointed he had not seen what Leah had. Had it been a vision? Why only to her?

He hurried back. She had moved away from the wall but was still not within sight of the door. "Did you see them?" she said.

"No."

"They were there, Rayford! I wasn't seeing things!"

"I believe you."

"Do you?"

"Of course! But Tsion said he didn't think they *would* be visible. He'll be glad to hear it."

"Where could they have gone? There were too many to move away that quickly."

"Leah," Rayford said carefully, "we're talking about the supernatural, good and evil, the battle of the ages. There are no rules, at least not human ones. If you saw the horsemen predicted in Revelation, who knows what power they might have to appear and disappear?"

She folded her arms and rocked. "I lived through the earthquake. I saw the locusts. Did you?"

He nodded.

"You got a close look, Rayford, really close?"

"T and I studied one."

"Then you know."

"I sure do."

"That was the most horrible thing I had ever

seen. I didn't get as close a look at these, but they're monstrous. I could tell they were near the horizon, but they were so big I could see every detail. Are they not allowed to hurt us?"

"Tsion says they have the power to kill a third of the population."

"But not believers?"

Rayford shook his head. "They kill those who have not repented of their sin."

"If I didn't repent before, I do now!" she said.

● ● ●

With the cook, his helpers, Fortunato, and his two aides aboard, Mac taxied out of the hangar and onto the airstrip south of the Global Community palace. Once airborne, he greeted the passengers over the intercom, informing them of the brief stop in Kuwait, then the four-thousand-plus mile flight to Johannesburg. Within seconds there came a loud rapping on the cockpit door.

"That would be Leon," Mac said, nodding for Abdullah to unlock the door. "It's time you met him anyway."

Leon ignored Abdullah. "What's with the stop in Kuwait, Captain? I have a schedule!"

"Good morning, Commander," Mac said. "Our new first officer assures me we will land in plenty of time for your meeting, sir. Abdullah Smith, meet Supreme C—"

"In due time," Fortunato said. "What's in Kuwait?"

"Two birds with one stone, sir," Mac said. "Director Hassid found a bargain on fuel, and our new cargo chief combined some deliveries, as long as we were headed that way. All told we've saved the administration thousands."

"You don't say."

"Yes, sir."

"And *your* name again, young man?"

"Abdullah Smith, sir."

"I'm hungry anyway. Could you use some eggs Benedict this morning, Officer Smith?"

"No, thank you, sir. I ate earlier."

"Captain McCullum, I would have appreciated knowing of the schedule change in advance."

"As I said, sir, it's really not a schedule change *per se*. Just a bit of a route ch—"

The door slapped shut. Abdullah looked at Mac with his brows raised. "Charming man," he said.

Mac depressed the button beneath his chair and listened to the cabin. "Karl, how are my eggs coming? Enough for all of us, yourself included?"

"Yes, sir, Supreme Commander, sir. I shall serve them on the ground—well, let me rephrase that. I shall serve them when we're on the ground temporarily in Kuwait."

"I'm hungry *now*, Karl."

"I'm sorry, sir. I was led to understand that you

preferred the quiet and lack of bouncing around that might be afforded while we're refueling."

"Who told you that?"

"The first officer, sir."

"The new man? He doesn't even know me!"

"Well—"

"We'll see about this."

Mac clicked the button and turned a switch so he could speak directly from his mouthpiece to Abdullah's headset. In one breath he repeated what he had just heard.

"Thank you," Abdullah said as the door resounded yet again.

"Your name again, officer?" Leon said.

"Smith, sir."

"You told the cook to serve breakfast in Kuwait rather than in the air?"

"I merely informed him of our slight route change and suggested that you might appreciate it more if—"

"So it *was* your idea. *You* told *him* what you thought I'd like, yet you and I had never met."

"I take responsibility, sir. If I was out of order, I—"

"You were only exactly right there, Smith. I just wondered how you knew how much I hate trying to eat, especially a dish like that, while bouncing around up here. No offense, Mac—er, Captain."

Mac was tempted to call him Leon and tell him no offense taken. But he just waved. The Condor virtually flew itself, but Mac liked to give the impression, as Rayford liked to say, "of keepin' my eye on the road and my hand on the wheel."

"So, how *did* you know that, Officer Smith?" Leon said.

"I only assumed," he said. "I would not want egg yolk or hollandaise on my shirt in an important meeting."

At the ensuing silence, Mac turned to see if Fortunato had left. He had not. He looked overcome. He rocked back with his mouth open so wide his eyes were shut. He lurched forward with a hacking, coughing laugh and a slap on the shoulder that drove Abdullah back into his seat. "Now that's good!" Fortunato roared. "I like that!" And as he backed out of the cockpit, pulling the door shut behind him, he repeated, "Yolk or hollandaise on my shirt!"

Mac depressed the button again. "I did not intend to implicate the first officer," Karl was saying.

"Nonsense! Good idea! Serve us in Kuwait. How long will that be?"

"Just minutes actually, sir, is my understanding."

"Good. This way I'll go into my meeting with a clean shirt. You should have thought of that, Karl."

EIGHT

LEAH'S safe was hidden behind her sons' moldy pup tent high on a deck. Rayford helped her climb a perfectly vertical board ladder to it, then waited until she had pushed aside the tent and other junk. He followed and crouched behind her, aiming the light over her shoulder at the combination lock.

"How'd you get this thing up here?" he whispered. "It must weigh a ton."

"We didn't want the neighbors to know," she said, her voice still shaky. "We were in here late, like now. My husband, Shannon, had had the safe delivered in a plain box, and he rented a hydraulic scaffold. One neighbor asked what it was for, and Shannon told him it was for roof repairs in the garage. Seemed to satisfy him."

"So, once you got it up here, what, you two wrestled it into place?"

She nodded. "We worried the deck wouldn't hold it."

The safe was about three feet high and two feet wide, and Leah had not been joking when she said it was stuffed with cash. As she opened the door, she said, "We had to keep our other valuables at the bank."

The safe was crammed with bundles of twenties. "We could use this at the safe house," Rayford said.

"That's why we're here."

"I mean the safe itself. We could never accept all this cash. There aren't enough years left to spend it."

"Nonsense. You're going to need more vehicles, and you never know how many people might have to live with you."

They quickly stuffed the bag with the cash. "This is going to be too heavy to carry," he said. "Help me push it over the side."

They duckwalked and grunted and dragged the bag to the edge of the deck. The bundles shifted, but they were finally able to push the bag free. It plopped to the floor, with a thud, sending up a cloud of dust. Rayford turned off the flashlight and held his breath, listening. "Can you see me?" he whispered.

"Barely."

He signaled her to follow, and it was as difficult

going down the boards as up. When he reached the floor he helped her the rest of the way.

"I suppose you think that makes you a gentleman," she whispered.

"Only if you're a lady."

They bent over the bag, feeling the edges in the dark for the best grip. A bright beam shined in their faces.

"Are you Mrs. Leah Rose?" a voice demanded.

She sighed and looked at Rayford. "Yes," she said quietly. "I'm so sorry, R—"

"Don't say my name!" he hissed. "And you shouldn't claim to be someone you're not."

"Are you Mrs. Rose or not?" came the voice again.

"I said I was, didn't I?" she said, suddenly sounding as if she were lying. Rayford was impressed she had caught on so quickly.

"And you, sir?"

"Me, what?" Rayford said.

"Your name."

"Who's asking?"

"GC Peacekeeping Forces."

"Oh, that's a relief," Rayford said. "Us too. I was asked by Commander Sullivan to mop up here. Looters ransacked the house after your boys finished up. He wanted us to secure the garage."

Someone flipped a switch and the bare bulb just above Rayford's head came on. He squinted before four armed GC officers, three men and a woman. "What were you doing in the dark?" the leader said. He wore lieutenant's bars.

Rayford looked up. The bulb was within an arm's length. "We heard something outside and doused the light."

"Mm-hm," the young man said, approaching. "I need to see some ID." Behind him the woman eyed Rayford with uncertainty. One of the other men looked up at the deck.

"I'm Pafko," Rayford said, desperately trying to remember which pocket he used for his phony ID. "Andrew. Here it is."

"And you, ma'am?"

"She's Fitzgerald."

"And my papers are in the car," she said.

"Lieutenant," the other guard said. "There's an open safe up there."

The lieutenant handed Rayford his ID. "You weren't planning on a little looting yourself, were you, Pafko?"

"Every penny will be accounted for."

"Mm-hm." He turned to the woman. "Double-check with Central. Pafko, Andrew, assigned out of Des Plaines. And Fitzgerald. First name, ma'am, and assignment city?"

"Pauline," Leah said. "Also Des Plaines."

The woman reached for the phone strapped to her shoulder.

Rayford almost skated, but the call would expose him. They would both be easily identified, maybe tortured and killed if they didn't reveal the rest of the Force. He deserved that for not being more careful, but Leah certainly didn't.

"No need for that, Lieutenant," Rayford said. "Before letting headquarters know where we are, shouldn't we have a look-see to find out if maybe all six of us would be better off forgetting we were here tonight? I'm as loyal as you are, but we both know the Rose woman was a rebel sympathizer. If this was her money, it's ours now, isn't it?"

The lieutenant hesitated, and the female guard took her hand away from the phone. The lieutenant knelt by the bag.

The woman said, "You're buying this? You think he's GC?"

He looked up at her. "How else would he know why we were looking for Mrs. Rose?"

She shrugged and went to peer at the safe. The other two guards moved to the door, apparently to check for curious eyes. Rayford ran a hand through his hair. Was it possible he had four willing accomplices?

He caught Leah's eye and tried to communicate to follow his lead. She looked as petrified as when she had seen the horses. Rayford casually stepped between the lieutenant and the door. Leah stayed with him.

The lieutenant saw the cash and whistled through his teeth. The men moseyed back in to look, and that brought the woman over too. With their attention on the bag, they allowed Rayford and Leah a step closer to the door than they were. Leah could have slipped out without being noticed, but Rayford couldn't say anything, and she didn't move.

"There's plenty for everybody all right," one of the men said. The lieutenant nodded, but Rayford noticed the woman staring at Leah. She dug a stack of sheets from her back pocket and riffled through them. She stopped and raised her eyes to Leah.

"Lieutenant," the woman said.

"Let me show you one thing," Rayford interrupted, reaching into the bag and pulling out a bundle of twenties. "Figure there's fifty twenties in each bundle." He held it at one end and let the stack flop back and forth. The woman reached for her weapon. Rayford raised the bundle. "Wouldn't it be nice to divide these, and—go! Now!" Rayford smacked the lightbulb with the cash, and the garage went black.

He spun and sprinted after Leah as she raced through the side door. He heard a shot and wood cracking and was aware that the lieutenant's big flashlight had come back on too. As he and Leah sprinted over the slippery ground, he guessed

their odds of reaching the Land Rover at no
better than one in five. But he wasn't about to
stand there and be arrested.

Someone hit the automatic door button, and
Rayford heard the garage door rise. He sneaked
a peek back, and the opener light showed all
four guards coming full speed, weapons raised.
"Faster!" Rayford shouted as he turned back
toward Leah. But she had stopped. He slammed
into her, and they both tumbled over and over in
the grass.

Something had given way. Had his leg broken,
or had he crushed one of hers? Why had she
stopped? She had been moving well! They'd had
a chance. The Land Rover was in sight. Would
the GC shoot? Or would they just arrest them?
Rayford would rather be in heaven than endanger
his loved ones. "Let's make them shoot," he
rasped and tried to rise. But Leah had drawn
up on all fours and was staring toward the car
through strands of hair in her face.

Rayford looked back. The guards were gone.
He looked the other way, where Leah's eyes were
transfixed. And there were the horses, not ten feet
from him—huge, monstrous, muscular things twice
the size of any he had ever seen. Leah was right,
their feet were not on the ground, yet they shifted
and stepped back and forth, turning, turning.

Flames came from their nostrils and mouths,

and thick yellow smoke billowed. The fire illumi-
nated their majestic wide heads, the heads of
lions with enormous canines and flowing manes.
Rayford slowly, painfully rose, no longer surprised that Leah had been rendered helpless when
first she had seen them. "They won't hurt us," he
said weakly, hopefully, panting.

He trembled, trying to take in the scene. The
first flank of steeds was backed by hundreds,
skittish and moving in place as if eager to charge
and run. The riders were proportioned every bit
as large as the animals. They appeared human,
but each had to be ten feet tall and weigh five
hundred pounds.

Rayford swallowed, his chest heaving. He
wanted to check on Leah, but he could not look
away. The horse in front of him, hardly three
paces away, stutter-stepped and turned in a circle.
Rayford gaped at a tail consisting not of hair but
rather a writhing, sinewy serpent with a head
twice the size of Rayford's fist. It writhed and
bared its fangs.

The riders seemed to gaze miles into the
distance, high over Rayford's head. Each horse-
man wore a breastplate that, illumined by the
flames, shone iridescent yellow, deep navy, and
fiery red. Massive biceps and forearms knotted
and rippling, the riders seemed to work to keep
the animals from stampeding.

Rayford neither heard nor smelled the horses or the fire and smoke. He only knew they whinnied and snorted because of the flame and clouds. No sound of reins, saddles, breastplates. And yet the lion/horses and their riders were more vivid than anything he had ever seen before.

Rayford finally stole a glance at Leah. She appeared catatonic, unblinking, mouth open. "Breathe," he told her.

Had God provided these beings to protect them? Surely the guards had run for their lives. Rayford turned again and at first saw nothing between him and the garage. But then he noticed all four guards on the ground, perfectly still.

He heard sirens, saw helicopters with searchlights, heard guards running, shouting. "We have to go, Leah," he said. "We can walk right through the horses. They're not physical."

"You there!"

Rayford whirled. Two guards nudged the fallen four with their boots while shouting at Rayford and Leah, "Stay where you are!"

They approached cautiously, and Leah finally turned from the horses to look over her shoulder. She whispered, "I think I broke a rib." She squinted at the guards. "Aren't they afraid of the horses?"

What was wrong with these two? As they drew near—men who appeared in their early

twenties—they leveled high-powered weapons at
Rayford and Leah. Rayford knew the horses were
still behind him because of the reflection of the
flames dancing off the guards' faces.

"What do you know about those dead security
guards?" one said.

"Nothing," Leah said, still on all fours. "What
do you think of our army?"

"Stand up, ma'am."

"They can't see them," Rayford said.

"Can't see who?" the guard said. "Come
with us."

"You don't see anything," Rayford said without inflection.

"I told you to stand up, ma'am!" the other
shouted. As he stepped toward her, Rayford
stepped in front of him.

"Son, let me warn you. If—"

"Warn me? I could shoot you and never have
to answer for it."

"You're in danger. We didn't kill those g—"

The guard burst into flames, his screaming,
spinning body lighting the area like day. A horse
moved past Rayford and silently spun, its tail
striking the other guard on the forehead. He flew
like a rag doll, his head crushed, into a tree ten
feet away.

Leah slowly came to her feet, sweat dripping
from her chin. She reached for Rayford as if in

slow motion. "We're . . . going . . . to . . . die,"
she managed.

"Not us," Rayford said, finding his breath.
"Where does it hurt? Press your palm over the
pain."

She held her left rib cage, and Rayford wrapped
his arm around her waist, walking toward the car.
He squinted against the flames, walking through
the horses as if through a hologram. Leah hid her
face behind his shoulder.

"Are they in another dimension? What is this?"

"A vision," he said, knowing for the first time
that they would escape. "Tsion was right. They're
not physical."

They were in the middle of the herd now,
Rayford unable to see the end, feeling like a child
in a sea of adults. Finally they passed through the
last row of horses and saw the Rover a hundred
feet away.

"You all right?" he asked.

"Except that I'm dreaming," she said. "I'll never
believe this tomorrow. I don't believe it now."

Rayford pointed half a mile to the west where
another cavalry of fiery horses and riders mustered.
Leah pointed the other way, where there were yet
more. Behind them the hundreds they had just
come through seemed to move toward Leah's
town house.

They got into the car and Rayford drove

straight down her street, something he had not dared earlier. The horses breathed great clouds of black and yellow smoke that chased GC forces out of the neighborhood, many falling and seemingly dying on the spot. As the smoke billowed through the area, people burst from their homes, gagging, coughing, falling. Here and there the horses snorted enough fire to incinerate homes.

"Wait here," Rayford said, shifting into park in front of Leah's garage.

"Rayford! No! Let's get back!"

He leapt out. "Yeah, I'm gonna leave that kind of money . . ."

"Please!" she called after him.

Rayford strode past bodies and into the garage. He zipped up the sack and just managed to hoist it over his shoulder. Walking through smoke and flames he neither smelled nor felt, he pushed the bag into the back of the Rover and slid behind the wheel. As he pulled away, he looked at Leah. "Welcome to the Trib Force," he said. She merely shook her head, still holding her ribs.

Rayford speed-dialed the safe house. He turned again to Leah. "Better buckle up," he said.

●　　●　　●

Mac slipped past the Fortunato party as they were being served and left the plane to monitor fueling. That allowed him to watch the cargo transfer.

Abdullah opened the hatch, and a squadron of forklift trucks buzzed onto the tarmac, up the aluminum ramp, and into the belly of the plane. While Fortunato was eating, 144 computers and more than a ton of foodstuffs were smuggled off the GC's own Condor 216 and would be appropriated by their enemy before sunset. *Brilliant, Abdullah,* Mac thought. *Nothing like breakfast to keep the supreme commander oblivious.*

●   ●   ●

Buck awoke when Chloe answered the phone.

"What time is it?" he said.

She pointed to the clock, which read 12:30.

"Shh," she said. "It's Daddy."

"His note said he and Leah—"

She shushed him again.

"Outside?" she said. "Why? . . . All right! I'll do it. . . . Tsion? Are you serious? You want me to wake him? . . . Well, hurry!"

She hung up.

"Buck, get up."

"What? Why?"

"Come on. Daddy wants you to wake Tsion and look out the window."

"What in—"

"Hurry! He and Leah are on their way."

"What are we looking for?"

"The 200 million horsemen."

"It's started? You can see them?"

"Get Tsion!"

●　　●　　●

Airborne again, Mac asked Abdullah to oversee the controls. "I want to see if Leon starts talking strategy."

He reached back to be sure the door was locked, unbuckled his seat belt, slouched in his seat, shut his eyes, and depressed the bug switch. One of Fortunato's aides was trying to impress the boss.

"It'll be so neat when he finds out Carpathia's not here, and that it's just you on the plane."

"I didn't just hear you refer to the potentate by merely his last—"

"I'm sorry, Commander. I meant His Excellency, the potentate. I would love to be there when Ngumo discovers that Potentate Rehoboth not only knows about the meeting, but that he has also been invited."

The other aide waded in. "What's the point of this trip if you're just going to put Ngumo in his place?"

"A valid question," Leon said. "Naïve, but valid. First, this is a particularly clever way to do it. It's not just an insult; it's a stinging insult. Despite our smiles and subservient attitudes, there will be no doubt in his mind that this is a slap in the face. It's not a meeting with His Excellency. It's not even a face-to-face with the supreme commander in private. He will get nothing he asks for and will be told to like it. It could have been done by phone, but I wouldn't have enjoyed it as much. Anyway, this is an alliance-building mission."

"With Rehoboth?"

"Of course. It is crucial that His Excellency be confident of his regional potentates. A few more accommodations to Bindura, and we'll guarantee his loyalty. There are rumors of insurrection, but we're dead certain of six potentates, 90 percent sure of Rehoboth, and not so sure of the other three. They will be in line by the time of the disposition of the Jerusalem problem, or they will be replaced."

"The Jerusalem problem?"

"Don't disappoint me. You have worked hand and glove with me this long and you don't know what I mean when I refer to the Jer—"

"The two witnesses."

"Well, yes . . . no! That's what the rebels call them. And they call themselves some biblical thing, lampstands or trees or some such. Don't stoop to their terms. They are the crazy preachers, the wall-bangers, the—"

That last had sent the aides into paroxysms of laughter, which served only to start Leon on a string of comments he thought funny. To listen to his yes-men, he had only underestimated his comedic gift. Mac was shaking his head at the absurdity when Abdullah startled him with a slap across the chest.

Mac straightened up as if snapped with a wet towel. "I'm sorry," Abdullah shouted, "but look! Look! Oh! It was there!"

"What?" Mac said. With the sun climbing behind them to the left, the cloudless expanse before them appeared an endless clear blue. Mac saw nothing, and so now, apparently, did Abdullah.

"I saw something, Captain. I swear I did."

"I don't doubt you. What was it?"

"You'd doubt me if I told you." Abdullah's eyes were still wide. He leaned forward and looked in every direction.

"Try me."

"An army."

"I'm sorry?"

"A cavalry, I mean."

"Abdullah, you're not even looking at the ground."

"I would not have woken you if I saw something on the ground!"

"I wasn't sleeping."

"I *expect* to see horses on the ground!"

"You saw horses in the sky?"

"Horses and riders."

"There aren't even clouds."

"I told you you wouldn't believe me."

"I believe you *think* you saw something."

"You might as well call me a liar."

"Never. Clearly, you thought you saw something. You weren't napping. Were you?"

"Now I am a liar *and* asleep on the job?"

Mac laughed. "If you say you saw something, I believe you."

"It didn't look like 200 million, but—"

"Ah, you've been reading Tsion's lesson—"

"Of course. Who hasn't?"

Mac cocked his head. "You were daydreaming, maybe dozing. Don't look at me like that. I'm saying just for a split second, thinking about Dr. Ben-Judah's message—"

"You are going to offend me if you continue this, Captain."

Mac clapped Abdullah on the shoulder. "I'm sorry, brother. You have to admit it's possible."

Abdullah shrank from Mac's hand. "You have to admit it's possible I saw horses and riders."

Mac smiled. "What were they doing? Staging? Marshaling for the big parade?"

"Captain! You're insulting me!"

"C'mon, Abdullah! Tsion says the horses and riders come from the pit, same as the locusts. What would they be doing up here?"

Abdullah looked disgusted and turned away.

"Do you think I'd insult you on purpose?" Mac said.

No response.

"Well, do you?"

Abdullah was silent.

"Now you're going to pout."

"I'm not familiar with *pout*."

"Well," Mac said, "for not being familiar with it, you're pretty good at it."

"If pout means being angry at someone you thought was your friend and brother, then I'm pout."

Mac laughed aloud. "You're pout? May I call you pout? This is my friend and brother, pout!"

And before Mac could blink, horses and riders blotted out the sky. Abdullah jerked the controls and the plane tilted nearly straight up, pinning Mac to his seat. He heard crashing and banging in the galley and lounge. Then Leon crying out.

Just as Mac realized he was going to regret being unbuckled, Abdullah overadjusted, and the plane dipped. Mac slammed into the ceiling, full force, turning his face just in time to take the damage on the left side of his head. Control knobs broke off, tearing his flesh and piercing his ear. Blood splattered onto the windshield and control panel.

Abdullah finally brought the craft under

control and sat staring straight ahead. "I did not do that to get back at you for sporting with me," he said, his voice shaky. "If you did not see what I almost hit, I am terribly sorry and hope you are not seriously injured."

"I saw them plain as day," Mac said, his heart thundering. "I'll never doubt you again. I've got to stop the bleeding. If you see them again, don't try to avoid them. Keep her steady. They're floating around in space. You're not going to hit them."

"My apologies. It was instinct."

"I understand."

"Are you all right, Captain?"

"Not totally, but it's superficial, I'm sure."

"Good," Abdullah said. He mimicked a flight attendant: "You should always keep your belt fastened when you are in your seat, even when the seat belt light has been turned off."

Mac rolled his eyes.

"Now is it time for *you* to be pout?" Abdullah said.

Mac stood and reached for the door, just as someone banged on it from the other side.

NINE

BUCK apologized profusely to Tsion, explaining, "Rayford and Leah went to her place to get something and just now called to tell us to look out the window."

Tsion, his hair wild, pulled on a robe and followed Buck downstairs. Chloe, holding Kenny, stood before the windows facing west. "Maybe we need the lights off," she said. "I see nothing."

"What are we looking for?" Tsion said.

"The 200 million horsemen," she said.

Tsion rushed to the front of the house and pulled back the curtain. "I would not be disappointed if God moved up the Glorious Appearing a few years," he said. "Must be cloudy. No stars. Where is the moon?"

"Back here," Buck said.

"I cannot imagine Rayford was serious," Tsion said, rejoining Buck and Chloe.

"He was excited," Chloe said. "Scared even."

Buck moseyed out the back door and looked east, where the horizon glowed red. "Wonder if this is it," he called out.

"Something is burning somewhere," Tsion said wearily. "But isn't Mrs. Rose's home in the other direction?"

"I ought to drive that way and see what I can see," Buck said.

It was clear Chloe didn't like that idea. "Let's wait and see. It's not worth the risk if it's just a fire."

The phone rang. Chloe handed the fussing Kenny to Buck and hurried to get it. "No, Dad," she said. "Maybe fires in the east. . . . Are you sure it's begun? . . . Here, talk to Tsion."

●   ●   ●

As soon as Mac unlatched the cockpit door, Leon barged in, disheveled, swearing.

"A little turbulence," Mac said.

"Turbulence?! What's with the smoke, the smell? I've got a man down, and Karl says one of *his* people is unconscious! We've got to land, man! We're going to suffocate! And you're bleeding!"

Mac followed him into the lounge, where one of Leon's aides frantically pumped the chest of the other. Karl screamed from the galley, "We're all going to die!"

Leon covered his own mouth with a handkerchief, gagging and coughing. "Sulfur! Where's that coming from! That's poison, isn't it? Won't it kill us?"

Mac smelled nothing. He would check the control panel, but the Condor had supersensitive smoke and fume alarms, none of which had engaged. Mac knew he'd look suspicious if he were not also suffering. He covered his mouth. "I'll turn up the ventilation system," he said, as Karl dragged his fallen worker from the galley. "Get those two into the sleeping quarters. There are enough oxygen canisters for everyone."

"Isn't there somewhere we can land?" Leon said.

"I'll find out," Mac said.

"Hurry!"

He rushed back into the cockpit and locked the door. "What's going on?" Abdullah said. "You're losing a lot of blood."

"I'm all right," Mac said. "Those horses have power up here, even inside a pressurized cabin. Everybody smells sulfur, they're gagging, using oxygen, passing out. Leon wants us to land."

"We should go straight on to Johannesburg," Abdullah said, working with Mac to check every gauge. "What is affecting them is not coming from this plane. They'd be no better off on the ground."

"They could get medical treatment."

Abdullah looked at Mac. "So could you, but if they are being plagued by the 200 million horsemen, no medicine will save them."

"What's our ETA?"

"Several hours."

Mac shook his head, his wounds making him wince. "We're going to have to put down or Leon is going to find out we're invulnerable."

Abdullah pointed to the controls, Mac took over, and Abdullah pulled charts from his flight bag.

● ● ●

"They will be here any minute," Tsion said, hanging up from Rayford. "The plagues of fire and smoke and sulfur have begun. I did not expect this, but the horsemen are visible, at least to some. Rayford and Mrs. Rose saw them. And unbelievers are being slain."

Buck turned on the television.

● ● ●

"Mayday! Mayday!" Mac heard over the radio.

"This is Condor, go ahead."

"Mayday! My pilot is dead! I'm choking! Cockpit full of smoke. Agh! The smell! I can't see! We're losing it! Going down!"

"What's your location?"

But all Mac heard was the unnerving wailing. This was like the day of the Rapture, only now it was unbelieving pilots whose planes would be lost, maybe a third of them.

Mayday calls filled the frequency. Mac was helpless. He was also light-headed. He switched to a news radio feed. "No one has an answer yet to the puzzling rash of fires, outbreaks of smoke, and noxious, sulfur-smelling emissions killing thousands all over the globe," the newsman said. "Emergency medical professionals are at a loss, frantic to determine the cause. Here's the head of the Global Community Emergency Management Association, Dr. Jurgen Haase."

"If this were isolated, we might attribute it to a natural disaster, a rupture of some natural gas source. But it seems random, and clearly the fumes are lethal. We urge citizens to use gas masks and work together to extinguish spontaneous fires."

The newsman asked, "Which is more dangerous, the black smoke or the yellow?"

Haase said, "First we believed the black smoke emanated from the fires, but it appears to be independent. It can be deadly, but the yellow smells of sulfur and has the power to kill instantly."

The reporter said he had just been handed a bulletin, and he sounded terrified. "While there are pockets in which no fire or smoke or sulfur have been reported, in other areas the death count is staggering, now estimated in the hundreds of thousands. His Excellency, Global Community Potentate Nicolae Carpathia, will address the world via radio and television and the Internet inside this half hour."

Abdullah shoved a map under Mac's nose. "We are equidistant from airports that can handle a heavy in both Addis Ababa and Khartoum."

"It's up to Leon," Mac said. "He's the one who wants to land."

Abdullah took over again, and Mac emerged from the cockpit to find Leon on the phone. Mac grabbed a cloth napkin from the galley, soaked it, and held it to his ear. He tossed another damp cloth into the cockpit so Abdullah could wipe down the window and panel.

"One moment, Excellency," Leon said, "the captain needs me. . . . Yes, I'll ask." Leon covered the phone. "His Excellency asks where we are."

"Over the Red Sea. We can either—"

Leon held up a hand to silence Mac and told Carpathia. He handed the phone to Mac. "The potentate wishes to speak with you."

"What is your plan, Captain?"

Mac told him the options.

"Can you not turn back to either Mecca or somewhere in Yemen?"

"They have no strip that will handle a craft this large, sir."

"Addis Ababa is in what used to be Ethiopia," Carpathia said, as if to himself.

"Correct," Mac said. "Khartoum is in old Sudan."

"Go there. I will contact Potentate Rehoboth in South Af—, in Johannesburg and have him ensure that his people in Sudan extend every courtesy. If you are then able to complete this journey, it will be very beneficial to the cause."

"May I ask how things are there?"

"Here? We have lost dozens, and the stench is abominable. I am convinced this is chemical warfare, but it will not surprise me if the opposition claims some supernatural source."

"Me either . . . sir."

"The Jerusalem Twosome are already carrying on about it."

"Sir?"

"My new name for them. You like it?"

Mac did not respond. People were dying all over the world, and Carpathia was playing word games.

"They are, of course, taking credit for what is happening," Carpathia said. "That makes my job easier. Their day will come, and the world will thank me."

● ● ●

Buck sat in front of the TV with Tsion and Chloe, waiting for Rayford and Leah. From countries in daylight came images of fire and billowing smoke, people gagging, gasping, coughing, falling. Panic.

The phone rang. It was Mac calling for Rayford. Buck filled him in and was stunned to hear Mac and Abdullah's account. Mac told him of Carpathia's nickname for the two witnesses.

"He's about to come on TV," Buck said. "I'll have Rayford call you."

Rayford and Leah pulled in as Carpathia was being introduced. The stateside Trib Force sat before the TV, watching cosmic history. Tsion stood and paced as Carpathia solemnly looked into the camera. The potentate was at his typically parental best, assuring the horrified masses that "the situation will soon be under control. We have mobilized every resource. Meanwhile, I ask citizens of the Global Community to report suspicious activity, particularly the manufacture or transport of noxious agents. Sadly, we have reason to believe that this massacre of innocent lives is being perpetrated by religious dissidents to whom we have extended every courtesy. Though they cross us at every turn, we have defended their right to dissent. Yet they continue to see the Global Community as an enemy. They feel they have a right to maintain an intolerant, close-minded cult that excludes anyone who disagrees.

"You have the right to live healthy, peaceful, and free. While I shall remain always a pacifist,

I pledge to rid the world of this cult, beginning with the Jerusalem Twosome, who even now express no remorse about the widespread loss of life that has resulted from this attack."

"You know," Tsion said, sitting on the arm of the couch next to Chloe, "I am going to have to ask forgiveness for the glee I will feel when *this* man's due time arrives."

Carpathia pushed a button that showed Eli and Moishe holding forth at the Wailing Wall. They spoke in unison in a loud, haunting, echoing tone that carried without amplification far across the Temple Mount.

The words flashed across the screen. "Woe to the enemies of the most high God!" they said. "Woe to the cowards who shake their fist at their creator and are now forced to flee his wrath! We beseech you, snakes and vipers, to see even this plague as more than judgment! Yea, it is yet another attempt to reach you by a loving God who has run out of patience. There is no more time to woo you. You must hearken to his call, see that it is he who loves you. Turn to the God of your fathers while there is still time. For the day will come when time shall be no more!"

Carpathia came back into view with a condescending smile. "The day will come, my friends, when these two shall no longer disseminate their venom. They shall no longer turn water to blood, hold back rain from the clouds, send plagues to the Holy Land and the rest of the globe. I upheld my end of the bargain negotiated with them months ago, allowing certain dissidents to go unpunished. Here is my reward. Here is how we are repaid for our largesse.

"But the gift train stops here, loyal citizens. Your patience and steadfastness shall be recompensed. The day will yet come when we live as one world, one faith, one family of man. We shall live in a utopia of peace and harmony with no more war, no more bloodshed, no more death. In the meantime, please accept my deepest personal condolences over the loss of your loved ones. They shall not have died in vain. Continue to trust in the ideals of the Global Community, in the tenets of peace, and in the genius of an all-inclusive universal faith that welcomes the devout of any religion, even that of those who now oppose us.

"Just four months from now we shall celebrate in the very city where the preachers now taunt and warn us. We shall applaud their demise and revel in a future without plague and disease and suffering and death. Keep the faith, and look forward to that day. And until I address you again, thank you for your loyal support of the Global Community."

•   •   •

The ultimate in medical technology was housed in two fully equipped ambulances that waited at the end of the primary runway in Khartoum. With the wet cloth still pressed against his left ear, Mac helped Abdullah open the door and lower the stairs as Leon and Karl staggered out, each with a failing aide in tow and each leaving a dying comrade aboard. Emergency medical technicians, gloved and gas-masked, hurried aboard, lugging metal boxes. Mac and Abdullah stood on the tarmac, refusing assistance until everyone else was attended to. The other four were treated in the ambulances, and soon the EMTs deplaned, then reboarded with gurneys. They emerged with both victims covered head to toe with sheets.

Fortunato stood sans suit coat outside an ambulance, tie loose, shirt sweat drenched. He wiped his brow, breathing heavily. "Precautionary?" he asked the EMTs as the victims rolled by.

They shook their heads.

"They aren't . . ."

"Yes, they are," one said. "Asphyxiated."

Leon turned to Mac. "Get that wound taken care of, and have the plane thoroughly checked out. We can't have another episode like that."

Mac had three puncture wounds in his scalp, a deep laceration in his neck that required twenty stitches, and a nearly severed ear requiring forty more. "That's going to smart something awful when the painkiller wears off," he was told.

Two young people were dead, four other passengers deathly ill, and the world in chaos. Mac decided he could live with pain.

● ● ●

Rayford sat in the living room at the safe house in the wee hours as the others drifted back to their beds. He had limped into the house behind Leah, wet, cold, and aching all over. After having run into her at full speed, he could only imagine her pain. The immediate concern and attention of the others—even during the broadcast of Carpathia's address—wounded him in its sweetness. Truly they were brothers and sisters in Christ, and there would be no surviving without them.

After they heard Rayford and Leah's story and thanked God for the provision of the money, Tsion had shared a little of what he would transmit the next day. He seemed especially intrigued that believers could see the horses and horsemen while the victims could not. Even on camera, people were shown recoiling from snakebites, enveloped by clouds of smoke, and consumed, seemingly by spontaneous fire from thin air. "I had envisioned the horsemen as one vast army riding together," Tsion said, "and perhaps at some point they will. But so far it appears they are assigned to various locations. How long this will continue, I do not know. Frankly, I am disappointed to not have seen them yet myself."

Eventually Rayford and Chloe were the only ones left in the living room. "Going to bed, Dad?" she said at last.

"In a while. Just need to unwind. Unique day, you know. Never saw anything like that before. Don't care to again."

She moved around behind him and massaged his neck and shoulders. "You need rest," she told him.

"I know." He patted her hand. "I'll be all right. You get your sleep so you can take care of that baby."

As he sat in the darkness, Rayford ran through the events of the last several days. His question had been how much more they could take. This was only the beginning, and he couldn't imagine enduring the next few years. He would lose more comrades, and at an accelerating pace.

His rage had not abated, but he had been able to somehow tuck it on a high deck behind a pup tent in his brain. Still longing for the privilege of being used in Carpathia's demise, he had to admit he was grateful for what he had seen that night. He was way past where he could deny God's forceful presence during this period. But to stand face-to-face with the horsemen of Revelation, to walk right through them to safety . . .

Had the horsemen been blinded to the believers as well? Surely, like the demonic locusts, they were agents of Satan who would rather kill believers than enemies of God.

Rayford still wasn't sure what he thought about Leah. She was difficult to identify with. Something about her seemed younger and more naïve than her years. They had been through a horrifying ordeal together, and yet his image of her as too strident and opinionated had not faded. He had been moved by her salvation account and did not doubt her sincerity. Was it sexist to be repulsed by her straightforwardness? Would he pass the same off as mere spunk in a man? He hoped not.

Rayford inventoried his injuries. He needed another long, hot shower. A toe throbbed and might be broken. His left knee ached as it had before surgery in college. His left elbow was tender. A finger was sprained. He felt a bump on the back of his head. Too bad he was pushing forty-six. Running into someone and tumbling to the ground was part of a typical day for a nine-year-old.

And he was stricken with thoughts of his son. Raymie had been twelve when he disappeared in the Rapture. Though Rayford had largely succeeded in refraining from pining over him, Raymie was always at the edge of his consciousness. He suffered the guilt of time lost, wasted, not carved out for his son. The memories of the times they *had* spent together brought a lump to his throat.

Rayford slid off the couch and onto his knees, thanking God for Irene and Raymie, grateful they were spared this torturous existence. He also thanked God for Amanda, whom he had enjoyed for such a short time, but who was no less a gift. Chloe, Kenny, Buck, Tsion, Mac, David, Bruce, Ken . . . they all came to mind and brought emotion, regret, gratefulness, worry, hope.

Rayford prayed he would be the kind of leader to the Tribulation Force that God wanted him to be. And he still held out hope that this somehow included his being in the proximity of Nicolae Carpathia three and a half years from the beginning of the Tribulation, just four months hence. And Carpathia had just announced where he would be.

● ● ●

Mac was grateful Abdullah supervised the fumigation and inspection of the aircraft. His head pulsated. He still had to fly, but he would rely on Abdullah more than ever.

Everyone, himself included, seemed jumpy,

keeping their eyes open for danger. Mac found himself starting at any movement in his peripheral vision, fully expecting to see the giant horses and riders. Abdullah appeared just as edgy.

Despite his trauma, Fortunato appeared eager to get going again. Karl was particularly agitated, alternately crying and bustling about to make certain everything was just so. As Mac and Abdullah walked through their preflight routine, Fortunato was ushered into the gleaming Khartoum terminal. He emerged in fresh clothes, apparently having also showered, and looked 100 percent better. Concern still clouded his face. He stopped by the cockpit to be sure Mac and the plane were flightworthy. "At the first unpleasant odor, I want this plane on the ground," he said.

●   ●   ●

At one in the afternoon in New Babylon, David Hassid finally got a break from his emergency duty. He had helped transport bodies to the morgue and ferry the ill to hospital rooms. He had not seen what had wrought the catastrophe, but he put two and two together when reports poured in of death from fire, smoke, and sulfur. Nowhere near a tenth of the GC employee population had been affected yet, but still hundreds had died. He knew his stateside comrades, at least Rayford and a new Trib Force member, had seen the horsemen. He felt better knowing he was not the only believer who had not seen them.

David was frantic about Annie. He had not seen her since the first alarm sounded, sending all personnel into preassigned emergency roles. He couldn't reach her by phone or computer, and no one had seen her. Her duty in an emergency was to punch a series of highly encrypted numbers into a remote-control box that secured the hangar. Once that was accomplished, she was to account for all staff in David's department. The hangar had been secured, but David had to check on staff himself.

It was grisly work. Of 140 people under his supervision, ten were dead, two were treated for smoke inhalation, and one was missing: Annie. Three of the dead had appeared to spontaneously combust. During the awful task David came to a conclusion. If Annie had somehow survived, he would make public their feelings for each other. He would even take the initiative to get her transferred, per policy, so it wouldn't appear a reprimand of either of them when it came through channels.

Once his report was filed David ran past dozens of employees who sat in clusters, crying, talking, commiserating. They would have been ripe for praying with, for sharing God with. But he was not yet prepared to sacrifice his potential benefit to the cause.

At his level of security clearance, David was able to obtain a key to Annie's quarters. She was not there. Despairing, he strode to the expansive hangar and entered the codes necessary to disengage the security locks. The huge side doors slid open to reveal the cavernous innards, which looked even bigger with the flagship aircraft away in service. The choppers and few fixed-wing craft didn't begin to fill the building.

David opened Annie's, Mac's, and Abdullah's offices and flipped on the lights. Nothing. But that's when he heard it, the muffled rhythmic pounding. It came from the utility room at the far corner of the structure. He soon recognized the thumps as Morse code. Someone was banging out an SOS. David broke into a sprint.

The utility room was double insulated for noise and steel reinforced for safety. This had been Annie's first time securing the hangar. Maybe she didn't know the utility room self-locked from the inside and was the last place a person wanted to be while remotely locking down the whole building. Once that room was locked, communicating from inside was impossible. Phone and even the remote control unit would not transmit past the heavy steel. To get out, someone inside had to first be discovered.

David reached the door. "Who goes there?" he hollered.

"David!" came Annie's frantic reply. "Get me out of here!"

"Thank God," he said, unlocking the door. She leapt into his arms, enveloping him so tight he had to fight to breathe.

"Learn something about the utility room today?" he said.

"I thought I'd be in here forever!" she said. "I checked the utilities and started punching in the codes as I was heading out, not realizing the doors would lock from inside. I've still got to account for your staff."

"Done."

"Good. Thanks for telling me about the utility room."

"Sorry. I'm just relieved I found you."

"*You're* relieved? I was scared to death. I imagined you could go days without thinking to look in here."

David could tell Annie was truly angry with him. "It was actually Mac's place to tell you about—"

She looked askance at him. "Don't tell me you're a finger-pointer. This seems like a major thing you could have told me."

He had no defense.

"So what was the big emergency?" she said. "Another false alarm?"

"You really don't know?"

"How would I, David?" she said. "I saw people running and heard a few coughing when I saw the alert. I came straight here."

"Come with me," he said.

They sat in her office, where he told her the whole story.

"I could have helped," she said. "I look like a coward, thanks to you."

"I just about died worrying about you," David said. "I thought I knew what you meant to me."

"You thought?"

"I was wrong. What can I say? I need you. I love you. I want everybody to know."

She shook her head and looked away. "You loved me enough to let me lock myself in."

Now David was angry. "Did you read the procedure manual like you were supposed to? It's clear."

"I suppose I'll get reprimanded."

"Probably. It's going to be hard to hide that I did your work."

"It was the least you could do," she said.

David fought to attribute her sudden unattractiveness to claustrophobia and frustration. "I love you even when you're ornery," he said.

"That's big of you."

He shrugged and turned his palms up in surrender. "I'd better get back. Until you and

I declare ourselves, we can't be seen together. For one thing, I have to account for your whereabouts."

"That's only fair."

He shook his head and rose.

"Someone should have told me," she said.

He didn't look at her. "I got that point."

"I'm just saying," she said, "that I'm the one who could get booted out of my job and reassigned. You know what that'll mean."

He turned back. "Ten minutes ago I would have loved that. It would have meant we could declare ourselves and I'd get more time with you."

David could tell he had wounded her. "And now?" she said.

"Like I said, I love you even when you're—"

"You know the price, David. I want what you want, but what's best for the Trib Force?"

"I can't be much good to the Force, frustrated without you."

"Who has the access to GC brass that you do?"

"I know. So, are we in love again or what?"

She came to him, and they held each other. "I'm sorry," she said.

"Me too."

TEN

MAC had not been to Johannesburg since before the great wrath of the Lamb earthquake. From the air it resembled New Babylon. The rebuilt airport served as a major hub of international travel. Regional Potentate Rehoboth's palace housed his several wives, children, and grandchildren, along with servants and aides.

The left side of Mac's head felt twice as big as the right, and pain stabbed each wound with every beat of his heart. Even applying his headphones was a chore, trying to keep the gauze from pressing tighter against his stitches.

Upon landing, Mac and Abdullah were to open the door and lower the steps. They could then leave the plane, retire to their quarters, or remain in the cockpit, as long as they did not interfere with the meeting. Karl and his assistant would remain on board to serve food. Mac told Leon that he and Abdullah would remain also, probably in their quarters. Of course, they stayed in the cockpit, where Mac listened in on Fortunato and his remaining aide.

"Clancy," Leon said, "I would like you to phone Ngumo at the VIP guesthouse. You can see it there at the end of the airport. Here's the number. He will not likely answer himself, but put the speakerphone on so I can hear, just in case."

Mac wished he could take notes, but he couldn't risk being found with them. He would just have to remember as much as he could— no easy task with the pain. He heard Clancy slowly enter the number. A mature woman answered. "You have reached Mwangati Ngumo's secretary. May I help you?"

"Yes, ma'am, thank you. I am Clancy Tiber, personal assistant to Global Community Supreme Commander Leon Fortunato. I am pleased to tell you that the supreme commander is prepared to receive Mr. Ngumo and two aides aboard *Global Community One*."

"Thank you, Mr. Tiber. You may expect them in five minutes. Mr. Ngumo is very much looking forward to his meeting with Potentate Carpathia."

Clancy hung up and said, "This is too delicious. Is it supposed to be this much fun?"

"There's more where this came from, son."

The flag-bedecked Botswanian limo stopped fifty feet from the plane, and Mac idly watched three dignitaries alight. Abdullah unstrapped himself and pressed his nose against the windshield. "Does that look like Ngumo to you, Mac?"

"Hm?"

"That's not Ngumo."

"I've never met him."

"Neither have I, but unless he's lost fifty pounds since I saw him on TV, that's not him. And since when does the big man carry a bag too?"

Mac removed his headset and leaned forward, but the men were already past where he could see them. He jumped as Fortunato blasted so hard against the locked cockpit door that it sprang open and banged against the wall. "Go! Go!" Leon said. "Take off now!"

"We're shut down, Leon."

"Start it up! Now! Those men have weapons!"

"The door's open, Leon! There's no time!"

"Do something!"

"Engage three and four," Mac said, and Abdullah flipped several switches. "Full power, now!"

The two engines on the right side of the plane burst to life with a roar, and Mac maneuvered the controls so the plane swung to the left. Mac saw the three would-be assassins blowing down the runway in the hot jet exhaust.

"You're a genius!" Leon said. "Now get us out of here!"

The men struggled to their feet, retrieved their high-powered rifles, and ran toward their limo. With the steps and open door of the Condor now facing away from them, Abdullah ran to pull up the stairs and shut the door.

"Now go!" Leon shouted. "Go!"

"We're low on fuel. We'd have to come back here to land."

"They're driving this way! Go!"

Mac started the sequence, knowing the plane was not prepped for takeoff again so quickly. The left side engines screamed to life, but until other crucial gauges caught up, the onboard computer would abort takeoff. If Mac overrode the fail-safe mechanism, he risked crashing.

He turned the jet rear side toward his pursuers, but they roared around front, showing their weapons. "Leave them in the dust!" Leon said. "Let's go!"

But the gunmen circled back out of sight of Mac and opened fire. The blowing of the tires was nearly as loud as the explosions from the weapons. The Condor was wounded. With more than half its tires shredded, the bird rested unevenly on the runway. Mac would never get it to roll, let alone achieve takeoff speed.

Strangely, not another plane was in sight. All the crazy activity, which had to have been witnessed by both air traffic and ground control personnel, had drawn no emergency attention. Mac realized they had been set up and would likely all die. He and Abdullah had been stranded before this band of killers. Whoever they were, they clearly had the cooperation of the Rehoboth regime.

Bullets ripped through the fuselage. Mac and Abdullah leaped from their seats and followed the screaming Leon through the galley, the lounge, and into the main cabin. "Lie on the floor and stay in the center!" Mac shouted.

The killers had apparently decided to make sure no one survived. Bullets tore through windows and walls up and down the plane. Mac noticed only five men on the floor. Abdullah, Leon, Clancy, Karl's helper, and he were curled beneath seats, their heads buried in their hands. "Where's Karl?" Mac shouted, but no one stirred.

Mac felt the pressure of footsteps near him and peeked up to see the cook staggering down the aisle, drenched in blood. "Karl! Get down!" As the man fell, wide-eyed, a gaping hole in his forehead evidenced a fatal wound.

"Do we have a weapon?" Leon shouted.

"Prohibited by your boss, Leon!" Mac said.

"Surely you sometimes break the rules! I'll pardon you if you produce one! We have no hope, Mac!"

There *were* two pistols in the cargo hold, and *yes,* Mac thought, *sometimes I break the rules.* But there was no getting to the guns, and what would he do with them anyway, outnumbered and facing heavy artillery?

"Do something!" Leon pleaded. "Do you have a phone?"

Mac dug his from his belt and flung it to Leon. The commander frantically poked in a special code, shuddering with every round that pierced the plane. "GC Mega-Alert, this is LF 999, secure line! Inform His Excellency *GC One* under heavy fire, Johannesburg International. Patch me through to Potentate Rehoboth directly, now!"

Mac heard the phone in the lounge. Dare he crawl out and see who it was? If there was a chance it was the shooters with a demand, it might be worth it. He crawled over Karl and into the lounge, where he grabbed the receiver as the base of the phone bounced on the floor. "Talk!" he barked.

It was the woman he had heard over the intercom, now hysterical. "Mr. Ngumo is not behind this attack! He was overtaken by—oh, no! Oh—"

A deafening fusillade made Mac pull the phone from his ear. When he listened again, the woman screamed, "They've killed him! No! Please!" More shots, and her phone had fallen.

Mac scrambled on all fours into the cockpit and grabbed the radio mike. "Mayday! Johannesburg runway! *GC One* under attack!" From the middle of the plane he heard Leon shriek into the phone, "You, Bindura? Why? Carpathia is not even on this plane! I'm telling the truth! Call them off! Please!"

If Rehoboth was behind this, they were as good as dead anyway. He would have thought of everything. Mac shouted over the radio, "Mayday! Johannesburg! Believers on board!" If by some stretch a Christian pilot was in the area, who knew what he or she might be able to do?

Mac was knocked on his face by the force of a concussion bomb, and the plane began to fill with smoke. Leon and Clancy screamed, "Fire!" and Abdullah ran forward.

"They may shoot us, Mac, but we have to jump ship! They've set us afire!"

Mac and Abdullah opened the main cabin door, trying to keep from being open targets. Leon pushed Clancy from behind, the young man stiff-legged with fear, crying, lurching toward the door. As soon as Abdullah lowered the stairs, Leon shoved Clancy's quivering mass down ahead of him as a shield. Clancy was torn apart by bullets, and Leon froze at the top of the steps. Only when a firebomb exploded in the lounge did he take his fateful plunge. Mac and Abdullah leaped aboard him and rode him down the steps as the inferno roared out the door behind them.

Mac believed he would never hit the pavement alive. He had lost all hope and leapt from the plane only to escape the flames. With deafening gunfire surrounding him and the Condor engulfed behind him, he shut his eyes so tight he felt as if his cheekbones were in his forehead. With one hand vise-gripped on Abdullah's wrist and a knee in Fortunato's fleshy back, Mac bet his life he would open his eyes in heaven.

But he did not.

Leon dropped to his hands and knees on the runway, Abdullah flipping over him. Mac landed flat on Leon's back, crushing him to the asphalt. A bullet ripped through Mac's right shoulder blade and another shattered his right hand, the blasts from the weapon not twenty feet away deafening his right ear.

"Oh, God!" Leon screamed beneath him. "Oh, God, help me!" Mac sensed his own head was the next target and that he would be mercifully put out of his misery.

Blackness.

Silence.

Nothing.

Only smell and taste and feeling.

Mac saw nothing because he chose to keep his eyes shut. He heard only Leon's raspy panting.

The smell was gunpowdery and metallic, the taste blood, the feeling a hot, deep, searing pain. The tear in his shoulder superseded the tender soreness of the side of Mac's head. His hand was worse. He almost dared not open his eyes. Nothing about that wound would surprise him. Mac felt as if his hand had been shattered.

Leon's body rose and fell beneath him as Leon gasped for air. Mac rolled off him onto the pavement on his left side, eyes still shut, mind spinning. Was it over, or would he open his eyes to assassins standing over him? Had Leon been hit? Abdullah?

Disappointed that he was not in heaven, Mac forced open one eye. Smoke was so dense and dark he couldn't see inches past his nose. He drew his ravaged hand to his face for a closer look and felt the devastation in his shoulder. His hand shivered so violently it shook his whole body, and blood splattered from it onto his face.

Mac reached with his other hand to steady the wounded appendage and saw he had all his fingers, though they were splayed in different directions, a bullet having ripped through the back of his hand. His whole body shook, and he feared he was going into shock.

As the smoke slowly cleared, he forced himself to sit up. Leon lay hyperventilating, eyes open, teeth bared. Clancy Tiber lay beside him, obviously dead.

"Abdullah?" Mac called out weakly.

"I am here," Abdullah said. "I have a bullet in my thigh. Were you hit?"

"At least twice. What happened to the—"

"Do you see the horses?"

"I can't even see you."

"I hope they stay long enough for you to see."

"So do I."

● ● ●

Rayford awoke after nine in the morning Saturday at the safe house. He could have slept another couple of hours after the night he'd had, but an unusual noise had niggled him awake. His eyes popped open and he lay still, hoping it was later, hoping his body had had time to recharge, wondering if he had lucked out and his aches and pains might have abated.

A rhythmic swishing sound, like someone rubbing their hands together every few seconds, made him sit up. Listening more closely, he thought it might be sniffing or even sniffling.

It came from the bedroom next door, where Tsion both slept and worked.

The rest had been good for Rayford's mind and spirit, but it had only stiffened his ailing joints and muscles. He groaned aloud, pulled on his robe, and peeked into Tsion's room through the door, which was open a few inches.

At first Rayford didn't see Dr. Ben-Judah. The chair before his computer screen was empty, as was the bed. But the sound was coming from that room. Rayford knocked gently and pushed the door open another foot. Beneath the window next to the bed, Tsion lay on the floor, his face buried in his hands. His shoulders heaved as he wept bitterly.

"Are you all right?" Rayford said softly, but Tsion did not respond. Rayford stepped beside him and sat on the bed so Tsion would know he was there. The rabbi prayed aloud. "Lord, if it is Hattie, I beg for her soul. If it is Chaim, I covet him for the kingdom. If it is someone in this house, protect them, shield them, equip them. Father, if it is one of the new brothers or sisters, someone I have not even met, I pray your protection and mercy." He wept more, moaning. "God, tell me how to pray."

Rayford put a hand on the teacher's back. Tsion turned. "Rayford, the Lord suddenly impressed deeply upon my heart that I should pray for someone in danger. I was writing my message, which is also weighing on me—probably the most difficult I have had to write. I thought the leading was to pray for my audience, but it seemed more specific, more urgent. I prayed the Lord would tell me who needed prayer, but I was then overcome with the immediacy of it. I knelt, and it was as if his Spirit pushed me to the floor and planted in my soul a burden for whoever was in need. I still do not know, and yet I cannot shake the feeling that this is more than just my imagination. Pray with me, would you?"

Rayford knelt awkwardly, feeling every injury from the night before and having less an idea what to say than Tsion did. "Lord, I agree with my brother in prayer. We don't understand how we finite beings can say or pray anything that affects what an infinite God wants to do, but we trust you. You tell us to pray, to boldly come to you. If someone we know and love is in danger, we pray your supernatural hedge of protection around them."

Rayford was moved by Tsion's emotion and could not continue. Tsion said, "Thank you," and gripped his hand.

They rose. Tsion sat before his computer and wiped his eyes. "I do not know what that was about," he said, "but I have stopped questioning how God communicates to us."

Tsion sat awhile collecting himself, then asked Rayford if he would look over his day's message. "I will be refining it before posting it this afternoon, but I would appreciate your input."

"I'd love to read it," Rayford said, "but I can't imagine what I have to offer."

Tsion rose and offered Rayford his chair. "I am going to get something to drink. I shall return for my grade."

● ● ●

Mac knew if he stayed on the steamy Johannesburg runway he would die. His hours-old ear and scalp wounds oozed from beneath the bandages, and the painkiller had long since worn off. His shoulder felt as if someone had smashed it with a red-hot hammer. His hand would never be the same. The best he could hope for was to save the fingers, which surely would never bend properly again.

The smoke wafted away with the hot late-afternoon wind, and Abdullah came into view fifteen feet to Mac's left. The young man rested on his knees, turban unwound, face tight with fear and fatigue. His right thigh bore a deep red wound. He pointed into the distance. "They're still here," he said.

Mac had had only the briefest glimpse of the

phantasmagoric cavalry of frightful men and beasts when Abdullah tried to avoid them in the sky. Now a legion mustered a hundred feet past the runway, snorting smoke and fire and sulfur, snake tails striking and snapping at victims who couldn't see them.

In their wake, the leonine steeds left bodies. Some jerked spastically before freezing in macabre repose. Others writhed ablaze until death brought relief. Or so they thought, Mac mused. In truth, the victims passed from one flame to another. One of the phony dignitaries ran top speed down the runway. The other two lay dead near the plane, close enough to have killed Mac with their next shots.

Even from behind and far away, Mac found the horsemen and their mounts dreadful. They hovered inches off the ground but galloped, trotted, stepped, and reared like physical horses. Their riders urged them on, stampeding people, buildings, vehicles, wreaking destruction.

The thick, swarthy Leon Fortunato appeared out of the haze, having rolled toward Mac. He grabbed Mac's face in both hands, and Mac nearly screamed from the pain on one side. "You saved my life, Mac!" Leon cried. "You protected me with your own body! Were you hit?"

"Twice," Mac said. He pulled back so Leon's

hands slipped away. Mac pointed to the horses. "What do you see over there?"

"Carnage," Leon said, squinting. "Fire, smoke. And what's that awful smell, like in the plane earlier? Agh!"

"We need to get away from the plane," Mac said. Flames poured out the windows.

"The beautiful Condor," Leon said. "His Excellency's pride and joy."

"Do you want to pull Clancy's body out of the way?" Mac said.

Leon struggled to his feet and staggered, trying to gain his balance. "No," he said, regaining his voice. "The world is short of graves. We would only cremate him anyway. Let this fire do it."

Leon turned slowly in a circle. "I thought we were dead," he said. "What happened?"

"You prayed."

"Excuse me?"

"You asked God to help you," Mac said.

"I consider myself religious."

"I'm sure you do. God must have answered."

"Why did the attackers stop shooting?"

Mac winced, wishing they had stopped sooner. "How can we know? One ran. The other two haven't moved."

Leon and Mac got on either side of Abdullah and slowly walked him toward the terminal.

●   ●   ●

It was not lost on Rayford, the privilege of having the first look at a message millions around the globe anticipated. Tsion had written:

My dear brothers and sisters in Christ:
I come to you today with a heavy heart, which is, of course, nothing new during this period of history. While the 144,000 evangelists raised up by God are seeing millions come to Christ, the one-world religion continues to become more powerful and—I must say it—more odious. Preach it from the mountaintops and into the valleys, my beloved siblings: There is one God and one Mediator between God and man, the Man Christ Jesus.
The deadly demon locusts prophesied in Revelation 9 died out *en masse* more than half a year ago, having tortured millions. But many bitten during the last month of that plague only stopped serving their sentences of agony three months ago.
While many have come to faith after being convinced by that horrible judgment, most have become even more set in their ways. It should have been obvious to the leader of the Enigma Babylon One World Faith that devotees of that religion suffered everywhere

in the world. But we followers of Christ, the so-called dissidents—enemies of tolerance and inclusion—were spared.

Our beloved preachers in Jerusalem, despite heinous opposition and persecution, continue to prophesy and win converts to Christ in that formerly holy city that now must be compared to Egypt and Sodom. So we have that for which to be thankful in this time of worsening turmoil.

But by now you know that the sixth Trumpet Judgment, the second woe (Revelation 9), has begun. Apparently I correctly assumed that the 200 million horsemen are spiritual and not physical beings but was wrong to speculate they would thus be invisible. People I know and trust have seen these beings kill by fire and smoke and sulfur as the Scripture predicts. Yet unbelievers charge we are making this up and only claiming to see things they themselves cannot.

That this current plague was wrought by the releasing of four angels bound in the Euphrates River should be instructive. We know that these are fallen angels, because nowhere in Scripture do we ever see good angels bound. These have apparently been bound because they were eager to wreak havoc upon the earth. Now, released, they are free to do so. In fact, the Bible tells us they were prepared for a specific hour, day, month, and year.

It is significant that the four angels, probably bound for centuries, have been in the Euphrates. It is the most prominent river in the Bible. It bordered the Garden of Eden, was a boundary for Israel, Egypt, and Persia, and is often used in Scripture as a symbol of Israel's enemies. It was near this river that man first sinned, the first murder was committed, the first war fought, the first tower built in defiance against God, and where Babylon was built. Babylon is where idolatry originated and has since surged throughout the world. The children of Israel were exiled there as captives, and it is there that the final sin of man will culminate.

Revelation 18 predicted that Babylon will be the center of commerce, religion, and world rule, but also that it will eventually fall to ruin, for strong is the Lord God who judges her.

This current plague, the Bible indicates, will result in the deaths of a third of the population left after the Rapture. Simple math portends a horrible result. One-fourth of the remaining population already died from plague, war, and natural disaster. That left, of course,

75 percent. One third of 75 percent is 25 percent, so the current wave of death will leave only 50 percent of the people left behind at the Rapture.

I must clarify that what follows is speculation. My belief after studying the original languages and the many commentaries on this prophecy is as follows: God is still trying to persuade mankind to come to him, yes, but this destruction of another third of the remaining unbelievers may have another purpose. In his preparation for the final battle between good and evil, God may be winnowing from the evil forces the incorrigibles whom he, in his omniscience, knows would never have turned to him regardless.

The Scriptures foretell that those unbelievers who do survive will refuse to turn from their wickedness. They will insist on continuing worshiping idols and demons, and engaging in murder, sorcery, sexual immorality, and theft. Even the Global Community's own news operations report that murder and theft are on the rise. As for idol and demon worship, sorcery, and illicit sex, these are actually applauded in the new tolerant society.

Sadly this last judgment before the second half of the Tribulation may well continue four more months until the three-and-half-year anniversary of the accord between the Global Community and the nation of Israel. That also coincides with the end of the ministry of the two witnesses. And it will usher in a period when believers will be martyred in multiples of the numbers who die now.

Many of you have written and asked me how I explain that a God of love and mercy could pour out such awful judgments upon the earth. God is more than a God of love and mercy. The Scriptures say God is love, yes. But they also say he is holy, holy, holy. He is just. His love was expressed in the gift of his Son as the means of redemption. But if we reject this love gift, we fall under God's judgment.

I know that many hundreds of thousands of readers of my daily messages must visit this site not as believers but as searchers for truth. So permit me to write directly to you if you do not call yourself my brother or sister in Christ. I plead with you as never before to receive Jesus Christ as God's gift of salvation. The sins that the stubborn unbelievers will not give up (see above) will be rampant during the last half of the Tribulation, referred to in the Bible as the Great Tribulation.

Imagine this world with half its population

gone. If you think it is bad now with millions having disappeared in the Rapture, children gone, services and conveniences affected, try to fathom life with half of all civil servants gone. Firemen, policemen, laborers, executives, teachers, doctors, nurses, scientists . . . the list goes on. We are coming to a period where survival will be a full-time occupation.

I would not want to be here without knowing God was with me, that I was on the side of good rather than evil, and that in the end, we win. Pray right now. Tell God you recognize your sin and need forgiveness and a Savior. Receive Christ today, and join the great family of God.

Sincerely, Tsion Ben-Judah

ELEVEN

MAC and Leon helped Abdullah toward the chaotic Johannesburg terminal.

"Rehoboth was behind the assassination attempt," Leon said. "He told me so himself. He thought His Excellency was on board. We must get help and regain authority here without risking our lives."

"A little late for that, isn't it?" Mac said. "Couldn't you have made it clear in advance that Carpathia was not with us?"

"We had our reasons to let Mr. Ngumo believe *His Excellency*—which is how you should refer to him, Captain—was aboard. Regional Potentate Rehoboth was invited, but we did not know he was subversive to His Excellency."

"I believe you're going to find Ngumo and his secretary dead," Mac said, and he told Leon of the phone call.

"We had better hope we find Rehoboth dead," Abdullah said. "He cannot afford to leave us alive."

Leon stopped, and his face blanched. "I assumed I spoke to him at his palace. He would not be here, would he?"

"We need to keep moving," Mac said, about to collapse. "If Rehoboth wants us dead, all he has to do is say the word to any one of these guards." But the guards looked as frightened as anyone else, gagging, coughing, attending to fallen comrades. Throughout the terminal people screamed, bodies lay about, luggage was strewn. The counters were empty, arrival and departure monitors blank.

Just after they stepped inside, Mac heard the scream of a Super J jet. The fighter-style knockoff of a Gulfstream was sleek, black, and incredibly aerodynamic—with power to burn and lots of room inside. It was the first plane to land at Johannesburg since the Condor. Above its identifying numbers were emblazoned an Australian flag and *Fair Dinkum*. As soon as the plane stopped, out jumped the pilot and a woman, who both sprinted toward the terminal.

"'Ey!" the man called out shrilly, making many turn. "'Oo called in a Mayday with believers on board!" He was tall, blond, and freckled. His Aussie accent was so thick Mac wouldn't have been surprised if it was put on. His wife was nearly as tall with thick, dark hair.

Mac and Abdullah glanced at each other, and Fortunato slowly turned. "I did," Mac said, noting the marks on both the man's and his wife's foreheads. The Aussie stared at his as well. "I was desperate," Mac added. "I thought that might draw someone who wouldn't otherwise stop. Did it work?"

"It sure did, mate," the pilot said, eyeing Abdullah's forehead as well. "We're believers all right and not ashamed of it, even if you hoodwinked us to get us here. Call me Dart. First name's not important. This here's my wife, Olivia."

"Liv," she said, "and you all need immediate attention."

"'Oo might you be?" Dart demanded of Fortunato.

"I am Supreme Commander Leon For—"

"That's what I figured," Dart said. "It's too early for your boss to be dead, so I won't ask if he's on board that fireball out there."

"Thankfully not," Fortunato said.

"So what happened, the horsemen get you?"

"Oh, you're one of those?" Fortunato said. "You see them too?"

"Sure do."

"Dart," his wife said softly, "we need to get them some help."

"Yeah, I guess we better," he said. "But I don't mind tellin' ya, I feel like I'm aidin' and abettin' the enemy. Personally, I'd leave you to die, but God's gonna get you in the end anyway. Read the Book. We win."

Fortunato turned on him. "You could be imprisoned for speaking disrespectfully of—"

"By the way, Mr. F.—you don't mind me callin' you Mr. F., do ya, because I'm gonna anyway—what's yer major complaint? You look to be ambulatin' all right."

"You are required by law, sir, to refer to me as Su—"

"Let me tell you something, Mr. F. I don't live under your laws no more. I answer to God. You can't do a thing to me he dud'n allow, so take your best shot. Your man here sent up a Mayday, pretended believers were in trouble, the wife and I were intrigued believers might be on board the Antichrist's own plane, so we—"

"Antichrist's?! To refer to His Excellency, Potentate Nic—"

"You don't get it yet, do you, F.? I think he's the Antichrist, and you know what that makes you."

"I'm not a student of that folderol, but I would advise you to—"

"Don't need any advice there, mate, but I can get you some medical help. Looks like your biggest complaint is some torn suit pants and a coupla owies on your hands. These boys here need some real help."

"Honestly, I—"

"There's a medical office in the wing behind this one, and with your clout you oughta be able to pull somebody away from all the other victims."

An announcement came over the public address system. "Attention! Attention please! Global Community Supreme Commander Leon Fortunato please report to GC Peacekeeping Forces headquarters in Wing B."

As the announcement was repeated, Dart said, "That's right next door to the infirmary, Mr. F. How 'bout you go on ahead and we'll get your comrades here to the doctors."

"I should have you arrested, you—"

"If that's your priority right now, you go right ahead. But if I was you, I'd run to safety and let these boys get patched up. There'll be plenty of time for chasin' us once you've caught your breath."

Fortunato's face and neck flushed, and he looked as if he might burst. He turned to Mac. "No doubt His Excellency has provided assistance for us."

"You should go on ahead, Commander," Mac said. "Find out about Rehoboth, check in with Carp—, with the potentate."

"I don't trust this man."

"Aw, c'mon, Mr. F. I'm harmless as a dove.

Much as I'd like to kill a couple of your staff, I promise I won't. We'll get 'em where they're goin' and be on our way."

Dart gently pushed Fortunato away from Abdullah and stuck his head under the Jordanian's arm. Liv grabbed Mac's belt with one hand and his left elbow with the other, leaving Fortunato free to go.

"You, sir," Fortunato said as he reluctantly strode on ahead, "are a disgrace to the Global Community."

"We'll wear that one as a badge of honor, won't we, Liv?"

"Oh, Dart," she said.

"Thanks for not giving us away," Mac said when Leon was out of earshot.

"Inside saints," Dart said, his accent now Southern U.S., more like Mac's. "I couldn't believe it. I almost blew it. I saw yours and the little guy's marks and figured the big man might be with us too. As soon as I saw him I knew who he was and had to cover."

"It was brilliant," Mac said, introducing himself and Abdullah.

"And how'd you like Dart and Olivia?" Dart said.

"That even threw me," Liv said.

"You covered perfectly, honey," Dart said. "'Liv' was a stroke of genius."

They introduced themselves as Dwayne and Trudy Tuttle from Oklahoma. "I change the flag and motto on that plane every few days. We've been Germans, Norwegians, Brits. We're with the International Commodity Co-op. Heard of it?"

"If big-mouth here doesn't get us killed," Trudy said.

"Never thought I'd get a chance to tell the False Prophet what I thought of him to his face."

"The False Prophet?" Mac said. "Leon?"

"Claims Carpathia raised him from the dead, didn't he? Worships the guy, calls him His Excellency. You watch and see if it doesn't turn out that way. So, what's your story? You infiltrate, or find Jesus after you were already with the GC?"

● ● ●

Buck looked in the mirror. His facial scars were still red and prominent more than a year after his injuries. The surgery he'd found in a makeshift Jerusalem clinic may have been better than he expected, but there was no hiding his disfigurement. Chloe appeared behind him and handed Kenny to him. "Stop thinking that," she said.

"What?"

"Don't play dumb. You think you can use your new face to your advantage."

"Of course," Buck said.

He wondered if handing him the baby was her

way of making him want to stay put. But they had been through this before too. She had accepted that her frontline globe-trotting was over. She wasn't about to drag a baby into danger, much as she wanted to be where the action was. Her running the Commodity Co-op was crucial not only to the Tribulation Force, but also to the millions of new believers who would soon have no other source for trade.

Chloe had told Buck she wished he could be content with his behind-the-scenes work, countering the propaganda of *Global Community Weekly* with his own *The Truth*. But with the new technology provided by David Hassid, Buck could do that from anywhere without being traced. The expansion of the cellar was nearly finished, and Buck felt needed in so many other places.

They had also discussed his responsibility to the baby. Sure, this was different from normal child rearing, knowing that Kenny's real growing-up years would be in Christ's earthly kingdom. Still, it was important for a young child to have both parents present as much as possible. Buck had argued that though he might be gone two to three weeks at a time, when he *was* home he was home twenty-four hours a day. "It's a wash," he'd say. "I'd net the same hours with him as I would if I were working away from home."

Buck took the baby to the kitchen and Chloe followed him. "You've got that look in your eye," she said. "A few more days cooped up here and there'll be no stopping you. Where you going?"

"You know me too well," he said. "Truth is, Tsion wants someone to go back to Israel. Check in on Chaim. He's encouraged by the E-mails they trade, but he believes someone has to be there face-to-face before the old man will make his decision."

Chloe shook her head. "I want to disagree, but I can't. Daddy can't risk it. He's got it in his head to track down Hattie before she blows our cover or gets herself killed. Tsion certainly can't go. I don't know what the world would do without him. I know God has everything under control and I suppose he could raise up someone like he did to replace Bruce, but—"

"I know. We ought to be hiring armed guards and moving him out of sight."

"When are you going, Buck?"

She had a way of cutting to the chase.

"Tsion wants to talk to you about it."

She smiled. "Like having a friend ask your parents for a favor? He thinks I can't turn him down."

"Well, can you?"

She snorted. "I can't even turn you down. But

if you get yourself killed, I'll hate you for the rest of my life."

"Thought I'd go see Zeke after dark."

She reached for Kenny. "That's what I thought. Stock up on stuff for the baby. I'll make a list of other stuff we need. Talk to Leah too. She says we're low on some basics."

That night Buck rolled into a dilapidated one-pump gas station in what had once been downtown Des Plaines. Believers knew the station as a source for fuel, foodstuffs, and assorted sundries. Zeke managed the place with Zeke Jr.—who went by Z—a middle-twenties longhair covered with tattoos. He had made his living tattooing, pinstriping cars and trucks, and airbrushing monsters and muscle cars onto T-shirts. He also airbrushed the occasional mural on the side of an 18-wheeler. That business, needless to say, had dried up long ago.

The Zekes had lost the Mrs. and two teenage daughters in a fire resulting from the disappearances. They had been led to Christ by a long-haul trucker. Zeke and his son now attended an underground meeting of believers in Arlington Heights, carefully keeping their faith hidden from unbelievers so they could serve as a major supplier and helper. Z had been a no-account druggie whose on-again off-again tattooing and art merely financed his daily high. Now he was the emotional, soft-spoken artist behind most of the fake IDs local Christians used to survive.

Zeke was filling the tank of Buck's Rover and watching for strangers or customers without the mark of God on their foreheads. "Need some stuff," Buck said. "Including Z's handiwork."

"Gotcha," Zeke said. "He's down there watchin' TV and doin' his Ben-Judah study. Lemme have your list. I'll drive your rig into the garage and load it for ya."

Buck got out to venture inside when another car pulled in behind his. "You got enough to fill me?" the man called out. "Or are you rationing today?"

"I can handle it," Zeke said. "Let me get this transmission job on the rack and I'll be right with you."

Buck empathized with the daily tension of living a lie just to stay alive. He moseyed inside, which to unknowing eyes looked a typical greasy station. Brand-name calendars, pictures of cars, an oily phone book, everything dingy. A panel in the tiny washroom, however, was a ruse. The sign said, Danger. High Voltage. Do Not Touch. And a low-level buzz in the fingers awaited anyone who doubted it.

That, however, was the extent of the danger. Knowing where to push and slide the panel

opened one into a wooden staircase that led to
Zeke's own shelter, fashioned out of the earth
beneath and behind the station. Deep in the
back, Zeke would fill Buck's list and transport
the goods up a rickety staircase into the garage,
where he would transfer them to the Rover. In a
cozy though windowless and cool earthen room
dominated by an oversized ventilation shaft sat
the fleshy Z, wearing black cowboy boots, black
jeans, and a black leather vest over bare arms
and chest. As Zeke had said, Z was watching the
news while scribbling notes on a dog-eared spiral
notebook with his laptop open.

"Hey, Buck," Z said flatly, putting his stuff
away and slowly rising. "What can I do ya for?"

"Need a new identity."

Z squatted behind a sagging lime green couch
and swung open a noisy two-drawer filing cabinet
that was clearly off its track. He finger-walked
his way through about ten files and yanked them
out. When the door wouldn't shut all the way,
Z resorted to slamming it with his boot. Papers
stuck out of the tightly jammed drawer, and
Z smiled sheepishly at Buck.

"Choose yer pick," he said, fanning the folders
onto the couch.

Buck sat and looked at each folder under the
lamp. Z's filing system may have been makeshift,
but he sure knew where everything was. Each

folder had vital statistics on white males approximately Buck's size and age. "Inventory's getting bigger," Buck said.

Z nodded, his eyes on the TV again. "These smokin' horses are leavin' bodies everywhere. You seen 'em suckers?"

"Not yet. Sound scary."

"Yep. 'Salmost too easy, though. All I got to do is get the wallets before the GC gets the body. Gives people a lot more to choose from."

"This guy," Buck said, putting an open folder at the top of the stack and handing it to Z.

Z tossed the extras behind the couch and studied the file as he set up his instant camera. Buck sat before a plain blue background and posed for straight-ons and profiles. "Thought of you when I seen him," Z said. "Driver's license, passport, citizen's card, anything else?"

"Yeah, make me a card-carrying member of Enigma Babylon Faith. And an organ donor. Why not?"

"Can do. Fast-track?"

"Couple of days?" Buck said.

"Easy."

By the time Buck found Zeke and exited through the garage, he knew Z was plying his trade under a magnifying light in the other room. The next time Buck ventured out in public, he would carry authentic-looking, well-used identification documents with his new face in place of that of the deceased Greg North.

● ● ●

Mac had never enjoyed such medical attention. While Johannesburg seemed in disarray, thousands of citizens dead or dying, Fortunato's clout opened every door. Regional GC Peacekeeping Forces swept in on Carpathia's own authority and took charge of Rehoboth's palace. He was discovered dead in his office, along with dozens more of his staff.

Mac and Abdullah had been examined and prepped at the airport infirmary, then transported to the palace for surgery. Leon told them, "You'll also hear that Rehoboth's family was wiped out by the smoke and fire plague. But the smell of GC gunfire may still hang in the air."

As Mac and Abdullah were wheeled into the palace, the bodies of Rehoboth's various families were wheeled out. "The news will be clear that Rehoboth failed in an assassination attempt, but we will likely explain the family deaths as plague related. Our enemies will know the truth."

"And Ngumo?" Mac asked.

"Oh, dead, of course. And his secretary, as you said. Rehoboth masterminded that and engineered it from his office. Ngumo was eliminated, Rehoboth's impostor/assassins were put in place,

and Rehoboth was ready to take over once His
Excellency was dead."

Mac underwent several hours of surgery by
a hand specialist, had major work done on his
shoulder, and doctors also redressed his scalp
and ear wounds. After several hours of anesthe-
tized sleep, he awoke on his left side, facing
Abdullah's bed. His first officer's leg was bandaged and elevated. Abdullah pointed to a jar on
his bedstand. It contained a mangled bullet that
had been dug from his quadriceps.

"Much damage," Abdullah said. "But not life
threatening."

Mac's heavily bandaged shoulder was still
numb. His right hand, thickly gauze-wrapped
and shaped like a gun, rested on his side.

A GC doctor, a native of India, entered the
recovery room. "I was told you were waking,"
he said. "Successful surgery on three major areas.
Your head was the least of it and will heal first.
The shoulder will have considerable scarring, but
only bullet fragments needed to be removed, and
there was no structural damage. You will feel
nerve numbness and may have limited mobility.
Your hand was saved, fingers intact. This will
cause you much discomfort for many weeks, and
you will likely require therapy to learn to use it.
The ring and middle fingers will be stationary
and stiff. We have curved them into a permanent

position. The little finger will have no use. You may get limited use from the index finger, but no promises. The thumb will not bend."

"If I can grip the controls with one finger, poke buttons, and flip switches, I can fly again," Mac said.

"I agree," the doctor said. "You were most fortunate."

Fortunato visited. "You will be pleased to know that you both will be receiving the highest award for bravery given by the Global Community," he said. "The Golden Circle, the potentate's prize for valor, will be presented by His Excellency himself as thanks for saving my life."

Neither Mac nor Abdullah responded.

"Well, I know you're pleased and that only your modesty prohibits you from feeling worthy. Now rest. You will recuperate and rehabilitate here as long as necessary, then you will be transported to New Babylon by your former first officer in the new *Global One*."

"How long will it take to build that?" Mac asked, knowing Fortunato had no clue how long it took to manufacture an airplane.

"It will be painted tomorrow," he said. "Peter the Second has graciously consented to make it a gift to His Excellency. Affairs of state will not be interrupted by this dark episode. The new regional potentate of the U.S. of Africa—a loyal-

ist handpicked by Potentate Carpathia himself—
will be installed within the week."

●　　●　　●

Buck drove home with a vehicle full of supplies,
a full tank of gas, and a preoccupation about
Mac and Abdullah. The radio was full of news
of the insurrection and death of Bindura Rehoboth. GC casualties had included a cook and two
aides, but accounts of the destruction of *Global
Community One* left Buck wondering. He called
home, pleased to discover that Rayford had
heard from David and that their compatriots
were worse for wear but alive.

●　　●　　●

A week later David and Annie sat in the Personnel office at the Global Community palace.
The personnel director held David's memo.
"So the bottom line, Mr. Hassid, is that you take
responsibility for Ms. Christopher's breach of
procedure protocol?"

David nodded. "I should have told her something that basic."

"Perhaps. Perhaps not. Why is it the department head's responsibility when the subordinate
has a procedure manual?"

David shifted. "Annie—Ms. Christopher—may

have been distracted by a romantic interest on the part of a coworker."

The director looked over the top of his glasses. "Really," he said, more statement than question. "That hardly excuses the violation. Are you interested in pursuing this relationship, Ms. Christopher?"

"Very much."

"And this coworker is in your department?"

"You're looking at him," David said.

"Brilliant. Well, look. . . . Ms. Christopher's file shows a list of minor offenses, insubordination and the like. But I'll waive the usual lowering of a grade level for this kind of a breach, provided she allows me to reassign her where she can be most profitable."

She hesitated. "And where might that be?"

"Administrative branch. This crisis has cost us more than a dozen analysts. Your profile shows you would excel."

"What does it entail?"

He flipped a page and mumbled as he read: "Administrative branch, chain of command: Potentate, Supreme Commander, Director of Intelligence, Analysis Department Director, Employee. Major duties and responsibilities: examining and interpreting data from sources not sympathetic to the Global blah, blah, blah. Intelligence Analyst, yes or no?"

"Yes."

"And try not to lock yourself in the office."

As soon as they were out of the Personnel office, David took her hand. He felt such freedom! Then he saw Leon Fortunato stride toward the elevator with Peter the Second barking at him from behind.

"I don't want a face-to-face with *you,* Leon."

Fortunato pushed the button and turned on him. *"Supreme Commander* to you, Peter."

"Then do me the courtesy of using *my*—"

"I will if you will," Leon said.

"All right, Commander! But I'll not have Carpathia appropriating my—"

"His Excel—"

"All right! But he must answer to me if he's going to abscond with my aircraft and—"

As they boarded the elevator Leon said, "If you think the potentate of the Global Community would ever answer to you . . ."

"I want to hear this one," David said. "I'll call you, Annie."

"Be careful," she said.

David sprinted to his quarters, locked the door, and called up on his computer the bug in Fortunato's office. Peter II was in midsentence:

". . . refuse to sit when this is not where I want to be."

"It's as close as you're going to get."

"Why does His Excellency duck me, Commander? You tell the world I offered my plane, which I might have been happy to do. But I was not consulted, not given a chance to—"

"Everything you have, you have because of the potentate. Do you think Enigma Babylon Faith is independent of the Global Community? Do you think you report other than to His Excellency?"

"I demand to see him this instant!"

"You *demand?* You demand of me? I am the gatekeeper, Supreme Pontiff. You are denied access, refused an audience with His Excellency. Do you understand?"

"I swear to you, Leon, you'll regret insulting me this way."

"I have asked you not to call me—"

"I will call you anything I please. You sit here in artificial authority not because of any following or accomplishments, but because you have mastered the art of kissing up to the boss. Well, I don't kiss up, and I will be heard."

There was a long silence.

"Maybe you will," Leon said. "But not today."

David heard heavy footsteps and a door slam. Then Leon's voice. "Margaret?"

Over the intercom: "Yes, sir?"

"See if the potentate has a moment. You may tell him who just stormed out of here."

"Right away, sir."

David switched to Carpathia's office and listened in on the exchange. His secretary had passed along the message from Fortunato's. "What does he want?" Carpathia asked.

"She says he just had a meeting with the supreme pontiff."

"Invite him up."

TWELVE

MAC was up and walking long before Abdullah and was eager to get back to New Babylon. Difficult as his job was, therapy had been no respite. He might have otherwise felt pampered in the Johannesburg palace, but his injuries negated any rest. Between painkillers his body was afire. He requested doses only large enough to take the edge off. The last thing he wanted was an addiction to pills.

Mac was disgusted with himself for two gaffes. He had hollered over the air that believers were on board *Global One*. Fortunately Dwayne Tuttle, the erstwhile "Dart," had covered for him. But Mac had also tossed Leon Fortunato, of all people, his secure phone.

It was nearly twice as heavy as a normal cell phone, packed with so much secure technology. Leon hadn't seemed to notice, but what if someone had called Mac while Leon had the phone? If they didn't recognize Leon's voice or had less than perfect reception, they could have compromised the whole Trib Force.

What troubled Mac was that neither lapse was a result of panic or desperation; both were due to lack of faith. He sincerely believed they were not going to survive the onslaught, and thus, what was the difference?

Fortunately, he had been wise in his selection of a new first officer. Abdullah had saved the day with the phone. Mac had awakened with a start late the first night during his recovery. He shook Abdullah awake. "Leon has my phone," he said. "One call from the wrong person and we're history."

"Sleep well, my friend," Abdullah said. "Your roommate is a pickpocket."

"Come again?"

"When you and Leon were helping me into the terminal, I retrieved your phone from his pocket."

"That's a heavy phone. Why didn't he notice?"

"He was scared to death. I picked my spot. The phone is in my possession."

"What time is it?"

Abdullah checked his watch. "Two in the morning."

"What time in the States?"

"They are nine hours behind us when we are in New Babylon. Eight here."

"Let me have that phone."

Mac called Rayford and filled him in on the Tuttles, who had disappeared shortly after delivering Mac and Abdullah to the infirmary. "I didn't even get a chance to tell them how connected we were to the co-op," Mac said, "but your daughter is surely aware of them."

● ● ●

Rayford found Chloe was aware of the Tuttles. "They're going to handle a huge South Sea area for us," she said. "That they were close enough to hear Mac's Mayday is nothing short of a miracle."

"It's a contact straight from God," Rayford said. "If you can spare them, I need them to get me to Europe."

"Why don't you fly yourself, Dad?"

"I don't want to fly alone and then try to be at my best incognito. I'd share the flying with Dwayne. We can take his Super J or the Gulf-stream."

"Do you know where you're going?"

"Beauregard Hanson is going to tell me, next time he shows up at Palwaukee. T is going to keep him there under some pretense, I'm going to wave a little cash under his nose, and he's going to sing. He just doesn't know it yet."

●   ●   ●

David Hassid sat transfixed before his computer, earplug in, listening to Carpathia and Fortunato.

"Leon, you must not feel obligated to kiss my ring every time you come into my presence. I appreciate it in public, but—"

"Begging your pardon, Excellency, but—"

"And you must also feel the freedom to address me informally in private. We go back a long way and—"

"Oh, but I could not. Not now. Not after all I have witnessed and experienced. You must understand, Potentate, that I do not do these things from any other motive than genuine devotion. I believe you to be inspired, sir, and while it is the highest honor that you consider me enough of a friend to call me by name, forgive me if I cannot reciprocate."

"Very well, then, Leon. Now tell me about your encounter with the man who would be king."

David listened as Fortunato recounted the conversation. Carpathia was silent a moment. Then, "Peter does not know, does he? He does not have any idea that I knew of his alliance with Rehoboth. He believes he can divide me from my regional potentates and conquer me."

"I'm sure that's what he believes, Excellency."

"What a fool!" Carpathia said.

"Shall we let him lead us to another subversive or two, or has his time come?"

David heard movement, as if Carpathia had stood. His voice quality had changed, so David assumed he was pacing. "I nearly lost patience with you months ago when he had not been eliminated. But in the end there was benefit. Not only did he lead us to Rehoboth, a recent communiqué from him proved most enlightening and may have bearing on our two friends to the south."

"The Jerusalem Twosome?"

"The same. You like that term, do you not?"

"Genius, sir. Only you . . ."

"I had asked him to put his scholars on all the mysterious manuscripts from the past, from Nostradamus to ancient holy writings and such, and see if there are any clues to the vulnerability of those two. I know the Ben-Judah-ites believe they are the two witnesses prophesied in the Christian Scriptures. In the unlikely event that they are, Mathews tells me they will be vulnerable four months from now. They themselves have spoken often of their being protected from harm until the due time."

"But, sir," Fortunato whined, "the people who say these men are the prophesied ones are the same who say you are the Antichrist."

"I know, Leon. You and I know I am merely doing what I have been called to do."

"But if they have a due time, so does their enemy!"

"Leon! Take a deep breath. Do I act like an Antichrist?"

"Certainly not, Excellency!"

"Who do you say that I am?"

"You know well that I believe in my heart you may be Christ himself."

"I shall not make that claim for myself, trusted friend. At least not yet. Only when it is obvious to the world that I have divine power could I personally make such a claim."

"I have spread far and wide the story of your resurrecting me—"

"I appreciate that and am confident many believe it. But it was not witnessed by anyone else, so there may be doubt. I have been ineffective in containing the two preachers, which has damaged my credibility. But I worship a deity determined to be the god above all gods, to sit high above the heavens, to evolve into the perfect eternal being. How can I fail if I pledge myself to him?"

"As I pledge myself to you, Excellency."

To David it seemed Carpathia had returned to his chair behind his desk, where the microphone fidelity was best. "Let us bide our time on Peter," he said. "Are the majority of the potentates at the limits of their patience with him?"

"They are, and, sir, despite that Potentate

Rehoboth misled me on this very issue, I believe most of the others were sincere. They assured me they were not only sympathetic to eliminating him, but that they would also be willing to participate in his demise."

"Leon, I have worked with rulers long enough to know that their word is worthless until it has been confirmed by action. We must allow Peter to believe that more regional potentates are disloyal to me. Clearly his goal is to usurp my role. Rehoboth would have been his Fortunato, had the assassination attempt succeeded. Surely Peter must believe he has the confidence of the others. Let us use that to our advantage."

"I will give this my full attention, sir. And thank you again for surrounding me with protection in Johannesburg."

"Think nothing of it. When will the pilots return so we may confer the medals upon them?"

"Soon, sir."

"The people love pageantry, do they not?" Leon agreed aloud, but Carpathia talked over him. "With the turmoil of late, we have had too few opportunities to make examples of model citizens, of heroes."

"Our workforce is depleted, Excellency, but with creativity we can rise to the occasion and make their return to New Babylon a world-class event."

To David, Carpathia sounded as if he were dreaming. "Yes, yes," he said. "I like that. I like that very much. And get someone on this timing issue with the Twosome. If the Ben-Judah-ites put the due time at the midpoint of our agreement with Israel, I want the precise date."

David's heart pounded as he could feel Carpathia's excitement. The potentate raised his voice, spoke more quickly. "Talk about pageantry, my friend! Talk about an event! Fool the two. Surprise them. Defer to them until that time. Give them the audience they think they deserve. Pull out all the stops, Leon. Global television coverage. Plan a happening. Put me there.

"Yes, I shall be in Jerusalem, the heart of the country with whom I have made a solemn pact. We will celebrate the halfway point of the peace that has been accomplished there. Produce the dignitaries. Get Peter there in all his laughable finery. My old friend Dr. Rosenzweig must be a guest of honor. We will do as the so-called saints do and recommit ourselves. I will dedicate myself anew to the protection of Israel!

"With all the world's eyes there, I shall personally take responsibility for the end of the preachers. How her citizens will love the end of plagues, harangues, drought, famine, bloody water! Leon, take a note. Get the potentates to encourage Peter in his scheming against me. Have them lead him to believe they are with him, that they are, are, yes, *unanimous* in their antipathy toward me. They *want* him to be their ruler. Be sure he comes to Jerusalem believing he has the confidence of every one of them."

"I will do my best, sir."

"We have only a few months. Make it your top priority. High level, confidential meetings whenever and wherever you need them. Full use of all our resources. This must be our proudest moment, the perfect performance. It shall be the end of insurrection, the end of opposition, the end of Enigma Babylon trying to assume my authority, the end of the Judah-ites, with no preachers in Jerusalem to worship."

"But Ben-Judah still has that vast audience—"

"Even he will lose heart when it becomes clear there is only one power on earth and that it resides in New Babylon. Invite him! Invite his followers! They were so buoyed by embarrassing me and trying to kill me there last year. Well, welcome them back, and watch their reaction!"

"You are brilliant, Excellency."

"If you like that, Leon, consider this. It will take the best you have to offer. But start confiding in Peter that all is not well between you and me."

"But, Excellency, I love—"

"I know, Leon."

"But the supreme pontiff knows too. I can't imagine convincing him that my unwavering loyalty has suddenly—"

"Of course! It must not be sudden. Let *him* suggest it! Surely he finds negative things to plant in your mind about me, does he not? Has he never criticized me?"

"Certainly, but I always defend your motives and—"

"Just hesitate once, Leon. Let him render you silent just once. I know him. He will pounce on it. He believes he can persuade anyone of anything. What an ego to believe the ten potentates admire him, when we know beyond doubt most of them would kill him themselves! Can you do it, Leon?"

"I'll try."

"I have every confidence in you. Within four months we will consolidate all power and authority and render opposition moot. Just the thought of it energizes me! Go now, friend. Hesitate to ask for nothing. All my—our—resources are at your disposal."

"Thank you, Excellency. Thank you for the privilege of serving you."

"What a nice thing to say," Carpathia said.

David had a headache from listening intently for so long. He was about to shut down the computer when he heard someone in Carpathia's office again. The secretary chatted with him for a minute, then he asked her to hold all calls and allow no visitors until further notice. David heard the door close and then a click, and he assumed Carpathia had locked it. He waited to see if Carpathia made a significant phone call.

He heard the squeak of Nicolae's chair, and then perhaps it rolled. Finally, he heard the potentate whispering. "O Lucifer, son of the morning! I have worshiped you since childhood." David shivered, his heart thudding. Carpathia continued, "How grateful I am for the creativity you imbue, O lion of glory, angel of light. I praise you for imaginative ideas that never cease to amaze me. You have given me the nations! You have promised that I shall ascend into heaven with you, that we will exalt our thrones above the stars of God. I rest in your promise that I will ascend above the heights of the clouds. I will be like the Most High.

"I shall do all your bidding so I may claim your promises to rule the universe by your side. You have chosen me and allowed me to make the earth tremble and to shake kingdoms. Your glory will be my glory, and like unto you, I will never die. I eagerly await the day when I may make plain your power and majesty."

● ● ●

Rayford got the call late on a Friday night. "He's here," T said. "And I told him someone was coming in with an interesting and potentially profitable proposition. So far he's bit, but I hadn't seen him since your woman friend disappeared, and I can tell he's waiting for me to raise the issue."

"I'll be there. Keep him warm."

Rayford sat down with Leah and asked if he could wave some of her cash before Bo Hanson to see if he'd sell information on the whereabouts of Hattie Durham.

"Well," she said, as if relishing her position, "you hardly speak to me for days, never ask how I'm doing, not even how or if the ribs are mending, but now you need something and here you are."

Rayford didn't know what to say. He hated her tone and her attitude, but he was guilty. "I have been remiss," he tried.

"I risk my life with you and donate my husband's and my entire life savings to the Tribulation Force, and you treat me like an intruder. That's remiss?"

"Apparently it's unforgivable," he said.

"Apparently? You say that as if conceding that *I've* decided you're without excuse."

Rayford stood. Leah said, "Please don't be rude enough to walk away from me."

He turned. "There are easier ways to say no. Could you try another?"

"But I'm not saying no."

"You could have fooled me."

"I enjoy rattling your cage."

"I'm glad one of us enjoys it."

"Rayford, please. I *have* been hurt by your avoidance of me, but I also realize that you have suffered many losses, including two wives in three years. I don't expect you to be comfortable with me. But I thought we patched up our rocky start, and going through what we went through together has to count for something."

He sat back down. "I don't know about you, Leah, but I found that as frightening as anything I've encountered—and that includes discovering my wife's body at the bottom of the Tigris. I don't like to think about it, and I sure don't want to dwell on it. This is no excuse, but maybe you remind me of it."

"I'm sure I do. But you're in charge here, and I need something to do. Assign me something, chief. I'm ready to offer every medical skill I have when necessary, but I don't want to work only when people are hurt or sick. I've tried to help Chloe with the baby and even some with the co-op, but she's too nice to ask. I have to push myself on her. Make that my job and she won't feel bad about counting on me."

"OK, consider that done."

"Tell *her.*"

"I will."

"And you people are so politically correct around here, no one's even suggested I do anything domestic. I happen to be a good cook and enjoy everything about it. Planning, food preparation, even cleanup. May I do that for you so you can all concentrate on what you're supposed to be doing?"

"You'd do that? That would help."

"I'd feel I was contributing. Forget the money. You didn't even have to ask. I told you from the beginning I was giving it to the cause, and I meant it. If circumstances changed and I left here tomorrow, I wouldn't take a penny with me. Can we put that to rest?"

"That's so above and beyond—"

"I already feel appropriately thanked. We bring to the table what we have, and none is more important than another. Except maybe Tsion."

"So you were giving me a hard time because . . . ?"

"You deserved it. You should have cared more and showed it. Have I asked about your knee?"

"Several times."

"I wasn't being polite. I caused that injury. I didn't know you weren't looking, but I shouldn't have stopped in front of you anyway. You're a wonderful man. You were hurt. I care. I asked. You gave me the cursory, macho answer, end of conversation. I was hurt too, and no one was responsible for that but you. You were following too close, moving too fast for conditions."

Rayford shook his head. "So how are the ribs coming?"

"Slow, as a matter of fact. I might have cracked more than one. I can go through a day hardly aware of them, then one false move and I'd like to scream."

"I'm sorry. I hope you feel better soon."

She looked at him.

"I mean it," he said.

"I know. And you have a lot more on your mind than my needs."

"Has everyone else been good to you?"

"The best. No complaints."

"I'm the only one who doesn't get a gold star."

"And since I have your attention, would you consider something, for when I get healthy? I am mobile. I am smart. I take risks, like I did for you all more than once at the hospital. I have no family, nothing to lose. If you need me to go somewhere, do something, deliver something, pick up something, communicate something, I can do the phony alias. All right, I almost blew it with the GC the other night—"

"You gave up too soon was all. Actually you caught on quickly and covered well."

"Keep me in mind is all I'm saying. With hair dye and makeup, women are harder to recognize than men. The GC won't keep my picture circulating for long. Get me a fake ID and put me to work."

"In good time. I've just gotten excited about having you in charge of eats."

"I was afraid I would regret that offer."

Rayford stood, his toe and knee still tender. Chloe stepped in from the front room. "Daddy, bad news. You know I've been trying to reach Nancy, Hattie's sister, to let her know we're sure Hattie's alive? I found her. She shows up on a confirmed dead list. Smoke inhalation."

Rayford looked at the floor. "Well," he said sadly, "another reason to find Hattie."

● ● ●

Mac and Abdullah were scheduled to board the new *Global Community One* early Friday evening to be ferried back to New Babylon by Mac's old first officer. The plane, appropriated from Peter II, had been rechristened from *II One* to *Phoenix 216*. Leon Fortunato would come to fetch the wounded heroes.

Mac just couldn't wait to get back to David and Annie. There was the chore of bugging the new plane and also something urgent David had to talk to him about and didn't dare by phone. When the world's leading communications security technician won't talk on the phone, it's big.

Mac was packing just after four o'clock when he got a call from Rayford. "I'm on my way to Palwaukee to put some pressure on this Bo character I told you about. I'm going to be in Europe soon and I need a few things. Albie still your best source?"

"By far. What do you need?"

"Oh, ah, I'd just as soon talk to him directly. Got his number?"

"Not with me. I expect to be home tonight. Can you wait till then?"

"I guess, if you can't get David to dig it out for me."

"It's in my computer. A few hours make that much difference?"

"I guess not."

●　　●　　●

With his new face and his fresh old-looking documents, Buck flew commercial to Tel Aviv. It had amazed him how difficult it was to find flights anymore. The plague of smoke and fire and sulfur continued to ravage the earth, and virtually every aspect of life was affected. The Rapture itself had changed the face of society, and life had not been the same since the great earthquake either, but Buck knew it would get worse. Virtually everyone had lost someone.

He found it hard to leave Chloe and the baby. He had been with them more than ten months, from the moment of Kenny's birth. Buck couldn't imagine the bond he'd developed and was shocked at how he physically ached to hold the baby. He had known that longing for Chloe, and sometimes it had nearly driven him mad. Somehow with Kenny it was even more intense.

On the plane an Asian woman a few rows behind him held a small boy, probably a few months younger than Kenny. Buck was so jealous it was all he could do to stay in his seat when the boy squalled during takeoff. As soon as he was able, he found his way back and asked the woman if she spoke English.

"Little," she said.

"What's your baby's name?"

"Li," she said, pronouncing it *Lee*.

"Hi, Li," he said, and the boy locked eyes with him. "How old?"

"Seven month," she said.

"Beautiful boy."

"Thank you very much, sir."

"Would he come to me?"

"Beg pardon?"

Buck held out his arms to the baby. "May I hold him?"

She hesitated. "I keep," she said.

"That's fine," he said. "I understand. I would not give my boy to a stranger either."

"You have boy baby?"

He showed her a picture and she cooed and showed it to her son, who tried to grab it. "Beautiful boy too. You miss?"

"Very much."

She nudged her baby toward him, and Buck reached for Li again. The boy eagerly went to him, but when Buck straightened and gathered him in, Li grew serious and squirmed to keep an eye on his mother.

"She's right there," Buck said. "Mama's right there." But Li squawked and she took him back.

Buck offered his hand, which she shook shyly. "Greg North," he said.

"Nice meet you, Mr. Greg," she said, but she did not offer her name.

Later in the flight, after Buck had eaten, he was thrilled when the young mother asked his help. He had seen her pacing the aisle with Li till he fell asleep. She said, "You hold, I eat?" Buck held the sleeping child for nearly twenty minutes before she came for him. He hated to give him up.

In Tel Aviv Buck searched every face for the sign of the cross. The only one he saw was on a man who was being interrogated, so Buck refrained from jeopardizing his situation.

It was nine in the morning in Israel when Buck slung his bag over his shoulder and stepped out of the Ben Gurion airport terminal to call Chaim Rosenzweig's home. A young female answered and spoke in Hebrew. Buck racked his brain. "English, please," he said, hoping he could come up with a name.

"Dr. Rosenzweig's," she said. "May I help you?"

"Hannelore?"

"Yes," she said tentatively. "Who's speaking please?"

"I'll tell you, but you must not say my name aloud, all right?"

"Who is it, please?"

"I want to surprise Chaim, all right?"

"Who?"

"Hannelore, it's Buck Williams."

"Buck!" she whispered with excitement. "No one can hear me. Where are you?"

"Ben Gurion."

"Can you come? The doctor and Jacov will be so excited!"

"I very much want to see everyone."

"Wait there. I will send Jacov."

"Tell him not to say my name, Hannelore. If he must call out for me, I am using the name Greg North."

"Greg North. He will come soon, Buck. Greg, I'm sorry. I will keep your secret from Dr. Rosenzweig. He will be so—"

"And how is Jonas?"

"Oh, Buck, I'm sorry. He has passed. Praise God he is in heaven. We'll tell you all about it."

THIRTEEN

RAYFORD grabbed his bag of cash and trotted up the tower stairs at Palwaukee Airport. Having seen two cars in the lot, he knew T had kept Bo Hanson from fleeing. Rayford's knee protested a few steps from the top, and he limped to the door.

He had been in the tower many times and knew anyone there had heard his every footfall. T waved him in from behind the desk, and Bo looked up from a side chair as if just realizing someone was coming in. Rayford had found Bo none too bright, despite his privileged upbringing. His bleached crew cut was caked in place, and he took a deep breath, Rayford assumed, to showcase his muscular physique. The pose didn't mask his fear.

"It's been a while, Bo."

He nodded. "Mr. Steeles."

"Steele."

"Sorry."

"What've you been up to, Bo?"

"Nothin' much. What about you?"

"Lost a dear friend recently. Two, matter of fact."

Rayford sat, setting the bag at his feet.

"Two?" Bo said.

"One was my doctor. You met him."

"Yeah. What happened?"

"Something he caught from Hattie."

"Oh. I heard about her. Bad news."

"What'd you hear?"

"It was all over the news," Bo said. "Plane crash. Spain, I think. I lost somebody too. Ernie got burned up the other day in California."

"I'm sorry to hear that."

"Thanks. Sorry about, ah, Hattie too."

"How much did she pay you, Bo?" Rayford said.

"Pay me?"

"To fly her out of here, concoct a story, fake her death."

"I don't know what you're talking about."

"You approved the flight. Your initials are on the log. You didn't think to alter the plane's identification, so even though the pilot never reported in, his plane was traced to your brother Sam in Baton Rouge."

"He—I—I still don't know what you're talking about."

"You fancy yourself a businessman, Bo?"

Bo looked at T. "I own part of this airport. I do all right."

"Five percent," T clarified.

Bo looked stricken. "I have other holdings, other interests, other concerns."

"Wow," Rayford said. "Impressive words. Any of those *other* things have names?"

"Yeah," Bo said. "One of 'em's named None of Your."

Rayford gave T a look and turned back to Bo, whose chest was heaving, his pulse visible at the neck. "I'll bite, Bo. None of Your?"

"Yeah, it's my business. It's called None of Your Business. Get it? Ha! None of Your Business!"

"Got it, Bo. Good one. So you need payoffs from young women who want to disappear."

"I told you I don't know what you're talking about."

"Yet you haven't denied it."

"Denied what?"

"That you put Hattie Durham on your brother's Quantum and got her flown out of here."

"I deny that."

"You do."

"I absolutely do. I had nothing to do with that."

"It happened, but you didn't do it?"

"Right."

"But now you know what I'm talking about."

"I don't know. I guess. But I wasn't even here."

"Why are your initials on the log?"

"The tower guy called me. Said a guy wanted to refuel a Quantum. I said OK. If it was my brother, I didn't know that. And if his passenger was Hattie, I didn't know that either. I told you. I wasn't here. I didn't put anybody on any plane."

"But you've got one heck of a memory. You know all the details of the flight you OK'd the night you weren't here."

"Prove it."

"Prove what?"

"Whatever you just said."

Rayford shook his head. "You want me to prove you have a good memory?"

"I don't know. You're making fun of me or something, and I don't get it."

Rayford leaned forward and clapped Bo on the thigh. "Tell you something, Bo," he said. "I'm a businessman too. What if I were to tell you I don't have a problem with Hattie flying off to Europe or even pretending to be dead?"

Bo shrugged. "OK."

"She's a grown woman, has her own money, makes her own decisions. She doesn't report to me. I mean, I care about her. She's not really

well. Isn't making smart decisions these days,
but that's her right, isn't it?"

Bo nodded solemnly.

"But, see, I need to find her."

"Can't help you."

"Don't be too sure. I need to talk to her, give her
some news she has to hear in person. Now what
am I gonna do, Bo? How am I gonna find her?"

"I dunno. I told you."

"You told me you were a businessman who did
all right. How much of a businessman are you, Bo?
This much of one?" Rayford bent and unzipped his
bag.

Bo leaned and peered into it. He looked up at
Rayford, then at T.

"Go ahead," Rayford said. "Grab a bundle.
They're real. Go on."

Bo grabbed a wrapped stack of twenties and
pressed his thumb against the end, letting the bills
flap in succession.

"You like?" Rayford said.

"'Course I like. How much you got?"

"See for yourself."

Bo bent to the bag in earnest and opened it
wide. "I could use some of this."

"Badly enough to tell me what I need to know?"

He still had his nose in the bag. "Nothing like
the smell of cash. What do you need to know?"

"I want to fly to Europe tomorrow and find

Hattie Durham alive and well within an hour after I hit the ground. Know anybody who can help me with that?"

"Maybe."

Rayford grabbed two handfuls of bundles from the bag and began setting them on the desk one by one. When three bundles were laid out, he said, "Would that buy me some information?"

"A little."

"Like what?"

"France."

"City?"

"More."

Rayford set another bundle.

"Coast."

"You drive a hard bargain. North or south?"

"Yes."

With every question, Rayford added cash. Finally he narrowed it to a city on the English Channel. "Le Havre."

"You've got a lot of money sitting there," Rayford said, "but every bill goes back into the bag without an exact address, who she's with, and what might otherwise surprise me. You write it down, I leave this money with T—"

"Hey, you're welshin'!"

"—and when I find her, I tell him, and you get the dough. But you've got to write it down."

"It's already written down," Bo said, and he

produced it from his wallet. Everything Rayford needed was hand printed in tiny letters. "You'll keep me out of this, right?"

"That I promise," Rayford said. "Now there is the matter of silence."

"Silence?"

"You haven't proven good at it, have you?"

"Guess not."

"I'm not good at it either."

"You said you'd keep me out of this."

"I assume you meant to not tell whoever is with Hattie, or Hattie herself."

"That *is* what I meant."

"But my *complete* silence can be bought."

"Silence from who?"

"The GC, of course. Defrauding an insurance company by a fake death or even causing rescue workers to search under false pretenses is an international class X felony under Global Community law. It is punishable by life imprisonment. As a citizen, I am bound to report any knowledge of a felony."

"I'll deny it."

"I have a witness." He nodded to T, who was staring down at the desk.

"You takin' his side, Delanty? You're scum."

T said, "This is between you and—"

"Forget it," Bo said. "I'll take my chances. This is ex—, extor—, blackmail."

"Bo," Rayford said, "can you reach that phone? You'd better call and report this extortion, and be sure to tell them what it is I'm blackmailing you over. You know, the felony."

Bo snorted and folded his arms.

"Oh, are you through with the phone?" Rayford said. "I need to report a crime."

"You wouldn't dare. You're hidin' out yourself."

"They accept anonymous reports, don't they, T?" T did not respond. "Let's find out." Rayford lifted the receiver and began to push buttons.

"All right! Hang it up!"

"Are we businessmen again, Bo? Ready to negotiate?"

"Yes!"

"How about I make it easy on you? How about I not let it cost you a penny you don't have yet? How's that?"

Bo shrugged.

"For instance, you don't have this yet." Rayford swept the bundles of cash off the desk and into the bag in one motion.

"Awright, fine! I'll just tell whoever I need to, you'll never find Hattie Durham."

"Now, you see, Bo, I had considered that. It's just a little shortsighted. I'm holding the cards now. If Hattie's gone for *any* reason, you're an international fugitive. Believe me, I've been there, and you don't want that."

Rayford thrust out his hand. "Nice doing business with you, Bo."

And Beauregard Hanson, intellect that he was, shook Rayford's hand. "Hey!" he said, yanking it away. "It wasn't nice doing business with you, you—you stupid guy!"

Bo slammed the door, marched down the stairs, slammed the tower door, slammed his car door, threw dirt and gravel as he spun out of the parking lot, raced out the gate, and ran out of gas. Rayford watched from above as he tried to flag down a ride.

● ● ●

Jacov pulled to the curb at Ben Gurion and leaped from the Mercedes.

"Greg!" he exulted, bear hugging Buck. As soon as they were in the car he said, "How are you, my brother?"

"Worried about Chaim. And eager to check in on you all."

"Hannelore told you about Jonas."

Buck nodded. "What happened?"

"Well, tell me, have you seen the horsemen?"

"No."

"Believe me, you don't want to. Frightful things. They were rampaging through our neighborhood while Jonas was in the security booth. You know it."

"Sure."

"A house burned across the street and a man driving past was overcome by smoke. He passed out and the car struck the booth. Chaim was most distressed. He did not believe we could see the creatures. He still thinks we are lying, but he laments Jonas's death. He says over and over, 'I thought he was one of you. I thought he would be protected.' And he has now gone from being very close, studying Dr. Ben-Judah's messages every day, to crying out at all times of the day and night, 'It's not true, any of it, is it? It's lies, all lies.'

"And, Buck, he has done something strange. We know he is old and eccentric, yet he is still brilliant. But he has purchased a wheelchair. Motorized. Very expensive."

"Does he need it?"

"No! He has recovered from the locust sting. He fears the current plagues like a man possessed, sitting by the window, watching for the vapors. Will not go out. Spends a lot of time in his workshop. You remember it?"

Buck nodded. "But the chair?"

"He rides around the house in it, and when he gets bored on one floor, he calls me and a valet, and we must carry it to another floor for him. Most heavy."

"What's it all about?"

"It is as if he is practicing with it, Buck. He was not good at first, always bumping things. Could not back up, could not turn around. Would get into impossible positions, then get angry, and finally call us to help him pull it free. But he has become proficient at it. He never has to back up and start over. He can go through narrow places, turn around in a confined place, quite remarkable. He is accomplished on every floor. He entertains himself, I think."

"What's he doing in the shop, Jacov?"

"No one knows. He locks himself in there for hours at a time, and we hear filing, filing, filing."

"Metal?"

"Yes! And we see the tiny shavings, but we never see what has been filed. He has never been good with his hands. He is a brilliant man, creative, analytical, but not one who spent time working with his hands. He still reads botany and writes for the technical journals. And he is studying biblical history."

Buck shot Jacov a double take as they pulled onto Chaim's street. "You're not serious."

"He is! He compares texts against the Bible and against what Tsion teaches. He and Tsion have corresponded."

"I know. That's why I'm here. Tsion is very concerned for him, believes he is close."

"I thought he was too, Buck. We believers surrounded him after you left. But then he watches the news and finds himself so disappointed in Carpathia. He feels betrayed, feels Israel has been betrayed. He cannot get through to Nicolae, is always stopped short by his commander."

"Fortunato."

"Yes. Most troubling. You will be alarmed at how he has aged, Buck, but it will lift his spirits to see you."

"Anything else?"

"Not that I can think of. Wait, yes. Do not mention strokes."

"Strokes?"

"You know, when the body—"

"I know what a stroke is, Jacov. Why would I ever mention such a thing?"

"He seems to have become obsessed with the subject."

"Of strokes." Buck let the statement hang in the air. "Whatever for?"

"He is beyond us, Buck. We have given up understanding him. A distant relative has had a stroke, and he has seen pictures of the man. A pitiful change. He must fear that for himself. That is not like him. You know."

●   ●   ●

The Global Community palace complex had become depressing. About 15 percent of the employees had been killed by smoke, fire, or sulfur. Carpathia publicly blamed Tsion Ben-Judah. Newscasts carried sound bites of the potentate averring, "The man tried to kill me before thousands of witnesses at Teddy Kolleck Stadium in Jerusalem more than a year ago. He is in league with the elderly radicals who spew their hatred from the Wailing Wall and boast that they have poisoned the drinking water. Is it so much of a stretch to believe that this cult would perpetrate germ warfare on the rest of the world? They themselves clearly have developed some antidote, because you do not hear of one of them falling victim. Rather, they have concocted a myth no thinking man or woman can be expected to swallow. They would have us believe that our loved ones and friends are being killed by roving bands of giant horsemen riding half horses/half lions, which breathe fire like dragons. Of course, the believers, the saints, the holier-than-thous can see these monstrous beasts. It is we, the uninitiated— in truth, the uninoculated—who are blind and vulnerable. The Ben-Judah-ites cannot persuade us with their exclusivistic, intolerant, hateful diatribes, so they choose to kill us!"

David's own department was slowly being

decimated. Survivors, scared to be outdoors and yet no less vulnerable indoors, worked double shifts and still walked around in terror.

Whatever joy David and Annie might have had in the first love stage of their relationship was dampened by the travail of so many. Those who knew them, who might have been excited for them and encouraged them, now considered personal relationships trivial. And as much as David and Annie loved each other, they couldn't argue that point. People were dying and going to hell. David was so saddened that he seriously considered escaping the palace with Annie and going somewhere where they could help evangelize people before it was too late.

Annie helped him realize anew the unique position he was in. They sat in his office one night, hunched over his computer, holding hands. A simple Y clip allowed them both to listen in on a conversation between Leon and Peter II in Peter's office at the Faith palace.

"Carpathia's day is past, Leon. Now, you must stop reacting that way every time I use other than those ridiculous titles you two have thrust upon each other."

"But you insist on being called—"

"I have earned my title, Leon. I am a man of God. I head the largest church in history. Millions around the world pay homage to my spiritual leadership. How long before they demand that I lead them politically as well? The religious Jews and the fundamentalist Christians are the only factions who have not brought themselves into step with Enigma Babylon Faith.

"Factions? Pontiff, we estimate that a billion people access Ben-Judah's Web site every day."

"That means nothing. I am one of them. How many of those are devotees? I certainly am not, yet I have to keep tabs on their nonsense. I have been patient with them, allowed them their uniqueness and dissidence in the name of tolerance, but that day is closing.

"I have begged Carpathia to make it illegal to practice religion outside the One World Faith. Soon I will step up the punishment for the same and dare him to do something about it. Does he really want to go on record as countering the most beloved religious figure of all time? My people expect no less of me than to take swift, definite action against intolerant apostates. But you believe Carpathia himself is deity."

"Yes, I do."

"Worthy of worship."

"I do, Pontifex."

"Why, then, is such a god/man impotent in the face of the two preachers? They have made him a laughingstock."

"But he negotiated with them and—"

"And gave away the store. He said himself he had upheld *his* end of the bargain, refusing to persecute believers if the two so-called witnesses would let the Israelis drink water instead of blood! Well, they may be drinking pure water, but they are also choking to death in droves! Who's been made the fool, Leon?"

No answer.

"You can't say it, can you, Leon? You can't admit your godlike boss is incapable of doing the right thing. You yourself would not stand for such insolence from your subjects. Rest assured, whoever those two codgers are, wherever they're from, and whatever magical powers they tap into, they are not above the law. They are subject to the Global Community, and if Leon Fortunato were potentate, that problem would have been taken care of long before now. Am I right? Huh, Leon? You'd do what I would do, wouldn't you? You'd have those two eliminated."

No response.

"Once I do that, Leon, you'll want to stay close, hear me? Stay close. If I am beloved now, if revered, if deferred to, imagine my subjects when I rid them of these plague-mongers. Admit it, Leon, Nicolae is biding his time. Isn't he? Waiting them out. Now there's courage. There's diplomacy. There's impotence! Defend him, Leon! You can't, can you? You can't."

"I must hurry to another appointment, Pontifex, but I must say that when I hear you speak so decisively, I do yearn for a return to that kind of leadership."

"There are regional potentates who agree with you, Leon," Mathews said.

"Well, if I may be perfectly frank, Pontifex, a man in my position would have to be deaf and blind to not see how the potentates, to a man, venerate *you*."

"Neither am I blind to their respect, Leon. I appreciate knowing you recognize it as well. I should like to think they would welcome my leadership in areas other than just spiritual."

FOURTEEN

THE NEW computers had been installed, and David Hassid's depleted workforce was grinding away. Bright young minds combined with the latest technology, driven and analyzed by the computers, to try to get a bead on the origin of the transmissions from Tsion Ben-Judah and Cameron Williams. The former had become the best-known name in the world, save Carpathia himself. He disseminated encouragement, exhortation, sermons, Bible teaching, even language and word studies based on his lifetime of study.

Buck, on the other hand, produced a weekly cybermagazine called *The Truth*. He too had a huge following who remembered when he was the celebrated youngest senior writer for *Global Weekly*. He became publisher when all news outlets, print and electronic, were taken over by Carpathia and the magazine had been renamed

Global Community Weekly. When Buck's true
sympathies were exposed and he became known
as a believer in Christ, he became a fugitive.
Linked with Carpathia's former lover, Hattie
Durham, as well as with Tsion Ben-Judah, he
had to live in hiding or travel incognito.

Buck urged his readers, "Keep your copy of
Global Community Weekly, the finest example
of newspeak since the term was coined. The day
before each new issue, visit *The Truth* on-line
and get the real story behind the propaganda the
government has foisted upon us."

David Hassid loved the reaction at the palace
to Buck's weekly counters of *GC Weekly. The
Truth* was indeed the truth, and everyone knew
it. David had written a program that allowed him
to monitor every computer in the vast compound.
His statistics showed that more than 90 percent
of GC employees visited Buck's magazine Web
site weekly, second in popularity only to the porn
and psychic sites.

Using the enormous satellite tracking dishes
and microwave technology, it was theoretically
possible to trace any cyberspace transmission to
its source. Most clandestine operators moved
around a lot or built in antitracking shields that
made detection difficult. Besides having helped
design the transmission protocol for the stateside
Trib Force, David took double precautions by

inserting a glitch into the computers in his department.

The complicator was purely mathematical. A key component in plotting coordinates, of course, is measuring angles and computing distances between various points. On paper such calculations would take hours. On a calculator, less time. But on a computer, the results are virtually instantaneous. David planted, however, what he called a floating multiplier. In layman's terms, any time the computer was assigned a calculation, a random component transposed side-by-side digits in either the third, fourth, or fifth step. Not even David knew which step it would select, let alone which digits. When the calculation was repeated, the error would be duplicated three times in a row, so checking the computer against itself was useless.

Should someone's suspicions be raised and they checked the computer against an uncontaminated calculator, the computer would eventually flush the bug and give a correct reading. Once the techie was convinced the previous had been human error or a temporary glitch, he would move on to the next calculation and probably not realize until hours or days later that the computer had a mind of its own again.

David assumed that by the time the inconsistencies of the machines became an issue, the project would fall so far behind that it would be scrapped. Meanwhile, the computers used to generate Tsion's teaching and Buck's magazine were programmed to change their signal randomly, changing every second between 9 trillion separate combinations of routes.

Under the guise of getting a bead on Williams's base, the techies in David's department spent a lot of time studying the on-line magazine itself. It was clear to everyone that Williams had inside information, but no one knew his sources. David knew Buck used dozens of contacts, including David himself, but Buck always cleverly shaded the input to protect his informants.

The last issue of *GC Weekly* had carried the story of the failed assassination attempt on Carpathia by Regional Potentate Rehoboth. The magazine pretended to be totally forthcoming by revealing that this had been a shock to the Carpathia regime. "Honest, forthright men of character seek to discuss their differences diplomatically," an editorial began.

Such a man of honor was Mwangati Ngumo of Botswana, who insisted more than three years ago that Nicolae Carpathia replace him as secretary-general of the United Nations. That selfless, forward-thinking gesture resulted in the great Global Community we enjoy today, a world divided into ten equal regions, each governed by a subpotentate.

His Excellency asked Supreme Commander Leon Fortunato to visit the honorable Mr. Ngumo and try to persuade him to let the potentate's reconstruction effort rebuild Botswana. Ngumo, the great African statesman, had insisted that his own nation wait until even poorer countries were helped. Mr. Ngumo had been so benevolent that the meeting had to be held in Johannesburg rather than Gaborone, because the Botswanian capital airport still could not accommodate the large GC plane.

When United States of Africa potentate Rehoboth learned of the meeting, he generously offered every courtesy and offered to sit in for the sake of diplomacy. This the Global Community politely declined, because the nature of the business was more personal than political. Potentate Rehoboth was promised his own meeting with His Excellency.

Rehoboth must have misunderstood somehow and assumed that Potentate Carpathia himself would attend the meeting with Mr. Ngumo. While the GC was unaware of any jealousy or anger over Rehoboth's exclusion from the meeting, clearly the regional potentate was murderously angry. He assigned assassins to murder Ngumo and his aides, replace them as impostors, and board *Global Community One* (the Condor 216) to murder His Excellency.

While his henchmen succeeded in destroying the plane and killing four staff personnel, heroic measures by both the pilot and first officer—Captain Montgomery (Mac) McCullum and Mr. Abdullah Smith— saved the life of the supreme commander. Immediate response by Global Community Peacekeeping Forces resulted in the deaths of the assassins.

Photos of the grand celebration honoring the wounded cockpit crew accompanied the article. *The Truth,* six days later, took the story apart. In his breezy style, Buck ran down the facts:

What the Global Community brass doesn't want citizens to know is that the relationship between Carpathia and Ngumo had long ago gone south. Ngumo had not been so magnanimous as we have been led to believe. He stepped down from his UN post under heavy pressure, believing he would receive one of the ten regional potentate positions and that Botswana would be awarded use of the agricultural formula discovered in Israel, which Carpathia has used in negotiating with many other countries.

Ngumo had gone from near deity to pariah in his own homeland because of the shameless neglect on the part of the Global Community. The formula was never delivered. Botswana was ignored in the reconstruction effort. Ngumo saw his potentate status bestowed instead on his archrival, the despot Rehoboth— who had pillaged his own nation of Sudan and made multimillionaires of his many wives and offspring. He was so unpopular in Sudan that he located the opulent GC regional palace in Johannesburg rather than Khartoum, as inconveniently noncentral as he could have without placing it in Cape Town.

The GC knew Rehoboth and Ngumo were bitter rivals, and by deliberately scheduling the high level meeting on board *GC One,* they forced it onto Rehoboth's own turf. Rehoboth assumed Carpathia was on board and vulnerable to attack because Ngumo thought he was on board as well. This ruse to slap Ngumo in the face also fooled Rehoboth, who had been invited to join the meeting as yet another surprising insult to Ngumo.

Personnel who escaped with their lives were more lucky than heroic. GC Peacekeeping Forces had been swayed by Rehoboth and did not respond for several minutes after the plane was fired upon. The assassins were not shot. One fled and two died from the smoke and fire and sulfur plague, as did many others that day.

Rehoboth knew enough to stay at his palace during what he hoped was Carpathia's execution. When it went awry and he himself was eliminated, the peacekeeping forces once again immediately fell into line and finally contained the area. The deaths of Rehoboth's entire family, attributed by the GC to the plague, were clearly executions. Thus far the plague has killed roughly 10 percent of the earth's population. What are the odds that every member of an extensive household would be stricken in one day?

Buck's cybermagazine commented on all the follies of the Carpathia regime, the "penchant for putting a pretty face on international tragedy, and an assumption that you care about parades in the potentate's honor when death marches the globe."

David enjoyed patching in to Carpathia and Fortunato's offices shortly after Buck's magazine hit the Net each week. "Where are we on tracing this?" Carpathia demanded of Leon that morning.

"We have an entire department section on it full-time, sir."

"How many?"

"I believe seventy were scheduled, but due to attrition, probably sixty."

"That should be plenty, should it not?"

"I should think so, sir."

"*Where* is he getting his information? It is as if he is camped outside our door."

"You said yourself he was the best journalist in the world."

"This goes beyond skill and writing ability, Leon! I would accuse him of making this up, but we both know he is not."

That afternoon David received a memo from Leon, asking that the metal detectors destroyed in the airplane be replaced "before His Excellency appears in public again." That gave David an idea. Might he have a role in Carpathia's demise if he could ensure the metal detectors would malfunction at strategic junctures? If he could make computers whimsical, could he make metal detectors fickle?

He wrote back: "Supreme Commander Fortunato, I shall have the new metal detectors delivered and operational and stored on the Phoenix 216 within ten days. In the meantime I have a crew thoroughly going over every detail of the plane so it meets the standards of the potentate.

I am personally overseeing this with the input
of the cockpit crew."

David and Annie, along with Mac and
Abdullah, both slowly mending, spent their off-
hours planting a bugging device in the Phoenix
216 so sophisticated that it delivered near record-
ing-studio sound quality to the headsets of both
pilot and first officer.

When it was finished, David asked his top technicians to check the plane for bugs. A unit of four
experts combed the fuselage for six hours and
judged it "clean."

● ● ●

Rayford was bemused by Bo Hanson, standing
outside the Palwaukee gate trying to flag down
help. "What an idiot," he said.

T, still sitting behind him at the tower desk,
said, "What's he doing?"

"Hitchhiking, I think. Ran out of gas." He
turned around to reach for the phone. "Well,
I've got to tell Dwayne Tuttle how to get here."
T was rising. "Don't get up," Rayford said.
"It'll be a short call."

"I've got something I have to do anyway,"
T said. "Then can we talk?"

Rayford looked at his watch as Tuttle's phone
rang. "I'm good for a little while."

Mrs. Tuttle answered, and as Rayford introduced himself and reminded her of his daughter's E-mails and how he had gotten their number, he idly strode back to the window. Trudy called Dwayne to the phone, and Rayford was glad he didn't have to speak for a few seconds. He had lost his breath. T had driven out to Bo's car and was pouring gasoline into his tank from a can. Was it possible they were in league with each other? Could T have fooled him all this time?

Something told him that if he had a moment to think about it, he could come up with some other explanation. The locusts had not bitten T. He had the mark of God on his forehead. He knew church people, said the right things, seemed genuine. But now aiding and abetting the enemy? Helping the man responsible for Hattie's flight?

"Mr. Steele!" Dwayne said.

"Mr. Tuttle, or should I call you Dart? That was quite a story, sir."

T returned and slowly mounted the stairs as Rayford finished making arrangements for the flight to France. When he hung up he looked askance at T as they sat across the desk from each other. T's dark face mirrored Rayford's own look.

"You think I didn't notice?" Rayford began.

"Notice what?"

"What you were just doing. That little something you had to do."

"So what was I doing?"

Rayford rolled his eyes. "I saw you, T. You were giving gas to Bo."

T gave him a "So?" look.

"The guy who—"

"I know who Bo is, Ray. I'm beginning to wonder who you are."

"Me? I'm not the one—"

T stood. "You want to check my mark, don't you? Well, come on and do it."

Rayford was stunned. How had it come to this? They had been friends, brothers. "I don't need to check your mark, T. I need to know what you thought you were doing."

"I asked to talk to *you*, Ray. Remember?"

"Yeah, so?"

"I wanted to know what you thought *you* were doing with Bo."

"What's the mystery, T? I got him to give me the information I needed. I didn't aid or abet him."

"Like I did."

"Like you did."

"That's what you call what I did."

"What do you call it, T? You guys working together against me, behind my back, what?"

T shook his head sadly. "Yeah, Ray. I'm in concert with a kid two sandwiches short of a picnic so I can turn the tables on my Christian brother."

"That's what it looks like. What am I supposed to think?"

T stood and walked to the window. Rayford couldn't make any of it make sense.

"What you're supposed to think, Ray, is that Bo Hanson is not likely long for this world. He's going to die and go to hell just like his buddy Ernie did the other day. He's the enemy, sure, but he's not one of those we treat like scum to make sure they don't find out who we really are. He already knows who we are, bro. We're the guys who follow Ben-Judah and believe in Jesus. We don't buy and sell guys like Bo, Rayford. We don't play them, lie to them, cheat them, steal from them, blackmail them. We love them. We plead with them.

"Bo is dumb enough to have given you what you needed without making him think his ship had come in and then sinking it for him. I'm not saying I have the answers, Ray. I don't know how we could have got the information another way, but what you did sure didn't feel loving and Christian to me. I'd rather you *had* bought the information. Let *him* be the bad guy. You were as bad as he was.

"Well, I said more than I planned. You play this one however you want, but keep me out of it from now on."

●   ●   ●

Buck half expected Chaim Rosenzweig to be in his wheelchair, but the old man was everything he had remembered. Small, wiry, aged more perhaps, wild white hair. A beatific smile. He opened his arms for an embrace. "Cameron! Cameron, my friend! How are you? Good to see you! A sight for old, tired eyes! What brings you to Israel?"

"You do, friend," Buck said as Chaim led him by the arm to the parlor. "We're all worried about you."

"Ach!" Chaim said, waving him off. "Tsion is worried he won't convert me before the horses trample me."

"Should he be? May I take back the news of your conversion?"

"You never know, Cameron. But you need not ask, am I right? You who can see the horses can also see each other's marks. So, tell me. Does mine show?"

The way he said *mine* made Buck's heart leap, and he leaned forward only to see nothing. "We *can* see each other's, you know," Buck said.

"And the mighty men on the lion horses too, I know."

"You don't believe it."

"Would you if you were I, Cameron?"

"Oh, Dr. Rosenzweig, I *was* you. Don't you

realize that? I was a journalist, a pragmatist, a realist. I could not be convinced until I *would* be convinced."

Chaim's eyes danced, and Buck was reminded how the man enjoyed a good debate. "So I am unwilling, that is my problem?"

"Perhaps."

"And yet that makes no sense, does it? Why should I be unwilling? I *want* it to be true! What a story! An answer to this madness, relief from the cruelty. Ah, Cameron, I am closer than you think."

"That's what you said last time. I fear you will wait too long."

"My house staff, they are all believers now, you know. Jacov, his wife, her mother, Stefan. Jonas, too, but we lost him. You heard?"

Buck nodded. "Sad."

Chaim had suddenly lost his humor. "You see, Cameron, these are the things I don't understand. If God is personal like you say, cares about his children, and is all-powerful, is there not a better way? Why the judgments, the plagues, the destruction, the death? Tsion says we had our chance. So now it's no more Mr. Nice Guy? There is a cruelty about it all that hides the love I am supposed to see."

Buck leaned forward. "Tsion also says that even allowing seven years of obvious tribulation is more than we deserve from God. We did not believe because we could not see it. Well, now there is no doubt. We're seeing, and yet people still resist and rebel."

Chaim fell silent, then clapped his palms to his knees. "Well," he said at last, "don't worry about me. I confess I am feeling my age. I am fearful, frightened, homebound, you know. I cannot bring myself to venture out. Carpathia, in whom I believed as I would my own son, has proven fraudulent."

Buck wanted to probe but dared not. Any decision had to be Rosenzweig's idea, not a plant from Buck or anyone else.

"I am studying. I am praying that Tsion is wrong, that the plagues and the torments do not keep getting worse. And I keep busy."

"How?"

"Projects."

"Your science and reading?"

"And more."

"Such as?"

"Oh, you are such the journalist today. All right, I'll tell you. My staff thinks me mad. Maybe I am. I have a wheelchair. You want to see it?"

"You need a wheelchair?"

"Not yet, but the day will come. The torment from the locust weakened me. I have blood counts and other test results that show me at high risk for stroke."

"You're healthy as a hor—as a mule."

Rosenzweig sat back and laughed. "Very good. No one wants to be healthy as a horse anymore. But I am not. I am high risk and I want to be ready."

"It sounds defeatist, Doctor. The right diet and exercise . . . fresh air."

"I knew you would get to that. I like to be prepared."

"How else are you preparing?"

"I'm sorry?"

"What are you working on? In your utility room?"

"Who told you about that?"

"No one who knew anything. Jacov merely mentioned that you spend a lot of time on projects in there."

"Yes."

"What is it? What are you doing?"

"Projects."

"I never knew you to be handy that way."

"There is a lot you don't know about me, Cameron."

"May I consider you a dear friend, sir?"

"I wish you would. But do dear friends refer to each other so formally?"

"It's difficult for me to call you Chaim."

"Call me what you wish, but you are my dear friend and so I am happy to call myself yours."

"Then I want to know more about you. If there is a lot about you I don't know, I don't feel like a friend."

Chaim pulled a drape back and peered out. "No smoke today. It will come again though. Tsion teaches that the horsemen will not leave us until a third of mankind is dead. Can you imagine that world, Cameron?"

"That will leave only half the population since the disappearances."

"Truly we are facing the end of civilization. It may not be what Tsion thinks it is, but it's something."

Buck said nothing. Chaim had ignored his salvos, but perhaps if he did not press . . .

•   •   •

Rayford hung his head. "T," he said, his voice suddenly hoarse and weak, "I don't know what to say."

"You knew what to say to Bo. You played him like a—"

Rayford held up a hand. "Please, T. You're right. I don't know what I was thinking."

"You seemed to enjoy it."

Rayford wished he could disappear. "God forgive me, I did enjoy it. What's the matter with me? It's like I've lost my mind. At the house I fly off the handle. Leah, the newcomer I told you about, she's brought out the worst in me—now, no, I can't put that on her either. I've been awful to her. I don't understand myself anymore."

"If you ever understood yourself you were way ahead of me. But don't be too hard on yourself, bro. You've got a modicum of stress in your life."

"We all do, T. Even Bo. You know, not just tonight, but never ever have I seen Bo as anything but a scoundrel."

"He *is* a scoundrel, Ray. But he's also—"

"I know. That's what I'm saying. The day I met him he was putting down believers, and I've had a thing about him since. I want him put in his place and I was glad for the chance to do it. Some saint, huh?"

T didn't counter. Rayford got the point.

"What do I do now, chase him down and start being Christlike to him?"

T shook his head and shrugged. "Got me. I'd sooner think your best approach is to disappear from his life. He's going to suspect any radical change."

"I should at least apologize."

"Not unless you're ready to prove it by paying him for the information he thought you were buying."

"Now he's the good guy and I'm the bad guy?"

"I'll never say Bo's the good guy, Ray. As for you being the bad guy, I didn't say it. You did."

Rayford sat slumped for several minutes while T busied himself with paperwork. "You're a good friend," Rayford said finally. "To be honest with me, I mean. Not a lot of guys would care enough."

T moved to the front of the desk and sat on it. "I like to think you'd do the same for me."

"Like you need it."

"Why not? I didn't expect you'd need it either."

"Well, anyway. Thanks."

T punched him on the shoulder. "So what's the deal with the Tuttles? You gonna get to fly a Super J?"

"Think I can handle it?"

"All the stuff you've flown? They say if you can drive a Gulfstream—the big one—this is like a fast version of that. Sort of a Porsche to a Chevy."

"I'll drive like a teenager."

"You can't wait."

● ● ●

David was at first warmed, then alarmed, when he received a personal E-mail early the next evening from Tsion Ben-Judah. After assuring

David he wished to meet him sometime before
the Glorious Appearing, Tsion came to his point.

I do not understand all that you are able to
do so miraculously for us there with your
marvelous technical genius. Normally I stay
out of the political aspects of our work and
do not even question what is going on. My
calling is to teach the Scriptures, and I want
to stay focused. Dr. Rosenzweig, whom I am
certain you have heard of, taught me much
when I was in way over my head in university
botany. My specialty is history, literature,
and languages; science was not my field.
Struggling, struggling, I finally went to him.
He told me, "The main thing is to keep the
main thing the main thing." In other words,
of course, focus!

So I am here focusing and letting Captain
Steele and his daughter put together the
co-op, Buck Williams his magazine and the
occasional furtive mission, and so forth. But,
Mr. Hassid, we have a problem. I let Captain
Steele run off on his mission to track down
Hattie Durham (I know you have been kept
abreast) without asking him what he had
found out about Carpathia's knowledge of
her whereabouts.

No one but the uncaring public believes she

went down in a plane. That the GC allowed that patent falsehood to be circulated tells me it somehow plays into their hands. My fear, of course, is that they now feel free to track her down and kill her, for in the mind of the public she is already dead. Her only advantage in pretending to be dead is to somehow embarrass or even endanger Carpathia.

All that to say this: I had been under the impression that none of your clandestine work there had turned up anything about knowledge of her whereabouts on Carpathia's part. I cannot help thinking Rayford would have been more prudent to wait on searching for Hattie until he knew for sure he would not be walking into a GC trap.

I may be a paranoid scholar who should stick to his work, but if you know my history, you know that even I have been thrust into violence and danger by this evil world system. I am asking you, Mr. Hassid, if there is any possibility of digging up the remotest clue that could be rushed to Captain Steele before he walks blindly into danger. If you would be so kind as to let me know you received this and also indicate whether you believe there is any hope of turning up anything helpful, I would be most grateful.

In the matchless name of Christ, Tsion Ben-Judah.

David quickly tapped a response:

"Am dubious about odds for success (as I have been monitoring computer and phone and personal interaction at the highest levels here and have not heard even a conversation about Hattie), but will give this my full attention immediately. I will transmit to Captain Steele's secure phone anything pertinent and fully understand your concern. More later, but don't want to lose a minute.

David frantically batted away on his laptop, accessing the massive hard drive, tapping into the palace mainframe and decodifying every encrypted file. He looked for any reference to *Hattie, Durham, HD, personal assistant, lover, pregnancy, child, fugitive, plane crash,* and anything else he could think of. Of course, everything that had been said in the administrative offices for weeks was recorded on his monster minidisk, but the only subtitles there would be dates and locations. There was no time to listen to everything Fortunato or Carpathia had said since Hattie was reported dead.

He called Annie, who rushed to his office. He

closed the blinds and locked the door so no night crew could see him pacing, running his hands through his hair. "What am I going to do, Annie? Tsion is right. Rayford is committing a huge blunder here, even if he lucks out. You know the GC either has to have Hattie in custody or have killed her. They'll be watching the site where she was supposed to have been hidden. Whoever comes looking for her is going to find not her but GC. She's just bait. Rayford had to know that."

"You'd think," she said.

"Help me," he said.

"It's not that I don't want to, David, but I agree you're looking for the proverbial needle in—"

"What were those stateside people thinking? That the GC bought the phony crash story? Surely they knew better! I didn't know Rayford had finally gotten a bead on her until he was already gone. Why wouldn't he have come to me for one last effort to dig up GC intelligence?"

She shook her head. "How secure are you, David?"

"Sorry, what?"

"You're in their computers, their offices, their plane, on their phones. Has anyone even begun to suspect you yet?"

He shook his head. "The computer installation slowdown should have raised a flag, but I didn't sense suspicion from Leon. If I had to guess, I'd say I'm in solid with them. I have too many irons in the fire to not get burned eventually, but for now I'm golden here."

"There's your answer then, superstar."

"Don't make me guess. Rayford's in the air."

"Just ask them."

"Come again?"

"Go straight to Leon, tell him it's none of your business but you've been noodling the plane crash news, you've always admired his insight and wisdom and street smarts—you know the drill. Suggest that maybe that plane crash wasn't all it appeared, and say you want his take on it."

"Annie, you're a genius."

FIFTEEN

"YOU want to see my projects, Cameron?"
Chaim Rosenzweig said. "That would make
you happy, make you feel like more of a friend?"
   "It would."
   "Promise you won't think me batty, an old
eccentric as my house staff does."
   Buck followed him, realizing that regardless
how Chaim appeared to the brothers and sisters
in the house, he was aware of everything.

● ● ●

Rayford found the Tuttles an all-American couple
who had lost all four of their grown sons in the
Rapture. "Did we ever miss it," Dwayne said in
the Super J, streaking across the eastern U.S.
"Oldest boy goes off to college, gets religion we
think. Doesn't seem to hurt him any, 'cept he
starts in on the other three and before you know

it, baby brother's goin' to church. That's OK, but we figure it's just little brother/big brother hero worship, know what I mean?

"Then the middle boys get invited to some church deal they probably wouldn't have gone to if their brothers hadn't already been Christians. They get asked to play on the church basketball team, go off to a week of camp, and come back saved. Man, I hated that word, and they used it all the time. I got saved, he got saved, she got saved, you need to be saved. I loved those boys like everything, but—"

Dwayne had gone from his rapid-fire delivery to choked up so fast Rayford hadn't seen it coming. Now the big man spoke in a little voice, fighting the sobs. Trudy reached from the seat behind his and laid a hand on his shoulder.

"I loved those boys," he squeaked, "and I didn't have a bit of a problem with 'em all wantin' to be religious, I really didn't. Did I, Tru?"

"They loved you, Dwayne," she drawled. "You never gave them a hard time."

"But they gave me a hard time, see? They were never mean, but they were pushy. I told 'em it was all right with me, 'slong as they didn't expect me to start goin' to church with 'em. Had enough of that as a kid, never liked it, bad memories. Their type a church was better, they said. I says fine, you go on then but leave me out of it. They told me their mom's soul was on my head. That got me mad, but how do you stay mad at your own flesh and blood when, even if they're wrong, they're worried about their mom's and dad's souls?"

Rayford shook his head. "You don't."

"You sure don't. They kep' after me. They got their stubbornness from me, after all. But I was good at it too. And I never caved. Tru almost did, didn't ya, hon?"

"Wish I had."

"Me too, sweetie. We wouldn'ta met Mr. Steele here till heaven, but I'd just as soon be there than here even now, all things considered. You too there, Cap?"

"Me too, Dwayne."

"You can guess the rest. Before we ever go to church one time, the thing they told us might happen happened. They were gone. We were left. So where'd we go first?"

"Church."

"Church! Not so stubborn now, are we? Doesn't sound so lame to be saved now, does it? Hardly anybody left at that place, but all we needed was one who knew how a person gets saved. Mr. Steele, I'm an actor myself. Well, aircraft salesman and demonstrator, but always actin' on the side since college. Specialize in voices."

"Mac told me about your Aussie."

"There, right, like 'at. He liked that, did he?"

"I don't know that he was feeling good enough to appreciate it, but he's sure you fooled Fortunato."

"A deaf turtle could fool 'at boy, Rafe. You don't mind if I call you Rafe, do ya? I like to find shortcuts so I can get more words in in a shorter time. Just kiddin', but you don't mind, do ya?"

"My first wife called me that. She was raptured."

"Then maybe you'd rather I not—"

"No, it's all right."

"Anyway, Rafe, I'm a gregarious guy—I guess you figured. Salesman has to be. But I always put all of my theater training into it. I was known as a straightforward, opinionated guy, and people pretty much liked me. Unless they was too sophisticated. If they was, I'd use the word *was* where I'm s'posed to use *were,* like I just did there, and tweak 'em to death. So, I'm this friendly, confident, outgoing guy who—"

"*Loud* is the word you're lookin' for there, hon," Trudy said.

Dwayne laughed as if at the first joke he'd ever heard. "OK, Tru, all right then, I'm this loud guy. But you gotta admit I was a people magnet. Only I wasn't a church guy, OK. Well, now all of a sudden, I am. I'm saved. I'm a day late and a dollar short, but I'm learnin' that it still counts. We're still gonna suffer, and we're never going to wish we hadn't got saved earlier—don't kid yerself—but all right, we're saved. So, now I'm still this gregar—"

"Loud."

"—loud guy but I got a whole new bee in my bonnet now. I'm knockin' people over with it. Even our pastor says sometimes he wonders if I don't turn people off rather than wooin' 'em— that's his term, not mine—wooin' 'em to Jesus. I learned that lesson in sales, but I figure it's different now. It's not about whether I'm gonna make my quota or get my bonus or whether you can afford *not* to have this beautiful new airplane. People got to know, brother, that this is no sales pitch. This is your everlasting soul. Well, I get wound up.

"I always wondered what I'd do if I met up with ol' Antichrist himself. I'll tell you what, I'll bet he'd either have me killed or get saved hisself, one of the two. Get it? Well, sir, I was encouraged that I didn't lose any of my braverido or brovura—"

"Bravado," Trudy offered.

"Right, I didn't lose any of that when I saw his number two boy t'other day. My heart was a-pumpin', I don't deny, but hey, I'm gonna die anyway. I'd like to be here when Jesus comes

back, but goin' on before can't be all bad either.
The day I got saved I decided I wasn't ever gonna
be ashamed of it. It was way too late for that. I'm
gonna see my boys again, and—"

As suddenly as before, big Dwayne clouded up.
This time he couldn't continue. Trudy put a hand
on his heaving shoulder again, he looked apolo-
getically at Rayford, who took over the controls,
and the Super J rocketed east into the night.

● ● ●

"What in the world is it?" Buck asked, looking
at a highly polished strip of metal.

Chaim mince-stepped over and shut the door,
and Buck realized he was privy to something
Rosenzweig had shared with no one else.

"Call it a hobby that has become an obsession.
This is nowhere near my field, and don't ask me
where the compulsion has come from. But I am
striving toward the sharpest edge ever fashioned
by hand. I know the big machines with their
micrometers, computers, lasers and all can reach
near perfection. I'm not interested in artificially
induced. I'm interested in the best I can do. My
skill has outstripped my eyesight. With simple
clamp-on angle-setters, I am filing blades so sharp
I can't see them with the naked eye. Not even
powerful bifocals do them justice. I must look at
them under much light with my magnifying glass.

Believe me, this is more appealing than those creatures you and I studied under it half a year ago. Here, look."

He handed Buck the magnifying glass and pointed him to a shiny blade, probably three feet long, clamped between two vises. "Whatever you do, Cameron, do not touch the edge. I say this with utmost gravity. You would lose a finger before you felt the edge touch your skin, let alone before you felt the pain."

Sufficiently warned, Buck peered at the magnified edge, amazed. The line looked multiple times thinner than any razor blade he had ever seen. "Wow."

"Here's the interesting part, Cameron. Back away carefully, please. The material is super-hardened carbon steel. What appears flexible as a razor because it is so microscopically sharp, is rigid and strong. You know how a conventional knife dulls with use? And usually the sharper the edge, the quicker the deterioration?" Buck nodded. "Watch this."

Rosenzweig produced from his pocket a dried date. "A snack for later," he explained. "But this one is fuzzy, I don't want to wash it, and I have more. So it becomes my object lesson. Notice."

He held the date delicately between his thumb and middle finger, barely pinching one end. He slowly, ever so lightly, drew it across the edge of the blade, reaching beneath it with his other palm. The severed half dropped into his hand as if it had not been touched. "Now let me show you something else."

Rosenzweig looked around the cluttered room and found a balled-up rag, stiff from neglect. He held the rag about eighteen inches above the blade and let it fall. Buck blinked, not believing his eyes. The rag had split without a sound and seemingly without resistance.

"You should see what it does to fruit," Rosenzweig said, his eyes bright.

"It's amazing, Doctor," Buck said. "But, why?"

The old man shook his head. "Don't ask. It's not that I have some deep dark secret. It's just that I don't know myself."

● ● ●

David didn't call Fortunato. He showed up in Leon's waiting room late that evening. "I just need a second with the commander, if possible," he told Margaret, who was packing up her stuff after an obviously long day.

"David Hassid?" Leon barked into the intercom. "Of course! Send him right in."

Leon stood when David appeared. "Tell me there's progress on the tracing operation," he said.

"Unfortunately not," David said. "Those people must be using some technology no one else has ever heard of. We're back to square one."

"Sit," Fortunato said.

"No, thanks," David said. "I'll just be a minute. You know I don't make a habit of bothering you about—"

"Please! I'm all ears!"

"—about matters outside my area of responsibility."

Fortunato's open look froze. "Of course there are many confidential matters at my level that I would not be at liberty to—"

"I just had a suggestion, but it's none of my business."

"Proceed."

"Well, the death of His Excellency's former personal assistant recently . . ."

Fortunato squinted. "Yes?"

"That was tragic, of course . . ."

"Yes . . ."

"Well, sir, it wasn't a secret that the woman, Miss Dunst—"

"Durham. Hattie Durham. Go on."

"That she was pregnant and that she wasn't happy."

"The fact is, Hassid, that she was trying to extort money from us to keep quiet. His Excellency felt he

owed her some recompense for the time they had,
ah, enjoyed together, and so a generous settlement
was paid. Miss Durham may have mistaken that
as money intended to guarantee her silence, but it
was not. You see, she was never privy to anything
that would threaten international security, had
no stories—true ones anyway—that could have
embarrassed the potentate. So when she sought
more money, she was rebuffed, and yes, it's fair
to say she was not happy."

"Well, thank you, sir. I know you told me
more than I am entitled to know, and you may
rest assured I will keep your confidence. I just
had a question about the whole plane crash thing,
but it's really moot now, so I'll just thank you for
your time."

"No, please. I'll tell you anything you want to
know."

"It's kind of embarrassing, because, like I say,
I know it's not my area—really none of my business. I'd really rather not pursue it, now that I
think about it."

"David, please. I want your thoughts."

"Well, OK. I know that with someone of your
ability and savvy here, nobody needs me worrying about security or public relations—"

"We should all worry about those things all the
time."

"It just seemed to me that the report of her

death looked suspicious. I mean, maybe I've read too many mystery novels, but wasn't it a little too convenient? Was any wreckage ever found, any bodies? Just enough of her stuff to make it look like she died?"

"David, sit down. Now I insist. That's good thinking. The truth is that Miss Durham's so-called fatal plane crash never happened. I put our intelligence enforcement chief on it as soon as word came in, and the fact is that Miss Durham, her amateur pilot, and the plane were quickly traced. The pilot unwisely put up a fight when our people asked to interrogate Miss Durham, and he was unfortunately killed in an exchange of gunfire. You understand that for reasons of security and morale, not all such incidents are covered in the press."

"Of course."

"Miss Durham is in custody."

"Custody?"

"She's in a comfortable but secure facility in Brussels, charged with the false report of a death. She really is no threat to the Global Community, but we're hoping to lure her compatriots to her original hiding place. She will be released once they have been dealt with."

"Her compatriots?"

"Former GC employees and Ben-Judah sympathizers had provided her asylum when her presence was required in New Babylon. They are much more of a threat than she is."

"So she became bait, and it was her own fault."

"Precisely."

"And this trap, it was your idea?"

"Well, we work as a team here, David."

"But it was, wasn't it? It's how you think. It's the street smarts."

Fortunato cocked his head. "We surround ourselves with good people, and when no one cares who gets the credit, much can be accomplished."

"But luring the compatriots, that was yours."

"I believe it may have been."

"And did it work?"

"It may yet. No one knows of the death of the pilot. We sent word to his brother, whom we know to have been an accomplice, that he was in hiding and would not hear from him for several months."

"Brilliant!"

Fortunato nodded as if he couldn't argue.

"I won't take any more of your time, Commander, and I don't guess I'll let this kind of stuff bother me anymore either, knowing you and your people are on top of everything."

"Well, don't feel bad about a good hunch there, and never hesitate to ask if something's not clear to you. We put a lot of confidence in a person at your level and with your scope of responsibilities. Not everyone has this kind of access or information, of course, so—"

"Say no more, sir," David said, rising. "I appreciate it more than I can say."

● ● ●

Rayford had handled a huge chunk of the flying across the Atlantic, but that hadn't slowed Dwayne's oral output. Rayford enjoyed it, actually, though he would have appreciated getting to know Trudy as well. When it was finally time to turn the controls back to Dwayne, Rayford decided to place his call to Albie (shortened from Al B., which in turn had been shortened from Al Basrah).

Albie was the chief air traffic controller at Al Basrah, a city on the southern end of the Tigris near the Persian Gulf. He was almost totally unknown far and wide as the best black marketer in the business. Mac had introduced him to Rayford, and it had been Albie who supplied the scuba equipment for Rayford's forage to the wreckage in the Tigris.

Albie, a devout Muslim, hated the Carpathia regime passionately and was one of few Gentile non-Christians who also steadfastly resisted Enigma Babylon One World Faith. His business was simple. To people he trusted with his life, he could provide anything for a price. That was double retail plus expenses, and if you were caught with contraband, he had never heard of you.

Dwayne was, for the moment, uncharacteristically quiet, and Trudy was dozing. Rayford dug through his bag and used his ultimate phone— Mac's term for David's hybrid because it could do anything from anywhere.

The number was ringing when Dwayne noticed the equipment. "Now that there is what I call a phone! Uh-*huh!* Yes, sir, that is a phone and a half. I'll bet that's got whistles and bells I've never even heard of and—"

Rayford held up a finger and said, "I'll let you take a look at it in a minute."

"I'll be countin' the seconds, pardner. I sure will."

"Al Basrah tower, Albie speaking."

"Albie, Rayford Steele. Can you talk?"

"From east at four knots. Your situation?"

"I want to meet with you about a purchase."

"Affirmative. Sorry for negative previous endeavor. First officer?"

"Mac is recovering. I'm sure you heard about—"

"Affirmative. Hold please." Albie covered the phone and Rayford heard him speaking in his own tongue. He came back on. "I'm alone now, Mr. Steele. I was so sorry to hear of your wife."

"Thank you."

"I've also been very worried about Mac. I have heard nothing from him for a while. Of course, as captain now he doesn't need my services as much. What can I do for you?"

"I need a weapon, concealable but powerful."

"In other words you want it to do what it is intended to do."

"You're reading loud and clear, Albie."

"Very difficult. The potentate being a pacifist—"

"Means you're the only reliable source."

"Very difficult."

"But not impossible for you, right?"

"Very difficult," Albie said.

"Expensive, in other words?"

"Now you're reading *me* loud and clear."

"If money were not an issue, does something come to mind?"

"How concealable are we talking about? You want one that'll hide from a metal detector?"

"That's possible?"

"Made of wood and plastic. Can fire two rounds, three tops, before it disintegrates. Limited range, of course. No kill power past twenty feet.

"This has to do the job from thirty yards. One shot."

"Mr. Steele, I have access to just the weapon. It is roughly the size of your hand. Heavy, thus accurate. Weight is due to firing mechanism, which is normally used in oversized high-powered rifles."

"What kind of action?"

"Unique. It employs both fuel injection and hydraulic vacuum."

"Sounds like an engine. I've never heard of such a thing."

"Who has? It propels a projectile at two thousand miles an hour."

"Ammunition?"

"Forty-eight caliber, high speed—naturally, soft tip, hollow point."

"In a handgun?"

"Mr. Steele, the air displacement caused by the spinning of the bullet alone has been known to sever human tissue from two inches away."

"I don't follow."

"A man was fired at with one of these pistols from approximately thirty feet away. The shot tore through his skin and damaged subcutaneous tissue in his upper arm. Doctors later determined that there were zero traces of metal in the tissue. The damage had been done by the speed with which the air around the spinning bullet was displaced."

"Oh, my. You know what I need to hear. Hundreds?"

"Thousands."

"Thousand?"

"Thous*ands* plural, my friend."

"How many?"

"Depends on where you take delivery, whether we meet—which I prefer."

●　　●　　●

David was frustrated. He had sprinted back to his quarters and called Rayford, whose phone was busy. That phone had everything but a signal that another caller was waiting. David had even installed a wake-up feature that made the phone ring when it was turned off, provided the user left it in sleep mode. Rayford always did.

He dialed again. Still busy.

●　　●　　●

"I didn't intend to listen in there, Cap, but that sounds like quite a piece of hardware you're orderin'. I like that you don't care if it's illegal. It's not like we're subject to the laws of the Antichrist."

"That's my view. You wanted to see the phone?"

"Yeah, thanks. Take over here, will ya?"

Dwayne turned the phone over and over, hefting it in his palm. "Heavy sucker. Probably does everything but cook your breakfast, am I right?"

"It'll even do that, unless you want scrambled."

"Ha! Tru, d'you hear that?! Oh!" He put his hand over his mouth when he saw his wife was sleeping. Then he whispered. "Is this one of them that'll send or receive from anywhere, all that?"

Rayford nodded. "Best part is it's secure. It uses four different channels a second, so it's untraceable, untappable. Lots of goodies."

"You keep it in your bag?" Dwayne said.

"Yeah, thanks."

Dwayne switched it off and reached behind Rayford to set it in his flight bag. On second thought, he pulled it back out and turned the main power toggle off as well.

"I'll take 'er now," Dwayne said, resuming control of the plane. "And if I'm not bein' too much of a nosy Nellie, can you tell me what you're gonna use such a powerful handgun for?"

Rayford thought a moment. He'd made it a practice to be open with fellow believers, even about Tribulation Force matters. He might not reveal the location of the safe house or tell someone's phony ID name, just so the hearer wouldn't have to suffer for something he didn't need to know. But the gun was personal, which stabbed at Rayford because he knew well where the big money was coming from. At the moment he couldn't imagine following through with his plan.

"The Global Community may be pacifistic and weaponless by law," he said. "But we lost a pilot to gunfire, and almost every one of us has been shot at, at least once, and a few hit. Buck and Tsion were shot at—Buck was hit—escaping Israel through Egypt. Buck was shot at helping Hattie escape a GC facility in Colorado. Our newest member and I were shot at recently. And you know what happened to Mac and Abdullah."

"I hear you, bro. You'll get no argument from me. Sounds like it would be pretty expensive to issue one of those babies to everybody though."

"I'll personally test it first," Rayford said.

"Good idea. 'Course, the two you just mentioned would never be able to carry weapons in their jobs. You'd almost have to plant theirs on board."

"We did that when I was captain of *Global Community One*. Had a couple of pistols secured in the cargo hold. Would have been awful hard to get to, but they were a last resort. Of course, now they're gone forever."

"By the way, Rafe," Dwayne said, pointing to the horizon, "that would be what we in the aviation trade refer to as the sun. Our ETA is forty minutes. Customs in Le Havre is pretty much by the book, if you haven't been there. You got the British visa stamp?"

Rayford nodded.

"Did I ask you who you are today and why I ferried you across the channel from England?"

Rayford pulled out his passport and flipped it open. "Thomas Agee. Import/export. And you are?"

Dwayne smiled and affected a dead-on British accent. He handed Rayford two United States of Britain passports. "At your service, sir."

Rayford read aloud, "Ian Hill. And the wife's . . . Elva. Nice to meet you both."

● ● ●

David wasn't getting a busy signal anymore. He carefully redialed to be certain he hadn't erred. The number was right. Either Rayford could not hear the ring, or the phone had been shut off. David called Tsion and woke him. Someone was going to have to contact that plane on an open frequency. And fast.

SIXTEEN

BUCK suffered from jet lag and the decision to stay up late with Dr. Rosenzweig. He had spent much of the night pleading with Chaim to come to Christ. "It's the reason I'm here," Buck told his old friend. "You must not put it off any longer. You're not getting younger. The judgments and woes get worse now until the end. Odds are you will not survive."

Chaim had nearly dozed off several times, lounging on the couch across from Buck. "I am at a crossroads, Cameron. I can tell you this: I am no longer an agnostic. Anyone who tells you he still is is a liar. I recognize the great supernatural war between good and evil."

Buck leaned forward. "What, then, Doctor? Can you remain neutral? Neutrality is death. Neutrality is a no vote. You pretend to leave the issue to others, but in the end you lose."

"There is so much I don't understand."

"Who, besides perhaps Tsion, understands much of anything? We're all new at this, just feeling our way. You don't have to be a theologian. You just need to know the basics, and you do. The question now is what you do with what you know. What do you do with Jesus? He has staked a claim on your soul. He wants you, and he has tried everything to convince you of that. What will it take, Chaim? Do you need to be trampled by the horses? Do they need to suffocate you with sulfur, set you afire? Do you have to be in terror for your life?"

Chaim sat shaking his head sadly.

"Doctor, let me be clear. Life will not get easier. We all missed that bus. It will get worse for all of us. But for believers it will be even worse than for unbelievers, because the day is coming—"

"I know this part, Cameron. I know what Tsion says about the mark necessary to buy or sell. So you are calling me to a life worse than the wretched existence mine has already come to be."

"I'm calling you to the truth. Your life may get worse, but your death will be the best! No matter how you die, you will wake up in heaven. If you survive until the Glorious Appearing . . . imagine! Those are the believer's options, Doctor. Die and be with Christ, only to return when he does. Or survive until his appearing.

"Chaim, we want you with us. We want you to be our brother, now and forever. We can't imagine losing you, knowing you are separated for eternity from the God who loves you." Buck could not hold back the tears. "Sir, if only I could trade places with you! Do you not know how we feel about you, how God feels about you? Jesus took your place so you don't have to pay the price."

Chaim looked up in surprise at the tears in Buck's voice. The alarm appeared to give way to some realization. Perhaps the old man had *not* known the depth of their feeling for him. Buck felt as if he were pleading God's case in God's absence. God was there, of course, but he apparently seemed distant to Chaim.

"I pledge this to you as I did once before to Tsion," Chaim said. "I will not take the mark of Nicolae Carpathia. If I should starve to death for taking that stand, I shall not be forced to bear a mark in order to live as a free man in this society."

That was a step, Buck decided. But it wasn't enough. In the guest room Buck had wept until he fell asleep, praying for Chaim. At nine in the morning he was still exhausted. He had hoped to get another firsthand look at the two witnesses, but he promised Chloe he would stay on schedule and visit Lukas Miklos in Greece on his way back. The new friend they called Laslos would be the key contact in that part of the world for the co-op.

● ● ●

It was 7 A.M. in Le Havre when Rayford and the Tuttles bluffed their way through customs as Thomas Agee and Ian and Elva Hill. Trudy was to rent a car and check into two rooms they had reserved at Le Petit Hotel south of the city. It was an expensive, secluded place unlikely to draw curious eyes.

Dwayne would use another rental car to drop Rayford off a couple of blocks from the address on Rue Marguerite where Bo Hanson had said his brother and Hattie were hiding out under assumed names. Rayford planned to simply show up at their apartment and talk them into opening the door by warning them that the GC was onto them and that they had to move. Rayford believed Hattie would deduce that Bo had led him to them and that thus the GC story must be true. Rayford would offer them a ride and to put them up in an obscure hotel if they were prepared to flee immediately.

The three would rendezvous with Dwayne and improvise. Either in the process of getting into the car or by some scheme along the way, Rayford and Dwayne would ditch Samuel Hanson and let him fend for himself. He was the one with a plane. They could sort out their differences back in the States.

Rayford wanted to surprise Hattie and Samuel as early in the day as possible, so he and Dwayne took the first available rental car. With a quick farewell to Trudy, who was to load all their bags into her car, they were off. Dwayne bubbled with ideas of how to outwit Samuel.

"Are you sure you want to insert yourself this far into a Tribulation Force operation?" Rayford said.

"Are you kiddin' me? I've been itchin' for some action ever since I got saved. Now listen, we can ditch this boy soon's we get in the car. You could tell him to step outside with you for a minute because, like, you've got a private message for him. Like from his brother. You get out and walk him behind the car, and then you tell him you forgot the note in the car. You jump back in, I take off, and there we go."

"Could work," Rayford said.

"Or how 'bout this one?" Dwayne said, following Rayford's directions as he sped through town. "When you first bring 'em to the car, I get out all mannerly and such and we do the formal introductions. I open the door for the lady and get her inside. Then I give this Hanson character a big ol' Oklahoma shove. He'll roll twenty feet, but it won't hurt him. By the time his head clears, we'll be long gone."

Rayford studied a city map and the note from Bo. "They're using the names James Dykes and Mae Willie. Sometimes you have to wonder. . . ."

"Here's another idea," Dwayne said, but Rayford cut him off.

"No offense, Dwayne, but I don't much care how we do it, as long as we get it done."

"You gotta have a plan."

"We have plenty. If it doesn't feel right for me to invite him out of the car, you know what to do."

"You got it, pardner."

●　　●　　●

By now David was despairing. It was midmorning in New Babylon, and he and Mac were huddled in Mac's office. David had programmed his own secure phone to dial Rayford's every sixty seconds and to leave a digital message that simply read ABORT and gave David's number.

"If I'd known it was gonna be this way," Mac said, "I could've flown to France and intercepted him myself by now."

David, feeling helpless, brought up on his computer phone calls between Leon and his intel-

ligence enforcement chief, Walter Moon, the day
before, the day of, and the day after the
announcement of Hattie's death. When David
finally hit pay dirt and heard something that
would help Rayford, he felt even worse.

"This'll make your day, Mac," he said. "Listen
to this. It's Leon and Moon."

"What's your plan on the Durham situation,
Wally?"

"It's done, Commander. She made it so
easy. How long we been looking for that—"

"Too long. Now what's done? What did
you do?"

"Like we said, we got rid of the pilot. He
was usin' the name Dykes, but we traced the
plane to Sam Hanson out of Louisiana."

"By got rid of . . ."

"You want to know or you want to not
know? Let's just say Sam's had his last
bowl o' gumbo. We put the filly in the
Brussels lockup. She was usin' the name
Mae Willie, so we booked her under that
so she could hide out even inside if she
wanted. I know the big boss—'scuse me,
the Excell—, *His* Excellency doesn't want
anything noisy."

"Right, and anyway, who'd believe she's
Hattie Durham? She's been reported dead."

"And she's the one who did it. We could leave her in Belgium forever."

"And we're taking advantage of this how?"

"We informed the pilot's only living kin, his brother, in a note that looks like it's from Sam, that Sam would be holing up in France for a while, so don't expect to hear from him. We figure the brother will eventually get suspicious or run out of patience and come looking for him. We just hope her Judah-ite friends will find her through the brother first, because we have a surprise for them.

"I'm listening."

"We've got a look-alike staying at the apartment, claiming to be Dykes. He plays coy but then promises to take any snoops to Hattie. They wind up in the same situation as the Cajun, if you get my drift."

"Excellent, Wally."

Mac shook his head. "You keeping Tsion informed? Rayford's walking into a hornet's nest, and those people over there, particularly his daughter, ought to be prepared, in case he never comes back."

David nodded and reached for his phone, but it was ringing. He zeroed in on the caller ID. "It's him!"

Mac leaned over to listen in, and David hit the

button. "Captain Steele, where are you, man? I've been trying to call you for—"

"Excuse me, sir. This is Mrs. Dwayne Tuttle. You can call me Trudy. My husband and Captain Steele left me to arrange for hotel rooms and take care of the luggage. I saw this phone in the captain's bag, and I'm sorry but I turned it on out of curiosity. Well, just dozens and dozens of messages have been scrollin' by, all with your number and this abort message, and I thought I ought to call."

"Ma'am, thank you. Where is Rayf—Captain Steele right now?"

"He and my husband are on their way to try to find Miss Durham."

"Does your husband have a phone?"

"No, sir, he sure doesn't—"

"Is there any way we can reach them?"

"I have the address where they're going, if you'd like to call the young lady."

Mac grabbed the phone. "Ma'am, this is Mac McCullum. Remember meeting me in Africa?"

"Yes, sir, how are you feel—"

"Trudy, listen to me and do exactly what I say. It's a matter of life and death. Do you know that town?"

"Just from the airport to here."

"Get yourself a map at the desk and have them tell you the fastest way to Hattie's address. Drive there as fast as you can. If anyone tries to stop you, don't let them and explain later. At all costs, you must tell Captain Steele to abort. He'll take it from there."

"Abort, yessir."

"Any questions?"

"No, sir."

"Then do it right now, Trudy. And call us to let us know what happens."

● ● ●

Dwayne drove past the address on Rue Marguerite and stopped a block and a half away.

"Seedy little dump, idn't it?" Dwayne said.

"It's perfect, really," Rayford said. "I'm impressed. This may be the best choice they made in the whole fiasco. Let's watch awhile and see if she comes or goes."

Rayford got antsy after ten minutes when only two people left the building, neither Hattie. "If I'm not back in five minutes, come looking for me."

"They armed?"

"Doubt it. If Sam's as bright as his brother, he wouldn't know which end to aim. Hattie would worry about breaking a nail."

Still, Rayford wished he was carrying the weapon Albie had described. He could never shoot Hattie, and he wouldn't risk the consequences for a small-time goon like Bo Hanson's brother. This shouldn't be that risky, he decided. Hattie would let him in. If she didn't, he had a story in mind to use on Sam Hanson.

The three-story building had three sets of ten mailboxes built into the wall in the lobby, which was neither manned nor secured. Rayford was surprised they had not chosen a building with at least a buzz-in system. He found "Dykes, J." on the box numbered 323 and mounted the stairs.

Each floor was reached by a series of four sets of steps in a square pattern. By the time Rayford reached the top floor, he was winded and his knee ached. Apartment 323 was on the front side of the building at the left end. He could have been watched from the time he stepped onto the property. Sam and Hattie could have even seen the car cruise by.

Rayford gathered himself and found the button in a metal box in the middle of the apartment door. His push resulted in a resounding two-tone ring that could have been heard in any flat on that floor. Rayford thought he heard movement, but no one answered. As he reached for the button again, he distinctly heard someone. He guessed they were pulling on a pair of pants. "Take your time," he called out. "No rush."

He imagined someone tiptoeing to the door and listening. There was no peephole. Rayford hoped whoever it was was listening to tell if he had retreated. He pushed the button quickly, giving them an earful.

A male voice: "Who is it?"

"Tom Agee."

"Who?"

"Thomas Agee."

"Don't know that name."

"I'm a friend of the woman who lives here."

"No woman here. Just me."

"Mae Willie doesn't live here?"

Silence.

"May I speak with Mae, please? Tell her it's a friend."

Rayford heard the unmistakable sliding action on a semiautomatic pistol. He considered a break for the stairs, but the door opened abruptly to reveal a muscular young man with one hand behind his back. He was barefoot and bare chested, wearing only jeans.

Rayford decided on a bold approach. "May I come in?"

"Who'd you say you were looking for?"

"You heard me or you wouldn't have opened the door. Now where is she?"

"I told you, it's just me here. What do you want with her?"

"Who? The one who doesn't live here?"

"State your business or hit the street."

"Are you Samuel Hanson?"

The man leveled his eyes. "Name's Jimmy Dykes."

"Then you *are* Samuel Hanson. Where's Hattie Durham?"

The man started to shut the door. "Buddy, you're lost. There's nobody here by that—"

Rayford stepped forward and the door stopped at his foot. "If I'm in the wrong place, how did I know yours and Hattie's real names? Now I need to speak with her."

"Dykes" seemed to be considering it.

"You're not GC, are you?"

"I'm a friend of Hattie's," Rayford said, loudly enough so Hattie might hear him.

"You're not really Tommy Agee, either, are you?"

"We all have to be careful, Samuel. I'm Rayford Steele. I bring you greetings from your brother, Bo."

Samuel had still not moved. "Hi, back. Hattie's not here, but I can take you to her. C'mon in while I get dressed."

Samuel pushed the door open wider and Rayford stepped in. As the door was swinging shut, Rayford heard footsteps flying up the stairs. Samuel headed for another room, and as he turned his back, Rayford saw him move a handgun from back to front.

Samuel set the weapon on the table, still blocking Rayford's view of it with his body. He grabbed a shirt and had one arm in it when frenzied banging on the door and ringing of the bell made both men start.

Rayford hoped it was Hattie. He ignored Samuel's look and swung the door open. *Trudy?!* His life shifted into slow motion as he desperately tried to remember her undercover name. He turned to look back at Samuel, who tore his shirt straightening his arm to reach for the gun.

Trudy screeched, "Abort!" and reached as if to pull Rayford from the room, but he knew neither of them could run from that weapon. The incongruity alone of Trudy showing up with an abort message told him that whoever this man was, he would kill them.

Trudy bounded down the stairs, and Rayford imagined taking a .45 bullet in the back and another in the top of the head. Trudy would be slain before she reached the first floor. Rayford simply could not let this man follow him out of the room unimpeded.

He turned from the slowly closing door and charged the man, who had just fought through his shredded shirt and had grabbed the handle of the weapon. One stride from him and accelerating, Rayford saw him lift the already cocked firearm and slip his index finger onto the trigger.

Rayford didn't want to take his chances wrestling a man with a gun. He could cover the man's hand with both of his, but he didn't like the odds. Instead he marshaled his adrenaline and left his feet, throwing himself at the gunman with his fists drawn into his chest, elbows akimbo, like a cornerback taking out a receiver who just got his fingers on the ball.

Rayford's man didn't fumble, but he did go flying. Rayford had caught him in the neck with one of his forearms, driving his body back as his head jerked forward. As his momentum carried him back, the man's bare feet hit the floor and a small table caught him behind his knees.

His feet flew straight up as the back of his head smashed through the front window. He lay there stunned, the gun in his hand, finger on the trigger, as Rayford scrambled toward the door. His feet were moving so fast he could hardly gain purchase on the floor. He felt as if he were in a nightmare, being chased by a monster, and running in muck.

He yanked the door open and peeked back as he fled. The gunman's head still stuck in the broken window. His torso had wound up lower than his feet, and his kicking and squirming only made it harder for him to get up.

It did not stop him from firing off two rounds, however, deafening, ugly explosions almost simultaneous with shattering wood and flying wallboard.

Rayford crashed down the steps three and four at a time, nearly overtaking Trudy, who was moving as fast as she could one step at a time. When Rayford reached the second floor, he grabbed the banister and, despite his protesting knee, swung into the middle of the staircase. He dropped to the floor as Trudy reached the last step.

She moaned as she ran as if certain she was about to be shot. Rayford felt a tingling in his back as if he, too, expected a bullet to rip through him.

Trudy had left her car idling, the door open, directly in front of the apartment building. Dwayne had noticed it and pulled up behind it, clearly puzzled. He looked up as Rayford and his wife hurried toward him, and he called out, "What the . . . ?"

"Go!" Rayford waved at him. "We'll catch up with you!"

Rayford ran to the driver's side and Trudy opened the passenger door as shots came from the third floor. As soon as Rayford heard her door shut, he floored the accelerator and threw dirt and stones as the car fishtailed down the street.

His instincts had saved them, he knew, but

as his heart shoved blood through him faster than ever, Rayford was unable to feel gratitude for that presence of mind. He knew God had been with him, protected him, helped spare him. But all Rayford felt was a resurgence of the rage that had plagued him for months.

This, all of it, started and ended with Nicolae Carpathia. He wanted to murder the man and he would, he decided, if it was the last thing he did on earth. And he didn't care if it was. He would spend whatever he had to for that weapon from Albie, and regardless what it took, he would be where he needed to be when the time came.

Trudy, gasping, wrestled her seat belt on. As Rayford followed Dwayne through the narrow streets, she fished around on the floor and came up with his phone. "Is—is—is there a sp—sp—speed dial number for Mac McCu—"

"Two."

She punched it and Rayford heard it ring, then Mac's voice. "Mrs. Tuttle?"

"M—m—mission accomplished!" Trudy said, and she handed Rayford the phone as she burst into tears.

SEVENTEEN

DAVID was spent.

He and Mac had listened to Rayford's debriefing as the two cars zipped through Le Havre on their way back to the hotel. All agreed that if they had not been followed they were safe briefly at the hotel under their aliases, but that they should leave the country as soon as possible. Rayford had used both his phony and his real name with "Samuel," who, of course, turned out to be a GC plant. Provided he hadn't bled to death from window injuries, he would have already spread the word that Rayford was in France.

That made it unlikely that Rayford could get out of the airport through customs. Fortunately, he had separated from the "Hills" as they passed through customs and was not linked to their party on the computer.

"We can't help you from here," David told him.

"I'll stay in touch," Rayford said. "But I'm not going straight home."

●   ●   ●

Buck left Israel without visiting the Wailing Wall. Neither had he reported to Tsion the details of his encounter with Chaim Rosenzweig. He wanted to do that in person, knowing Tsion would be as heavyhearted as he was. How they had grown to love Chaim! It wasn't enough to say that you couldn't make a person's decision for him. The believers who loved Chaim wanted to do just that.

Buck enjoyed a warm reunion with Lukas Miklos and his wife. In her broken English, Mrs. Miklos told Buck with relish, "Laslos loves the intrigue. He tells me day and night for week, remember our friend be Greg North, not you-know-who."

Laslos had done his homework. He had made his lignite business so profitable that he was stockpiling profits and planned to sell the operation to the Global Community just before trading restrictions were predicted to go into effect.

Laslos showed Buck an expansive site at a new location where he would house trucks and loading equipment to ship commodities to co-op

locations. His new concern would look like a
GC-sanctioned shipping business, but it would
be ten times larger than it appeared and would
be the hub of co-op activity in that part of the
world.

Buck also visited Laslos' underground church,
a vast group of believers led by a converted Jew
whose main dilemma was how large the body
had grown. Buck flew back to the States encouraged by what he had seen in Greece but saddened
by the lack of spiritual movement on Chaim
Rosenzweig's part.

At home he found Tsion and Chloe skittish
about a decision they had come to about Leah.
Buck thought it a great idea, but they wondered
whether they should have proceeded without
consulting Rayford. Due to the near disaster with
Rayford and the complexity of the communications between Force members from all over the
world, Tsion suggested putting one person in
charge of centralized information. Leah immediately volunteered, saying she found herself looking for things to do between preparing meals.
Chloe had spent hours with her, bringing her
up to speed on the computer, and Leah said she
had never felt more fulfilled.

The four gathered around the computer, and
Leah showed how she had found a program that
helped her consolidate everything coming into or

going out from the safe house. With a little thought and a few keystrokes, she then transmitted to everyone what the others had communicated. "This way we'll never wonder who's in the loop, who knows what, and who doesn't. If Mac or David writes up an incident that everyone should know about, I see that everyone gets it."

As they hurtled toward the midpoint of the Tribulation, Buck sensed they were as prepared as they could be.

●　　●　　●

Rayford had to give Dwayne his due. He may have been a loudmouth, but he had come up with the best plan for spiriting Rayford out of Le Havre. "We didn't get to use my ideas for ditchin' Hattie's boyfriend," he said, "so this is only fair."

It was clear Trudy was proud of what she had accomplished that morning, but she was also still shaken and wanted no responsibility for another caper on their way out of the country.

She and her husband preceded Rayford to the airport by fifteen minutes to drop off their rental and get the plane ready for takeoff. Rayford would follow and drop off his car, then casually move to the back side of the lot where a fence separated the cars from the terminal. Dwayne had noticed that the area behind the fence led around the end of the terminal building and directly out to the runway. "You can either hop that fence and run to the plane—once you've heard it screamin' and know we're ready to go— or I can bring the plane close to that fence and make it easier for you."

"Pros and cons?" Rayford said.

"It could be a long run to the plane, and you've been gimpy on that knee. On the other hand, if I bring the Super J to the fence, that'll draw a lot of eyes and maybe even some freaked-out officials trying to keep me out of that area."

They finally decided that Dwayne would get the plane into takeoff position and then ask permission to taxi out of the sun near the terminal to check out something underneath. That would put him closer to where Rayford could vault the fence. "I'll tell 'em I heard a squeak in a wheel bearing and see if I can't get 'em to poke around under there with me while you're slipping aboard."

All went well until Rayford pulled into the rental lot. The Super J was on the runway, engines whining. The rental attendant asked him something in French, then translated into English. "Are you keeping it on the charge card?"

Rayford nodded as the young man printed the receipt and kept looking from the handheld machine to Rayford's eyes. "Excuse me," he said, turning his back to Rayford and talking into his walkie-talkie. Rayford didn't understand much of the French, but he was certain the man was asking a coworker something about "Agee, Thomas."

The receipt was printing as the man spoke, but when he tore it off he didn't hand it to Rayford. "No did go through," he said.

"What do you mean?" Rayford said. "It's right there."

"Please to wait and I try again."

"I'm late," Rayford said, backing away and aware of movement near the terminal. "Send me a bill."

"No, must you wait. Need new card."

"Bill me," Rayford said, looking over his shoulder to see the Super J slowly taxiing his direction. Three men ran from the terminal toward the rental lot. Rayford sprinted toward the fence, and the agent yelled for help.

Rayford guessed the fence was four and a half feet high and the Super J more than a hundred yards away, moving slowly. If Dwayne had succeeded, an inspector would likely walk out to meet the plane. The men racing into the lot were a hundred feet behind Rayford. They all looked young and athletic.

Rayford tried to scissor-kick his way over the fence but caught his lead heel on the top. That

caused him to slow enough that gravity brought
his seat down on the middle of the fence, and his
momentum took him over. He grabbed the top
to keep from slamming to the ground, but until
he extricated his heel he hung upside down for
a few seconds. He wiggled free and landed hard
on his shoulder, jumped up, and lit out for the
plane.

A look back revealed his pursuers clearing the
fence with ease. If Dwayne didn't increase his
speed, Rayford would never outrun them. Rayford heard the acceleration of rpm's and saw a
man with a clipboard waving at Dwayne to slow.
Fortunately he didn't comply, and Trudy lowered
the steps as Rayford headed for the door.

The men behind yelled at him to halt, and as
Trudy leaned out, reaching, he heard their footsteps. Just as he left the ground to leap for the
steps the fastest of the men dove and slapped
Rayford's trailing foot. He was thrown off
balance and nearly flipped off the side of the
stairs, but Trudy proved stronger than she looked.
Rayford grabbed her wrist and was afraid he
would pull her out the door with him, but as his
weight dragged her to the floor, she turned length-
wise, her shoulders on one side of the opening
and her knees on the other. He vaulted over her,
Dwayne throttled up, and Rayford helped Trudy
shut the door.

"That's twice today you've saved my bacon," Rayford said.

She smiled, shaking as she collapsed into a seat. "It's the last time, too. I just retired."

Dwayne whooped and hollered like a rodeo cowboy as the Super J shot into the sky. "She's somethin', ain't she? Whoo boy!"

"Quite a machine," Rayford said, dreading what he was going to feel like the next morning.

Dwayne gave him a puzzled look. "I wudd'n talkin' about the Super J, pardner. I was talkin' about the little woman."

Trudy leaned forward and wrapped both arms around her husband's neck. "Maybe you'll quit calling me that now."

"Darlin'," he said, "I'll call you anything your little ol' heart desires. Whoo boy!"

"You heading west?" Rayford said suddenly.

"I can head any direction you want, Rafe. Say the word."

"East."

"East it is, and I'll stay below the radar level awhile so they can forget about tracking us. Buckle up and hang on."

He wasn't kidding. Dwayne made the Super J change direction so fast, Rayford's head was pinned to the chair.

"Like a roller coaster, eh? You gotta love this!"

Rayford muttered to himself.

"How's that, Cap?" Dwayne said.

"I said you need to work up a little enthusiasm."

Dwayne laughed until tears rolled.

● ● ●

Late in the day David received a private E-mail message from Annie, reporting that the head of her department and a couple of the other higher-ups had met briefly in Fortunato's office. David wrote back, "I'd love you with all my heart even if you weren't the most valuable mole in the place."

While he skipped around his hard drive trying to retrieve the audio of the meeting in question, his status bar told him he had another message. Again it was from Annie. "I never dreamed of so lofty a compliment from the love of my life. Thank you from the bottom of my moley little heart. Love and kisses, AC."

When David found the recording, he recognized the voice of his peer, the head of Annie's department. He rambled through the obligatory kissing up, then turned the floor over to his intelligence analysis chief. Jim Hickman was brilliant but self-possessed and clearly enjoyed the sound of his own voice.

"These cultists," Hickman began, "are what I like to call literalists. They believe ancient writings, particularly the Jewish Torah and the

Christian New Testament, and they make no
distinction between historical records—many
of which have proved accurate—and figurative,
symbolic languages of the so-called prophetic
passages. For instance, anyone—myself
included—with even a cursory background in the
history of ancient civilizations knows that much
of the so-called prophetic books of the Bible are
not prophetic at all. Oh, after the fact of some
strange natural phenomenon one could make
some of the imaginative and descriptive language
fit the event. For instance, the current rash of
death by fire, smoke, and sulfur—which is clearly
poison-vapor warfare, probably by this very
group—becomes the fulfillment of what they
believe is a prophecy that includes monstrous
horses with lions' heads, ridden by 200 million
men."

"Are we going somewhere with this, Jim?"
Fortunato said. "His Excellency is looking for
specifics."

"Oh, yes, Commander. All that to say this: as
these people take these writings literally, they
attribute to these two crazy preachers—"

"The potentate calls them the Jerusalem
Twosome!" Fortunato said.

"Yes!" Hickman cried. "I love that! Anyway, the
Ben-Judah-ites believe that these old coots are the
so-called witnesses of the eleventh chapter of the

book of Revelation. In their precious old King James translation the operative verse reads like this: 'And I will give power unto my two witnesses, and they shall prophesy a thousand two hundred and threescore days, clothed in sackcloth.'"

"So that's why those two dress in those burlap bags," Fortunato said. "They're *trying* to make us think they're these—what did it say?—witnesses."

Hickman dripped with condescension. "Exactly, Commander. And Ben-Judah has always held that this period began the day the one-world government entered into a peace agreement with Israel. You count exactly twelve hundred and sixty days from then, and you must have what the preachers themselves call the 'due time.'"

Fortunato asked the others if they minded leaving him alone with Hickman for a moment. David heard the sliding of chairs, the door, people moving about. Then, "Jim, I need to confide something that's troubling me. You're a smart guy—"

"Thank you, sir."

"And you and I both know there are things in those ancient writings that would be hard to fake."

"Oh, I don't know. Turning water to blood is being perpetrated by the same people who are killing us with germ warfare. It's a trick, something planted in the water supply."

"But at Kollek Stadium it seemed to happen to water already in bottles."

"I've seen magicians do the same thing. Something in the mix responds to weather conditions—maybe when the temperature drops at a certain time in the evening. If you have an idea when that is, you can make it look like you caused the phenomenon."

"But what about keeping it from raining for so long?"

"Coincidence! I've seen Israel go months without rain. What is new? It's easy to claim you're keeping it from raining when there is no rain. What will they say when the rain comes, that they decided to give us a break?"

"People who try to kill them wind up incinerated."

"Someone said the two conceal a flamethrower they produce when the crowd has been distracted. Really, Commander, you're not suggesting these two breathe fire."

Fortunato was silent. Then, "Well, if they are not who they claim to be, how do we know they will be vulnerable at the prescribed moment?"

"We don't. But either they are vulnerable or they are not who they say they are. Either way, we win. They lose."

David would transmit the information to Tsion, but first he wanted to eavesdrop on

Fortunato when he reported to Carpathia. He checked Fortunato's and Margaret's phones. Nothing. Fortunato's office was quiet. He hit the mother lode when he tapped into Carpathia's office. Fortunato had just summarized his conversation with Hickman.

"Twelve hundred and sixty days since the treaty," Carpathia repeated. "We had already decided on a pageant. Now we know precisely when to stage it. You have your work cut out for you, Leon. You must turn the regional potentates against Peter the Second—not that they are not against him already, but it must result in his demise. I will leave it to you. Leave to me the so-called witnesses. The world, especially Israel, has long since looked forward to their end. For months I have believed it beneath me to personally rid the world of those two. I wondered about the public-relations fallout and considered merely sanctioning and ordering their killing by GC troops. But they will have so alienated even their own followers by then that doing it personally will be considered my crowning achievement so far."

"If you're certain."

"You do not agree?"

"It would be so easy, Excellency. We could have it done without your being implicated. You could even decry the deed publicly, restating that you encourage freedom of speech and thought."

"But not freedom to torment the world with plagues and judgments, Leon!"

"But doesn't that imply that these men are who they say they are?"

"It makes no difference, do you not see? I want responsibility, credit, points for standing up to these impostors."

"Of course, as always, Excellency, you know best."

●   ●   ●

The Super J sat at the end of the runway at Al Basrah. Upon arrival, several airport workers had run barefoot to the plane, gawking at the sleek lines and the British flag. Where Dwayne's Aussie alter ego "Dart" had "Fair Dinkum" emblazoned on the side, the decal now read "Black Angus."

Rayford was impressed with how the British accent affected Dwayne's posture and bearing and even his vocal volume. "Very good then, gents," he said. "Ian Hill, proprietor, and the wife, Elva. Thanks so much for looking after the refueling."

Rayford introduced himself as Jesse Gonder, and one of the workers gave him an envelope with keys and a note enclosed. "You remember the truck. Take it to this address and I will be along. Al B."

Rayford found Albie's ancient vehicle, and they

chugged into town and a crowded marketplace. He and Dwayne and Trudy sat awaiting Albie in a bustling stone hewn café under a cloth roof.

Dwayne apparently knew enough to keep his voice down in public, especially while losing the British accent. The three sipped warm cans of soda as they—at least Rayford and Dwayne—spoke guardedly about the Tribulation Force. Trudy seemed to nap between sips. "I'm sorry," she slurred. "Too much excitement for one day."

"She's a trooper," Dwayne whispered, eyeing patrons at nearby tables who likely couldn't understand anyway. "But I don't guess she's been this scared in her life."

Trudy shook her head, then nodded, and her head bobbed again.

"That daughter of yours is smart as a whip, I don't mind tellin' ya, Rafe. I know you all must pitch in with ideas and such, but she's got this co-op organized and coming along like nobody's business. You know I've had a thing for bein' bold about my beliefs."

"I heard."

"I'm gonna hafta put the *ki*bosh on that as soon as the mark is required for buying and selling. It'll be obvious enough where I stand, and the way I get it, at least from Pastor Ben-Judah's messages, eventually I could lose my head. We all could."

Rayford allowed a tired smile. His mind had been on Hattie and how foolishly she had allowed herself to be imprisoned. But he had never heard Tsion referred to as Pastor Ben-Judah, and he liked it. It fit. He was more than the pastor of the Trib Force. He was anybody's pastor who chose to engage his daily cyberpulpit.

As Dwayne carried on about the honor of his and Trudy's being the key southwest operatives of the Commodity Co-op, Rayford's mind wandered to Leah's suggestion. She was right; she was free of family obligations. Maybe she *could* be mobile. She was a small-time fugitive compared with the rest in the safe house. Her face wouldn't be recognized by more than the local GC. With makeup, contact lenses, and hair dye, she could travel anywhere.

Even to Brussels.

She could pose as a relative of Hattie's. Someone had to share the bad news of Hattie's sister. Rayford hoped the GC would keep Hattie alive until she became a believer, but he didn't mind their keeping her incarcerated until after the midpoint of the Tribulation. If she was free, she would try to get herself in position to kill Nicolae. Rayford had to admit to himself that he coveted that role. Though he knew it was ludicrous, his doing the deed wouldn't be any more disastrous than Hattie's doing it. Whoever did it was not going to get away with it. He prayed silently, "Lord, search my motives. I want what you want. I want Hattie saved before she does something to get herself killed."

"I'd like to meet that Greek you told me about," Dwayne was saying. "Harvesting the ocean out of the Bering Strait, shipping grain from the southwest, and bartering produce in Greece is just part of what Miz Williams has ready to roll. It's gonna be something, Rafe."

A truck creakier than the dilapidated junker Albie lent them squealed to a stop in the narrow street and Albie hopped out. He smacked the truck on the side panel, and it roared off. Rayford stood to welcome him, but Albie—carrying a rolled-up brown paper bag—motioned that he should stay seated. Albie bowed to Trudy, but she was asleep, her chin in her hand.

"One of my people reports strangers about," he whispered as he pulled up a chair.

"You can trust us, Mr. Albie," Dwayne said.

"I trust by referral, sir," Albie said. "You're with him. Him I trust, you I trust."

"Strangers where?" Rayford said, not eager to engage the GC again. "Here?"

"You would never see them here," Albie said. "That doesn't mean they are not here. They have learned to blend."

"Where then?"

"At the airport."

"We have to have access to that plane, Albie."

"Don't worry. I had someone slap a GC quarantine sign on the door, warning of sulfur vapors on board. No one will dare go near it. And as far as I know, for now no GC craft are at the airstrip. If you can get up and away and stay below radar awhile, you can escape."

"But are they looking for us?"

Albie shrugged. "I am an entrepreneur, not a spy. You would know better than I. Come, let me show you your merchandise. Do you want your friends to see it too?"

"I don't mind."

"We will go far away and test it."

"I'm gonna stay here with Trudy," Dwayne said. She seemed to be sleeping soundly, her head on her arms on the table. "Don't forget us now, hear?"

"Stay alert," Rayford whispered as he rose.

"Don't worry about me, pardner. You won't catch me napping. I haven't had this much fun since the pigs ate my sister."

Rayford narrowed his eyes at Dwayne.

"I'm joshin', Rafe. It's a country expression."

●　　●　　●

"Is it true?" Leon wanted to know.

"Sir?" David asked, sitting in Fortunato's office.

"You haven't seen the internal audit on your department?"

David fought to keep calm. "I knew they were doing a report, but I didn't have the sense they had been there long enough to file a report."

"Well, they *have* come to some conclusions, and I don't like them one bit."

"They didn't talk to me."

"When does Internal Auditing ever talk to anybody? They're supposed to, but they never do. Anyway, you're not going to like what they found, but I'm still going to ask you to answer for it."

David was aware of his pulse and tried to regulate his breathing. "I'd be happy to study their findings and respond as thoroughly as I can."

"They give *you* high marks. They say it's not your fault."

"Fault?"

"For the fiasco, the disaster. They say it's not because of your leadership, which they find stellar."

"What are they calling a disaster?"

"Not the morale of your troops, that's for sure. Or your own work ethic. Seems you put in more hours than anybody but the potentate and me."

"Well, I don't know about that . . ."

"Bottom line, Hassid, they're recommending

pulling the plug on the cyber-transmission detection project."

"Oh, no. I'd like to keep trying."

"I know it's been a pet of yours and that you've put heart and soul into it. Fact is, it's not cost efficient."

"But wouldn't a little more time be worth it if we *did* turn up something?"

"You're not going to turn up anything now, are you, David? Be honest. Internal Audit says you're no closer than you were the day we installed the equipment, and with the thousands of man-hours and the budget thrown at it, it doesn't make sense anymore."

David worked up his most disappointed expression.

"So, I ask you again," Leon said. "Is it true? Is it more trouble than it's worth? Should we pull the plug?"

"What will the potentate say?"

"That's my worry. I'm going to take the tack that we don't need to know the source location that badly and that the Judah-ites are making fools of us this way. He'll agree. How about you?"

"Who am I to disagree with the potentate and the supreme commander?"

"Atta boy."

"Not to mention Internal Audit."

"There you go. Now I have an idea for the use of those man-hours and computers."

"Good. I'd hate to see them go to waste."

"Now that the cockpit crew is back to work and the Phoenix 216 is appropriately outfitted, His Excellency has assigned me a rather ambitious ten-region tour over the next few weeks. In preparation for a gala celebration of reaching the halfway point of the Global Community's seven-year protection agreement with Israel, he would like me to meet personally with each of the regional potentates, including the new African leader. I would like your staff, the ones who will be freed up by the dissolution of the other project—"

"Excuse me, Commander, but I have a dumb question. . . ."

"The only dumb question is the one that isn't asked."

Never heard that *one before!* David thought. "Well, again, it's outside my area."

"Fire away."

"Wouldn't it be more cost efficient to just have the ten, ah, potentates come here or meet somewhere else with you?"

"Good thinking, but there are reasons for doing it this way." Leon had shifted into his patronizing teaching mode. He steepled his fingers and studied them. "His Excellency

Nicolae Carpathia is, along with his many other
stellar leadership qualities, a diplomat nonpareil.
He leads by example. He leads by serving. He
leads by listening. He leads by delegating, thus
my trip. The potentate knows that each of his ten
subpotentates, as it were, needs to keep a sense of
his own presence. To keep them loyal, energized,
and inspired, he prefers to defer to their own
orbits of authority and autonomy. By sending me
as his emissary to, how shall we put it, their turf,
he is honoring them.

"This gives them the opportunity to roll out
the red carpet, to have their subjects see that they
are being honored by a visit from the palace. In
each international capital I will publicly, officially
invite the regional potentate to the Global Gala
in September. His subjects will be invited as well
and urged to combine their trip to Jerusalem with
an additional pilgrimage to New Babylon."

"Interesting," David said.

"I thought you'd think so. And this is where
you and your people and all those freed-up
computers come in. His Excellency has always
been a matchless role model to me as a public
speaker. You're well aware of his proficiency
in many languages. I can't hope to match that,
though I would like to understand a phrase or
two in each major language group I will be
addressing. The potentate also, I don't know

whether you've noticed, never, and I mean absolutely never, uses a contraction, not even in informal conversation."

"I've had so little personal contact with him. . . ."

"Naturally. But let me tell you his most enormous oratorical gift, and this is besides his unequaled ability to memorize pages of material and make even a lengthy speech appear extemporaneous. It is this: Potentate Carpathia knows the history, even the nuances, of his audience as well as they know it themselves. Have you ever seen the tapes of his first address to the United Nations three years ago?"

"I'm sure everyone has by now."

"That speech alone, David, virtually sealed his appointment as secretary-general and eventual leader of the new world order. He took that podium as merely a guest speaker, president of a smallish country in the eastern European bloc. The position he ascended to was not even vacant when first he opened his mouth. Yet with brilliance, charm, wit, mastery of his subject, the use of every language of the U.N., and an astounding recitation of the history of that great institution, he had the entire world eating out of his hand. I grant that had we not just suffered the global vanishings that plunged us all into a grieving, terror-filled malaise, perhaps the size of the audience would not have been appropriate for the greatness of the address. But it was as if God ordained it, and His Excellency was the perfect man for the moment."

Fortunato's eyes had glazed over. "Ah, it was magical," he said. "I knew in my soul that if I ever had the privilege to contribute even in a minuscule way to the ideals and objectives of that man, I would pledge my life to him. Have you ever felt that way about someone, David?"

"I believe I can empathize with that devotion, yes sir."

That seemed to snap Leon from his reverie. "*Really*," he said. "May I ask whom?"

"Whom? You mean who I, ah, idolize enough to pledge my life to? Yeah. My Father, actually."

"That's beautiful, David. He must be a wonderful man."

"Oh, he is. He's, like, God to me."

"Indeed? What does he do?"

"He's creative, works with his hands."

"But his character, that's what inspires you."

"More than you'll ever know. More than I can say."

"That's very special. I'd love to meet him someday."

"Oh, you will," David said. "I'm certain you'll meet one day, face-to-face."

"I'll look forward to that. But I've completely

left my train of thought. Let me make my point and then I'll let you go. Forgive me, but I enjoy bringing along a young loyalist with promise."

"Think nothing of it."

"Anyway, I would like your people to use those computers to dig out important facts about each man I am visiting, his region, its history. By knowing as much as I can and being accurate about the details, I honor them. Can you provide me with that, David? Make me look good, which makes His Excellency look good, which is good for the Global Community."

"I'll take it as a personal challenge, sir."

EIGHTEEN

STARS dotted an inky sky when Albie finally skidded to a dusty stop in a deserted plain. He left the old truck's headlights burning, illuminating a boulder next to a mature tree about a hundred yards away. Albie hopped into the bed of the truck and scampered atop the cab. He peered behind them.

"Let my eyes grow accustomed to the darkness," he said, "and I'll be sure we're alone." Satisfied, he hopped down the way he had gone up. "I used to be able to drop all the way from the top to the ground. But the ankle . . . remember?"

"The earthquake," Rayford said.

"Not a high medical priority, all things considered."

He motioned for Rayford to follow him to the front of the truck, where he squatted before a headlamp and reached into his paper sack. He produced a rectangular block of black metal that looked like a box. It was about ten inches long, five inches wide, and an inch and a half deep.

"Captain Steele, this is ingenious. It costs extra, but I know you will want it. Watch carefully so you can see how easily it is done. Unless you know the trick, you cannot do it. First, get the feel of this in your hands."

Rayford took the block and was impressed with its weight and density. There were no visible seams, and the block felt solid.

"Open it," Albie said.

Rayford turned it every which way in the light, looking for a place to get a grip, trip a switch, squeeze a spring, anything. He saw nothing.

"Try," Albie said.

Rayford gripped the block at both ends and pulled. He pushed to see if the sides had any give. He twisted it and shook it, pressed around the edges. "I'm convinced," he said, handing it back.

"What does it remind you of?"

"Ballast. Maybe a weight of some kind. An old computer battery?"

"What would you tell a customs agent it is when it shows up black and ugly under the radar?"

"One of the above, I guess. Probably say it's for the computer I left at my destination last time."

"That will work, because he will not be able to open it either. Unless he does this, and the odds are he never would."

Holding the block before him horizontally, Albie put his left thumb in the upper left corner with his left middle finger on the back of the lower left corner. He did the opposite with his right hand, thumb on the lower right corner, middle finger on the back of the upper corner. "I am pushing gently with my thumbs, which forces my fingers to resist. When I feel a most delicate disengagement, I then slide my thumbs along the bottom edge, put my index fingers along the top edge, grip tightly, and pull. See how easily it slides apart."

Rayford felt as if he were witnessing a magic trick from a foot away without a clue how it was accomplished. Albie had slid the block apart only an inch or so, then quickly snapped it back shut. "The seams seem to disappear because this was fashioned from a solid block of steel. Try it, Captain."

Rayford placed his thumbs and middle fingers where Albie had. When he pressed slightly with his thumbs and felt the pressure on his fingers, he sensed an ever so slight give. He was reminded of his penny toys as a kid when he tried to make a BB drop into a shallow hole in a piece of cardboard by tilting it this way and that. It worked only when you tilted just so far but not too much.

He grasped the ends of the block as Albie had done, and the unit smoothly slid apart. In his left hand was solid steel in the shape of a large jigsaw puzzle that perfectly aligned with the heavy handgun in his right. Amazing.

"Is it loaded?"

"I was taught there's no such thing as an unloaded gun. Many people have been killed by guns they were certain were unloaded."

"Granted. But if I aimed and shot . . ."

"Would a bullet be fired? Yes."

"Got anything you don't care about that could be set atop that rock?"

"Just aim at the rock for now. It takes getting used to."

"I was a fair marksman in the military years ago."

"Only years? Not decades?"

"Cute. Insulted by my fence."

"Familiarize yourself with your weapon."

Rayford set the block on the ground and turned the gun over and over in his hand. Heavy as it was, it had excellent balance and settled easily into his palm. He worried it might be difficult to hold steady due to the weight.

"That mechanism," Albie said, "is found in no other handgun. Only in high-powered rifles. It does not cock. It is semiautomatic. You have to pull the trigger anew for each shot, but it will fire off a round as quickly as you can release the trigger and trip it again. It is probably the loudest handgun made, and I recommend something in the ear nearest the weapon. For now, just plug your ear with your other hand."

"I don't see a safety."

"There is none. You simply aim and fire. The rationale behind this piece is that you do not separate the block and produce it unless you intend to shoot it. You do not shoot it unless you intend to destroy what you are shooting. If you shoot at that rock enough times, you will destroy it. If you shoot a person in a kill zone from within two hundred feet, you will kill him. If you hit him in a neutral zone from that same distance, your ammunition will sever skin, flesh, fat, tendon, ligament, muscle, and bone and will pass through the body leaving two holes. Provided you are at least ten feet away, the soft hollow-point shell has time to spread out due to the heat of the firing explosion and the centrifugal force caused by the spinning. Rifling grooves etched inside the barrel induce the spin. The projectile then will be roughly an inch and a half in diameter."

"The bullet spreads into a spinning disk?"

"Exactly. And as I told you on the phone, a man *missed* by the projectile by two inches from thirty feet away suffered a deep laceration from the air displacement alone. Should you hit someone from between ten feet and two hundred feet, the bullet will leave an exit wound of nearly six inches in diameter, depending on what body part is expelled with it. The thin, jagged, spinning bullet bores through anything in its path, gathers the gore around it like grass in a power-mower blade, and turns itself into a larger object of destruction. During the testing of this weapon a technician was accidentally shot just above the knee from approximately twenty feet away. His leg was effectively amputated, the lower portion attached by a thin ribbon of skin on each side of the knee."

Rayford shook his head and gazed at the ugliness in his hand. What was he thinking? That he would ever dare carry such a monstrosity, let alone use it? He would be hard pressed to justify this as a defensive weapon.

"Are you trying to talk me into this or out of it?"

Albie shrugged. "I want you satisfied with your purchase. No complaints. I said you could go cheaper. You said you wanted performance. What you do with this is your business, and I wouldn't even want to make it mine. But I guarantee you, Captain, if you ever have to use it on someone, you won't have to use it twice."

"I don't know," Rayford said, his haunches aching from crouching. He shifted his weight, picked up the other half of the block, and held it facing the gun to see how they aligned.

"At least try it," Albie said. "It's an experience."

"I'll bet it is."

Rayford dropped the block again, stood between the headlights, spread his legs, aimed the gun at the rock, and steadied his shooting hand at the wrist with his other hand.

Albie covered both ears, then interrupted. "You really should put something in that right ear."

Rayford dug in his pocket for the note Albie had written. He tore a piece from it, moistened it with his tongue, and crumpled it into a small ball. He pushed it into his ear and resumed firing position. "I wish I could cock it just for timing," he said. "It's as if the gun's ready and I'm not."

"I'm not hearing you," Albie said, too loudly. "I'm afraid you'll shoot when I take my hands from my ears."

The gun was only slightly closer to Rayford's protected ear. When he squeezed the trigger, the recoil drove him back against the hood of the truck. He slid to where his seat hit the bumper, but there wasn't enough room to hold him, and he plopped in the dirt. The explosion sounded like a bomb and then like nothing, as he was temporarily deafened and didn't even hear the echo. Rayford was glad he had not squeezed off another round when he flopped.

Albie looked at him expectantly.

"You're right," Rayford said, his ear ringing. "An experience."

"Look," Albie said, pointing into the distance.

Rayford squinted. The rock looked none the worse for wear. "Did I hit it?"

"You hit the tree!"

Rayford could hardly believe it. The bullet had hit the trunk about eight feet off the ground, just below the branches. "I need to see this," he said, struggling to his feet. Albie followed him as he got close enough to see that a gash had been taken out of the tree that left less than half the trunk intact. The weight of the branches finally overtook the gaping hole and the top of the tree came crashing down, bouncing off the rock.

"I've heard of tree surgeons," Albie said. "But . . ."

"How many rounds does it hold?"

"Nine. Want to try again and see if you can hit what you're aiming at?"

"I'll have to compensate. It pulls up and to the right."

"No, it doesn't."

"You saw what I hit. I was aiming into the middle of the rock."

"Pardon me, Captain, but the problem was not the gun. It was the shooter."

"What?"

"In your profession they would call it pilot error."

"What did I do?"

"You flinched."

"I didn't."

"You did. You expected the powerful sound and action, and you caused the barrel to point up and to the right. This time, concentrate not only on not doing that, but also on planting your back foot and taking the recoil in your legs."

"Too much to think about."

"But try. Otherwise, you're on the ground again and the tree has been put out of its misery."

Rayford filled both ears this time, made sure his right leg was planted behind his left with the knee slightly bent. Indeed, he had to fight the urge to flinch as he squeezed the trigger. This time, not dazed by the sound and not driven back against the truck, his eyes were on the rock when a huge chuck of it was blown off the top. Rayford retrieved a piece at least ten inches in diameter and three inches thick.

"Who makes this thing, anyway?"

"Those who need to know, know."

"There's no signage on it," Rayford said. "What do they call it?"

"People who know the weapon have nick-
named it the Saber."

"Why?"

Albie shrugged. "Probably because the other
piece could be called a sheath. When it's pieced
together it's like a sword in its sheath."

Albie showed him how to reassemble the
block, returned it to the sack, and drove him
back toward the marketplace.

"Needless to say, I don't carry that kind of
cash," Rayford said.

"I got it on consignment. Can you get it to me
in two weeks?"

"It'll come from Mac."

"Good enough. . . . Uh-oh."

Rayford looked up. The road into the crowded
commercial area was blocked by GC Peacekeepers, lights flashing. Albie took to the side streets.
As he drew within sight of the café he stopped
abruptly and sighed. Rayford sat forward, his
head touching the windshield. The crowd was
in the street, the café empty save for the table
where Rayford and Albie had left the Tuttles.

Trudy sat in the same pose as when they had
left, head nestled in her forearms on the table.
But a huge chunk was missing from the back of
her head and her arms were covered with blood
that still dripped from the table.

Next to her, facing Rayford, sat the big, blond,

freckle-faced Dwayne. His head had fallen back and his arms hung at his sides, palms up, thumbs pointing out. His forehead bore a neat round hole and his chair rested in a pool of his blood.

Rayford grabbed the door handle, but Albie's fingers dug into his arm like talons. "You can do nothing for them, friend. Don't reveal yourself to your enemies. Give me your phone."

In a daze, Rayford handed it to him, then pounded his fists into the dash as Albie backed out of the area and drove across the sand. He spoke quickly in his native tongue, then slapped the phone shut and set it on the seat next to Rayford.

Rayford could not stop pounding. His head throbbed, the heels of his hands shot through with pain. His teeth were clenched and a buzz had invaded his brain. He felt as if his head might explode. Instinct told him to pray, but he could not. His strength left him as if he had opened a drainpipe and let it escape. He slumped in the seat.

"Listen carefully to me," Albie said. "You know whoever did that is after you. They will be lying in wait at the airport and there'll likely be a fighter or two in the air somewhere. Can you fly that plane?"

"Yes."

"I told my man there to announce that due to

winds and curfews in surrounding areas he was
shutting down the airport. He will give people ten
minutes to leave before turning off the runway
lights. He tells me no one is near your plane, but
that the airport is busier than normal with pedes-
trian traffic. The place will be dark and hopefully
empty by the time we get there. Still, to be safe,
I will let you out before I enter the tower. Stay
in the darkness until you reach the plane. When
I hear your engines, I will light the runway for
you."

Rayford could not speak, not even to thank
Albie. Here was a man who was not even a
believer. But he was an enemy of Carpathia and
willing to do anything to thwart him. He didn't
know Rayford's situation and told him repeatedly
he didn't want to know. But he was risking his
own life by trying to get Rayford into the air,
and Rayford would never forget it.

They were within sight of the airport when
the lights went off and a short line of cars snaked
out of the lot. Albie stopped and nodded that
Rayford should go, pointing wide to the right
around the airfield, which was now a sea of
blackness. Rayford grabbed the bag and started
to leave, but Albie caught him and took the block
out. He opened the gun and handed Rayford
both pieces. He poured extra ammunition into
his palm and stuffed it in Rayford's pocket.

"Just in case," he said, stuffing the bag beneath the seat.

Fury had again constricted Rayford's throat, and he could not emit a sound. He slipped the gun in one pocket and the block in another, gathered up his phone, and thrust out his hand toward Albie. They squeezed hard and Albie said, "I know. Now go."

Rayford loped across the sand and scrub grass in the darkness, hearing his own panting. When finally his vocal chords loosened, he moaned with each breath. Then he emitted a closed-mouth growl so loud and fierce that it dizzied him, and he nearly tumbled. He was within a hundred feet of the plane when he heard footsteps angling toward him and a shout. "Rayford Steele! Halt! GC Peacekeeper!"

Rayford gave off a guttural, "No!" and kept moving, reaching into his pocket for the gun.

"You're under arrest!"

He kept moving.

"Stop or I'll shoot!"

Rayford felt that tingle in his back. Had it really been that very morning that he had eluded another GC gun? He whirled, his own weapon raised.

The faint light from the road in the distance silhouetted the GC man, closing on him, weapon aimed.

Rayford stopped. "Don't make me shoot you!" he screamed, but the man kept coming. Rayford fired at his feet, hitting the ground a yard in front of the man.

A huge cloud of sand erupted and the man flipped over backward, landing on his stomach with a loud "Unh!" His weapon clattered free. Rayford made a dash for the plane, peeking over his shoulder to see the man lying motionless.

"God, don't let him die!" he said, yanking open the door and diving aboard. He pulled the door shut, realizing he was drenched with sweat. "I don't want to kill a man!"

Rayford jumped over the back of the seat into the pilot's chair and fired up the engines. The fuel tank showed full, the other gauges danced to life, and the runway lights came on. He grabbed the radio. "All clear?" he said, careful to not mention Albie's name.

"Two bogies six miles due north," came the reply. They could be upon him in seconds, but they would look for him to head west and climb quickly.

Rayford looked far to his left just before reaching takeoff speed. The GC man had labored to his feet and staggered as if catching his breath and looking for his weapon. The Super J smoothly took to the air, and Rayford headed south, staying below radar level until he was sure he was not being pursued. Then he gave the craft full power, and the thrust drove him back in his seat as he set the nose to the stars and the west. All he wanted was to reach maximum cruising speed at optimum altitude and get home to his comrades in one piece.

● ● ●

It was just after noon in Illinois as Tsion Ben-Judah stood gazing out the upstairs window of the safe house. Summer was coming on. He had just enjoyed a light lunch with Buck, Chloe, the baby, and Leah. What a strange and wonderful, warm woman she had turned out to be. He did not know what bothered Rayford so about her. Tsion found her most engaging.

He had nearly finished his message to the faithful and would begin polishing it for transmission in a few minutes. In it he warned that the closer the calendar drew to September, the forty-second month into the Tribulation, the more likely it was that the death toll of the 200 million horsemen would reach a third of the population. The gravity of his missive weighed on him, and he felt a sudden need to pray for his old mentor and fellow countryman, Chaim Rosenzweig.

"Father," he began, "I do not even know how to pray for my friend anymore." Tsion quoted,

"'Likewise the Spirit also helps in our weaknesses. For we do not know what we should pray for as we ought, but the Spirit Himself makes intercession for us with groanings which cannot be uttered. Now He who searches the hearts knows what the mind of the Spirit is, because He makes intercession for the saints according to the will of God.'

"Thank you, Lord," he said.

And when he opened his eyes he at first thought he was dreaming. Filling his entire field of vision through the window was an army of horsemen and their steeds. Hundreds and hundreds of thousands of them, riding, riding. The horses' heads were as the heads of lions, and from their mouths poured fire and smoke.

Tsion had written of these, had heard others' accounts, secretly wished he might get a glimpse. But now as he stared, unblinking, wanting to call the others, especially Buck, who also had not seen these, he could not find voice.

In the middle of the day with the harsh late spring sun bathing the scene, the massive horsemen looked angry and determined. Their brightly colored breastplates gleamed as the immense beasts beneath them rumbled side by side, picking up speed from trotting to galloping to stampeding. It was as if their time had come. The occasional forays had been mere rehearsal. The demonic cavalry, limited only by God's choosing whom they might slay, stormed across the earth for what would surely be their final attack.

"Tsion!" Buck called from downstairs. "Look out the window! Quick!"

● ● ●

Rayford had the Super J at peak performance on autopilot. Fatigue swept over him, but he dared not doze, regardless of the technology within reach. He picked up his phone to dial home when something caught his eye miles below. Fire and smoke, billowing black and yellow, rose from a boundless stretch of millions of horsemen and horses on the run across the ocean, heading for land.

NINETEEN

Three Months Later

AUGUST broke hot and humid in Mount Prospect, and Rayford was nearly as motionless as the wind. The safe house was not air-conditioned, and with the death of half the world's population since the Rapture, nothing was as it once had been.

An ominous foreboding settled over the house. Tempers were short, nerves raw. The baby was walking now and talking a bit, proving to be the only entertaining diversion. But Kenny was also cranky in the heat, and even Tsion had been known to leave the room when he fussed and Chloe wasn't quick enough to mollify him.

If the Rapture had brought a collective global wail over the loss of loved ones and all children, and the great wrath of the Lamb earthquake had changed where people lived and how they moved about, the judgments since had been even worse. The temporary darkening of the sun, moon, and stars, the scorching of a third of the earth, the poisoning of a third of the water, and now the slaying of more than a billion people . . . well, Rayford thought, it was a wonder anyone remained sane.

Maybe they hadn't. Maybe they had all gone mad. Rayford entertained thoughts he knew were ludicrous. Might he still wake up beside his precious but neglected and unappreciated wife Irene, with Raymie down the hall, only twelve, Rayford still with time to become the husband and father he should have been? Had this all been a Scrooge-type dream giving him a glimpse of what life would be like if he didn't change his ways?

Could he wake up a new man, ready to give his life to God, to be the right kind of influence on his daughter, his wife, his son?

It was possible, wasn't it? Couldn't it still have been simply the worst imaginable nightmare? Rayford knew his finite brain had not been programmed to assimilate everything he had been through. He never again wanted to catalog all he had seen, all he had lost. It had been more than a mortal could endure, and yet here he was.

The world had been invited to the Global Gala a month hence in Jerusalem. How dare Carpathia do it? How dare he deem it acceptable to celebrate when more people had been slain in the latest plague than had been raptured three and a half years before?

Tsion warned his audience not to go, to not be tempted by the prophecies that pointed to that date as the downfall of the one-world faith, the due time for the two witnesses, and the death of even Carpathia himself. Though he lived in the same house, like everyone else who resided there, Rayford also read Tsion's missives each day. On the subject of the despicable Global Gala, Tsion had written:

> Strangely, I have been invited as an "international statesman." All has been forgiven, amnesty declared for dissidents, our security guaranteed. Well, dear loved ones, friends, and brothers and sisters in Christ, I shall not attend. An earthquake is prophesied that will wipe out a tenth of that city. I do not fear for my own well-being, as my future is secure— as is yours if you have trusted Christ for forgiveness and eternal life.
>
> But I do not choose to personally witness even such unique, historic events when it is clear by their very nature that Satan himself will make his presence felt. My own family was butchered in retaliation for my "sin" of

going public with my belief that Jesus is the long-sought Messiah. During my flight from my homeland and even all the way to where I am exiled, I was oppressed by the awful presence of the author of death.

Death will be in the air in Jerusalem next month, my friends, regardless how the event is packaged and sold to the world. It is an outrage that a festival is the excuse given to bring these parties together. On the one hand the so-called world potentate decrees an end to sacrifices and offerings in the temple, because they violate the tenets of tolerance espoused by the Enigma Babylon One World Faith. On the other he aims to celebrate the agreement between the Global Community and Israel. How do these figure together? While it is true he has intimidated the impotent world and kept potential enemies from attacking Israel, he tramples upon her centuries-old traditions and betrays her heritage and religious autonomy.

Like the rest of the world, I will follow the proceedings on the Internet or on television. But no, dear ones, I shall not accept the invitation to attend. This event portends the second half of the Tribulation, called the Great Tribulation, which will make these horrific days seem languorous.

Even the GC-controlled news media can no longer sugarcoat what we know to be true. Crime and sin are beyond control. The necessities of life are in short supply due to lack of a workforce and ways to manufacture and distribute them. Yet there is not a neighborhood on earth that does not have a brothel, a séance and fortune-telling parlor, or a pagan temple expressly for worshiping idols. Life is cheap, and our fellow citizens die every day as marauders loot their homes and businesses and persons. There are not enough Peacekeepers still alive to do police work, and the ones who are on the job are either overwhelmed or corrupt.

With people simply gone from every walk of life, it is amazing what continues to flourish. New movies and television programming are virtually nonexistent, but there is no shortage of pornography and perversion on the hundreds of channels still available to anyone with a receiver.

We are not surprised that these are dark days, brothers and sisters, and I pray you would hold on and maintain and continue to try to share the truth of Jesus until he comes. Merely surviving from this point will occupy most of your time. But I urge you to prepare, have a plan for what you will do when that inevitable day arrives where it is not just illegal to tap into this Web site or declare yourself a believer. Be ready for that day when the insidious mark of the beast is required on your forehead or hand for you to legally buy or sell.

And above all, do not make the fatal mistake of thinking that you can take that mark for the sake of expediency while privately believing in Christ. He has made plain that those who deny him before men, he will deny before God. And in later teachings I will elucidate on why the mark of the evil one is irrevocable.

If you have already trusted Christ for your salvation, you have the mark of the seal of God on your forehead, visible only to other believers. Fortunately, this decision, mark, and seal is also irrevocable, so you never need fear losing your standing with him. For who shall separate us from the love of Christ? Shall tribulation, or distress, or persecution, or famine, or nakedness, or peril, or sword? In all these things we are more than conquerors through him that loved us. With the apostle Paul, I am persuaded that neither death, nor life, nor angels, nor principalities, nor powers, nor things present, nor things to come, nor

height, nor depth, nor any other creature
shall be able to separate us from the love
of God, which is in Christ Jesus our Lord.

In spite of and in the midst of every trial
and tribulation, let us continue to give thanks
to God, who gives us the victory through
our Lord Jesus Christ. And as the Scriptures
say, "Therefore, my beloved brethren, be
steadfast, immovable, always abounding in
the work of the Lord, knowing that your
labor is not in vain in the Lord."

Steadfast in love for you all, your friend,
Tsion Ben-Judah.

● ● ●

Hattie was in prison and without knowledge of
her sister's death, and Rayford felt responsible
for her.

The murders of Dwayne and Trudy Tuttle had
broken his heart.

The reaction of Bo Hanson to the loss of his
brother served only as another nail in the coffin
that bore Rayford's despair. Rayford and T
had agreed that T should break the news to Bo.
T had befriended him, despite their differences,
while Rayford had estranged him. Rayford
hoped that T might open a door of witness
to Bo by compassionately bearing the awful
news. Then perhaps Rayford would be able to

apologize for his behavior and have a part in seeing Bo come to Christ.

T had returned encouraged from his meeting with Bo. He had called him, met him in his apartment, and told him what had happened. He reported that the tearful Bo had asked, "What about the note I got from Sam?"

"I told him it had been forged by the GC, Ray," T said. "He seemed to be all right. He cried a lot, blamed himself. Said he sold his brother out just for money. But he hadn't sold him out. He had merely made the mistake of getting him involved in an ill-conceived plan. He was down when I left him, but he let me pray with him. I thought that was a huge step."

"I'm sure it was," Rayford said, "but you didn't ask to see me so you could give me good news. What happened?"

T sat back and sighed. "Bo killed himself last night, Ray. Drank himself sick at a bar, waved a gun around, cursed Carpathia and the world, and shot himself."

Rayford had been inconsolable for days. "I might as well have pulled the trigger myself," he said.

The rest of the Trib Force offered the usual "can't blame yourself" speeches, and in the end he came to agree. He turned the blame on the one who had all the blame he needed: Nicolae Carpathia.

Rayford immersed himself in the prophetic passages about the death of Antichrist, never seeking Tsion's counsel or interpretation. In his feverish state he interpreted the Scripture the way he wanted to, shoehorning himself into the agent God would use to do the deed. When he read that "He who kills with the sword must be killed with the sword," and knew that even Tsion believed this was a reference to Antichrist, Rayford shuddered. Was this a message just for him? A later verse referred to "the beast who was wounded by the sword and lived." That had to be a reference to one of the heads of the beast "as if it had been mortally wounded, and his deadly wound was healed."

He didn't understand it all. Who could? But without Tsion's analysis, Rayford believed he had figured out these verses. Carpathia was to be mortally wounded in the head by a sword and then come back to life. A sword? What was it Albie called the superb killing machine Rayford had stashed behind loose bricks in the basement? Saber.

Could he—would he do it? Was it his duty? He shook his head. What was he thinking?

●　　●　　●

Mac missed Rayford. He had been the voice of reason, a mentor, a spiritual model. Mac enjoyed

David and Annie. Great kids. But hard to identify
with. Abdullah was a good first officer and a
wonderful flyer, but he could go days without
saying anything except in response to Mac.

Life was interesting, but it sure wasn't fun
anymore. Flying to the major capitals and listening in on Fortunato's incessant courting of the
ten kings was as sickening as it was fascinating.
Behind a podium on the tarmac at the airport in
Nairobi, Leon grandly welcomed to "His Excellency Nicolae Carpathia's cabinet of esteemed
regional potentates, the honorable Mr. Enoch
Litwala. How this great leader and renowned
pacifist was overlooked during the initial search
for a regional potentate of the United States of
Africa will go in the embarrassment file of the
history of the Global Community. We may have
come to him late, but we found him, didn't we?"

The crowds cheered their favorite son. Leon
continued, "His Excellency sends his heartfelt
greetings to Africa and his highest compliments
on your achievement of international goals.
And it is my singular pleasure, on his behalf, to
personally invite your new potentate to Jerusalem
in September for the Global Gala!"

After waiting for the crowd to quiet, Leon
affected a serious tone. "We have endured rough
times and much loss of life. But His Excellency is
sparing no expense for an international festival

like nothing ever seen before. Besides celebrating the halfway mark of the agreement with Israel, and I am so pleased he has given me permission to share this publicly with you, His Excellency is guaranteeing—you heard that right—guaranteeing an end to killer plagues. You ask how can he do this? The potentate is on record that if the two so-called witnesses at the Wailing Wall do not cease and desist their torment of Israel and the rest of the world, he will personally deal with them."

This message was repeated in every capital to enthusiastic response. Mac believed people were so tired of death and devastation and so addicted to their own sin that they looked forward to a return to life before the two prophets of doom had seemed to unleash the anger of heaven. Was it possible Carpathia would literally kill the pair? Hadn't he threatened to do that before? They had made a fool of him. But now he was making a guarantee. And he was also pledging to help people get to the Gala in spite of the disastrous loss of public services due to the decreased population.

"We are about to see a dramatic turn back toward our goals and ideals for a utopian society," Fortunato quoted Carpathia, and the Global Gala would mark the first step.

Bizarre, Mac thought, to see Antichrist himself

in a public relations nightmare, trying to salvage
his image.

In the capitals, Leon followed his praising of
the regional potentates with promises from the
Global Community for better services. "We're
going to work smarter *and* harder," he would
say, "to meet your needs. Within a decade, the
only memory of the population attrition will be
sadness for those we have lost. Inconvenience will
be a thing of the past as we work together until
cutting-edge technology brings us to a higher
level of services than we ever dreamed."

There were always photo opportunities for the
Carpathia-controlled press, in which Fortunato
gravely studied underdeveloped areas due to the
widespread deaths. Then he would kiss babies
and hold them aloft, proclaiming "the future of
the Global Community." Finally, with people in
the area encouraged and inspired, he would invite
the potentate back onto the opulent Phoenix 216
for "a high-level confidential meeting where your
leader can best represent the needs of this
region."

Fortunato would listen to the potentates, of
course, and make promises a million Carpathias
could never keep. But each private confab eventually centered on the "Enigma Babylon situation."
As Mac listened in, he found that most of the
potentates knew exactly what Leon was talking

about as soon as he raised the issue. A few wanted to know, "What situation is that?" but either way, by the time Leon took off for his next appearance, it was clear which potentates could be counted on. Stunning to Mac was that every one was on record in opposition to the overbearing Peter II.

That was so amazing that Mac requested a private phone chat with Tsion, despite the time difference. He went through Leah, as did all communication now, and assured her that he would understand if Tsion didn't have the time. But within a day, the two were on secure phones together.

"Captain McCullum, my friend, I am so grateful for all the inside information you have sent my way. It makes my work so much easier and gives me insights into the inner workings that I would never otherwise have. What can I do for you?"

"Well, sir, just a quick question, I hope. I know David has kept everybody up-to-date, through Leah, about the plot to rally the ten kings against Peter the Second. We know that not all the kings are even loyal to Carpathia, but every one of them is on board with this anti-Peter thing. Are they just blowing smoke with Fortunato, or am I naïve to believe what sounds like true anger and agreement?"

"Excellent question, Captain, and the only reason I have not dealt with it on the Net is that I feel it might be too revealing and I would then be inserting myself into history in the making. That is a dangerous precedent, and we must guard against trying to help God, as it were, fulfill his promises. If he says it will happen, it will happen.

"But as for the ten kings and their willingness to conspire against Peter the Second: This is biblical. God is working out his eternal plan. Just as in the Old Testament he used pagan armies to punish his own people and today he uses demon hordes to get the attention of unbelievers, he is also using these kings. Revelation 17 says, 'And the ten horns which you saw on the beast' (these are the kings, Mac), 'these will hate the harlot' (that is the false religion, represented now by Peter the Second), 'make her desolate and naked, eat her flesh and burn her with fire.'

"Now get this, Captain. The next verse answers your question. The reason they are agreeing on this when in truth they are all egomaniacs who agree on little—not even on Carpathia—is this. Listen as I read. 'God has put it into their hearts to fulfill His purpose, to be of one mind, and to give their kingdom to the beast, until the words of God are fulfilled.'"

"Wow."

"Isn't that something? It is amazing to witness the fulfillment of prophecy."

"Thank you, sir."

"You will find these kings of one mind, because God said so. And you know it will mean the demise of Peter, don't you?"

"I figured that."

"The question is how and where it will happen."

"I have an idea," Mac said.

"*Really*," Tsion said.

Mac told him of the private conversation between Leon and the newest king, Kenyan Enoch Litwala. Fortunato had listened through Litwala's list of suggestions and demands, taking notes, telling him what he thought he heard him saying, and so forth, then got to the Peter the Second issue:

"His Excellency has asked that I raise with you personally a most delicate situation. He most admires your wisdom and ability to size up circumstances, but this is a matter with which you may not be familiar. Are you aware of any, shall we say, hesitation on the part of the other regional potentates concerning the, ah, visibility of Peter the Second?"

Litwala had responded so quickly that Mac had sat up in the cockpit and pressed the earphone tighter. "I don't know or care what my colleagues think," Litwala said, "but I will speak my own heart. I despise the man. He is egotistical, legalistic, self-possessed. He has appropriated huge amounts of money for his Enigma Babylon that should have been used in my country for my people. I do not find him loyal to His Excellency the potentate, and—"

"Indeed?"

"As soon as he heard I was being considered for this post he came to see me, flew all the way here, I believe on this very plane. Was this not his before?"

"It was."

"He tried to elicit my support for his playing a larger role in world governance, aside from religion. I said nothing. I believe he has too much influence *now*. Why would I want him to have more? I told him I would study his proposals and, should I be so honored as to be chosen for this position, I would consult more experienced regional potentates about their views. That seemed to please him. He tried to pry from me any negative thoughts I had about His Excellency, but I just listened. I did not challenge or counter him, but neither did I reveal precisely where I stood. That might prove valuable later."

"It's good, Potentate Litwala. He believes he has the support of the others and likely assumes you will fall in line. Do you agree he is potentially a danger to the harmony of Global Community leadership?"

"Not potentially. Presently."

"What would you propose we do about it? That is His Excellency's question of you."

"He would not appreciate my deepest feelings."

"You might be surprised."

"If the potentate appreciates that I believe Peter needs to be eliminated, yes, that would surprise me."

"By eliminated, you mean diplomatically removed from—"

"By eliminated, Supreme Commander, I mean eliminated."

There was silence over the reverse intercom for a moment. Litwala spoke first. "My problem is that I trust few. After what I have endured with Rehoboth and others . . ."

"I'm telling you the other potentates are agreed on this," Leon said.

"They would have him eliminated?"

"They would."

Another pause. "But who would do it?"

"You need to talk with them about that."

"There must be a way to ensure we're in it together, without the possibility of betrayal. We must all be equally culpable."

"Like all contributing to the remuneration for the—"

"No," Litwala said. "We must all have equal responsibility and liability."

After Litwala left the aircraft, Mac heard Fortunato on the phone with Carpathia. "Did you pick a winner with the new African potentate! . . . You did? . . . You're not serious. . . . You are! . . . That is amazing. Have you ever done that to me? . . . Planted thoughts? . . . Tell me what he'll suggest. . . . All ten of them? At the same time? So no one can point the finger at another. Brilliant."

Mac called David. "Have you got a tap on Carpathia's phone?"

"Always."

"Check it. You remember the story Buck Williams tells about how Nicolae told people what they saw and what they would remember? I think Nicolae just revealed to Leon that he's done something like that again."

"They're talking now?"

"Right now."

"I'll listen to 'em live, Mac. Safe trip."

● ● ●

By the time David got patched in to Carpathia's phone, Nicolae and Leon were finishing their conversation.

"I can be totally free of it that way," Carpathia was saying. "No one willing to talk, no weapon, no body. Enough DNA in the ashes to identify the body if there is any question, but as Peter will never turn up again, I cannot imagine there being a doubt."

"And who would corroborate the disease? Dare they involve yet another party?"

"Leon! Think! Od Gustav."

"Ah, yes! *Doctor* Gustav. Who needs an outsider when one of the ten can sign the death certificate? Did I say you were brilliant, Excellency?"

"Probably, but even the confident man can take hearing that more than once."

"Well, the ice idea. I mean, really. There's no other word for that."

"Thank you, Commander. Safe trip."

David smirked at the repeat of how he had signed off with Mac. Two buddies saying good-bye. Dave and Mac; Nick and Lee. Both pairs playing games, outsmarting the competition. He sighed. The difference between the pairs of friends was only eternal.

David quickly moved from listening live to listening to the recording from the beginning, when Fortunato had said, "Did you pick a winner with the new African potentate!"

"How well I know," Carpathia said. "I hand-picked him the day I first visited the U.N. I knew I would have to wait while we worked our way through either Ngumo or Rehoboth. I found him *very* suggestible."

"You did?"

"From the beginning. I hypnotized him on the phone once. Told him he would be unswervingly loyal to me, that my enemies would be his enemies and my friends his friends."

"You're not serious."

"Shall I prove it? He is willing to eliminate Peter, and he means eliminate."

"You are!"

"But he wants them all in on it, all ten of them. How am I doing?"

"That is amazing. Have you ever done that to me?"

"Done what?"

"Planted thoughts?"

"I do not need to, Leon. You are my most trusted friend and adviser. With Enoch I have even verbally implanted a whole plan in his mind. He will think about it, and when he comes back, he will suggest what is already in his head."

"Tell me what he'll suggest," Leon said.

"A meeting in Jerusalem the morning before the gala. He will invite Peter and tell him it is to discuss his succession to my role if a certain plan of theirs is carried out. It would be a meeting of just Peter and the potentates."

"All ten of them?"

"Yes. And it will be at the fancy new Global Community Grand Hotel, where the ice sculptures have become so popular. For the meeting they will order the large sculpture of Peter himself, the one that depicts him as a mighty angel, life size, with the huge wings with pointed feathers. As the ten are admiring it, each will break off one of those thick feathers with the sharp ends, and as Peter is wondering what in the world it is all about, each will plunge his into him from different angles—neck, eye, temple, heart."

"At the same time?" Leon said. "So no one can point the finger at another. Brilliant."

"The weapons will melt, the body will be transported to a crematorium in a bag brought in Scandinavian Potentate Gustav's briefcase. The body will be burned to avoid the spread of the deadly disease that causes one to bleed to death through his mucous membranes."

"Which will explain any blood in the meeting room."

"Exactly. I can be totally free of it that way. No one willing to talk, no weapon, no body. Enough DNA in the ashes . . ."

TWENTY

BUCK was getting the cold shoulder.

It had been a long time since he and Chloe had found themselves at loggerheads. "I know it's only three and a half more years," she said, "but do you think I want to raise this child alone?"

"Nothing's going to happen," he said, reaching for her. She turned away.

"You're going," she said. "It's written all over you. I love Chaim, but it was unfair of him to ask."

"If I don't go, Tsion's going to go, and we don't want that."

Chaim Rosenzweig had been invited to appear at the Global Gala as an honored guest of His Excellency the potentate. Chaim had Jacov communicate to the Tribulation Force by posting a cryptic message on Tsion's Web site. Leah had found it, almost by accident.

"Is this anything?" she asked Rayford late one

night when the two were working at their computers in the kitchen. "The initials aren't a coincidence, are they?"

She turned her laptop so he could see. The message was one of thousands posted on the site, most encouraging Dr. Ben-Judah, some asking questions, some criticizing or threatening. Part of Leah's job was to monitor those and see if any required personal responses. Most didn't. This post stuck out due to its brevity and the unique initials. It read: "C (B) W call J re boss. Signed, H's."

"I don't know who *J* is or what *H*'s means," she said, "but how many people know they can reach Cameron (Buck) Williams at this site? Or am I reading into it?"

Rayford studied it and summoned Buck. The three huddled in front of Leah's screen and stared. Buck suddenly stood. "Jacov," he said. "Pretty crafty. He's Hannelore's husband, and he wants to talk about Chaim."

Buck checked his watch and phoned. It was seven in the morning in Israel. Jacov was an early riser. "He's been invited to the Gala," Jacov said quickly. "None of us thinks he should go. He has not been well, staying up all hours. He looks terrible. Talk him out of it."

Chaim didn't sound well. He seemed to be trying to be his jovial self, but his thick Israeli

accent sounded weary and sometimes slurred.
"I will not be dissuaded, Cameron, but I have
insisted that I be allowed to bring my valet and
two guests. I was assured I could bring anyone
I wanted. Stefan is petrified of Carpathia and
insists he will quit my staff before he would
attend. Jacov has agreed to serve as both driver
and valet."

"Dr. Rosenzweig, you don't want to do this.
You've read Tsion's warnings, and—"

"Tsion's warning is for what the Global Community calls the Judah-ites. I love Tsion and
consider him one of my own, but I am *not* that
kind of Judah-ite. I am going, but I want you and
Tsion there with me."

Buck rolled his eyes. "Forgive me, Doctor, but
that is naïve. We are both persona non grata with
the GC, and we trust Carpathia's security pledge
as far as we can throw it."

"They said I could bring any guests I wanted."

"They didn't know whom you had in mind."

"Cameron, you and I have become close, have
we not?"

"Of course."

"More than just a journalist and a subject, am
I right?"

"Certainly, but—"

"You are a cosmopolitan person. You should
know that in my culture it is highly offensive

to rebuff a formal invitation. I am formally inviting you and Tsion to attend the Gala with me, and I will take it as a personal insult if you do not."

"Doctor, I have a family. Dr. Ben-Judah has millions who count on his—"

"You would both be with *me!* The Carpathia regime has committed some heinous acts, but to threaten the safety of someone as prominent as Tsion in the presence of a guest of honor . . ."

"I can tell you right now, sir, that Tsion will not be coming. I'm not even sure I will pass along the invitation. He would want to do what you ask because he loves you so, but it would be irresponsible of me to—"

"Do you not love me also, Cameron?"

"Yes, enough to tell you that this is—"

"I will withdraw my invitation of Tsion if I know you will be there."

Buck hesitated. "I couldn't come under my own name anyway. And though I look different enough to get through customs, I could never appear with you if you are close to GC brass. They would recognize me instantly."

Chaim was silent for a moment. Then, "I am very sad that two of my dearest friends, friends who say they care deeply about me—"

"Sir, don't. This is not becoming. You want

me to come because you've made me feel guilty? Is that fair? Are you thinking of me and my wife and my child?"

Rosenzweig, totally out of character, ignored Buck's mention of his family. "What would Tsion say if you told him I might be ready to become a Judah-ite?"

Buck sighed. "For one thing, he hates that term with a passion. You of all people should know Tsion well enough to know that this is not about him, not about his developing a following. And to dangle a decision about your eternal soul as a bargaining ch—"

"Cameron, have I ever asked for anything? For years I have considered you a young man whose admiration for me is unwarranted but cherished. I don't believe I have ever taken advantage of that. Have I?"

"No, and that's why this—"

"You are a journalist! How can you not want to be here for this?"

Buck had no answer. In truth he had wanted to attend since the moment he heard of the Gala. He could hardly believe Carpathia himself was hosting the event at which so much prophecy would culminate. But he had never seriously considered going. He had been encouraged by how easily he had traveled to and from Israel under an alias not long before. But Chloe. Kenny.

Tsion's stance on any believer attending. Buck considered it out of the question.

Now Chaim had finally tapped into the core of Buck's being. Pagan or believer, single or married, childless or a father, he had been a journalist for as long as he could remember. He had been curious as a child—nosy, his friends and family said—before he'd ever had a conduit through which he could publish his findings. His trademark was incisive eyewitness reporting, and he was never happier than when he was on a story, not hidden away in a safe house where all he could do was comment on previously published material.

His hesitation seemed to feed Rosenzweig, as if he knew Buck had taken the bait and now all the old man had to do was yank the line to set the hook.

"It's not that I don't *want* to be there," Buck said weakly, hating the whine in his voice.

"Then you'll come? That would mean so much to—"

"This is not a decision I can make independently," Buck said, and he realized he had turned a corner. He had gone from a flat refusal to mulling a full-blown prospect that had to be decided.

"That is another distinction between our cultures," Chaim said. "A Middle Eastern man is his own person, charting his own course, not answerable to—"

"I cannot be seen with you," Buck said.

"Just knowing you are there will warm me, Cameron, and surely we will be able to interact privately at some point. I will withdraw my formal invitation to Tsion, and I will not procrastinate about our spiritual discussions any longer."

"You don't need to wait for me for that, Doctor. In fact, I would urge that before you even dream of attending the Gala you would—"

"I need to discuss these things in person, Cameron. You understand."

Buck didn't, but he feared if he spent any more time on the phone he would make more concessions. He was sure to incur the wrath of the rest of the Trib Force regardless, so Buck negotiated one condition.

"I must insist on one thing," he said.

"Oh, Cameron, you're not going to go back on your word now, are you?"

"I could not sanction your being there on the second day of the pageant."

Chaim was silent, but Buck heard papers rustling in the background. "It is a five-day event," Rosenzweig said, "Monday through Friday next week. Monday is the anniversary of the treaty. Nicolae wants me on the platform for that celebration. Tuesday is a party at the Temple Mount, which I fear will turn into a confrontation between him and your preacher friends. That is what you want me to avoid?"

"Exactly."

"Granted."

"Thank you, sir."

"My packet of information requests the honor of my presence at both the opening and closing ceremonies. That would be Monday night and Friday night."

"My preference is that you not go at all."

"I heard you say you would be there."

●　　●　　●

Annie and David had become even closer. He felt bad when she told him that sometimes she felt he appreciated her more as a co-subversive than as one who loved him. Glancing around to be sure they were alone at the end of a corridor, he took her face in his hands and touched the tip of his nose to hers. "I love you," he said. "Under any other circumstances, I'd marry you."

"Is that a proposal?"

"I wish. You can imagine the pressure, the stress. You have it too. The only other two believers I've seen here besides us and Mac and Abdullah, those two women in inventory, were somehow found out last night."

"Oh, no! We hadn't even made contact yet. They probably thought they were alone."

"They were shipped to Brussels this morning."

"Oh, David."

"Odds are we aren't going to be here much longer either. I don't know exactly when the mark requirement is coming, but we have to escape first."

"I want to be your wife, even if only for a few years."

"And I want you to be, but we can't do anything like that until we know whether we can get out of here together. If one escapes and the other doesn't, that's no kind of life."

"I know," she said. "We're likely to be the first to know when Carpathia does start requiring a mark of loyalty. And you know he'll start right here in the palace."

"Probably."

"Meanwhile, David, you might want to tell the stateside Force that if they need to travel, now's the best time. I saw a document that's going to the Peacekeeping Force around the world. It calls for a moratorium on arrests or detainment, even of enemies of the Global Community, until after the Gala."

● ● ●

There had been no keeping the Rosenzweig request from Tsion, of course, and Tsion had been unusually melancholic ever since. "I will not tell you what to do, Buck," he said in front of Rayford, "but I wish your father-in-law would pull rank on you."

"Frankly," Rayford said, at the next meeting of the household, "I wish I were going with Buck."

"You're letting him go," Chloe said, with her fourteen-month-old on her lap. Kenny turned to face her and put his hands over her eyes as she spoke. She turned her head so she could see. "I can't believe it. Well, why don't you go with him, Dad? Why don't we all go? Bad enough we won't all make it to the end of the Tribulation anyway, why don't we throw caution to the wind? Why don't we make sure Kenny is an orphan without even a grandfather?"

"Kenny!" the baby said. "Grandpa!"

Rayford slapped his thighs and opened his arms, and Kenny slid off Chloe's lap and ran to him. Rayford lifted him over his head, making him squeal, then sat him on his lap. "The fact is, I have a different trip in mind for me."

"This is just great," Chloe said. "Do we vote on anything anymore, or do we all just pull a Hattie and run off to wherever we want?"

"This is not really a democracy," Rayford said, and judging by the look he got from Tsion, realized he was on shaky ground. The baby climbed off him and toddled into the other room. "Leah and I have been talking, and—"

"Leah's going somewhere too?" Chloe said. "She's invaluable to me here."

"I won't be gone long," Leah said.

"It's a foregone conclusion then?"

"This is more announcement than discussion," Rayford said.

"Clearly. Well, let's hear it."

Rayford began carefully, fearing his own motive. In his heart of hearts he wanted to get to Jerusalem with his Saber. But he said, "We need to make contact with Hattie. I feel responsible for her, and I want to know she's all right, let her know we're still standing with her, see what we can do for her. Mostly, I want to make sure she's not given us away."

Even Chloe did not argue. "She deserves to know about her sister," she said. "But the GC will be watching for you, Dad."

"They will be less likely to suspect a woman. We're thinking of making Leah Hattie's aunt on her mother's side, giving her a new look and, of course, a new ID. She'll say she's heard a rumor or got word smuggled out somehow that Hattie's there. If they don't associate Leah with us, why shouldn't they allow the contact?"

"But now, Dad? With Buck going?"

"David's told us now is the best time to travel. It's going to become nearly impossible soon."

"That is true," Tsion said.

Rayford looked up in surprise, and he noticed others did too.

"I'm not supporting this," Tsion said. "But if that poor child dies in prison apart from God, when we had her under our own roof for so long . . ." His voice quavered and he paused. "I don't know why God has given me such a tenderness toward that woman."

Chloe sat shaking her head, and Rayford knew she was not happy, but through arguing.

"T believes it would be too risky for me to start cruising around in the Super J, so he's prepping the Gulfstream."

"It shouldn't surprise me that this is virtually set," Chloe said. Rayford sensed a resigned admiration, as if she had conceded that once he got something in his brain, it happened.

"Buck can fly with us to Brussels—that'll save us a few dollars—and continue commercially to Tel Aviv. I'll stay out of sight in Belgium and meet up with Leah when she's ready."

"Maybe Buck could fly back with you too," Chloe said. "Depending on how long you want to wait for him in Brussels."

"Maybe," Rayford said. "Would you prefer that?"

"Would I prefer he fly home with my dad rather than taking his chances with a commercial system that is half what it used to be? Yes, I would prefer that. Of course, I prefer he not go, but short of that, humor me."

●　　●　　●

The mood was festive on the Phoenix 216 when Mac and Abdullah took off Saturday morning for Israel with a full load. It seemed the entire Carpathia administrative team was on board, and Nicolae was in his glory. Mac listened in as Leon clapped for attention and asked people to gather. "Welcome, everyone," he said. "And to our very special guest, who selflessly bequeathed His Excellency this aircraft at a time of dire need, a special welcome to you, sir."

There was polite applause, and Mac wished he could see Peter Mathews's face. "Would you care to say a word before His Excellency addresses us, Pontifex?"

"Oh, why, yes, thank you, Commander. I, we, at Enigma Babylon look forward to the Gala with much anticipation—Israel is, as you know, one of the last areas to acquiesce to our ideals. I believe that we will have the opportunity to put our best face on the one-world faith and that we will come away from this week with many more members. I frankly relish opportunities to challenge dissidents, and with the two preachers and the history of the Judah-ite rallies here, this is the place to do just that. Good to be with you."

"Thank you, Supreme Pontiff," Leon said. "Now, Your Excellency . . ."

Carpathia sounded ecstatic with expectation. "My personal greetings and welcome to you all," he said. "I believe you will one day look back on this coming week as the beginning of our finest hour. I know we have suffered the way the whole world has with the plagues and death. But the future is clear. We know what we have to do, and we will do it. Enjoy yourselves. It is a festival, a party. Personal, individual freedom has never been more celebrated. And may I say, there are more places in Jerusalem than anywhere to indulge yourselves. Revel in the Epicurean and physical pleasures that appeal to you. Show the rest of the Global Community that they are allowed to pamper the flesh even after times of hardship and chaos. Let us ring in the new world with a festival like no one has ever seen. Many of you have been responsible for arranging entertainment and diversion, and for that I am grateful. I cannot wait to see the spectacle myself."

Mac and Abdullah enjoyed private rooms next to each other in the palatial King David Hotel, where Carpathia had reserved two entire floors. The rest of the entourage stayed not far away in accommodations no less opulent. The ten regional potentates would be housed at the GC Grand, another quarter mile away.

During the two days before the official opening
of the Gala, the cockpit crew was required to conduct tours of the 216 back in Tel Aviv. Early Monday morning they helped arrange transport from
Ben Gurion Airport to Jerusalem for the potentates
and their extensive entourages. Mac worked with
GC Security to off-load the metal detectors David
had put into the cargo hold, and these were set
up on either side of the gigantic outdoor platform
that had been erected not a half mile from the
Temple Mount and the Wailing Wall. Everyone
who would be on the platform, from entertainers
to VIPs, would pass through a metal detector on
one side of the platform or the other.

The stage floor was twelve feet off the ground
and a hundred feet square. A vast green tar-
paulin was canopied atop it to block the sun,
and massive scaffolding towers held the speaker
systems that would boom the music and speeches
to an expected two million revelers. All across
the back of the stage, filling a flowing curtain
designed to coordinate with the canopy, were
various messages in every major language. These
welcomed the delegates, announced the dates of
the five days of the Global Gala, and featured
huge sparkling logos of the Global Community.

The largest statement printed on the back-
drop, Mac noticed, read, One World, One Truth:
Individual Freedom for All. All around the plaza,

on every lamppost, fence, and wall, was the slogan
Today Is the First Day of the Rest of Utopia.

As Mac and Abdullah aided with the placement
of the metal detectors, several bands and dance
troupes rehearsed and sound technicians swarmed
the area. Mac pulled Abdullah close and whispered, "I must be seeing things. Who does that
girl, second from the left, look like to you?"

"I was trying not to watch," Abdullah said.
"But if you insist. Oh, my, I see the resemblance,
of course. But it is not possible. Is it?"

Mac shook his head. Hattie was in Brussels.
They knew that. This woman merely stuck out
from the other dancers because she looked a bit
older. The rest looked barely out of their teens.

The security chief reminded musicians and
dancers that none would be allowed on stage
beginning with Monday evening's opening ceremony without proper identification and without
passing through a metal detector. "If you've
got the big buttons or buckles and jewelry, be
prepared to take those off and have them checked
before you go through."

At a briefing of the security staff, Mac heard
the chief instruct the teams of plainclothes guards
who would work in shifts in the front of the
stage. "Particularly when the potentate is at the
microphone," he said, "maintain your position.
Let the audience move if you're blocking their

vision. You stand in a semicircle, eight at a time, four feet apart, hands clasped at your belt. Eyes forward, no talking, no smiling, no gesturing. If you are summoned through your earpiece, do not respond orally. Just do what you're told."

Mac felt a deep sadness as he walked to a shuttle van that was to take him and Abdullah back to the King David. He glanced back at the stage from across a wide expanse of asphalt. Backed by deafening music, the dance troupe ended a lascivious routine.

"This is the new world, Abdullah. This is individual freedom, sanctioned by the international government."

"Celebrated even," Abdullah said. Suddenly he stopped and leaned against a fence. "Captain, these are the times when I long for heaven. I don't want to die, especially the way I have seen others' lives end. But to survive until the Glorious Appearing will be no easy thing."

Mac nodded. "What happened to the Tuttles was awful," he said. "But they probably never knew what hit them. They woke up in heaven."

Abdullah turned his face to the sun and a cloudless sky. "God forgive me if that is what I wish for. Quick and painless."

Mac could hear Eli and Moishe preaching from half a mile away but couldn't make out their words. "I've heard so much about them," he said. "I don't suppose we should risk being seen there."

"I would love to see them," Abdullah said. "How about we walk back to the hotel and at least go past there. We do not have to join the crowd, just see what we can see and hear what we can hear."

"Say no more, Smitty," Mac said.

All along the way Mac and Abdullah passed bars, strip clubs, massage parlors, brothels, pagan sanctuaries, and fortune-telling establishments. In a city with a history of religion dating back millennia, and where—like in the rest of the world—half the population had been wiped out since the Rapture, these businesses were not hidden. They were not seedy, not relegated to a certain inevitable section of town. Neither were they operating in darkness behind black doors or labyrinthine entrances that saved the "real" treats for those who were there on purpose.

Rather, while the rest of the Holy City seemed to crumble for neglect and lack of manpower, here were gleaming storefronts, well lit and obvious to every eye, proudly exhibiting every perversion and fleshly evil known to man.

Mac quickened his pace despite Abdullah's pronounced limp, and the two hurried toward the Temple Mount and the two witnesses as if from a sewer to a spring.

TWENTY-ONE

As HE was sure was true with others in the safe
house, Buck could not figure the relationship
between his father-in-law and Leah Rose. She
seemed a burr to Rayford, and yet surely he
had to appreciate what she had brought to the
Tribulation Force, besides her fortune.

Rayford was not above squabbling with her,
and she held her own. Yet they had seemed to
spend more and more time together as the time
drew near the halfway point of the Tribulation.
The announcement of Rayford's plan to fly her to
Brussels made their new closeness less mysterious
to Buck. Rayford apparently needed her to do
a job, and she was eager to do it. Maybe there
was nothing more to the relationship than that.

Zeke Jr., the tattooed Z for short, dolled up
splendid documents for Leah. With bleached-
blonde hair, darker contact lenses, and a tiny

dental appliance that gave her a not unattractive overbite and slightly bucked teeth, she was transformed. Leah was now Donna Clendenon from California, formerly married to one of Hattie Durham's mother's brothers. She carried news of Hattie's sister Nancy's demise (which was, unfortunately, true). That, Rayford speculated, would get her visitation privileges at the Global Community lockup in Brussels, which, typically, had been christened the Belgium Facility for Female Rehabilitation. Those familiar with it knew the BFFR, or Buffer, as a maximum-security prison. Dissident women went in, but they rarely came out. When they did, they were anything but rehabilitated.

Buck's hope—which he assumed was also Rayford's—was that the GC saw enough value in Hattie that they would not simply eliminate her. Carpathia must have seen her, at the very least, as bait to help lure Rayford, Buck, or even Tsion Ben-Judah. Those in the safe house hoped the GC hadn't lost patience with Hattie in frustration over twice nearly having had Rayford in their grasp.

Buck appreciated that the good-bye was not as bad as it would have been if Chloe had wanted to again vent her feelings. She had told him in private, as well as at the meeting, that she considered his interest in the Gala a reckless obsession.

"It's not that I would deprive you of covering one of the great historical events ever, but you're willingly walking into an earthquake, and the stakes are greater for you now than ever. You're more committed to your word to Chaim than to protecting your family."

But the day she and Tsion and the baby saw the other three off, Chloe had apparently decided she had no more need to make her points. Buck assumed she had resigned herself to his going. She gave him plenty of time with Kenny, then held him tight and promised her prayers and undying love. "And yours had better be undying too," she said.

"My love will not die, even if I do," he had said.

"That was not exactly what I wanted to hear."

He thanked her for letting him go. She punched him on the arm. "Like I had a choice. Didn't I make your life sufficiently miserable? I'm probably the reason you're going."

She seemed to maintain her good spirits, though tears came as Buck and Rayford and Leah pulled away from the house under Tsion's prayer, blessing, and "Godspeed!"

●   ●   ●

"Do you believe this?" Mac asked Abdullah as they gawked at the television lights and cables and satellites erected near the Wailing Wall. There seemed nearly as many cameras as at the festival site.

Abdullah, typically brief, merely shook his head.

Mac felt a thrill at seeing Eli and Moishe, even from a distance. They were preaching loudly and evangelistically, and the crowd seemed schizophrenic. Mac had heard that the preachers' audience was usually quiet, either out of respect or fear. They kept their distance from the strange pair—who had been known to incinerate attackers, leaving charred remains. No one wanted to be mistaken for a threat.

This crowd—larger than normal and boisterous—was apparently made up of early arrivers for the Gala. Some responded to the pair's every sentence, cheering, clapping, whistling, amen-ing. Others booed, hooted, catcalled. Mac could only gawk at several on the edge of the crowd who danced and ran toward the fence, as if showing their bravado. It was clear the preachers could distinguish would-be assassins from foolish newcomers who considered this just part of the Gala hullabaloo.

Strangest, however, was a group of about two dozen who seemed moved by the preaching. They knelt within ten feet of the fence and appeared to be weeping. Eli and Moishe traded sentences, pleading with the crowd to come to Christ before it was too late. These evidently were doing just that.

"One reason to be grateful," Mac said, "in the middle of all this."

The two witnesses seemed especially urgent. The timing was not lost on Mac. He was a student of Tsion's as much as anyone else was, and he knew the "due time" they had so often mentioned coincided with the opening day of the Global Gala half a mile away.

●　　●　　●

Further insight into the relationship—or the lack of one—between Rayford and Leah came to Buck on the drive to Palwaukee. Her conversation centered on Tsion.

Tsion?

"He seems so lonely," she said.

"He is," Rayford said. "Except for Chloe and Buck, we're single people in very artificial close quarters."

"Don't I know it," she said. She asked about the details of Tsion's life before he joined the Trib Force, so Buck filled her in.

At Palwaukee, T had the Gulfstream fueled and the charts on board. He had even stocked the refrigerator.

"That's above and beyond the call, T," Rayford said.

"Don't mention it. Our little church body is praying for you all, though I have, obviously, given them no details."

• • •

From Israel, Mac checked in with David in New Babylon late Sunday night. "It's like a ghost town here," David said. "I have free reign but no one to spy on. Annie and I are getting time together, but we spend it planning to escape from here and deciding where we'll go."

"Don't leave before you have to," Mac said. "We need you right where you are."

• • •

The clock showed two hours earlier, Belgian time, when Rayford put down in Brussels. He was as nervous as when he had approached Hattie's apartment door in Le Havre. He had to cover his feelings. For all his son-in-law and Leah knew, his job here was just chauffeur. How would they interpret uncalled-for nervousness?

"Donna" would check into a hotel not far from the infamous Buffer, planning to attempt a visit the next day. Buck, under his new alias, Russell Staub, would head for his commercial connection to Tel Aviv.

"You've memorized my secure phone number?"

Rayford asked Leah as he taxied closer to the terminal.

"Yours and Buck's."

"There's not much I can do for you if you can't reach Ray," Buck said.

"If I can't get hold of Rayford," she said, gathering her stuff, "I'll need someone to say good-bye to. Wish me luck."

"We don't do luck," Buck said. "Remember?"

"Oh, yeah," she said. "Pray for me then."

Rayford knew he should respond, but he was preoccupied. And Leah was gone.

"Where are you going to be, Ray?" Buck asked him.

Rayford shot him a look. "The less you know, the less you're accountable for."

Buck held up his hands. "Ray! I just mean generally. Have you got a place, things to do, ways to blend in?"

"I'm covered," Rayford said.

"And Leah knows everything we want to communicate to Hattie?"

"I wouldn't bring her all this way and have her go in there unprepared." He could tell he was annoying Buck. What was the matter with him?

"I'm just getting everything set in my head for my own peace of mind, Ray. I'm going into a stressful situation, and I want fewer things to worry about."

"You'd better get going," Rayford said, looking at his watch. "If you find a way to worry
about fewer things, let me know. We're sending
a brand-new mole to a prison, and smart as
she is, who knows what she'll do or say under
pressure?"

"*That* puts me at ease."

"Time to grow up, Buck."

"Time to lighten up, Dad."

"Be careful, hear?" Rayford said.

Rayford felt very lonely when Buck left the
plane. He was undecided about his quest, and he
knew what the others would think of it. If God
did use him to kill Carpathia, he couldn't imagine
escaping. He feared he had seen his loved ones
for the last time. And he hoped he wasn't putting
too much on Buck, who would have to somehow
get Leah back to the States.

Ten minutes after Buck disappeared into the
terminal, Rayford refueled and asked the tower
for clearance to take off. He had considered looking for any airstrip other than Ben Gurion or
Jerusalem, but decided his best chance at slipping
through under his new alias—Marv Berry—was
to go where the most traffic was. Ben Gurion.

●　　●　　●

It was all David could do, even with Annie's help,
to keep straight who was who now that three

stateside Trib Forcers were using aliases overseas. He made himself a card that listed the real initials, in reverse order, next to the alias. Thus: "RL Donna Clendenon; SR Marvin Berry; WC Russell Staub." For good measure he added Hattie's: "DH Mae Willie."

●   ●   ●

Buck flew directly into Jerusalem on a late flight and checked into a hostel under his alias. At midnight he took a cab to the Wailing Wall and found himself at the back of a crowd so large he could not see Moishe and Eli. He used the occasion to check in by phone with David, then Chloe, then Mac. Finally he called Chaim's number, and Jacov answered.

"Oh, Buck!" he said. "I had so hoped you would call! It's awful, terrible!"

"What?"

"Dr. Rosenzweig could not get out of bed this morning, and he could not communicate. He appeared paralyzed and afraid. He drooled and moaned and his left hand was curled, his arm straight. His mouth drooped. We called for an ambulance, but it took so long, I was afraid he would die."

"A stroke?"

"That's the diagnosis. They finally took him to the hospital and are running tests. We won't know the results until tomorrow, but it does not look good."

"Where is he?"

"I can tell you, Buck, but you will not be allowed in. Not even any of us have been allowed to see him. He's in intensive care, and they say his vital signs look good for now, everything considered. But we are worried. All the time before the ambulance arrived, we prayed over him and pled with him to become a believer. Because he could not talk, I kept watching his forehead for evidence that he had prayed. But I saw nothing. He looked angry and frightened and kept waving me away with his good hand."

"Jacov, I'm so sorry. Keep me posted any time there's even a small change."

"We don't dare call your number from here. Your phone is secure, but ours isn't."

"Good thinking. I'll check in whenever I can. And I'll pray."

●   ●   ●

Rayford—as Marv Berry—was detained only briefly in the busy customs area, where an agent bought his story that the heavy metal box in his suitcase was a computer battery. Rayford rented a tiny car and checked into a seedy hotel on the west side of Tel Aviv. He called Leah's hotel in Brussels. It was well after midnight there, but he hoped with the time change and jet lag, she might be awake.

The hotel operator was unwilling to ring Mrs. Clendenon's room, but "Mr. Berry" insisted it was an emergency. Leah answered groggily on the sixth ring, and Rayford was impressed that she had her wits about her. "This is Donna," she said.

"It's Marv. Did I wake you?"

"Yes. What's wrong?"

"Everything's fine. Listen, it's going to be impossible to pick you up until Friday."

"What?"

"I can't get into details. Just be ready Friday."

"Well, ah, Marv, I should be ready Tuesday."

"Don't try to call me before Friday, all right?"

"All right, but—"

"All right, Donna?"

"All right! You can't tell me anything more specific?"

"I would if I could."

● ● ●

Buck awoke early Monday and hurried to the Wailing Wall. The night before he had not been able to get close to Eli and Moishe, though he thrilled to see people coming out of the crowd and kneeling by the fence to receive Christ.

The witnesses had always spoken with power

and urgency, but Buck could tell from their delivery that they knew as well as anyone they were running out of time. The world had been left depleted of population with the plagues wrought by the 200 million horsemen, and those who survived seemed determined as ever to continue in their sin. Now it seemed the witnesses were making their last concerted effort to wrest souls from the evil one.

Monday crowds at the Temple Mount were even bigger, because the Gala would not begin until early evening, and hundreds of thousands of delegates were curious about the preachers they had only heard about before. The sophisticated sin businesses in the center of Jerusalem were crowded too, but the majority of tourists were gaping at the strange men preaching from behind the fence.

This was their 1260th and last day to preach and prophesy before the due time. Buck felt unspeakably privileged to be there. He shouldered his way through the crowd until he popped out of the front row, striding past new converts kneeling before the fence. Buck stood close enough that he could have touched the fence, closer to Eli and Moishe than anyone else was. Some from the crowd cautioned him, reminding him that people had died for such boldness. He knelt, his eyes on the two, and settled in to listen.

Eli held forth with Moishe sitting behind him, his back against the wall of a small stone building. "Watch that one!" someone shouted. "He's hiding the flamethrower!" Many laughed, but more shushed them. Buck was overwhelmed at the emotion in Eli's voice. Eli cried out, near tears, loud enough to be heard for blocks, though he was also being broadcast frequently over GC CNN. TV reporters throughout Jerusalem filed stories about the excitement building for the Gala that evening, and every other one, it seemed, came from right here at the Wall.

Eli shouted, "How the Messiah despaired when he looked out over this very city! God the Father promised to bless Jerusalem if her people would obey his commandment and put no other God before him. We come in the name of the Father, and you do not receive us. Jesus himself said, 'O Jerusalem, Jerusalem, thou that killest the prophets, and stonest them which are sent unto thee, how often would I have gathered thy children together, even as a hen gathereth her chickens under her wings, and ye would not! Behold, your house is left unto you desolate. For I say unto you, Ye shall not see me henceforth, till ye shall say, Blessed is he that cometh in the name of the Lord.' "

The crowd had fallen silent. Eli continued, "God sent his Son, the promised Messiah, who fulfilled more than one hundred ancient prophecies, including being crucified in this city. Christ's love compels us to tell you that he died for all, that those who live should no longer live for themselves but for him who died for them and was raised again.

"We are ambassadors for Christ, as though God did beseech you by us: we pray you in Christ's stead, be ye reconciled to God. For he hath made him to be sin for us, who knew no sin; that we might be made the righteousness of God in him. Behold, now is the accepted time; behold, now is the day of salvation.

"Neither is there salvation in any other: for there is none other name under heaven given among men, whereby we must be saved. Though this world and its false rulers promise that all religions lead to God, this is a lie. Jesus is the only way to God, as he himself declared, 'I am the way, the truth, and the life: no man cometh unto the Father, but by me.'"

Eli appeared exhausted and backed away from the fence. Moishe rose and proclaimed, "This world may have seen the last of us, but you have not seen the last of Jesus the Christ! As the prophets foretold, he will come again in power and great glory to establish his kingdom on this earth. The Lord is coming with thousands upon thousands of his holy ones to judge everyone, and to convict all the ungodly of all the ungodly acts they have done in the ungodly way, and of all the harsh words ungodly sinners have spoken against him.

"His dominion is an everlasting dominion, which shall not pass away, and his kingdom that which shall not be destroyed. Come to him this day, this hour! The Lord is not willing that any should perish, but that all should come to repentance. Thus saith the Lord."

Eli rose and joined Moishe and they called out in unison, "We have served the Lord God Almighty, maker of heaven and earth, and Jesus Christ, his only begotten son. Lo, we have fulfilled our duty and finished our task until the due time. O Jerusalem, Jerusalem . . ."

The two stood before the fence, unmoving, not blinking; their hair, beards, and robes wafting gently in the breeze. The crowd grew restless. Some called out for more preaching; others taunted. Buck slowly rose and backed away, knowing the two were finished with their proclamations. To many it would appear that Nicolae Carpathia had won. He had brought his Global Gala to Jerusalem and silenced the preachers.

●　　●　　●

Rayford was as afraid to run into Buck as into the GC. He had purposely not shaved the day of the flight or since. Late Monday he drove to Jerusalem, parked on the outskirts, and walked into the city. He wore a drab green turban over a longish gray wig, and dark sunglasses with tiny holes that allowed him to see almost as well as normal while hiding his eyes.

He wore a light ankle-length robe, common to the area. Deep in an inside pocket he carried the Saber. The robe was roomy enough that he could pull his hands inside through the armholes and separate the weapon without anyone seeing. Though he saw metal detectors on either side of the great stage, the thousands and thousands of onlookers were allowed into the area without being searched. He felt a tingle from the back of his head to his tailbone, knowing he was carrying a high-powered weapon with kill power from hundreds of feet away. After having been so eager to do this thing, he now pleaded with God to spare him the task. Would he be willing to follow through and kill Carpathia if God made *that* clear?

The crowd had gathered early, and the preopening act, a Latin band, was loud, the beat addictive. Half the crowd danced and sang, and more joined them as the afternoon wore on. Music, singing, and dancing, interspersed with excited predictions about the soon arrival of the potentate himself, whipped the crowd into delirium.

As the sky gradually darkened, Rayford kept

moving, milling about to ensure he would remain unnoticed. Once he nearly stopped and whipped off his sunglasses. He could have sworn Hattie had brushed past him. Heart racing, he turned and watched her go. Same height, same figure, same gait. Couldn't be. Simply couldn't be.

●　　　●　　　●

Mac and Abdullah strolled into the Gala plaza, now jammed with delegates. "You want to hang together or split up this week?" Mac said.

Abdullah shrugged. "If you want to be alone, it's no problem."

"It's not that," Mac said. "I just want you to feel free to be by yourself whenever you want."

Abdullah shrugged again. Truth was, Mac wouldn't have minded being alone. Alone in the huge crowd. Alone with his thoughts about how the world, and his life, had changed. He had come to a decision. If Carpathia somehow survived this event, if for some strange reason even Tsion Ben-Judah had been wrong in his assessment of the prophecies, Mac had a plan. Rayford had had a point. One of them should have pointed Nicolae's plane toward a mountain long ago, sacrificing himself for the good of all. Mac wouldn't be so selfish as to involve Abdullah. Somehow he would have to devise an exception that would allow him to fly the potentate by himself. He wouldn't even need a mountain, really. All he needed was to cut the power and let gravity take over.

Could he? Would he? He looked at Abdullah and scanned the crowd. This was no way to live.

●   ●   ●

Finally, helicopters appeared. Rayford looked up as the people cheered. The choppers landed on either end of the stage, and the dignitaries bounded out to thunderous applause. All ten regional potentates, the supreme commander, and a woman in gaudy Enigma Babylon vestments trotted up the stairs. From under the stage came the burly security detail that formed a half-circle around the lectern.

Only when everyone else was in place did Carpathia arrive alone in another copter. To deafening roars he was welcomed to the stage by the standing VIPs, all seeming eager to shake his hand. Fortunato was last and led the potentate to a chair big and ornate as a throne.

The rest sat when he did, but the seemingly endless applause brought Carpathia to his feet again and again to shyly, humbly wave. Each time he stood, so did all the others on stage. Rayford was about two hundred feet from the man and twice had drawn his hands inside his robe and fingered the Saber, sliding it open an inch, then closing it. He did not have a clear shot with so many people in front of him. If he was to do this, God would have to orchestrate it. Rayford would bide his time, see if God provided an opening or opened a path to the front. If anyone in that crowd fired at Carpathia, no one would notice him until after the first shot, so enamored were they with their potentate.

●   ●   ●

Buck, having reluctantly left the Wailing Wall, arrived late and stood at the back of the crowd of nearly two million. He watched the pageant unfold but could not bring himself to applaud. He worried about Chaim, tried to call Jacov, but found he couldn't hear anyway.

When the crowd finally quieted enough to allow Leon to have the floor, he turned to make sure Carpathia was seated for good, then mounted the lectern. "Welcome, fellow citizens of the new world," he began and was interrupted by applause for the first of dozens of times. Every phrase elicited enthusiasm, making Buck wonder what planet the crowd was from. Did no one hold the leadership responsible for all the death and grief? The population had been cut in half in three and a half years, and these people celebrated?

"My name is Leonardo Fortunato, and it is my privilege to serve you and His Excellency as

supreme commander of the Global Community.
I want to introduce your regional potentates,
whom I know you will welcome with the enthusiasm they deserve. But first, to seek the blessing
of the great god of nature, I call upon the assistant to the supreme pontiff of Enigma Babylon
One World Faith, who also has an announcement. Please welcome Deputy Pontiff Francesca
D'Angelo."

Buck was amazed that the deputy was apparently unfazed by catcalls and whistles. Suddenly
Buck was overcome with a chill that made goose-
flesh stand on his arms. As Ms. D'Angelo stood
at the lectern, Carpathia rose and the crowd—
rather than exult—fell deathly silent. Buck felt as
if he were the only one able to look anywhere but
at Carpathia. The potentates looked at him from
where they sat, and Fortunato too turned toward
him.

Carpathia spoke in the haunting, hypnotic
voice Buck had heard only one time. Three and
a half years before, Nicolae had committed a
double murder after having told everyone in the
room what they would remember and what they
would not. Buck, as a brand-new believer, had
been the only one protected from that mind
control. Later, no one else even remembered
Buck had been in the room.

Now the potentate spoke, yet his voice was not

projected over the loudspeakers. Buck, as far from the stage as anyone could get, heard him plain as day, as if standing next to him.

"You will not remember that I have interrupted," Nicolae said.

"Oh, God," Buck prayed silently, "protect me! Don't let me be swayed."

"You are about to hear of a death that will surprise you," Carpathia said, and no one moved. "It will strike you as old news. You will not care."

Carpathia sat down and the crowd buzz picked up where it left off. Ms. D'Angelo said, "Before I pray to the great one-gender deity in whom we all rest and who also rests in all of us, I have an announcement. Pontifex Maximus Peter the Second died suddenly earlier today. He was overtaken by a highly contagious virus that made it necessary that he be cremated. Our condolences to his loved ones. A memorial service will be held tomorrow morning at this site. Now let us pray."

Tomorrow morning? Buck thought. The Gala program called for a "debate" between Carpathia and "the Jerusalem Twosome" at 10 A.M. Tuesday, followed by a "noon to midnight party" in the hedonist district. Buck looked into the faces of delegates around him. They seemed unfazed. Buck was shaken. So Nicolae was capable of controlling the minds of two million at once.

The crowd applauded the prayer—which seemed to pay homage to every living cell. They cheered the introduction of each subpotentate, especially the newest, Mr. Litwala from Africa. The delegates seemed equally impressed with each potentate's samish speech, which praised Carpathia in every other sentence. Finally the moment came for the man of the hour.

"And now," Fortunato began, and the assembled sent up a roar that drowned out the rest of his introduction, except that Buck was standing under one of the speaker towers. "The man God chose to lead the world from war and bloodshed to a single utopian community of harmony, your supreme potentate and mine, His Excellency, Nicolae Carpathia!"

The rest of the VIPs—save Fortunato—humbly left the platform, leaving Carpathia waving with both hands and smiling, striding back and forth behind the sober security team. Leon, leading the ovation, stood behind Nicolae in front of a chair to the right of the throne.

TWENTY-TWO

IF ANYTHING, Buck decided, the speaking gift
Nicolae Carpathia had first demonstrated at the
United Nations three and a half years before
had only improved with time. Back then he had
used his prodigious memory, grasp of facts and
history, and mastery of several languages to wow
even the press. Who could remember when the
working media had risen as one to endorse a
rousing speaker?

Of course, that first internationally publicized
speech had come within days of the disappearance from the earth of millions of people, including all babies and most children. Carpathia had
appeared the perfect man for the perfect moment,
and a terrified world—including at first Buck—
embraced him. The globe seemed as one to
look to Carpathia as a voice of peace, harmony,
and reason. He was young, handsome, dynamic,

charismatic, articulate, brilliant, decisive, and—
incongruously—humble. It appeared he reluctantly accepted the mantle of leadership thrust
upon him by an adoring populace.

Nicolae had reinvented the world, dividing it
into ten regions, each with its own potentate. In
the midst of increasing strife that impacted the
globe even worse than the loss of millions at
the Rapture, he stood as the paternal voice of
comfort and encouragement. Through World
War 3, famine, the great wrath of the Lamb
earthquake, meteor strikes, maritime disasters,
contamination of waterways, global darkening
and cooling, swarms of scorpion locusts, and
more recently the plagues of fire, smoke, and
sulfur that had taken yet another third of the
population, still Carpathia held firm control.

There were rumors of insurrection on the
parts of at least three subpotentates, but nothing
had yet come of that. Grieving, desperate people
often railed about the new world and why it
seemed to get worse, only to have Nicolae calm
them over the airwaves with promises, sympathy,
and pledges of tireless effort.

They believed him, especially those whose lives
were dedicated to personal freedom at all cost.
While the Global Community rebuilt cities and
airports and roadways and communications
systems, murder, theft, sorcery, idol worship, and

sexual sin were on the rise. These latter three were actually applauded by Carpathia and by all who called bad good and good bad.

The only chink in Carpathia's armor was that he seemed impotent before the two witnesses in Jerusalem. That he would schedule his Global Gala to usher in "the first day of the rest of utopia" in the city where the two had held sway for so long appeared the height of cheek. If Nicolae was again humiliated by his inability to control them, if they could not be stopped from turning the water to blood and withholding rain, the fabric of his leadership might finally begin to fray.

Yet here he was, facing cameras that broadcast his image to international TV and the Internet. Now thirty-six, confident and charming as ever, he strode back and forth across the stage behind his security team. Not content to stay at the lectern, he kept moving, making sure his wave and smile reached every segment of the live audience that seemed unable to get enough of him.

Finally, finally he raised his hands and received undivided attention. Without notes, without pause, without a misspeak, Carpathia performed for forty-five minutes. He was interrupted by enthusiastic applause with nearly every phrase, and if he was animated at the beginning, he seemed even more energized by the end.

He acknowledged the hardships, the grief and sadness that came with individual loss, and the work that still needed to be done. He allowed a tear in his voice as he spoke of so many of "you beloved compatriots who have suffered bereavement."

As Carpathia surged toward his dramatic, flourishing conclusion, he spoke louder, more directly, even more confidently. To Buck it seemed the crowd was ready to burst with love. They trusted him, believed in him, worshiped him, counted on him for sustenance.

Nicolae took one dramatic interlude where he strode back to the side of the lectern, leaned against it with one hand, crossed his feet at the ankles, and put his other fist on his hip. His look, on the giant screens throughout the plaza, was cocky and arrogant and pregnant with promise. With an are-you-ready-for-this smirk that created murmurs of excitement, laughter, whistles, and applause, plainly he was ready to make some bold pronouncement.

Carpathia let the tension build, then stepped purposefully behind the lectern and gripped it with both hands. "Tomorrow morning," he said, "as you can see on your program, we will reassemble near the Temple Mount. There we shall establish the authority of the Global Community over ev-er-y geographic location."

Cheers and more cheers. "Regardless who is proclaiming this or warning that or taking credit for all manner of insidious attacks on this city, this area, this state . . . I will personally put an end to the religious terrorism perpetrated by two murderous imposters. I, for one, am tired of superstitious oppression, tired of drought, tired of bloody water. I am tired of pompous so-called prophecies, of gloom and doom, and of pie in the sky by and by!

"If the Jerusalem Twosome does not cease and desist tomorrow, I shall not rest until I have personally dealt with them. And once that is accomplished, we shall dance in the streets!"

The throng surged toward the stage, lustily cheering and chanting, "Nicolae, Nicolae, Nicolae!"

He shouted over the din, "Have fun tonight! Indulge yourselves! But sleep well so tomorrow we can enjoy the party that shall have no end!"

As the helicopters reappeared and people were cleared from the landing area, Carpathia waved and smiled as he headed toward the steps. Leon followed quickly and knelt, thrusting out his arms and waving in gestures of unworthiness. To Buck's amazement, most of the crowd followed suit. Tens of thousands dropped to their knees and worshiped Carpathia as they would an athlete or a performer . . . or a god.

● ● ●

Rayford was beside himself. To keep from being conspicuous in his refusal to kneel, he kept moving. Each step brought him closer to the front, and inside his robe he pulled the Saber from its block. The heavy, solid, lethal feel both invigorated and scared him. He felt as if he were dreaming, watching himself from afar. Had it come to this? Had he become this crazy man who had won out over the pragmatist? Unless he could somehow be sure this was God's plan, he didn't dare inject himself into history. Whoever was the assassin, he would never again be free, that was sure. The perpetrator would be identified on tape and wouldn't get far.

Rayford was within fifty feet of the stage when Carpathia gave a final wave, ducked, and disappeared aboard the helicopter. The chopper lifted off directly over Rayford's head, and he could have shot it from the sky. He gritted his teeth and slammed the Saber back into the block. He replaced it in the big inside pocket, pushed his hands back out through the armholes. Clenched teeth made his temples throb.

As the crowd flooded out to play, Rayford determinedly marched the miles back to his car, jaw still set, hands hidden by the billowy sleeves. Unless God made him, he would not do anything rash.

●   ●   ●

Buck missed his family. The spectacle at the Gala plaza left him sad. He sleepwalked the streets, idly following the crowd but making sure he was headed back toward his hostel. He called home, talked to Chloe, talked to Kenny, talked to Tsion. Called New Babylon, talked to David, "met" Annie. He hated to beg off after having talked to her for the first time, but a beep told him he had another call, and the readout showed it was Leah.

"Sorry to bother you, Buck," she said, "but I had a disconcerting day at Buffer and wanted to tell someone."

"No problem, but you're supposed to be briefing Rayford, aren't you?"

"I'm not supposed to even call him until Friday."

"What?"

She told him of Rayford's instructions.

"And if there's trouble?"

"I guess I'm to call you."

"What can I do? Rent a car and drive to France?"

"No, I know."

"Did you see Hattie?"

"They're considering my request and will let me know."

"Doesn't sound good."

"Seems fishy, Buck. I don't know whether to bolt or play it out."

"Let me call Rayford and find out what the deal is."

"Would you?"

Buck stopped under a streetlight within blocks of the Wailing Wall and called Rayford's personal phone. He would know who was calling from his own readout. Rayford answered. "This had better be important, Buck."

"I'd say hanging one of our own out to dry is important. How can you strand her like that?"

Rayford sounded bored. "What's her problem? She get herself in trouble?"

Buck brought him up to date.

"Tell her to stay with the plan and not to call you or me until Friday."

"What've you got going, Ray?"

"Buck, listen. When I told Leah I didn't want her to call me till Friday, I didn't expect her to run to you. I need you to trust me."

Buck sighed and reluctantly agreed. He decided not to tell Chloe that he and her dad might eventually have to have it out. He didn't know what the problem was.

Buck climbed a tree so he could see the Wailing Wall, and there were Eli and Moishe. They still stood shoulder to shoulder, staring, unmoving, in the same position as he had last seen them. Crowds taunted.

He called Jacov for a report on Chaim. "Good news and bad news," Jacov said. "The tests are positive."

"What can be bad?"

"The doctor can't determine the cause of the paralysis or the speech loss. It looks and acts like a stroke, but there doesn't seem to have been one."

●   ●   ●

The next morning Rayford rose and got an early start toward the Wailing Wall. The path was wet in spots, and from more than dew. He was stunned to find the crowds huge two hours before the vaunted confrontation. Rumors flew that the memorial service for Pontifex Maximus Peter the Second had been cancelled due to lack of interest and that Ms. D'Angelo had already been defrocked. Apparently Enigma Babylon would die with its founder. No room even for pagan religion in Carpathia's orbit.

With his Saber inside his robe, Rayford elbowed his way to the middle of the bustling crowd. He had not slept well, praying most of the night, and now he wished he could sit. But he endured. The witnesses stood like statues, as people said they had for hours. Surely they would become animated when Carpathia arrived to challenge them.

A block away loud bands rehearsed for the all day/all night party.

●   ●   ●

Buck tried to climb the same tree he had the night before, but GC Security shooed him away. He found a spot on a rocky ledge with a clear view over the crowd. He was saddened by the silence of the witnesses, wishing that when Carpathia arrived they would at least go down swinging. But the due time was upon them; this was the 1261st day. The Bible said they would be overcome.

At a minute to ten the sky came alive with helicopter rotors. As at the Gala site, three choppers brought the potentates, Fortunato, no Enigma Babylon rep this time, and finally Carpathia. It marked the first time Buck had seen him without a tie. He wore expensive shoes and slacks, an open-collar shirt, and a cashmere sport coat with what looked like a Bible protruding from one of the pockets.

The potentates and Fortunato stepped behind a barrier that separated them from the crowd. Lights beamed, cameras whirred, and Carpathia swept to the fence. His shirt was equipped with a wireless mike, and he stopped for a dab of powder from a makeup artist. He smiled to the noisy crowd and approached the witnesses, who stood still, only their chests moving with their breathing.

Carpathia, like a magician, whipped off his sport coat and hung it from the top of a pointed bar in the fence. Whatever was in the pocket made the coat sag to that side. When Nicolae rolled up his sleeves as if to fight, the crowd went wild.

"And what do you gentlemen have to say for yourselves this morning?" he said, looking first to the witnesses and then to the crowd. Buck prayed they would be eloquent, challenging, forceful.

● ● ●

In Illinois it was the wee hours of the morning. Tsion sat before the television in his pajamas and robe and slippers. Chloe sat in a chair.

"The baby sleeping?" Tsion said.

Chloe nodded. "I pray he sleeps through this."

When Carpathia began with the challenging question, Chloe said quietly, "Give it to 'im, Eli. C'mon, Moishe."

But they did not respond.

"Oh, God," Tsion prayed. "Oh, God, oh, God. They are oppressed and they are afflicted, yet they open not their mouths; they are led as lambs to the slaughter, and as a sheep before its shearers is silent, so they open not their mouths."

●   ●   ●

For a second Buck wished he had a weapon. He had a clear sight path to Carpathia. What arrogance! What ego! How he would love to pop Nicolae between the eyes, even with a slingshot. He shook his head. He was a journalist, an observer. He didn't claim to be objective. His heart was with the witnesses. But neither was he a participant.

●   ●   ●

Rayford could hardly keep still. He bit his tongue to keep from shouting at Carpathia. He slipped his arms inside his robe and held the box in both hands. If Nicolae was going to make fools of the witnesses, maybe he would wind up the fool, lying in his own blood.

Carpathia was in his glory. "Cat got your tongues?" he said, pacing before the silent saints, peeking at the crowd for encouragement. "The water in Jerusalem tastes cold and refreshing today! Run out of poison? Coconspirators run away? Lose access to the water supply?"

The people cheered and mocked. "Throw them out!" someone yelled.

"Arrest them!"

"Jail them!"

"Kill them!"

Rayford wanted to shout, "Shut up!" but would have been drowned out by the blood-thirsty mob anyway. And Carpathia played them.

"Was that rain on my window this morning? What happened to the drought? Say, does anyone see locusts? Horsemen? Smoke? Gentlemen! You are impotent!"

The crowd ate it up. Rayford seethed.

"I proclaimed this area off-limits to you two years ago!" Carpathia said, his back to the crowd but the microphone allowing him to be heard everywhere, including on TV. "Why are you still here? You must leave or be arrested! In fact, did I not say that if you were seen in public *any*where after the meeting of the cultists that you would be executed?"

Carpathia turned to the crowd. "I did say that, did I not?"

"Yes! Yes! Execute them!"

"I have been remiss! I have not carried out my duties! How can I stand before the citizens who have charged me with upholding the dictates of my office when I have allowed this crime to go unpunished? I do not want to be shamed before my people! I do not want to be embarrassed at their party today!

"Come! Come out from behind that fence and

face me! Challenge me! Answer me! Climb over, fly over, transport yourselves if you are able! Do not make me open the gate!"

Carpathia turned to the crowd again. "Should I fear their very breath? Will these dragons incinerate and slay even me?"

The crowd was not as loud now, laughing nervously. The witnesses did not move.

"I am at the end of patience!" Nicolae said. The head of the GC Peacekeeping Force produced a key from his pocket and handed it to Nicolae. He unlocked the gate, and the crowd edged back. Some gasped. Then they fell silent.

Carpathia opened the gate with a flourish and rushed the witnesses. "Outside!" he shouted, but the two ignored him still. He moved right of Eli and shoved him into Moishe, making them both stumble toward the gate. He herded them through, pushing, bumping, jostling.

The crowd fell back more. Carpathia grabbed Eli and Moishe by their robes and slammed them back against the fence, then turned his back on them and smiled at the crowd. "Here are your tormentors!" he said. "Your judges! Your *prophets!*" He spat that last. "And what do they have to say for themselves now? Nothing! They have been tried and convicted and sentenced. All that is left is the rendering of justice, and as *I* have decreed it, *I shall carry it out!*"

He turned to the two, tugging their robes again until they stood six feet in front of the bars.

"Any last words?"

Eli and Moishe looked at each other and lifted their heads to heaven.

Carpathia strode to his jacket and removed the black object from the pocket. Rayford was stunned to recognize it. Nicolae hid the box from the crowd, his back to them, as he separated a Saber handgun from its adjoining piece. He backed about ten feet away from the witnesses and pointed the weapon at Eli, on his right. The sudden explosion made everyone recoil and cover their ears. The bullet entered Eli at the neck, and the force knocked him off his feet, his head slamming into the fence before his body crumpled to the ground, blood gushing. The huge exit wound splattered gore on the fence and the stone building behind.

Moishe knelt and covered his eyes as if in prayer. Carpathia shot him through the top of the head, making him flop into the fence and land on his chin, limbs splayed.

Rayford's mouth was dry, his breath short, his pulse reverberating to fingers and toes. All around him people held their ears and gawked at the remains. Carpathia fitted the gun back together, slipped it into the jacket pocket, put the jacket back on, and with a closed-mouth smile executed a deep bow to the crowd.

Rayford was overcome with such a passion to shoot Carpathia that he lowered his shoulder and rammed into the man in front of him, who let out a horrific grunt just as the crowd responded to Carpathia. They jumped and spun and cheered and laughed and shouted and danced. Rayford bulled forward, trying to get to Carpathia, all the while trying to detach his own Saber.

The crowd swayed together, falling, wrestling, enjoying themselves. Rayford tumbled in the middle of it, his arms inside his coat, unable to get up. He forced one hand out of a sleeve so he could push off the ground to stand, but he was knocked over halfway up. He swung his elbows to clear space, but in the process the Saber box rattled to the ground. He felt for it as he sat there, battered back and forth by waves of revelers. He forced both arms out just as someone knocked him back and his head slammed the concrete. He rolled and jumped up, a bump rising on the back of his head. Where was the Saber? Had it stayed together? It was fully loaded, and there was no safety.

● ● ●

Buck stood on the rocky ledge, drained. He watched the dancing, the carousing, the helicopters collecting Carpathia and the other VIPs and whisking them to the party site. Buck hated the sight of the grisly bodies of his beloved preachers. How he had come to cherish their dark, leathery skin, their thick, dirty feet, their smoky sackcloth robes! They had been so regal, majestic, patriarchal. Their bony hands and shoulders, wrinkled necks and faces, long gray hair and beards only added to their wonderful, supernatural mystery.

Their bodies had been destroyed. Formerly invincible, they had been blasted against the iron fence, leaving them next to each other in grotesque heaps. Buck was embarrassed for them, exposed in death. Their robes rode high on their legs, their hands curled beneath them, eyes open, mouths agape. Their blood ran the blackest red under bodies torn apart by a weapon so technologically advanced that calling it a handgun was the ultimate understatement.

Buck knew what came next. He did not need to witness the celebrating that had been scheduled for noon to midnight but which would last more than three days. He looked with deep sadness on sin come to fruition, on evil personified in people who had had every chance, been given every warning.

● ● ●

Tsion lowered his head, "I could not have imagined how ghastly . . ."

Chloe appeared unable to tear her eyes from the screen. "Buck must be there."

Tsion rose. "Chloe, we have turned a terrible corner. This is only the beginning. Soon Carpathia will not even pretend propriety. Most will be powerless to resist him."

● ● ●

Rayford spun and crouched, desperate for the Saber. He stepped on it, reached for it, and was knocked about again by crazed dancers. He dropped to his knees and grabbed it with both hands, hugging it to his chest as people climbed over him. Finally he tucked it back inside his robe and fought to the edge of the crowd. Carpathia was long gone by now.

● ● ●

Buck headed back to the hostel, passing celebrants on every corner, crowded around TV sets. He phoned Leah. No answer.

● ● ●

For the next three days the Gala was centered at the party venue. Music blared and speeches decried the Jerusalem Twosome and praised Nicolae. Fortunato urged everyone to view Carpathia as a deity, "perhaps *the* deity, the creator God and savior of all mankind." And the people cheered.

The only mention of the death of Peter the

Second came from Carpathia himself, who said, "Not only was I tired of the pseudoreligious preachers and their legalistic imperialism, but I was also tired of the intrusive Enigma Babylon Faith, which shall not be reinstituted. Individual souls can find within themselves the deity necessary to conduct their lives as they wish. I esteem individual freedom over organized religion."

Rayford began to spend time near the Gala stage where the closing ceremony would be held Friday night. He calculated angles, lines of sight, when to arrive, where to stand, where to move, how to get himself in position should God choose to use him. The ceremony would end after dark with a speech by Carpathia. Perhaps that would be the moment.

● ● ●

All over Jerusalem, people celebrated. Buck was sickened that every newscast showed Eli's and Moishe's bloated, fetid bodies, decayed and steaming in the sun. Day and night crowds danced around them, holding their noses, sometimes venturing close to kick the corpses. Blood and tissue formed a sticky mess around them.

From all over the world came reports of celebrations, of people exchanging gifts as they would at Christmas. From the occasional commentator came the suggestion that it was "time to get past this, to give these men a proper burial and move on." But the celebrants would have none of it, and global polls showed huge majorities favored refusing them burial, letting them lie.

On Wednesday evening, Buck had finally been permitted to see Chaim in the hospital. Though his color was good and his speech had improved, his face drooped. His left side was stiff. His right hand was curled. Chaim's doctor was still puzzled by the results of his tests, but he was reluctant to accede to Chaim's request to "go home and die in peace."

Chaim pleaded pitifully to Buck, slurring, "Just wheel me out of here! Please! I want to go home."

By Friday dawn, Buck had still been unable to reach either Leah or Rayford. He did, however, receive a surprising call from Jacov. "I don't know how he did it, but Chaim talked his way out of there. He has improved enough to come home, and the doctor now believes he may have had a small stroke that acted like a big one. He looks no better to me, but he can make himself understood. And he's ordering me to take him to the closing ceremony tonight."

TWENTY-THREE

As Buck showered Friday morning he realized he would do anything but sacrifice his identity to be at the Wailing Wall that day. He believed Tsion, he believed the Bible, he believed the prophecies. He couldn't imagine anything as satisfying as seeing the mockers of Eli and Moishe get theirs.

Buck had promised to help Jacov persuade Chaim to stay home from the Gala finale that evening, provided he was fortunate enough to find himself in the 90 percent of Jerusalem that would be spared the foretold earthquake.

● ● ●

Rayford slept most of the morning, ignoring his beeping cell phone except to note that the caller, every time, was Leah. What could he say? Sorry I can't pick you up tonight and ferry you back to the States, but I might be in prison or dead?

He was careful to be well rested and well fed. He wanted to be prepared and sharp, regardless which way the day went. Rayford was also careful to pray that God would tell him if he were heading off on his own. He was willing to get to the plaza at least three hours before sundown, stay in the middle of crowds, and make sure he was in the spot he had scouted. Past that, God would have to pull the trigger.

Rayford glanced at his phone and punched up Leah's last message readout: "Our bird has left the cage. Now what?"

Hattie was not at Buffer? Now what, indeed? He phoned her. But now Leah wasn't answering.

● ● ●

Buck was angry with himself for not going even earlier to the Wailing Wall. His spot on the rocky ledge was taken. GC guards let no one up the trees. The area teemed with drunken celebrants, some Buck would have sworn had been there for days. How long could this party last? Dancing, public lewdness, shouting, singing, drinking, people staggering about . . .

Thousands chanted in various languages, only the bravest now approaching the blackening, oozing carcasses that had split in the heat of the sun. Buck smelled the rancid cadavers from a hundred yards. Still, he was determined to get closer. He walked far around the left side of the Wall and found himself in a grove of trees and high shrubbery. Buck couldn't risk being recognized, but this gambit was worth the danger. If it led, as he hoped, to the same underbrush that had allowed him to get close to Eli and Moishe once before without drawing the ire of the guards, he could be an eyewitness to one of the greatest miracles of history.

● ● ●

Tsion and Chloe, up before dawn and watching TV again, took turns distracting Kenny when the cameras showed Eli and Moishe's gruesome remains. "Awful as the deaths were," Tsion said, "what is coming should be exquisite." He sat rocking on the couch, unable to sit still. Anytime he caught Chloe's eye he was reminded of his daughter when she was a little girl on the morning of her birthday.

● ● ●

Buck slithered through the brush past two guard outposts and around the opposite side, where he was finally as close to the fence as he could be without being seen. He could not believe his luck. Unless by accident, Buck would not be discovered. He was reminded of his admonition to Leah. *We don't do luck.*

"Thank you, Lord," he whispered.

Buck could barely stand the sight of what was left of the mighty men he had come to love. Except for the occasional kicks from the most irreverent of the partiers, the bodies had not moved in three and a half days. Animals picked at them, birds pecked, bugs crawled. Buck decided he would not let his worst enemy rot in the sun.

A raucous band invaded the area, and the carousers became feverish. The bravest danced side by side, arms interlocked at the shoulders, encircling the bodies. Buck feared he would miss the miracle now, blocked by these crazy drunks. Their misshapen circle flattened as it snaked between the bodies and the fence.

Faster and faster they danced until someone reversed direction. The whole line stopped and went the other way, but soon several had ideas of their own and the thing disintegrated. Dancers collided, laughing, hollering, guffawing until tears rolled. A middle-aged woman, one shoe missing, bent to vomit and was bowled over by some who thought the circle was still going.

Several went down, giving Buck a clear view of Eli and Moishe, now just hideous, distorted, repulsive collections of body parts in putrid piles. A sob of pity rose in his throat.

Without warning the dead men stirred. Buck held his breath. One by one the crazies shrieked, fell back, and drew the attention of the rest of the throng. Word spread that the corpses were moving, and the inner circle stampeded back while those hearing the commotion from farther back surged forward.

The music stopped, the singing turned to screams and agonizing wails. Many covered their eyes or hid their faces. Thousands fled. Thousands more came running.

Eli and Moishe struggled to their knees, filthy bodies in slow motion, chests heaving. Rugged, long-fingered hands on their thighs, they blinked and turned to take in the sight. In tandem they each put one hand on the pavement and straightened, slowly rising, eliciting terrible moans from the paralyzed onlookers.

As they deliberately rose to full height, the dried puddles around them stirred into liquid. Their gaping wounds mended, skin—stretched and split from swelling—contracted, purple and black blotches fading, fading. Hair and tissue from the fence and wall beyond disappeared as the men became whole.

Buck heard every screech from the crowd, but he could not take his eyes from Eli and Moishe. They gathered the folds of their robes into their fists at the chest, and the rest of the sackcloth fluttered clean in the breeze. They were again tall and strong, victorious and noble and stately.

Eli and Moishe looked on the crowd with what Buck read as regret and longing, then turned their faces heavenward. They looked so expectant that Buck noticed many in the crowd looking skyward too.

Snow-white clouds rolled in deep blue and purple skies. The sun was hidden, then reappeared in a beautiful sky of moving colors and pure white vapors.

A voice from above, so loud people covered their ears and ducked from it, said, "COME UP HERE!"

Faces still upturned, Eli and Moishe rose. A collective gasp echoed through the Temple Mount as people fell to their knees, some onto their faces, weeping, crying out, praying, groaning. The witnesses disappeared into a cloud that rose so quickly it soon became a speck before it too vanished.

Buck's knees buckled and he dropped to the soft soil, tears finally coming. "Praise God," he breathed. "Thank you, Lord!" All around, thousands lay prostrate, keening, lamenting, pleading with God.

Buck began to rise, but before his legs were straight the ground snapped beneath him like a towel. He flew back into a tree, scraping his neck and back as he tumbled. He leapt to his feet to see hundreds of people landing after being thrown even higher.

The sky turned black, and cold rain pelted the area. From blocks away came the ominous crash of buildings, the crack and boom of falling trees, the smash of metal and glass as vehicles were tossed about.

"Earthquake!" people shouted, running. Buck tottered out of his hiding place, amazed at how short and severe had been the tremor. The sun peeked through fast moving clouds, creating an eerie green atmosphere. Buck walked in a daze in the direction of Chaim's home.

● ● ●

Rayford had been watching on television from his hotel room. The quake cut the power and threw everything to the floor, including him. Almost immediately GC public address trucks rolled through the streets.

"Attention, citizens! Volunteers are needed on the east side of the city. Closing ceremonies will take place tonight as planned. Zealots have made off with the bodies of the preachers. Do not fall for fairy tales of their disappearing or their having had anything to do with this act of nature. Repeat: Closing ceremonies will take place tonight as planned."

●   ●   ●

Mac had slept late, then turned on the television
to watch the day's news. He wept as TV cameras
showed Eli and Moishe resurrect and rise into
the clouds. How would the GC refute what had
been broadcast around the globe? David Hassid
had reported that he had seen Carpathia's eerie
interruption on TV Monday night, but that
the incident did not appear on any tapes of the
event. And now, no replays of the resurrections
appeared on the news.

What power, Mac thought. What pervasive
control, even of technology. If by some stretch
Carpathia left Israel alive, Mac would not allow
him to land alive. Not on any plane he was pilot-
ing. But should he wait that long? He dug in
the bottom compartment of his flight bag and
fingered the contraband pistol just like the one
Abdullah also carried. If Mac carried it that
night, he would have to stay far from the metal
detectors.

●   ●   ●

Chaim's neighborhood had been hit hard. Bricks
had been loosened and a section of his garage had
disintegrated, but unlike the flattened residences
around his, Chaim's house had largely escaped
damage.

Power returned quickly to that area, and Buck

watched the television reports with Chaim and the rest of the household. The death toll was announced in the hundreds but quickly climbed into the thousands.

Most of the damage indeed centered on the east side of Jerusalem, where buildings fell, apartment complexes collapsed, roads became upturned ribbons of asphalt and mud, and thousands perished. By early evening it was clear that about a tenth of the Holy City had been destroyed and that the death toll would reach at least seven thousand by morning.

Every newscast repeated the insistence on the part of the GC that delegates should still attend the final ceremony. "It will be abbreviated," an appropriately morose Leon Fortunato intoned. "The potentate is involved in the search-and-rescue operation, but he asked that I extend his heartfelt condolences to all who have suffered loss. These are his words: 'Reconstruction begins immediately. We will not be defeated by one defeat. The character of a people is revealed by its reaction to tragedy. We shall rise because we are the Global Community.

"'There is tremendous morale-building value in our coming together as planned. Music and dancing will not be appropriate, but we shall stand together, encourage each other, and dedicate ourselves anew to the ideals we hold dear.'

"Let me add a personal word," Fortunato said. "It would be most encouraging to Potentate Carpathia if you were to attend in overwhelming numbers. We will commemorate the dead and the valor of those involved in the rescue effort, and the healing process will begin."

Buck had no interest in the maudlin imitation of the opening night—the potentates praising their fearless leader and he piously charming the crowd.

"You promised to be there," Chaim rasped.

"Oh, sir, the roads will be impassable, wheelchair ramps may have been damaged. Just watch it on—"

"Jacov can drive through anything and get me anywhere."

Jacov shrugged. Buck made a face as if to ask why he hadn't supported Buck's refusal. "He's right," Jacov said. "Get him and his chair into the car, and I'll get him there."

"I can't risk being recognized," Buck told Chaim.

"I just want to know you are in the crowd, supporting me."

●   ●   ●

The sun slipped out from under a bank of clouds and warmed Jerusalem. The orange highlight on the old city shocked Rayford in its beauty, but so did the devastation. Rayford couldn't imagine why Carpathia was so determined to go through with the schedule. But the potentate was playing right into God's hands.

Rayford stayed behind various groups, finally camping out in a cluster of people near the speaker tower to Carpathia's left as he faced the audience. Rayford guessed he was sixty or seventy feet from the lectern.

● ● ●

"I am not going," Abdullah announced. "I will watch on television."

"Suit yourself," Mac said. "I'll probably regret going myself."

Mac sat in the shuttle van for more than twenty minutes before it finally pulled away. He glanced back to see Abdullah stride quickly from the hotel, hands inside the pockets of a light jacket.

● ● ●

Buck arrived at the plaza before Jacov and Chaim and waited near the entrance, emboldened by being patently ignored. His new look was working, and anyway it appeared GC workers were preoccupied preparing for a guest of honor. And here he came.

Someone parked Chaim's vehicle while Jacov

wheeled Chaim to the metal detector at stage right. "Your name, sir," a guard asked.

"Jac—"

"He's with me, young man," Chaim spat. "Leave him alone."

"I'm sorry, sir," the guard said. "We are on heightened security alert, as you can imagine."

"I said he's with me!"

"That's fine, sir, but once he helps you onto the platform, he'll have to find a seat or stand elsewhere."

"Nonsense!" Chaim said. "Now—"

"Oh, boss," Jacov said quickly. "I don't want to be up there anyway. Please."

Buck saw Chaim close his eyes wearily and wave with the back of his hand. "Just get me up there."

"You have to go through the metal detector," the guard said. "No exceptions."

"Fine! Let's go!"

"You first, son."

Jacov's keys set off the alarm. He succeeded on his second try.

"I'll need you out of the chair briefly, Dr. Rosenzweig," the guard said. "My men can support you."

"No they can't!" Chaim said.

"Sir," Jacov said, "he had a stroke Mon—"

"I know all about that."

"Do you want to insult an Israeli, and may I say, global statesman?"

The guard appeared at a loss. "I have to at least search him."

"Very well," Chaim growled. "Be quick!"

The guard felt Chaim's arms and legs and back, patting him down all over. "Your getaway would have been a little slow anyway," he said.

Jacov and three guards lifted the chair to the stage and rolled Chaim to the left end of the row of chairs. The guard signaled Jacov to return. "I'm to leave him up here alone now?"

"I'm sorry," the guard said.

Jacov shrugged. Chaim said, "Go on! I'll be fine."

Jacov descended and joined Buck near the front. They watched as Chaim amused himself by steering the motorized wheelchair back and forth across the vast, empty stage, to the delight of the growing crowd.

● ● ●

The sky was dark, but the vast lighting system bathed the plaza. Rayford guessed the crowd bigger than on opening day, but subdued.

Their helicopters having been pressed into earthquake relief, the VIPs were transported in a motor coach. No fanfare or music or dancing, no opening prayer. The potentates mounted the steps, shook hands with each other and with Chaim, and waited in front of their chairs. Leon walked Nicolae up, surrounded by the security detail. The assembled broke into warm, sustained applause, no cheering or whistling.

Leon quickly introduced the potentates, then said, "There is one other *very* special guest we are particularly pleased to welcome, but His Excellency has requested that privilege. And so, with heartfelt thanks for your support during this time, I give you once again, His Excellency, Nicolae Carpathia."

Rayford reached inside his robe with both hands, separated the Saber, and silently told God he was prepared to produce it at the right moment.

A restrained Carpathia quickly quieted the applause. "Let me add my deep thanks to that of our supreme commander's and also my abject sympathies to you who have suffered. I will not keep you long, because I know many of you need to return to your homelands and are concerned about transportation. Flights are going from both airports, though there are, of course, delays.

"Now before my remarks, let me introduce my guest of honor. He was to have been here Monday, but he was overtaken by an untimely stroke. It gives me great pleasure to announce the miraculous rallying of this great man, enough so that he joins us tonight in his wheelchair, with wonderful prospects for complete recovery. Ladies and gentlemen of the Global Community, a statesman, a scientist, a loyal citizen, and my dear friend, the distinguished Dr. Chaim Rosenzweig!"

The crowd erupted as Carpathia pointed toward Chaim, and Rayford sensed his opportunity. People in front of him lifted their arms to clap and wave, and he quickly raised the weapon and took aim. But Chaim reached with his good arm as if to offer it to Carpathia, and Nicolae bounded over to the wheelchair to embrace the old man.

No way Rayford would fire that close to Rosenzweig. He lowered the weapon, hidden under the folds of his billowy sleeve, and watched the awkward embrace. Nicolae raised Chaim's good arm, and the crowd cheered again. Carpathia returned to the lectern and the moment was lost.

● ● ●

Mac McCullum knew Buck Williams was somewhere in the crowd. Maybe he would try to make contact when it was over. Was Abdullah also there? And why had he said he wasn't coming?

● ● ●

Quivering from the close call, Rayford tasted bile, Carpathia so repulsed him.

"Fellow citizens," Nicolae began somberly, "in the very young history of our one-world government, we have stood shoulder to shoulder against great odds, as we do tonight.

"I had planned a speech to send us back to our homes with renewed vigor and a rededication to Global Community ideals. Tragedy has made that talk unnecessary. We have proven again that we are a people of purpose and ideals, of servant-hood and good deeds."

From behind Carpathia, three potentates rose. That seemed to obligate the other seven, who slowly and seemingly reluctantly stood. Carpathia noticed the attention of the crowd was behind him and turned, seeing first three, then all ten potentates stand and clap. The crowd joined the applause, and Rayford thought he saw Carpathia and Fortunato trade glances.

Was something afoot? Were those the three Mac had said might not be so loyal as Nicolae thought?

The potentates sat again, and for the first time since the meetings at Kollek Stadium, Carpathia seemed at a loss for words. He started again, paused, repeated himself, then turned back to the potentates and joked, "Do not do that to me."

The crowd applauded anew, and Nicolae milked the situation for a bigger laugh. Obviously covering his own concern, he began to speak, looked back quickly, and turned again, engendering titters from the audience.

Suddenly the three potentates stood again and applauded as if trying to make points with Nicolae, though Rayford noticed one had reached into the inside pocket of his jacket as he rose. It was clear the crowd thought the clapping potentates were some sort of an impromptu bit. When Chaim suddenly steered his chair out of place and rolled toward Fortunato, the crowd laughed and exulted in earnest.

Rayford was distracted from his left. Hattie? There was no way. He tried to keep her in sight, but the people in front of him raised their hands again, shouting, clapping, jumping. He leveled the gun between them, aimed betwixt two security guards at Nicolae, and tried to squeeze the trigger. He could not! His arm was paralyzed, his hand shaking, his vision swimming. Would God not allow it? Had he run too far ahead? He felt a fool, a coward, powerless despite the weapon. He stood shaking, Carpathia in his sights. As the crowd celebrated, Rayford was bumped from the back and side and the gun went off. At the explosion the sea of panicked people parted around him. Rayford ran with a bunch of them, dropping the weapon and letting the other half of the box fall. People screamed and trampled each other.

As Rayford pushed his way into a gridlock of

bodies, he sneaked a peek at the stage. Carpathia was not in sight. The potentates scattered and dived for cover, one dropping something as he tumbled off the platform. Rayford could not see Fortunato either, at first. The lectern had been shattered and the entire one-hundred-foot-wide back curtain ripped off its frame and blown away from the stage. Rayford imagined the bullet passing through Nicolae and taking out the back-drop.

Had God used him in spite of his cowardice? Could he have fulfilled prophecy? The shooting had been a mistake! He had not meant to do it!

● ● ●

Buck had ducked under a scaffold at the sound of the gun. A tidal wave of humanity swept past him on both sides, and he saw glee on some faces. Converts from the Wailing Wall who had seen Carpathia murder their heroes?

By the time Buck looked to the stage, the potentates were leaping off, the drapery was flying into the distance, and Chaim appeared catatonic, his head rigid.

Carpathia lay on the platform, blood running from eyes, nose, and mouth, and—it appeared to Buck—from the top of his head. His lapel mike was still hot, and because Buck was directly under a speaker tower, he heard Nicolae's liquid, guttural murmur, "But I thought . . . I thought . . . I did everything you asked."

Fortunato draped his stocky body over Carpathia's chest, reached beneath him, and cradled him. Sitting on the stage, he rocked his potentate, wailing.

"Don't die, Excellency!" Fortunato bawled. "We need you! The world needs you! *I* need you!"

Security forces surrounded them, brandishing Uzis. Buck had experienced enough trauma for one day. He stood transfixed, with a clear view of the back of Carpathia's blood-matted skull.

The wound was unmistakably fatal. And from where Buck stood, it was obvious what had caused it.

●   ●   ●

"I did not expect a gunshot," Tsion said, staring at the television as GC Security cleared the stage and whisked Carpathia away.

Two hours later GC CNN confirmed the death and played over and over the grieving pronouncement of Supreme Commander Leon Fortunato. "We shall carry on in the courageous spirit of our founder and moral anchor, Potentate Nicolae Carpathia. The cause of death will remain confidential until the investigation is complete. But you may rest assured the guilty party will be brought to justice."

The news media reported that the slain potentate's body would lie in state in the New Babylon palace before entombment there on Sunday.

"Don't leave the TV, Chloe," Tsion said. "You have to assume the resurrection will be caught on camera."

But when Friday became Saturday in Mount Prospect and Saturday night approached, even Tsion began to wonder. The Scriptures had not foretold of death by projectile. Antichrist was to die from a specific wound to the head and then come back to life. Carpathia still lay in state.

By dawn Sunday, as Tsion gloomily watched mourners pass the glass bier in the sun-drenched courtyard of the GC palace, he had begun to doubt himself.

Had he been wrong all along?

● ● ●

Two hours before the burial, David Hassid was called in to Leon Fortunato's office. Leon and his directors of Intelligence and Security huddled before a TV monitor. Leon's face revealed abject grief and the promise of vengeance. "Once His Excellency is in the tomb," he said, his voice thick, "the world can approach closure. Prosecuting his murderer can only help. Watch with us, David. The primary angles were blocked, but look at this collateral view. Tell me if you see what we see."

David watched.

Oh, no! he thought. *It couldn't be!*

"Well?" Leon said, peering at him. "Is there any doubt?"

David stalled, but that only made the other two glance at him.

"The camera doesn't lie," Leon said. "We have our assassin, don't we?"

Much as he wanted to come up with some other explanation for what was clear, David would jeopardize his position if he proved illogical. He nodded. "We sure do."

EPILOGUE

"The second woe is past. Behold, the third woe is coming quickly."
   Revelation 11:14

ABOUT THE AUTHORS

Jerry B. Jenkins (www.jerryjenkins.com) is the writer of the Left Behind series. He owns the Jerry B. Jenkins Christian Writers Guild, an organization dedicated to mentoring aspiring authors. Former vice president for publishing for the Moody Bible Institute of Chicago, he also served many years as editor of *Moody* magazine and is now Moody's writer-at-large.

His writing has appeared in publications as varied as *Reader's Digest, Parade, Guideposts,* in-flight magazines, and dozens of other periodicals. Jenkins's biographies include books with Billy Graham, Hank Aaron, Bill Gaither, Luis Palau, Walter Payton, Orel Hershiser, and Nolan Ryan, among many others. His books appear regularly on the *New York Times, USA Today, Wall Street Journal,* and *Publishers Weekly* best-seller lists.

Jerry is also the writer of the nationally syndicated sports story comic strip *Gil Thorp,* distributed to newspapers across the United States by Tribune Media Services.

Jerry and his wife, Dianna, live in Colorado and have three grown sons.

Dr. Tim LaHaye (www.timlahaye.com), who conceived the idea of fictionalizing an account of the Rapture and the Tribulation, is a noted author, minister, and nationally recognized speaker on Bible prophecy. Dr. LaHaye was chosen the "Most Influential Evangelical of the Last Twenty-Five Years" by the Institute for the Study of

American Evangelicals at Wheaton College. He is the founder of both Tim LaHaye Ministries and The Pre-Trib Research Center. He also recently cofounded the Tim LaHaye School of Prophecy at Liberty University. Presently Dr. LaHaye speaks at many of the major Bible prophecy conferences in the U.S. and Canada, where his current prophecy books are very popular.

Dr. LaHaye holds a doctor of ministry degree from Western Theological Seminary and a doctor of literature degree from Liberty University. For twenty-five years he pastored one of the nation's outstanding churches in San Diego, which grew to three locations. It was during that time that he founded two accredited Christian high schools, a Christian school system of ten schools, and Christian Heritage College.

Dr. LaHaye has written over forty books that have been published in more than thirty languages. He has written books on a wide variety of subjects, such as family life, temperaments, and Bible prophecy. His current fiction works, the Left Behind series, written with Jerry B. Jenkins, continue to appear on the best-seller lists of the Christian Booksellers Association, *Publishers Weekly*, *Wall Street Journal*, *USA Today*, and the *New York Times*.

He is the father of four grown children and grandfather of nine. Snow skiing, waterskiing, motorcycling, golfing, vacationing with family, and jogging are among his leisure activities.

IN ONE CATACLYSMIC MOMENT
MILLIONS AROUND THE WORLD DISAPPEAR

Experience the suspense of the end times for yourself. The best-selling Left Behind series is now available in hardcover, softcover, and large-print editions.

1 LEFT BEHIND
A novel of the earth's last days . . .

2 TRIBULATION FORCE
The continuing drama of those left behind . . .

3 NICOLAE
The rise of Antichrist . . .

4 SOUL HARVEST
The world takes sides . . .

5 APOLLYON
The Destroyer is unleashed . . .

6 ASSASSINS
Assignment: Jerusalem, Target: Antichrist

7 THE INDWELLING
The Beast takes possession . . .

8 THE MARK
The Beast rules the world . . .

9 DESECRATION
Antichrist takes the throne . . .

10 THE REMNANT
On the brink of Armageddon . . .

FOR THE MOST

ACCURATE INFORMATION,

VISIT

www.leftbehind.com

ABRIDGED AUDIO Available on three CDs or two cassettes for each title. (Books 1–9 read by Frank Muller, one of the most talented readers of audio books today.)

AN EXPERIENCE IN SOUND AND DRAMA Dramatic broadcast performances of the best-selling Left Behind series. Twelve half-hour episodes on four CDs or three cassettes for each title.

GRAPHIC NOVELS Created by a leader in the graphic novel market, the series is now available in this exciting new format.

LEFT BEHIND®: THE KIDS Four teens are left behind after the Rapture and band together to fight Satan's forces in this series for ten- to fourteen-year-olds.

LEFT BEHIND® > THE KIDS < LIVE-ACTION AUDIO Feel the reality, listen as the drama unfolds. . . . Twelve action-packed episodes available on four CDs or three cassettes.

CALENDARS, DEVOTIONALS, GIFT BOOKS . . .

FOR THE LATEST INFORMATION ON INDIVIDUAL PRODUCTS, RELEASE DATES, AND FUTURE PROJECTS, VISIT

w w w . l e f t b e h i n d . c o m

Sign up and receive free E-mail updates!